# BULL DANCERS
## OF
# KNOSSOS

# THE BULL DANCERS OF KNOSSOS

**PAM AND JOHN RAGGATT**

HarperCollins*Publishers*

**HarperCollins***Publishers*

First published in Australia in 1998
by HarperCollins*Publishers* Pty Limited
ACN 009 913 517
A member of HarperCollins*Publishers* (Australia) Pty Limited Group
http://www.harpercollins.com.au

Copyright © Pam Raggatt 1998

This book is copyright.
Apart from any fair dealing for the purposes of private study, research,
criticism or review, as permitted under the Copyright Act, no part may
be reproduced by any process without written permission.
Inquiries should be addressed to the publishers.

**HarperCollins***Publishers*
25 Ryde Road, Pymble, Sydney, NSW 2073, Australia
31 View Road, Glenfield, Auckland 10, New Zealand
77–85 Fulham Palace Road, London W6 8JB, United Kingdom
Hazelton Lanes, 55 Avenue Road, Suite 2900, Toronto, Ontario M5R 3L2
*and* 1995 Markham Road, Scarborough, Ontario M1B 5M8, Canada
10 East 53rd Street, New York NY 10032, USA

National Library Cataloguing-in-Publication data:

Raggatt, Pam.
    The bull dancers of Knossos.
    ISBN 0 7322 5994 0.
    I. Raggatt, John. II. Title.
A823.3

Typeset in Sabon 10 on 13.5
The cover painting can be seen in the museum at Heraklion
Printed in Australia by Griffin Press Pty Ltd on 50 gsm Ensobulky

5 4 3 2 1
02 01 00 99 98

*To John Albert Raggatt,
died November 18, 1994,
my very dear husband, without whose
collaboration this work would not have
been completed.*

I would like to express my thanks for advice and assistance to Professor Colin Roderick, Dr Peter Raggatt and Anthony Raggatt. And for assistance with the production of the manuscript to: Kathleen Burnett, Shirley Morrissey and the late Gail Kern.

Thanks also to Rod Morrison, and the staff at HarperCollins Publishers

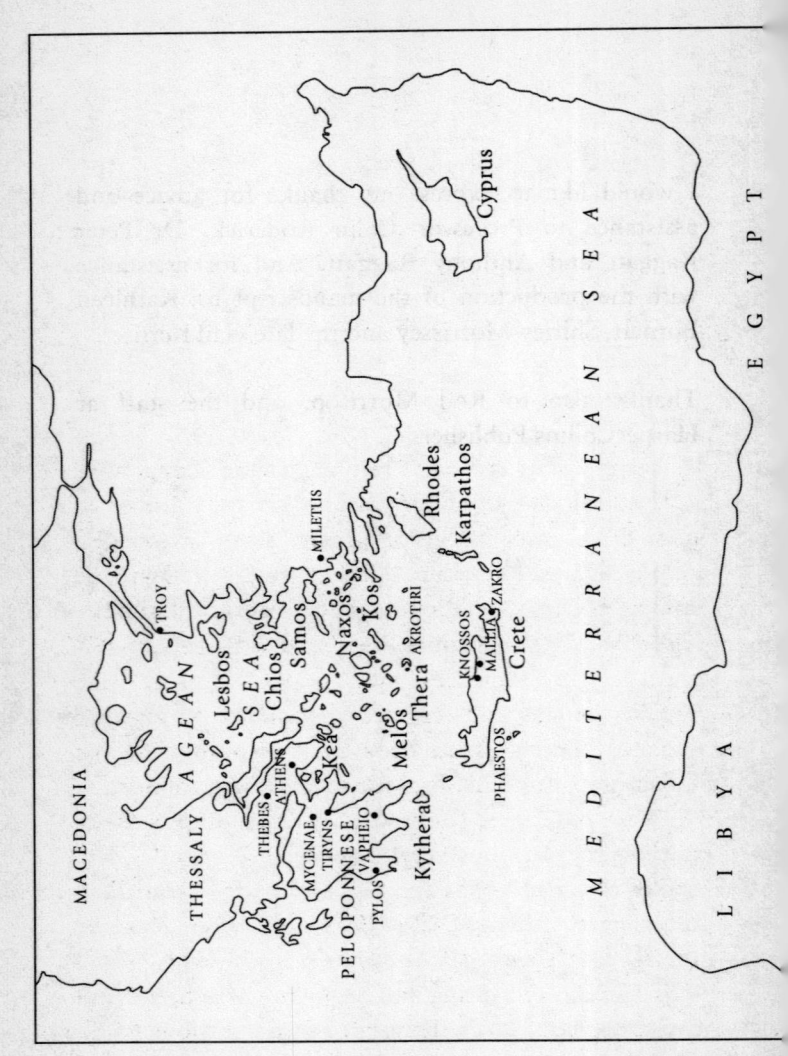

# PROLOGUE

Spring came late to Crete that year. Long after Festival time the high pastures lay buried deep in snowdrifts and the olive groves were silhouetted darkly against the white stillness. In the valleys, the lowing of cattle and mountain goats echoed dismally.

In the Minoan cities men and women covered their bright necklaces and golden armlets with woollen cloaks and warmed themselves by glowing braziers. The peasants scoured the countryside for fallen timber to build fires for warmth and comfort.

This bitter and prolonged winter, after a poor harvest the previous year, made people afraid. They spoke of omens. Was the Goddess angry? Had they offended the Great Earth Mother on whose bounty their lives depended? She, whose son, mighty Zeus, was reborn each spring and brought warmth, life and joy to the cold earth. This great Goddess alone could conquer the fearful Earth Shaker, the sinister God of the Underworld, who could make the earth tremble and devastate their homes, palaces and cities. They knew that Pasterion, the Chief Priest, was ill and had lost the power of speech. Did this forebode some great and terrible calamity?

Many people had made that long, hard climb to the sacred cave on Mount Jukto, the poor trudging on foot, the rich riding in palanquins or chariots, till the snow was muddy and churned up. To propitiate the Great Goddess hundreds of votive offerings were left among the Sacred Pillars which stood so mysteriously, deep in the cave. Some of the gifts were valuable — small bronze images of bulls, golden anklets, jewelled bracelets and carved seal-stones of ivory and amber. The peasants carried more humble gifts — simple things that were part of their daily lives: a knife, a pin, clay models of cats, mice or hedgehogs fashioned and baked in their ovens at home.

But, at last, when despair numbed their hearts and the poor suffered the pangs of hunger, the miracle of spring returned. The sun rose, warm and life-giving. When the snow melted on the uplands, clear, icy water rushed down through a thousand rocky crevices and fresh green covered the valleys and fields. The shepherds set out with their flocks for the lush, high plateaux, to doze through summer days while their beasts grew fat again.

The ports reopened and trade resumed. On the farms, the peasants ploughed and sowed, tidied and pruned in the orchards and vineyards. In the cities, the potter's wheel spun merrily; stonecutters and lamp-makers advertised their wares and the painters were everywhere, freshening up walls, pillars and stairways with blue and vermilion and saffron. The artists, too, were busy creating the frescoes which decorated the Palace and the houses of the wealthy in the smart suburbs of Knossos.

The people danced, twirling and leaping, till the grass in the Sacred Grove was quite flattened down. Truly the Great Goddess, the Earth Mother, loved her children. She held forth her breasts to nourish the earth and all who lived upon it.

It was now early summer, but the scents of spring flowers still lingered in the air and blended with the perfume of jasmine and dog roses.

# CHAPTER 1

On the terrace of his villa, overlooking the city of Knossos, Andreas Micalidos, as was his custom, enjoyed the cool evening breeze. In the sunset hour, he loved the clear quality of light which enveloped the houses and streets of the city.

But today Andreas was tired. He frowned, his dark eyes clouded with anxiety. His face, with its broad, strong features, mirrored his thoughts like an actor's — humorous or melancholy, compassionate or arrogant, idealistic or cynical according to his mood. His nature was compounded of all these elements.

Behind him rose his villa, graceful and elegant, the walls covered with blue tiles. On the upper storey there were windows with balconies of white stone. Buff-coloured columns with russet capitals supported the flat roof on either side. At ground level, a row of slender colonnades of dark red stone, smooth and polished, ran the length of the paved terrace.

Leaning against the stone balustrade, Andreas surveyed the Cretan landscape. To the north, across farms and villages, he could discern the blue haze of the sea. There, in the crowded port of Amnissos, merchant ships landed their cargoes — cedar wood from Phoenician Byblos, tin from Troy, Cyprian copper, bronze and silver from the Hittites of Anatolia. There, too, fishing boats danced jauntily and the tall masts and high painted prows of the Cretan fleet could be seen, loading stores, or anchored in the bay.

Eastward the valley sloped down to the silver gleam of the River Kairatos. To the south, the jagged mountainous backbone of Crete reared up to snowy peaks, shadowed here and there with the dark green of cypress groves, forming a backdrop for the most dramatic scene of all — the Palace of Knossos — which dominated the city and all the countryside around.

After more than forty years Andreas could not gaze on this great edifice without a sense of wonder. From where he stood only the west façade was clearly visible. A high portico over the main entrance gave grandeur and nobility to the Palace and a pair of gigantic stone horns, gold-tipped symbol of the Bull of Minos, curved upward, into the Cretan sky. This was a sight which filled newcomers with awe and the citizens with an admiration and love that was religious in its fervour.

Andreas thought now of the man who ruled there, that strange, enigmatic personality, Minos, the Priest-King. He recalled the frustrations and anxieties which attended his unwilling involvement with the Palace and the man who reigned in it.

As he gazed silently across the city toward the towering mountains, the last rays of the sun glinted on the Palace rooftops.

He turned at the sound of footsteps. His Egyptian friend, Ahmed, the family doctor, had joined him for their customary evening stroll. They greeted each other and walked along the terrace.

"My mother's in good spirits this evening," Andreas remarked, as they passed the loggia, visible through the colonnade.

The old lady was seated on a settee, enjoying the evening sunshine. Her five-year-old grandson, Timon, was beside her, chattering and attempting to cool her with a palm leaf fan. They called a greeting to Andreas and the doctor as they passed which each returned cheerfully.

"Indeed, sir," Ahmed said with a smile. "Old Madam seems to grow younger every day."

Andreas' mother approved the title of "Old Madam", which distinguished her from her daughter-in-law, known as "Young Madam".

The doctor, though middle-aged, was still youthful himself. His tall, lean figure and smoothly shaven face were in complete contrast to Andreas' strong muscular frame and dark beard.

From within the villa they could hear the murmur of talk and laughter. Andreas' wife, Zanthope, was entertaining her friends and admirers.

The two men turned down the side of the house and crossed a courtyard at the back. As they passed a small fountain, which splashed coolly over ornamental rocks, Andreas grasped a handful of rosemary and crushed it, enjoying the sweet pungent smell. They walked in companionable silence, their footsteps muffled on the sandy path. They saw the lamps being lit ready for the evening meal as Credon, the old steward, directed the servants.

The garden was quiet and peaceful. Here Andreas escaped from the incessant gossiping of his wife's friends and the rowdy young people his son, Antonius, occasionally brought home. But he only comes now when he's short of money, Andreas thought. He thrust aside a branch which overgrew the path. "I must speak to Dorcas about pruning these shrubs," he said.

The villa was not large for one of Andreas' position and wealth. It had belonged originally to his mother's family and held happy memories of his childhood, when he, and his brother, Miklos, had climbed the trees and raced reed boats with his sister Korynna in the stream which flowed through the garden.

When his father became a member of King Minos' Council, they had moved to an apartment in the Palace. The boys had missed the garden, and, as he grew up, Andreas disliked the overcrowded conditions in the Palace, and the scandal and gossip, which bored and irritated him.

After his marriage, Zanthope had pleaded, stormed and coaxed. Though he wished to please her, he was adamant on this one point — he would never live in the Palace. Not even after his father's death, when as a Councillor himself he found it difficult to distance himself from the affairs and political intrigues of the Throne.

For a time, however, the villa was a haven and he had preserved the illusion of freedom. The buildings had been damaged in an earthquake some years before, he rebuilt and enlarged them, adding an extra wing on the south side for his own use.

A garden was a luxury in that crowded city, thronged with immigrants. Tall terraced buildings and broad paved streets surrounded the Palace and even encroached to its walls. As the city expanded rapidly, most city dwellers had to content themselves with window boxes or potted plants and perhaps a cypress in the courtyard.

So Andreas never ceased to be grateful. Here, on hot summer days great trees spread a cool shade. A spring flowed through a series of rock pools, where clumps of iris and lilies growing at the pool verges were mirrored in patches of purple, white and yellow. In spring, jonquils and freesias filled the air with sweet perfume. The stream fed the fountain in the courtyard and the water was piped into the house and down into large, stone storage cisterns beneath.

After Andreas and Ahmed had walked for some minutes they sat together on a stone bench overlooking the city. Daylight was fading. A few stars showed faintly in the pale sky. Dr Ahmed gazed searchingly at Andreas, who seemed to be more tired than usual. He had seen these signs of tension before. His concern was both personal and professional. He knew that a conference of the Kings' Council had sat all through the afternoon. However, although he was Andreas' closest friend, he hesitated to broach the matter as he could not forget that Andreas was also his patron. A certain reticence in his employer warned Ahmed that his curiosity would be resented. Besides, he guessed from experience that in due course he would be told everything. He wished at this moment that he could be flippant or lighthearted like Andreas' son, Antonius, who was never short of witty remarks to amuse people.

"The summer flowers should be out in the high pastures now, sir," he said.

His remark was contrived, but it served its purpose. Andreas laughed. "So, you and my mother have put your heads together and decided that a week up at the farm smelling the flowers will do me good. You're probably right!"

"You should take things more easily, you know." Ahmed tried to speak lightly but there was an underlying seriousness in his tone.

Andreas shifted irritably. "There's nothing wrong with me, I'm as healthy as you are. I haven't needed your services these last few years..." The humour in his eyes softened the last remark.

"There could be a reason for your good health, sir," Ahmed said.

"Because I follow my doctor's advice, you mean?"

They fell silent, each deep in his own thoughts. In his youth, Andreas had been robustly healthy. He'd enjoyed all the pleasures and amusements readily available to a rich man's son — hunting, boxing, chariot racing — and as for women, although he never had the slim-waisted elegance that Cretans admired, he could never complain.

Some years after his marriage, he had sailed to Egypt on family business. There he had the misfortune to be infected with the plague, which was endemic in the Delta. Ahmed, then a young doctor, was called in and under his care Andreas made a complete recovery — or so it seemed. On his return from Egypt, he immediately reported to his father at the Palace. Entering at the South Gate, he began to climb the grand staircase in his usual energetic way, two steps at a time.

Without warning, he was startled by an attack of dizziness. The smooth white surface of the stairs spun in frightening confusion and his heart pounded as though it would burst from his chest. The pain made him sweat. Breathless, he grasped the balustrade to steady himself. The dizziness soon passed.

He told no one. But soon, when he discovered that any sudden exertion brought the same unpleasant result, he wrote to Ahmed in Egypt seeking an explanation. The reply had angered him. At first he refused to consider himself a semi-invalid who must avoid all vigorous exercise. But other attacks, more painful than the first, made him cautious. He was obliged to change his lifestyle.

An anguish which struck him far more deeply was his wife's indifference. Zanthope was scornful of his plan to live in the country and refused to go with him. Unhappy and depressed, he had left the city without her and had bought a farm, which he still owned, on the slopes of Mount Ida. There he retired with his books to find what comfort he could in the beauty of nature. He thought perhaps he would paint. He planned to bring his children to the farm for the whole summer where they could play in the meadows, climb the rocks and run wild as children love to do. He would get to know them better. He had been away from home so often that he sometimes felt like a stranger.

All these plans and dreams were swept away in one moment of disaster. His father and elder brother were driving in a chariot through the mountains on their way to inspect a new ship which was soon to be launched at Phaestos. His brother always drove too fast. A narrow road, a loose stone and a frightened horse — the bank on the steep road gave way. It was all over very quickly.

Suddenly Andreas Micalidos, at thirty years of age, found himself the head of the family. And it was no ordinary family. Through his mother he could claim a distant relationship to King Minos. Later on, it would be closer still.

The Micalidos family interests covered a wide range of enterprises. The most important of these was a merchant fleet of some thirty galleys. In the years before his marriage, and afterwards, when his wife's promiscuity began to break his heart, he had sailed the length and breadth of the Great Green Sea — to Egypt and Libya, to Phoenicia and Cyprus, to Troy and the Cyclades. Now that the fleet was his, these fine ships with their high painted prows and flying fish-tail pennants were the pride of his heart. He revelled in the joy of ownership.

There was also a large shipyard for building and repairs at Nirou-Khani, a few miles away, and a summer villa at nearby Mallia; an olive grove on the warm, southern slopes, high above Phaestos and a pottery at Zakro in the east. Sixty craftsmen worked there, making delicate and beautiful wares, so unique in design and decoration that they found a ready market, even in far off Troy and Byblos. Andreas found the responsibility for all these concerns and the people they employed an absorbing interest. He had of necessity to spare himself physically and so discovered a talent for administration. He delegated much of the work to agents.

Travelling in easy stages, he had inspected the ships and every concern on the island. He was surprised and shocked to discover inefficiency and carelessness in affairs under his brother's control — the brother who his father had respected and valued so much. What was more disturbing was the realization that while the family lived its carefree life, the business was obviously running down. It was held together largely through goodwill and the family name. Over the years, he had managed to set things right. The agents who carried reports, such as the price of cedar in Byblos or a new silver strike in Cilicia, also brought news of political developments abroad.

At first these things interested him only in so far as they concerned the safety of his ships. Lately, however, their significance to Crete had become very apparent to him. Reports coming in now were disturbing. Several weeks ago he had sent one of his best agents, Tarsis, to discover what the situation was in Troy. He now awaited his return with some anxiety.

At the villa darkness had fallen and the valley was bathed in a soft glow from lamps burning in the terraced houses where the well-to-do citizens of Knossos lived their comfortable and carefree lives. The Palace shone like a great lamp, ablaze with light. Smaller flickers of candles in the distance were from the sun-dried brick homes of the craftsmen and artisans, who gave thanks with their families to the Earth Mother with gifts of fruit and oil at the small shrines which stood in every home.

Andreas roused himself regretfully. "We must go in. They'll be waiting."

As they went toward the house the air was sweet with the fragrance of night-scented flowers. Most of Zanthope's friends had made their noisy departure. Those who remained she had invited to dinner. They included the Finance Minister, Councillor Brecchius, handsome, smooth and cold-eyed, his dull wife and their younger daughter, Leda, a shy, beautiful girl; Grinkos, bald and rotund, the Overseer of the Records Office and Doxa, his thin elegant wife. Though grey-haired, she was still an attractive woman. Her sharp eyes could price at a glance another woman's clothes and ornaments to the nearest coin. Doxa was ambitious and eager to advance her husband's career; she therefore valued her friendship with Zanthope. Her paid companion, Olivia, was also a guest.

Old Madam Micalidos, with Timon beside her, was now seated in a high-backed chair. She was awaiting the return of her son with some impatience.

"The master should come in, Credon," she said to the steward, who was watching for Andreas and Ahmed's return from the garden. "The air grows cooler when the sun goes down."

"For Zeus' sake stop fussing, one would think he was still a child," said Zanthope, who was reclining languidly on a couch. Noticing Timon she snapped her fingers at him. The boy immediately bolted from the room.

"Here they come now, Old Madam," Credon said and stood aside as the two men came in.

"Well, here is the great man at last. You know everyone here, Andreas," Zanthope waved an elegant hand, "except perhaps Leda Brecchius. I don't think you've been here before, Leda?" She glanced briefly at the girl. Leda blushed. Old Madam drew attention away from the young girl by telling Andreas that if he had not caught cold he certainly deserved to do so. Her son greeted her affectionately and then asked in a low voice, "Why did Timon run off like that?" She had not noticed that the boy was gone. "I suppose he went to get his supper," she replied.

Andreas glanced quickly at his wife. At forty she was still very beautiful. She was not Cretan. The daughter of an immigrant from a small town in Attica, she had fine, straight features, golden hair, grey-green eyes and a tall, slender figure. Her beauty had attracted many suitors, in spite of her family's obscure background. Of these, Andreas had been the most eager and determined. Perhaps it was her misfortune, rather than her fault, that she could not return his passion in equal measure.

Both Zanthope and Doxa, who was seated nearby, were dressed in the sophisticated style of the day. At that time, it was customary for fashionable women to reveal their breasts. Zanthope's deep crimson gown had a full skirt, embroidered with gold thread and the high-waisted bodice was tightly laced. A loose, short-sleeved jacket was also embroidered. Doxa wore a deep blue dress with a cream coloured jacket embroidered in red and silver. Both women wore pendant earrings and elaborate necklaces. The two older women and Leda were modestly dressed with the addition of a linen chemise to their jacket and bell-shaped skirts.

Andreas gave a general and peremptory greeting to the guests and made as if to follow the boy. "Andreas," he paused as his wife stretched out her hand, "look at these beautiful skins. I bought them from Agidor this morning."

Zanthope pointed to a pile of black and white zebra skins which violently contrasted with the vermilion floor tiles. "And he, no doubt, had them off a Libyan merchant in Phaestos and charged you ten times more than he paid for them," Andreas said dryly.

"I don't believe they're real," Doxa laughed, "striped horses indeed! Whoever heard of such a thing? They're probably dyed and it will all wash off!"

"You're envious, dear, because you haven't any yourself," her hostess replied with a smile.

"They're real enough," Andreas said, "they've come a long way — from Nubia, probably — perhaps from beyond the fourth cataract." He examined the skins with some interest, passing one to Ahmed who showed it to Old Madam.

"There you are," Zanthope cried triumphantly, "from the ends of the earth!"

"Real or not real, they'll make a fine couch cover on which to display your beauty, my dear." The voice, unusually deep, came from Olivia. She was a dark, handsome woman becomingly dressed in saffron yellow, her large soft eyes oddly at variance with a cruel, bitter mouth. "But to gain the best effect," she continued, "you must wear that crimson gown and your ruby necklace. Then you will create a sensation, darling. All Knossos will be at your feet!"

Credon announced that the meal was ready. It was served in an adjoining room which looked out over the courtyard and the fountain. The walls were decorated with murals, depicting flowers and birds in the formal fashion of an earlier generation. Silver bowls and dishes shone on the long table of dark, polished wood. Lamps were supported on bronze brackets at intervals along the walls and large, stone bowls, delicately veined, filled with oils and floating wicks, rested on the table. The guests were soon seated in carved, high-backed chairs. The women sat bathed in soft light and their jewels sparkled at the tilt of a head or the turn of a wrist.

As the servants began bringing in the food, two latecomers came in quickly and sat down with murmured apologies — a tall, middle-aged lady, Andreas' widowed sister Korynna, and his secretary, Sharim Senekor, a handsome young immigrant from the Phoenician coast, nicknamed Senka. He was much liked in Knossos. There remained still one empty place, but Andreas, with an impatient gesture, signalled for the meal to commence.

Seafood came first, bowls of shrimp and lobster, squid in spicy sauce and parrot fish fried crisp. Then followed roast pork and veal with savoury herbs.

While they ate, Credon poured red wine into silver goblets, wrought with a pattern of vine leaves and twining tendrils. Doxa Grinkos, who was seated next to Old Madam, began telling her about a new gaming board which King Minos had acquired.

"It is intricate and beautiful beyond belief, so I hear — made of gold, ivory and crystal, with blue enamel flowers all round the edge. Quite a work of art — everyone admires it."

"It must be quite exquisite," Old Madam said, "do you know whose work it is?"

"Oh, some fellow in the Palace workshop, I suppose," Doxa replied indifferently.

"Perhaps it was Phylon, he has a fine reputation," Senka broke in from the other end of the table, "I hear he has thirty men employed in his workshop."

"In that case, Andreas, I insist that he designs the lamp-holders for Mallia." Zanthope, more lively now after a goblet of wine, directed this remark, more of a command than a request, to her husband at the far end of the table. Andreas shrugged his shoulders and said, "He may be too busy."

"You must insist," his wife retorted, "summon him to discuss the designs tomorrow."

Andreas was tired of the subject of Mallia. He could see nothing wrong with the old summer villa, overlooking the sea, which had belonged to his father. However, Zanthope wanted a new villa. He had thwarted her lifelong ambition to live in the

Palace. He had forced her to live in this poky old place that really belonged to his mother, and the summer villa was no better. He had conceded that she had some grounds for complaint, so the old villa at Mallia was pulled down and a larger one built in its place.

Grinkos, greedily stuffing food into his mouth from a heaped plate, spoke with his mouth full. "How's the villa going, Micalidos? Costing you a pretty sum, I'll be bound."

"It's coming along well enough. If some decision can be made regarding the frescoes, it will soon be finished." A glance at his wife accompanied this remark. She was talking to Senka, with her face a little too close to his and sat up quickly. "It's those fools of artists. They just can't understand my instructions," Zanthope said.

She did not acknowledge the fact that she had changed her mind a dozen times until no one really knew what she wanted. "I hope the place is ready before the summer heat comes," she continued, "I want you all to join us there." She included everyone in a graceful gesture and her slim, elegant hand rested for a moment on Senka's arm. "And, of course, Antonius will come and bring his friends. We shall have such a delightful time."

A shadow passed over Andreas' face at the mention of his son. Suddenly, while conversation continued at the other end of the table, he heard a low voice saying, "Will Antonius return this evening?"

He looked at the girl on his right and could not recall her name but he noticed her eyes were large and full of expression. Old Madam, who was seated opposite, heard the question too and answered kindly, "We expect him, Leda, my dear, but he's never very punctual." The girl lost courage and blushed. Grinkos, guffawing loudly, blundered into the conversation.

"Love's young dream, eh?" He poked Leda in the ribs and leered familiarly. "You'll be going some to catch him — he's a wild one." The girl's face flamed in embarrassment. Andreas made a mental note to forbid his wife ever to invite this obnoxious fool to his house again.

"Andreas, my dear," his mother said gently, "you're looking very tired, are you working too hard? A week of mountain air would do you so much good."

"I know you and Dr Ahmed have put your heads together, but I really can't get away just now," Andreas said with a smile. "I must go to the shipyard tomorrow — there's some trouble over the timber."

"Surely you could send the agent. You'll wear yourself out. I can see what's going on. I know what I'm talking about." The old lady was so earnest that Andreas put his hand on hers and told her gently not to worry, he would be able to take a holiday soon.

The servants had cleared the table and brought dishes of cream cheese, honey cakes and large bowls of fruit, for the guests to help themselves. The wine was plentiful and Grinkos was already half drunk. He became garrulous and said thickly, "Heard you had trouble at the shipyard, Micalidos. Refused to work, did they? You'll have mutiny on the ships next, if you don't put these troublemakers down. Throw 'em in the dungeons in the North Keep, that's how I'd handle it!" He drank some more wine.

"Then it's just as well you don't have to handle it," Andreas remarked casually. But Grinkos continued undeterred. "So you didn't make much progress in the Council today. Heard you had a brush with Eburninos — he's a pretty smart young fellow, by all accounts." His speech was slurred. Leda shrank back in her chair, praying silently to the Earth Mother to protect her from any further attention from him.

An awkward silence followed Grinkos' outburst. Andreas was concerned, not by the man's vulgarity and rudeness, but by his knowledge of what had happened at a Council meeting behind closed doors. Some one in the Council must be talking unwisely. He glanced at Brecchius, but the minister was studying the design on his wine goblet and did not look up. If this trivial incident was common knowledge, might not other, more vital matters, be in danger of disclosure?

Andreas was angry, but controlled himself. "The Priest Eburninos will have to stop meddling," he said evenly, "he's an ignorant upstart who will shortly be put in his place." He relapsed into silence and no one dared address him again. The tension was relieved when Olivia admired the design on the fruit bowls, a swirling pattern of seaweed and sea-creatures that suggested the ebb and flow of the tide.

"This is some of the stuff we're turning out at Zakro," Zanthope said, "far more elegant than these old designs." She threw a deprecating hand at a row of beautiful black vases, decorated in geometric patterns of red, blue and yellow, standing on a shelf along the back wall.

"Surely it's just a matter of taste," Ahmed said. He admired the strong contrast of colour in the dark vases. Old Madam agreed with him. "I remember so clearly the day my father brought them home. My mother always treasured them. We children were never allowed to touch them." They continued to discuss the merits of the two styles, when Doxa broke in rudely, "Has anyone news of the Bull Ring? Who retires this year?"

"Paulius will retire," replied Senka, "and the Libyan girl, what's her name?" He snapped his fingers. "M'boola, that's it — and one other, I believe."

"Yes, — the vaulter, Asteria," Brecchius said, "they'll all be missed. We haven't had three such outstanding dancers for a long time."

"They'll certainly be hard to replace," agreed his wife.

"The bulls will get 'em all, you'll see," Grinkos belched and laughed, as though relishing the idea of these graceful and daring acrobats being gored and trampled by the bull.

"We shall have at least three new dancers, then," Doxa said, ignoring her husband, "I wonder if any of them will be worth watching."

"I heard that one of the new girls is very beautiful," Olivia began, "and the other —" Doxa, annoyed, interrupted her, "Where did you pick that up?"

"People were talking in the Courtyard this morning," her friend replied.

The great Courtyard of the Palace of Knossos was a popular meeting place for friends to gossip and exchange news. Usually Doxa would send Olivia on some errand or other, then elicit from her the latest story so that *she* might have the satisfaction of announcing it herself.

"Well, what did you hear?" she asked impatiently. "Only that one of the girls, Freyna, is very blonde and comes from the far, far north, beyond Troy."

"She must be a savage then," muttered Grinkos, banging his goblet on the table for more wine.

"And the other," Olivia continued, "according to Naxos, the Chief Trainer, has the makings of a vaulter. It seems she has remarkable ability."

"Isn't that the girl they call Belia," Senka broke in, "I heard something about her too."

"Belia," repeated Doxa, "that's an unusual name. Where does she come from?"

"That's the odd thing," Senka replied, "nobody seems to know. Apparently she was shipwrecked and brought by fishermen to one of the small islands to the north. The islanders took her for a gift from the Sea God, Poseidon, and put her to serve in their temple. When the Cretan ship arrived — for the tribute — they saved their money and gave her instead, for the Bull Ring."

"What a romantic story," Zanthope said, "she must be destined for success."

"The bulls will get her, you'll see," Grinkos mumbled.

The meal was finished and Zanthope stood up. Everyone followed her back to the front room, leaving Grinkos to the servants. Andreas felt leaden with weariness. He declined to join his mother and Ahmed at cards, so they settled together to play "Storm the Castle" at a small gaming board. Old Madam liked a contest in the evening before retiring.

Senka picked up a lyre and began to entertain the guests with a song in his pleasant voice. Andreas' sister, who had taken little part in the dinner conversation, preferring to listen, came up to say a quiet good night.

"I'm sorry I was late at table, Andreas," she said, "I had some trouble with Eleothi — he wouldn't drink his milk."

Eleothi was one of her pet snakes. She had several in a room built specially for them at the back of the house. Every evening, at sundown, she brought them milk and honey cakes. Andreas knew that she held the popular belief that snakes possess the reincarnated souls of the dead. Pathetically, she was convinced that Eleothi was her dead husband, returned to her in serpent form. Andreas believed his sister was a little mad.

"Don't worry about it, Korynna," he said wearily. He wondered if he could slip quietly away to his own apartment. After all he hadn't invited these people, they were his wife's responsibility. The sound of voices outside in the courtyard made him pause. Old Madam heard it, too.

"That must be Antonius, Andreas," she said with a smiling glance at Leda.

Andreas noticed the girl's reaction. He hoped she would not be another casualty of his son's charm and good looks.

Leda would make a delightful daughter-in-law, Andreas thought, but feared she was too shy and unobtrusive to attract his son.

Antonius Micalidos walked quickly into the room, greeted his father cheerfully with the remark that he was sorry to miss dinner, but he had a winning streak at Klonka's Club and didn't want to leave it. He jingled the coins in a small leather purse. He kissed his grandmother, blew a kiss across the room to his mother and slapped Senka on the back, saying with a wink, "I heard a new song tonight, but it's not for mixed company."

Antonius was tall for a Cretan, though scarcely six feet in height. He was very handsome, with his mother's Greek features and slender figure and his father's fine eyes and thick, dark hair. He had an infectious humour and the kind of magnetism that awakened interest whenever he entered a room or joined a gathering. He was dressed fashionably, wearing a blue and white striped loincloth, somewhat longer at the back and sides, with a tight belt to accentuate his narrow waist. On his chest he wore a collar of crystal and lapis lazuli. A bracelet on his left arm carried his personal seal, carved in agate; a gold anklet and two armlets were also set with crystal and lapis. Leather sandals and a dark blue headband completed his attire. His hair, held by the band in front, fell in thick curls to the back of his neck, and one long strand snaked forward, over the headband — this was the "Love-lock", then fashionable for young men and women in Knossos.

Andreas considered his son's style of dress exaggerated and foppish, but this was not the only subject on which they disagreed. Andreas asked Antonius if he had met Leda Brecchius. "Yes, indeed," Antonius replied, with a brief glance at her. Then, announcing to the room that he was famished, he disappeared as quickly as he had come. Leda watched the door hopefully, anticipating his return with some eagerness.

In the kitchen, Antonius and Deva, the cook, were enjoying their customary argument. Deva was fat and good-natured. She liked young men and Antonius most of all. He was often late for meals and would come pleading for a snack. She always pretended anger and refused. He would then coax, cajole and tickle her till she collapsed in merriment and gave in. Tonight was no exception and the racket woke Timon, who slept in an alcove in the kitchen wall. Peering out, like a rabbit from a burrow, he begged for a mug of goat's milk.

"Where have you been, Antonius," asked the child, a white moustache of milk on his upper lip.

"Playing cards," Antonius replied as he demolished a plate of shrimps. Timon adored his tall half-brother and Antonius treated him with the off-hand affection one might give to a friendly puppy. "Did you win?"

"Yes."

"Will you buy me a pony?"

"I didn't win that much — you'll have to ask Father."

"Will he let me have one?"

"I don't know. Thanks Deva, you saved my life."

"Ho, ho!" she said, hands on hips, "now you want cheese and oatcakes, I suppose."

"Why not, and why aren't you asleep at this time of night, small brother?"

"I was — you woke me up."

Antonius shared his oatcake with Timon, then ruffled his hair and drew the curtain across the alcove once more. "Well, back to sleep again. Good night."

"Good night, 'tonius," the child said sleepily.

Antonius went out through the kitchen to the stable to ensure his mare, Lorca, was comfortable. Lorca was a fine black Arab, a present from his mother. He stayed for some time, talking softly to the mare, stroking her sleek coat and feeling the velvet muzzle against his cheek.

When he returned to the house, the guests had left and everyone else had gone to bed. He was about to go himself when Credon, the steward, appeared and told him his father wished to speak with him.

Antonius climbed the short stairway to the apartment. As he knocked on the door, he expected a reproof for his absence at the evening meal, or even a lecture on the evils of gambling. He was surprised when his father, who was seated in a carved wooden chair, motioned him to sit down and refilling his own goblet, poured some wine for his son.

The room was not large but seemed spacious nonetheless. One end opened onto a small paved court, where a young cypress tree grew and clumps of iris and lilies flowered in large earthenware pots. One long wall of the room was decorated with frescoes of sea scenes in pastel tones of blue and green. The floor was tiled in a blue and white chequer-board pattern. On one side, some shelves held papyrus rolls and beneath stood a table with a silver ink-well in the shape of a dog and a jar full of reed pens. Through a partly drawn curtain a raised platform could be seen, covered with a high feather mattress and a coverlet of white fleece. Beyond, a tiled passage led to the bathroom and toilet. Two chairs, a polished table and a thick, bearskin rug were the only other furnishings, except for a small shrine with a tripod altar. A stand supported a pair of gold bull's horns in the centre of which was slotted the haft of a double-headed axe. This small shrine had been accepted as a concession to Old Madam and her daughter, who were religious. They believed it would give Andreas protection. He seldom addressed himself to the Goddess.

When his son was seated, Andreas came straight to the point. "I shan't keep you long, Antonius. I've had a busy day and I'm tired. However, as I see you so seldom these days," the older man paused for a moment while the younger studied the tiles on the floor, "I thought I'd take this opportunity of saying what's on my mind."

He paused again, considering his words. "Since your elder brother died, I've had no one with whom to discuss problems that come up from time to time. It would be both a help and a pleasure for me to have you take a more active interest in our affairs — after all, these things will be your inheritance one day."

Andreas waited and drank his wine, hoping that his son would reply. Antonius remained silent, staring into his wine-cup. Weariness and exasperation began to take possession of the older man. His inability to reach any kind of understanding with his second son often filled him with great sorrow. He was painfully reminded of a much greater and disastrous failure with the boy's mother years ago. It had been so different with his elder son, Myclos, who had died the previous year. There had been real comradeship between them. Myclos had enjoyed his missions on the trading galleys, as Andreas had done for his father before him.

On a short journey to a nearby island, Myclos and his friends had been involved in a stupid argument after too much wine. Knives had been drawn and he had been stabbed in the arm.

"Just a scratch, Father," Myclos had said hoarsely, when they brought him home, burning and shaking with fever. Even Dr Ahmed could do nothing for him and his death had been a terrible blow for Andreas.

"After all, I'm not getting any younger," Andreas said quietly. But when Antonius still did not reply, he said abruptly, "When are you going to get married, Antonius?" He was going to add, "and settle down and raise a family", but he could feel the young man's antagonism. "Would you like some more wine?" He held out the jug.

"No thank you, Father," Antonius said, placing his wine-cup on the table with deliberation. Suddenly he was seized with a fit of yawning.

"What about doing some military service," Andreas said shortly, "there are serious reports coming in from the north. There could be a war soon. There should be more in your life than gambling, whores and gossip!" He tried not to express his anger and disappointment.

"Father, we've had all this out before," Antonius spoke quietly, "my answer is still the same. No I do not wish to get married. Nor do I wish to undertake military service. As for your serious reports — everyone knows they're always scrapping about something on the mainland. Why worry? Our Cretan Navy will keep them in order. It always has. Neither do I wish to be involved in commerce. I've not the skill nor the inclination for it."

"Skill comes with practice," Andreas interjected.

"But not inclination, Father. The agents you employ do a far better job that I ever could." A faint edge of irritation crept into his voice. "It's not as though it was necessary. Surely I can enjoy myself and lead the kind of life I want, as the sons of other rich men do, without being made to feel guilty about it? Who knows — one day I might write some poetry that's good enough to publish!"

The last remark was made with an attempt at his usual light-hearted manner, but they were both tired and it fell flat. Andreas poured some more wine and refilled his son's cup. "I think you should know," he said, "that I intend to adopt Timon legally." Antonius looked puzzled.

"Well, sir, he's your son."

"Yes, but, if I recognize him legally, then on my death, he will divide the inheritance with you."

"Well," Antonius shrugged his shoulders, "there's plenty for both of us, I've no doubt."

"Are you fond of him?" Andreas asked.

"He seems a harmless little monkey."

"Your mother dislikes him."

"Perhaps women see these things differently." Antonius was wary. He had no wish to be drawn into taking sides.

"But, if I should die..." Andreas persisted.

"Nonsense, Father, you've another twenty years at least."

Andreas ignored the interruption. "The boy will need a guardian. I intend to appoint you."

"Why not Dr Ahmed? He's almost one of the family and he's far more the guardian type than I."

"I'd sooner it was you, Antonius."

"As you wish then, Father."

There was a moment of awkward silence. Antonius was impatient to leave, but he knew he had hurt his father and wanted to make amends. "Did the Council meeting go well for you today, sir?"

He did not ask because he was interested but because he thought it would please his father to discuss it. Andreas grunted in disgust. "No, indeed. I had little opportunity to state my views. We need money for ships and the priests want to build a new temple. We need to raise stronger fortifications around the Palace and the Council votes money to increase seating in the boxing ring! I can't make them appreciate the dangers of our situation."

"Perhaps you are tired, sir. That makes things seem worse than they are."

"You think I'm wrong, too, then," Andreas murmured. His son did not answer. It was all so hard to grasp. Crete had flourished for a thousand years, safe, secure and prosperous. There had been periods of internal discord, but even these problems were settled long ago. Knossos was supreme and Cretan ships sailed unchallenged throughout the Great Green Sea, from Troy to Egypt, from Libya to the coast of Sicily. Andreas broke the silence.

"Well, if the Goddess pleases, I am wrong and there is no threat to our island and empire."

"I shall drink to that, Father." They raised their cups and drank — "to Crete".

"Good night, Father."

"Good night, my boy."

Andreas watched as his son left the room with a light, confident step. If only his life had more purpose, he thought. He rose stiffly and walked through the open court. The night air was soft and balmy around him. He breathed it in deeply.

Below, in the dark valley, a lamp still burned in the Palace. Somewhere in the distance, a night-owl hunted and presently the muffled shriek of its prey broke the stillness of the night.

He lingered a few moments, gazing at that hypnotic light and then turned and went back into the house.

# CHAPTER 2

The next day, Andreas left Knossos in his chariot with Dr Ahmed and Senka, while morning mists still wreathed the valley in skeins of white. Progress was slow at first. The city streets were crowded with artisans and craftsmen on their way to the Palace workshops and carts bringing produce to market.

Once clear of the city, the driver headed the chariot eastward and settled the horses to a brisk trot. Early sunlight hung crystal beads in the meadow grass. Peasants tending their crops waved cheerfully as they sped by and Andreas remarked that the harvest showed more promise than the previous year, thank the Goddess.

"Yes, indeed, sir," Ahmed replied, "I don't ever remember seeing the countryside look better."

"How long is it since you came to us?"

"Twelve years."

Dr Ahmed was not likely to forget. In one tragic

night he had lost both his wife and newborn son. He owed much to Andreas, who had sympathetically invited him to visit Crete and then persuaded him to remain as personal physician to the household. Ahmed had established a surgery in a poor quarter of the city. Andreas financed the purchase of drugs and the service of assistants the doctor had trained. One of these, Iros, a young Corinthian, was now able to take charge when Ahmed was absent.

Andreas shifted as they rounded a bend. "I hope you've no regrets at making your life with us."

"No, sir, no regrets," the doctor replied with a smile.

Andreas always enjoyed visiting his shipyard at Nirou-Khani. However, on this day his pleasure was spoiled by reports of trouble and quarrelling among his shipwrights.

"Well, Senka," he said to the young man who had not spoken since they left Knossos, "I hope that rogue, Karkoran, has exaggerated this trouble."

"Yes, sir, so do I," Senka replied. "Perhaps it will all blow over," he added, feeling that some comment was necessary.

Andreas had observed his secretary's preoccupation and suspected he knew its cause. He recalled his impression of Senka and his wife at the dinner table the previous night, heads close together.

As they clattered through a small village, dogs barked and children waved from a cottage doorway. Andreas noted how peaceful and prosperous the countryside looked. Why should he be so filled with foreboding?

They turned north, heading towards the coast, through wooded country, fresh with the new green of summer.

"I think I'll pack Timon off to the farm for a few months," Andreas remarked, as they checked for a moment at the guard station on the Mallia road.

"It certainly wouldn't do him any harm," Ahmed said, "he might not get into so much mischief up there."

"There's no one to look after him properly since his mother died ..." Andreas broke off suddenly, exclaiming, "Just look at this!"

The wooded countryside through which they had travelled had given way to an area where the young trees had been lopped down and only the stumps remained.

"It's the same all over the country. These trees should have been left another ten years at least, before being felled."

Ships and palaces were threatening to swallow up Crete's vast forests. Andreas had tried to encourage reafforestation, without success. His efforts to persuade the King to forbid the felling of trees without a licence had been brushed aside. The priests, who dominated the Council, were not interested in timber unless it was for themselves.

Now, the sea was visible and Andreas ordered the driver to pause for a moment. They admired the wild, rocky coastline and the sea-shades changing from green to blue as the eye travelled from shoreline to horizon. There all colour dissolved into a haze and the vague outline of distant islands.

"Magnificent," Andreas spoke with quiet conviction, "we're lucky to live in such a beautiful place." Ahmed and Senka murmured their agreement and they descended the winding road to the shipyard.

It was situated at the head of a deep inlet, its buildings sprawled untidily along the shoreline. Large sheds stored rope, sailcloth, pigments and caulking pitch. Outside was a stone water cistern, a large copper cauldron for steaming and stacks of cedar planks. Workbenches on trestles held bronze saws, mallets, boxes of copper nails and wooden rivets. But the shipwrights stood in groups, idle and sour-faced.

Most of Andreas' fleet was now at sea, but one galley was propped on stilts for recaulking and the keel of another was laid, with the bare frames curving upwards like the skeletal ribs of some prehistoric beast.

Andreas viewed the scene with displeasure. The foreman, Cibaros, a dark sinewy man, stepped forward and respectfully raised his fist to his forehead.

"What's going on here, Cibaros?" Andreas said sternly.

"There's been some trouble, sir. I've spoken to the men, but they won't listen, they won't see sense."

Cibaros was as concerned as Andreas. He had served the family faithfully for thirty years and had been an apprentice when Andreas was in the schoolroom. There had never been trouble like this before.

Andreas was unimpressed. Containing his anger he said evenly: "I'm still waiting for an explanation."

"It's the poor quality of the timber. It's not what the men are accustomed to."

"What's wrong with it?"

"It's unseasoned — these men are craftsmen, as I am. They only turn out first class work ... it's a matter of pride. We can't work with green wood — it doesn't set true. And then, there's a shortage of special cuts — elbows and so on. It's not like the old days. In my father's time we were never held up for supplies like this. He'd as soon have jumped overboard as try to work with ..."

"Yes, I know," Andreas said tersely, "what's wrong with this stuff?" He pointed to the stacks outside the sheds.

"It's full of splits, knots and odd lengths," Cibaros said gloomily. He paused, rubbing his hand across his brow, "then, there's this other business."

"What other business?" As Cibaros hesitated, Andreas snapped, "Well, come on, out with it."

"The men are grumbling about those two," the foreman jerked his thumb at the two tall men who stood apart. One of them had a black eye.

"The Egyptians — isn't their work satisfactory?"

"Yes, indeed, sir, they're good workmen all right. There's no complaint on that score. It's just ... the men don't like having them in the yard." Andreas frowned angrily. Cibaros went on: "You see sir, the men blame these migrants for the shortage of timber. It's them that's cutting down all the trees for their homes and buying up all the wood for fuel. If supplies get any shorter, we'll all be out of work."

"No one will be out of work here. You have my word on that. Tell the men to gather round." Andreas assured the shipwrights they would have good timber soon. He appealed to them to accept the foreigners. "They have wives and children to feed, just as you have," he said reasonably.

"Why don't they go home and work there?" The voice came from the back. Andreas knew the man as a troublemaker.

"They'll work here as long as I say — anyone who doesn't like it can leave now. You men get back to work." Andreas turned to Cibaros and concluded, "Get the men busy on the caulking. You'll have fresh timber by noon. If that fellow makes any more trouble, sack him."

"Very good, sir."

Andreas, Ahmed and Senka immediately set off on the return journey. Andreas was silent. The timber business was getting beyond a joke. The merchants were wise to it and prices were soaring. The timber in the yard had cost enough, he thought. Mother of Zeus — it should have been checked before delivery — "I'll have the ears off that agent, Karkoran," he muttered to himself.

Andreas soon realized that his promise to find "fresh timber by noon" was overly optimistic. The merchants of Nirou-Khani were sold out. The most likely place was the port, Amnissos, directly north of Knossos. Andreas knew a merchant there named Praxitor, a Phoenician of Byblos, sharp and resourceful. He imported cedar wood through family contacts in his native city. In winter, when the ports closed, he sold at high profit. He seemed to Andreas the most likely source of good timber.

When they arrived at Amnissos they went directly to Praxitor's warehouse and timber yard. They passed through an unpretentious entrance which led to a large yard at the back of the house. The rich smell of cedar permeated everywhere. Some lay unsawn, the great logs still bearing the marks where they had been secured on the decks of the trading galleys.

Andreas was astonished at the quantity and quality of Praxitor's timber. The merchant allowed him to examine it all thoroughly, drawing out individual planks from the stacks to show off the grain. Andreas felt there was an ulterior motive in this, but could not conjecture what it was. Even if he had wished to rebuild his entire merchant fleet, he would not have needed half the timber here. But he was taken aback by the prices Praxitor quoted. He tried to bargain with him, but the merchant remained firm.

"My lord," he said in a harsh, thick accent, "I am not greedy. Next month this timber is worth more and the next, more again." He then remarked casually, "The royal fleet needs cedar planks ... so the rumour goes."

"The fleet is supplied through the Palace," Andreas snapped, annoyed at the fellow's impudence.

"Then, if the price does not suit my lord, he can no doubt find an alternative supply." The insinuation that he could get timber for his own use from the Palace stores infuriated Andreas. It was common knowledge that some people did this, but he had nothing but contempt for them.

"Deliver the order at once. My agent will bring your money tomorrow." Praxitor bowed low. "Our terms are — payment in full, delivery after."

"My credit is good!" Andreas turned to his secretary. "Senka, hire a horse and fetch the money from Knossos and make sure this barbarian delivers the timber immediately."

"Yes, sir," Senka replied.

Andreas, with a stern face, marched out of the yard, followed by Ahmed. They were about to climb into the chariot when they saw a man alight from a chair at a nearby wine-shop. It was Andreas' agent Karkoran.

"Tell that fellow to come here," Andreas ordered the chariot driver. He indicated to Ahmed to get in and wait for him.

Karkoran was a grey, flabby man, generally reliable when he was sober and of an ingratiatingly amiable disposition. He approached nervously when he saw Andreas' face, anticipating trouble.

"Were you drunk or half asleep when you had that rubbish delivered to my yard?" his employer snarled.

Karkoran cringed but diverted the blame to the timber merchants. "I selected first quality, sir ..." he began.

"Zeus! Don't lie to me! You'll answer to the magistrates if this happens again. Think yourself lucky not to be dismissed." Andreas turned abruptly and climbed into the chariot. Karkoran, muttering apologies, escaped into the wine-shop. Still fuming, Andreas directed the driver to a house further down the street. It was the noon siesta, very hot and quiet. A trader slumbered peacefully beneath his cart. When they alighted and made themselves known, Loren, the Harbour Master, was thrown into great confusion by the honour of a visit from the Minister for Trade, Councillor Micalidos and his friend, Dr Ahmed. He fussed at his young wife, Diora, snapped at the slaves and ordered them to serve "the best dry wine", and then ushered his guests to his small terrace overlooking the harbour. Vines, trained over a trellis, gave a pleasant shade.

"This is perfect," Andreas said, sitting thankfully. The wine was cool and Diora offered oatcakes and fresh cream cheese. The guests indicated their pleasure and their host relaxed. Their talk ran easily on matters concerning the port. Looking down at the busy wharves, they saw a trading galley loaded with crates of pottery and large jars of oil. At an adjacent berth another vessel unloaded a cargo of tanned hides and furs from Troy. Immigrants, with baggage and livestock, were on deck impatiently waiting to disembark.

"It's time some kind of check was made on the number of foreigners landing here," Andreas remarked.

"They bring us new skills and trade," the Harbour Master replied, "exports this year look like breaking all records."

Andreas drank his wine thoughtfully. "We pay a high price in overcrowded cities — and this timber shortage is far more serious than most people realize," he said.

"It's odd that you should mention that, Minister," Loren said, "there was trouble last month down at the naval repair yard."

Andreas was alert at once he asked. "What sort of trouble?"

"Well, I understand it concerned the flagship — the *Griffon*. You would remember, sir, when she was commissioned — by the King's father before he visited Sicily?"

Andreas remembered the day perfectly. It was shortly after his marriage. Zanthope had ridden, laughing beside him in the chariot, her golden hair streaming out as they raced along the highway to Amnissos. The fleet had been decked out with flags and pennants. Minos had worn ceremonial dress with a crown of peacock feathers.

With an effort Andreas brought his mind back to the present, as Loren continued. "Well, the *Griffon* was slipped to be recaulked and painted. When the paint and weed were stripped off, some planks — so they say — were found to be rotten. She was sitting, like a broody duck, for weeks waiting on new planking. In the end they recaulked her ... patched her up with pitch and paint and put her back in the water, rotten planks and all — there she is, in the bay." He pointed to the big galley, swinging at anchor and looking handsome enough. "How long she'll stay watertight is anybody's guess," he added tersely.

"Where did you hear this story?" Ahmed asked as Diora was refilled their wine-cups.

"We have an unending source of information in dear old Ptyrron," she remarked.

Ptyrron, an ex-sailor, had retired, she said, from the royal galleys and now acted as handyman for the Harbour Master. "He goes down in the taverns," she added, "to relive his seafaring days over a jug of beer and brings us all the gossip of the port. He's most entertaining."

Andreas encouraged her. "What other tales has he brought home lately?"

"Let me see," she replied thoughtfully, "oh, yes, I remember — they said they had some trouble a week ago on another galley, the *Eagle*. She apparently sprung a leak — the crew were kept bailing day and night. The captain wouldn't let them go ashore, but one of the sailors disobeyed and swam across, to see some girl, I suppose. When he returned, the watch caught him and he was flogged half to death, poor man! They say the crew were close to mutiny!"

The harbour master reproved her. "There's no proof of this, Diora. It's probably just another tall story."

Andreas was disturbed by what he had heard. He recalled that at the Council meeting yesterday, the Navy Minister, Markos, had not mentioned any timber shortage. On the contrary, he had expressed himself more than satisfied with the fleet.

Andreas was determined to discover the truth of these matters. He and Dr Ahmed thanked Loren and Diora for their hospitality and set off down the steep, narrow road to the main naval base of Crete's northern coastline. As they made their way across the deserted shipyard, Andreas looked around in disgust. "The place looks derelict!" Ahmed agreed with him. "Where in the name of Zeus are all the shipwrights?" Andreas exclaimed.

They stepped out of the sunlight into a dark shed and, for a moment, could see nothing until their eyes became accustomed to the gloom. They saw a group of men, who looked up uneasily from a gaming board set on a makeshift table.

"Which of you hard-working gentlemen is the foreman?" Andreas inquired. The foreman was, at that moment, enjoying a jug of wine at the Sailmaker's Haven.

"He's busy on a job, sir, on one of the galleys," said a brawny tough-looking shipwright.

"Which galley?"

"The *Griffon*, sir."

"How many men are with him?"

"Two, I think."

"Haven't you got anything better to do?"

"We're waiting on the timber."

"Try cleaning up the yard — it looks like a pigsty."

"Who are you to tell us what to do?" the man asked.

"I am Councillor Micalidos, Minister for Trade," Andreas said quietly, "I am on a tour of inspection, I'll see the Palace has a full report on conditions here."

Andreas found pleasure in matching the man's lies with one of his own. The effect was immediate. The workmen abandoned their game and protested loudly. They had no timber, no orders, there was nothing to keep them occupied. Another shipwright came forward: "It's no fault of ours the keels aren't laid yet — you can't build ships out of rotten wood, sand and seaweed!"

"How long have you been delayed?"

"Nearly four months. We filled in with a few repair jobs — used up every piece of timber in the place. And the new galleys ordered last winter are held up till we can lay the keels. And the stems and frames need special cuts — the stuff's just not coming in. Promises is all we get! Next month, they say — next month, next bloody year, more likely!" He spat angrily.

"I'll see you get timber," Andreas said, "if it's the last thing I do," he added half to himself as he and Ahmed left the shed. The chariot driver was sunning himself on a rock. "Ask one of those fishermen to ferry us out to the *Griffon*," Andreas ordered.

The man walked over to a group of fishermen spreading their nets out to dry. One of them pushed his boat out and rowed towards the end of a narrow landing-stage. They clambered in and were several yards away before Andreas said with a smile, "Would you have rather stayed on shore, Ahmed?"

"No, indeed, sir," the doctor replied. He was no seaman, but he was delighted to have this opportunity to see a royal galley at close quarters.

There was a gentle breeze as they moved out towards the *Griffon*. The squalor of the yard was soon lost to sight and they enjoyed the view of the rocky headland and the houses, painted in pastel colours on the steep hillside. As they approached the *Griffon*, Ahmed was amazed at its size. From the shore she appeared to be a large and handsome ship, but from a small boat at sea level the *Griffon* seemed massive. The hull rose in a broad, bellying curve towards the high carved prow, towering higher than the height of three men above them. A sailor leaned over the rail and inquired as to their business.

"Micalidos of the King's Council. I wish to come aboard."

The seaman disappeared. Andreas felt a bold front was most likely to succeed. The ship looked magnificent, painted scarlet, with two narrow strakes of white and pale blue at the sheer line. The notion that she had rotten planks below seemed ridiculous. Perhaps the rumours were exaggerated.

After a moment a rope ladder was dropped over the side. "Shall I wait while you're on board, sir?" asked the fisherman.

"No, thank you," Andreas said, giving the man a coin. They can ferry us back he said to himself. He intended to stay and learn as much as possible.

Andreas and Ahmed climbed the ladder with some difficulty. Once they were on deck the ship was even more impressive, from the magnificent cedar planking of the deck to the masts and spars varnished till they shone like glass. Many of the fittings, the lamp-holders and shroud plates were gilded. The poop, which seemed to tower up many feet above their heads, even at deck level, was crowned with a great bull's head, carved in wood and painted in the most realistic manner. The horns flashed gold in the sun and the eyes glowed red. The stem supporting the figurehead was carved in wave-like scrolls, decorated with the figures of sea-maidens, their ivory breasts gold-tipped and their legs and buttocks sheathed in scales, like fishes tails. Aft, above the transom, the stern reared up as high as the prow in the form of a great fish-tail. Two upright rudders rose on either side, where the helmsmen stood. The hand-grips of the tillers were banded in leather.

Three seamen sat on the forward deck splicing rope. They wore short, dark blue loin cloths and head bands to hold their long black hair in place. On their left wrist they carried a carved stone identity tag attached to a bronze bracelet. Their sunburnt skin was almost as dark as the timber planking. Andreas was about to remark to Dr Ahmed that the men looked healthy and well fed, when a seaman asked them to follow him aft, where three steps led up to a small quarterdeck. A young man stood waiting and bowed, fist to forehead.

"Captain Keridos, sir, welcome aboard the *Griffon*."

Captain Keridos was about thirty, not tall but well built. A touch of quizzical humour in the lift of one eyebrow softened the arrogance of his face. In his dress he was something of a dandy, even for a Cretan. He wore a handsome chest-piece of gold and silver chain. Andreas realized that he belonged to one of the leading families of Knossos. Keridos carried his command with ease. He was affable and invited them to his cabin and offered them a drink. However, Andreas sensed an underlying tension, even wariness in his manner. Well aware of the delicacy of the situation, Andreas realized that tactlessness would gain nothing. He introduced Dr Ahmed, remarked on the excellence of the ship, the convenience of the anchorage and the good bearing of the men.

Keridos accepted the compliments coolly, but he could not altogether conceal from Andreas, who knew ships and seamen, the intense love and pride he felt for his ship. Andreas felt a sudden compassion for this arrogant young captain, lavishing care and attention on a ship which could be rotten below the water-line. A servant offered them a bowl of figs and sweet melon. "The first ripe figs I've seen this year," Andreas said, taking one.

"I had them sent from the south," Keridos replied casually, "while in port I always provide fresh fruit for my crew, it keeps them healthy." He went on in the same tone: "If I had been informed of your visit, I would have sent a boat for you, sir."

"We preferred to come in an unobtrusive manner."

"Your visit is not official then?"

"No. As a member of the Council, I like to take an interest in the welfare of His Majesty's fleet."

"I am always glad to be of service."

After a moment's pause Andreas said: "Captain Keridos, I'll be honest with you. I've heard rumours concerning the fleet — of course, they may only be tavern gossip, but I felt I should investigate them."

"How does this concern me, sir?" Keridos asked quietly.

"I understand the *Griffon* was held up some weeks in the repair yard."

"We did have some delay, but it was of no consequence."

"But I understand you needed new planking and did not obtain it."

Keridos replied sharply, "The ship has been completely overhauled. She was recaulked and painted and is perfectly watertight."

"Is the ship sound," Andreas persisted, "will she stand up to rough weather?"

"I believe so. Of course we do not expect rough weather at this time of year."

Andreas was puzzled by the captain's attitude. If this young man loved his ship so much and the vessel needed new planking, why did he not press for it now he had the opportunity? If the rumours were groundless, why was he so reticent? But he saw no point in pressing him further. He changed the subject.

"What ships are out on patrol now, Captain?"

"The *Swan* and *Peacock*, sir."

"There are only two ships to patrol the north coast?"

"The Minister, Councillor Markos, considers that this is sufficient."

"Where are the *Dolphin*, *Porpoise* and the rest of the fleet?"

"They were ordered south to Phaestos, to take part in the Spring Festival. They have not yet returned."

Andreas was surprised to hear this. He asked Keridos if the three galleys lying at anchor nearby were ready for sea. The captain replied that one of them, the *Eagle*, was due for a refit, but the other two were ready for immediate duty.

"Yes, I heard that the *Eagle* was leaking badly," Andreas remarked. Keridos did not reply. Andreas wondered why, in Zeus' name, was this young man so evasive. He decided the interview must end and thanked the captain warmly for his hospitality. Keridos smiled politely and ordered a boat to convey them away.

Two smaller galleys, the *Gull* and the *Gannet*, lay about a hundred yards to port beyond the *Eagle*. Andreas asked the boatman to row them to the *Gannet*, commanded by a Lieutenant Dessios, a friend of Antonius, who had once dined at the villa. Dessios was a pleasant, open-faced young man, good humoured and talkative. He welcomed Andreas and Ahmed, inquired after Antonius and took them on a tour of his ship. "She's as sound as a bell, sir," he said proudly.

They saw the narrow benches where the oarsmen sat. It was hot and stuffy below decks. Not the place to be in bad weather, Ahmed thought. Andreas saw that everything was in order.

Seated in Lieutenant Dessios' small cabin they accepted a drink of local wine and their host introduced his friend, Lieutenant Rekkyn, who commanded the *Gull*, anchored nearby.

"The *Griffon* is a fine old ship," Ahmed remarked.

"Isn't she magnificent!" Dessios agreed, "Captain Keridos is fortunate to have command of her — of course, it's no more than he deserves."

"We heard there was some trouble with her planking."

"Yes, I believe there was," Dessios replied quietly.

"Do you know what happened?"

"I think they patched her up in the yard, sir."

"With new planks, or with pitch and canvas?"

"I couldn't say, sir, I was on patrol at the time."

"Has the *Griffon* been to sea since she was repaired?"

"I don't think so, sir. I believe she's to be held in reserve ... for emergencies."

Andreas pressed his advantage. "What you mean is, she's not really seaworthy if a storm blows up?"

"We don't usually get storms at this time of year, sir."

"I am aware of the prevailing weather at this season," Andreas said tersely. Turning to Rekkyn he inquired as to the condition of his ship. "*Gull* was built at the same time as this vessel, sir, only two seasons ago. I suppose these two ships are the most seaworthy of the northern fleet."

"What do you mean by the 'northern fleet'?" Andreas asked.

"This is the new ordinance, sir. The main fleet is now based on Phaestos in the south. We are to be known as the northern fleet."

Andreas could scarcely believe his ears. "How many galleys?"

Rekkyn looked inquiringly across the polished wood table at Dessios. "Four at anchor here and four on patrol, isn't it?"

"Only two on patrol, Rekkyn," Dessios replied, "I heard the other day that *Swordfish* was sent east to Zakro with despatches and *Ibis* sprang a leak and is beached for repairs on the coast near Nirou-Khani."

"Where'd you hear that?" Rekkyn asked.

"From old Ptyrron, of course, where else?" They both laughed. Andreas stared out at the busy wharves, but he saw nothing. He was considering the alarming discovery that the northern coast of Crete was now apparently defended by eight ships, three of which were unseaworthy and one was far off at Zakro.

"The two galleys on patrol," he said suddenly, "are they new ships like these?"

"No, sir," Rekkyn replied, "they're as old as *Griffon*."

"But they were recaulked and painted during the winter," Dessios said.

"What about gear — rope, rigging, sailcloth — are supplies adequate?" Andreas' persistence was embarrassing the young officers. After a moment's silence Rekkyn said, "There is a shortage at the moment, sir. But Captain Keridos says it's only temporary."

"Yes," Dessios broke in, "we have to make do — improvise. The Captain says it's excellent training for the men." His boyish face beamed enthusiastically. Andreas rose and thanked them for their hospitality. At that moment, Ahmed, on the other side of the cabin, pointed through the open port.

"What ship is that, out there? Is that one of our galleys?"

They turned to have a look. "No, sir, it's not one of ours," Dessios said.

"Mycenaean, by the lines of her," Andreas muttered. Sacred Mother, he thought, a Mycenaean galley sailing into Amnissos unchallenged. Such a thing would never had happened in the late King's reign. Why in holy snakes doesn't Keridos send her about her business? "Has this ship been here before?" he asked.

"They came to buy oil last month," Dessios replied.

Well, it might be legitimate business, but this was no trading vessel. Andreas was impatient to be gone. Could they have a boat to ferry them ashore? He tried not to sound too abrupt. Dessios was eager to help and they sailed shore-wards on the incoming tide. As they stepped ashore, a man detached himself from a group who were clearing up the yard. He raised his fist to his forehead respectfully, but his manner was nervous.

"Are you the foreman?" Andreas asked.

"Yes, sir. Achnos. May I ask your business here?"

Andreas ignored the question. "They said you were working on the *Griffon*, but you were not there?"

"I was there — before you came, sir. I had to come back for some gear; at the chandler's."

"You should let the apprentices run the errands. So, you had no timber to repair the *Griffon*?"

"That's right, sir. Just as well, if you ask me."

"What do you mean?"

"Be a waste of good timber — she's too far gone. Well, after all, she's twenty years old. Better to use the timber for new ships ... if we ever get any."

"I'm going to the Palace now. You will have timber, soon."

Andreas summoned the chariot driver and he and Ahmed began their journey back to Knossos. As they were passing the wine-shop, Andreas decided that he must speak with his agent, Karkoran. He sent the driver in to seek him. Karkoran came out with a nervous and ingratiating smile.

"Listen," Andreas said quietly, "there's an old fellow who frequents the wine-shops — Ptyrron's his name. Seek him out and buy him a drink — not too much — get him to talk. Find out what's going on in the naval galleys and the repair yard, and any other gossip you can pick up. Report to me as soon as you can, it's very important."

Karkoran nodded. As they resumed their journey Andreas reviewed his impressions of the day. A shortage of timber in the naval repair yards was extraordinary. However, Praxitor's yard had proved that timber was not unobtainable, though expensive and in short supply elsewhere. And the continued absence of the main fleet on a ceremonial visit south was quite beyond comprehension. Could these two circumstances be mere incompetence or was there a more sinister explanation?

Andreas knew he must tread carefully at the Palace. He had sometimes given offence by speaking too bluntly. He wondered who he could trust in an emergency. Brecchius, the Minister for Finance? — clever, but not dependable — a fair weather friend; Markos, the Navy Minister? honest, loyal and upright, but so difficult, touchy and jealous of his authority that he would take no criticism of his department. And Markos was the Councillor with whom he must contend — he and Xanthios, the Minister for Supply. "And I wouldn't trust him further that I could spit!" Andreas murmured. Dr Ahmed glanced at him inquiringly.

"My dear friend, I hope this day hasn't proved too tedious for you?"

"No, indeed," Ahmed replied smiling, "I've enjoyed this break from the surgery."

"I'm in a quandary. I don't know who I can really trust on the Council. I know I can rely on Chancellor

Darien and General Imanos — they were my father's friends. But the rest — the priests!" Andreas gave an expressive gesture. "It's sad the old priest, Pasterion, is ill. He's no fool." Andreas smiled wryly. "Perhaps the people are right and the Goddess really is angry!"

# CHAPTER 3

Andreas and Ahmed alighted at the North Gate of the Palace. Under the portico, a huge bas-relief of a bull menaced all comers. Andreas preferred other frescoes, but this work was powerful and demanded attention. Children would cry out in fear sometimes on seeing it and some people even said they could feel his hot breath on their faces.

The sentry saluted the two men and, after checking Ahmed's identity, let them enter. They passed through a shrine, gaily festooned with coloured ribbons and gifts left by departing visitors. A slave brought bowls of fresh, cool water. After removing their sandals, they thankfully bathed their faces, hands and feet. A tiled pathway ascended in a gentle slope to the central Courtyard. From this vantage point they were aware of the immense size of the Palace, but there was something more overpowering than its size. There was a sinister atmosphere about the place, an ambience at once disturbing and compelling. This was Labrynthos, the home of Minos, the Priest-King, the House of the Double Axes.

The Palace Courtyard was entirely closed. On either side great buildings rose up with balconied windows supported by russet pillars. White walls reflected the afternoon sun. Stylized golden bull's horns decorated the pale blue lintels above the windows, and the capitals and bases of the pillars were painted blue or black.

The East Palace was the royal residence of King Minos and his family, and those whose rank or position entitled them to apartments there. Others had acquired a place by wealth or influence. In consequence the Palace was very overcrowded. The West Palace, in its apparently endless maze of rooms, offices, shrines and corridors, accommodated official Government Departments. Justice, Trade, Local and Colonial Government, Treasury and Storehouse, and Embassies were all located here. It was the administrative hub of the nation. From it extended all power, and all wealth converged upon it. At the northern entrance was the Keep, with its massive ancient stonework. Those who offended authority vanished into its dungeons, deep in the foundations of earlier palaces, which the Earth Shaker had ravaged so long ago.

At the southern end of the Courtyard a wide, covered promenade connected the two palaces. A gateway through stone walls led out to a paved road which ran down the hill to the city.

It was now late in the afternoon. Heat radiated from the polished stone slabs which paved the

Courtyard, deserted except for the guards standing like statues at the doorways.

As Andreas and Ahmed approached the East Palace, the sounds of voices and laughter floated down from the upper balconies where some women sat idly gossiping and fanning themselves, while servants prepared the evening meal.

Andreas and Ahmed were about to enter when they heard shouts of applause in the distance. "Is there some contest on today," Andreas inquired of the sentry who saluted them.

"Yes, my lord, the wrestling tournament. Theseus, the Greek, challenges our champion, Varkos." Tournaments were held at regular intervals in the boxing ring outside the Palace and a great deal of money was wagered on the contestants.

They entered a lofty hall with a gallery at the second story. A large statue of the Goddess, Earth Mother, gazed benevolently down, extending her ivory hands in a welcoming gesture. Her flounced skirt shone with sapphires as blue as her eyes. Ivory breasts, with gold-tipped nipples, curved out from the tight bodice. Her dark hair was held by a blue and gold band. Gold edged the flounces of her skirt and gleamed in the bracelets on her arms. Two carved doves perched on her left shoulder and her lips were parted in a welcoming smile. A young slave boy sat before the image on a low stool, trimming the wick in a large lamp bowl.

Whenever possible, Andreas avoided going to the East Palace. He asked the boy if he knew the apartment of Councillor Markos and the lad beckoned them to follow him. They walked up a narrow, dimly lit stairway, along a winding, tiled passage and across a small court. Here a woman sat sewing on a stone bench, while two young children played at her feet. They ascended once more and, turning at right angles down another passage, the slave boy knocked on the door. The sound echoed loudly in the enclosed space. Presently another slave answered and, on hearing that they wished to see his master, replied: "My lord Markos is attending the tournament."

Andreas cursed and stood for a moment, uncertain what to do. Ahmed placed a hand on his arm. "Would it not be advisable, sir, to leave a message for the Minister and arrange a meeting tomorrow?" he asked.

"A message, yes — but I must see him tonight — the matter is urgent. Tell your master, when he returns, that I wish to see him as soon as possible. I will be at the apartment of Councillor Brecchius."

"Yes, Councillor Micalidos," the slave replied.

Turning to the boy who waited in the passage, Andreas asked him if he knew Councillor Brecchius' apartment. "Yes, my lord, it's not far."

Ahmed wished fervently that they were at home, enjoying the peace of the garden and the prospect of his evening meal. What an endless and exhausting day he thought and stole a glance at Andreas who looked worn out but determined. The doctor knew from experience that it was useless to remonstrate.

Madam Brecchius heard them asking for her husband at the door and came herself to welcome them. She wore a long, old-fashioned bell-shaped skirt and a linen chemise under her jacket. Leading them into a pleasant airy room surrounding a wide light well, she insisted that they stay and take some refreshment, her husband was at the tournament but would surely return soon.

Madam Brecchius loved flowers. She was delighted when Dr Ahmed complimented her on the array of large pots of roses and lilies. Across the room, her daughter, Leda, was working on a piece of embroidery. "Leda, dear, we have guests. For goodness sake put that sewing away." The girl put her work aside and exchanged greetings with Andreas and Dr Ahmed. Her mother continued in an upbraiding tone: "I wanted her to go to the tournament with her father and sister this afternoon, but nothing would budge her. She's far too much of a stay-at-home. When she does go out, she's overcome with nerves — if she went out more often, she would get used to it."

Leda flushed with embarrassment. Andreas came to her defence: "She does very well as she is." Leda smiled gratefully. The servants offered wine and dishes of olives and fish savouries and they sat on cushioned benches round the walls.

Andreas was becoming increasingly obsessed with his problems, but politeness demanded that they make conversation. Madam Brecchius chatted on about her flowers and her elder daughter, Chryssa, who was married to the Captain of the Palace Guard, and was everything, apparently, any mother could wish for in a daughter.

At last, Andreas' patience ended. He asked if he might have a pen and some papyrus with which to write a letter. He wrote:

> To Markos, King's Councillor,
> Minister of the Fleet,
> Greetings,
> It is imperative that I see you at your earliest convenience. The business I would discuss with you concerns the security of our country. You will appreciate the urgency. Would you care to dine at my villa tonight? Or we could meet in the Palace if you prefer.
> Regards,
> Micalidos

The letter was despatched with the instruction that an immediate answer was necessary.

After a few moments there was a loud knock on the door. They expected Brecchius, but the slave admitted an attractive young woman and a soldier, who wore an officer's corselet and carried a bronze-studded helmet.

"Well, Chryssa, how did it go?" Madam Brecchius asked, rising quickly to greet her favourite daughter.

"I won three gold pieces on Theseus, the bull dancer, mother. He's champion of the day!"

Chryssa threw up her purse jubilantly and caught it. Madam Brecchius presented her daughter and son-in-law, Captain Dino Senthios, to her guests. She then inquired if they would all be staying for dinner. Andreas and Ahmed politely declined. "I can, mother, but Dino must eat at once, he goes on duty in a few minutes," said Chryssa.

"Well come along Dino. Chrys, you entertain the guests; please excuse me, for a moment, gentlemen." Madam Brecchius beckoned to her son-in-law, who followed her into another room.

Chryssa Senthios was one of the most beautiful young women in Knossos. Her black hair lay in curls across her forehead and hung down her back from beneath a scarlet headband, accentuating the creamy pallor of her skin. Her dark, heavy-lidded eyes usually lacked animation, which gave her gaze a secret, enigmatic quality which the young men of Knossos found fascinating. Half of them imagined themselves in love with her. Her features were firm and straight. When she grew old they would be hard and sharp, but just now they seemed perfect. As she moved across the room, her flounced skirt of vivid red and blue swayed with the movement of her hips; a narrow belt encircled her waist and the low-cut, tightly laced bodice showed off her breasts to advantage. Her jewellery clinked and jingled at every step.

"You had good luck at the tournament, then?" Ahmed said.

"Yes, indeed, Theseus was magnificent! His style is quite superb." Chryssa had slender, expressive hands and gestured frequently as she spoke. "At first the contest was equal, hold for hold, we nearly died of excitement," she laughed, aware of her attentive audience, "but in the last round Varkos tired and was forced to yield. You should have heard the cheers!"

Andreas watched her appreciatively. What a contrast between the two sisters he thought, this one's a baggage and Leda's a mouse. Aloud he said, "Who is this Theseus, Madam Senthios?"

"They say he's a Greek Prince."

"A Prince? Do you believe that?"

"Yes, he could be a Prince. He has a noble bearing — he's tall, handsome, athletic. Somebody said he was the son of King Aegeus."

"Really?" Andreas was surprised, "if he's a Prince I wonder what he's doing here as a bull dancer."

"You'd have to ask the Princess," Chryssa said with a smile.

Andreas changed the subject. "Do you think your father will return soon, Madam Senthios?"

"Why, yes — he just stopped to collect his winnings."

There was a knock on the door. It was a message for Madam Brecchius. Her husband would not come home to dinner. There was also a letter for Andreas. He excused himself to read it. It was from Markos. He stated that he was otherwise engaged and that requests for interviews should be made in writing to his secretary! The letter infuriated Andreas and he smiled with some contempt at Brecchius' unwillingness to face him. In an argument he would prefer to sit on the fence.

However, Markos' ill-mannered reply could mean that either someone had informed him of Andreas' visit to the galleys and the repair yard or that the Minister had something to hide. Obviously, he could not pursue the matter further tonight. By the Goddess he thought, tomorrow I'll see the king!

Taking the bull by the horns was sometimes the best course of action. Politely declining Madam Brecchius' invitation to dinner, Andreas and Ahmed took their leave.

As her mother went to supervise the dinner preparations, Chryssa glanced mischievously at Leda. "Guess who was seated near us at the Tournament?" Leda knew that tone. She concentrated on her needlework.

"Yes, it was him," laughed Chryssa, "the one and only Antonius Micalidos — not alone, of course." Leda did not reply. "Don't you want to know who was with him?"

"No," replied her sister quietly.

"Well, pigeon, he changes his mistresses every week. He doesn't seem to care for any of them. They're just amusements. You have nothing to be jealous of," she said sitting down beside Leda.

"Chrys, how can you speak like this? What has jealousy to do with it? I don't care about these women."

"Poor lamb, you have got it badly. Why don't you get father to arrange a marriage? You have a good dowry."

"Please don't be silly. He never pays me the least attention."

Chryssa stood up to admire her image in a polished copper mirror on the wall. She held out one of her necklaces. "Look what Dino gave me." It was very beautiful, dark amethyst and crystal set in a silver chain. Leda admired it obediently.

"There's a husband for you. He knows my taste all right."

"I don't know how he can afford it on a Captain's pay."

"You are a simpleton. He doesn't pay. His father does," Chryssa spoke casually.

"I'd sooner have a small gift my husband could buy himself," Leda said quietly.

"Well, I wouldn't. Anything he could afford wouldn't suit me at all." Her gaze returned to the mirror. After a moment a thoughtful look came into her eyes. "Do you remember the necklace his mother was wearing at the last Palace reception?"

"Whose mother?"

"Antonius' mother, silly, Zanthope Micalidos. She has the most wonderful necklace I've ever seen. I don't think the Queen has anything better."

Captain Senthios returned, wiping his mouth and fingers on a linen napkin. He threw it down and took hold of Chryssa's shoulders and buried his face in her long, dark hair. She freed herself from the embrace.

"You'll be late on duty, my dearest Dino."

He was a good-looking young man, with an earnest expression. He took his military duties very seriously. "Yes, Chryssa, I must go. I'm on till midnight. Shall I call for you here?"

"Do you think I'll get lost if I go home alone?" Her tone mocked him. Their apartment was directly above on the next floor. "Please yourself," he said strapping on his helmet. "I must go. I'll call in here, just in case you decide to stay." He kissed her lightly on the forehead, saluted Leda and went out.

The three women dined together, Leda silent, while her mother and sister exchanged gossip, much of which was scandalous. Zanthope Micalidos did not escape their attention.

"I hear she's making a play for the young secretary now," Chryssa said.

"So we noticed last night! Poor Andreas Micalidos." Madam Brecchius told Chryssa about the dinner party at Andreas' villa the previous evening. "She rested her hand on Senka's arm at the table and pushed her face close to his ..."

"Really! That's going a bit far, he's only a paid servant," Chryssa sounded shocked.

"But he's quite one of the family," her mother said.

"Well, they ought to be more discreet." Leda found this conversation distasteful. What would Antonius think, she wondered. She hoped he would agree with her.

The King's sister, Princess Ariadne, was their next target. "You should have seen her, Mother," said Chryssa, devouring a leg of cold duckling, "she nearly went mad with joy when Theseus won the championship. I thought she was going to embrace him in public!"

"Indeed!" Madam Brecchius' eyebrows nearly disappeared beneath the fringe of greying hair on her forehead.

"They say she wants to marry Theseus, Mother. The King spoils her so, he won't refuse her anything."

"I don't believe he'd allow that, Chryssy — a royal marriage to a Greek bull dancer! Besides, it has to be approved in Council."

"The Council can be influenced!" Chryssa smiled.

They chattered on till the meal was finished. Madam Brecchius was disappointed when Chryssa refused to spend the evening with them. It was so dull without her. But Chryssa told her that she had promised to be with a friend, Pashote, who was ill and needed company.

Shortly afterwards, when Chryssa knocked, her friend came to the door half-naked. Pashote was, in fact, entertaining a lover. Chryssa stayed only a brief moment, showed off her new necklace and arranged that, if any questions were asked, they spent the evening together playing cards.

Few merchants were able to secure apartments in the East Palace, but Chryssa's father-in-law, Old Papa Senthios, was very rich. His money bought him most of the things he wanted, including acceptance of his son in the Palace Guard, a corps reserved usually for the sons of distinguished families. However, to give Dinos Senthios credit, his own merit gained him promotion.

When Chryssa tapped softly on the big, bronze door, it opened swiftly. "By the Goddess, you're in a hurry," she said, "take your time, he's on duty till midnight."

As Andreas and Ahmed made their way homeward through the maze of passages in the East Palace, they emerged into a wide, dimly lit hallway.

"Now I know where we are," Andreas said, "this is the Hall of the Double Axes."

They were now close to the royal apartments. On state occasions, when large numbers of guests filled the Throne Room, people overflowed into this long gallery. It was strangely quiet now, almost sinister. On every pillar the gilded images of the double axe and the sacred word 'LABRYS' glowed in the half light. By these signs the Palace stood secure against the wrath of the Earth Shaker and the Underworld.

The Hall opened into a large ante-room from which a magnificent stone staircase ascended around a square garden. Ahmed sighed with relief. He knew the stairway led up to the main Courtyard. They would soon be home. On the left, two sentries guarded tall, double doors. Smaller doors led off on the right at the far end. Andreas thanked the guide and dismissed him. As they crossed toward the stairway, one of the small doors opened and a distinguished, white-haired man came out, recognized Andreas at once and with a smile of pleasure, stretched out his arms to embrace him.

"Zaron, how are you keeping?" Andreas said. He then introduced Dr Ahmed.

"I am well, Andreas, thank the Gods, and yourself?"

"Very well — thanks to my friend here, " Andreas said with a smile at Ahmed.

"This is an unexpected pleasure, sir. What brings you here to the East Palace? Have you seen the King?"

Old Zaron had been nearly sixty years in the service of the royal family, as personal secretary to the late King Minos. He retained his privileged position. The Queen was very fond of him and the Princesses called him "Uncle Zaron".

Andreas put his arm around Zaron's shoulders and they walked over to a bench in the garden court. "Dear old friend, tell me, does His Majesty grant private audiences at this time of day?"

"Yes, Andreas, he does sometimes," Zaron said. The first name came quite naturally as Zaron had known Andreas since he was a boy, living in the Palace with his father.

"Let me see," he continued, "only the other week, the High Priest's secretary — er, oh, dear me — Eburninos, that's it — had quite a long audience. Over an hour."

"Do you think the King would see me now?" Andreas said, frowning.

Zaron looked perplexed. He could think of no good reason why Minos should refuse to see one of his Councillors. "Perhaps we could ask Her Majesty, the Queen, to help us. She's generally in her salon at this hour with Prince Nikos and Princess Phaedre. Sometimes His Majesty joins them. We might be lucky."

As he was speaking, he took Andreas by the arm and led him and Dr Ahmed towards the Queen's apartments. The old man was delighted to have an excuse to visit her and in spite of his weariness Ahmed felt a keen sense of pleasure and anticipation. Queen Kara was by birth an Egyptian princess and she had received him kindly on the few occasions they had met. As he followed Andreas and Zaron his step was a little lighter.

# CHAPTER 4

Queen Kara's salon was as charming as its owner. It had an atmosphere of warmth, colour and luxury. Two open courts at either end gave an airy spaciousness to the apartment. In one of these a mural showed dolphins plunging in the green sea. There were flowers in large china and terracotta vases, patterned carpets lay on the tiled floor, frescoes depicted young girls dancing, woven cushions filled the benches which lined the walls and the ceiling was ornamented with lotus flowers and papyrus fronds.

When Andreas, Zaron, and Ahmed entered, they stood for a moment in the doorway, too astonished to speak.

Two women were seated some distance apart on the cushioned bench. They were watching the scene before them so intently that they did not notice the visitors' arrival.

The rugs had been pushed back and on the smooth tiled surface a game was in progress. A beautiful girl of about twelve years old and a small delicate boy, perhaps half her age, were laughing and romping with a dark handsome man. They were playing at being bull vaulters. His Majesty, Priest-King Minos of Knossos, ruler of Crete and its maritime empire, was imitating a charging bull. On hands and knees, head down, he pawed the ground, tossing imaginary horns and making loud bellowing noises. The children shrieked with delight, jumping over his head and onto his back just as the real bull dancers did. However, unlike them, they lost their balance and slipped to the floor, laughing helplessly.

Queen Kara, dressed in the Egyptian style, watched with a tender smile. Dr Ahmed had seen her before only on state occasions. Then she had worn the formal Cretan fashion, with an elaborate headdress. Her beauty had seemed remote, almost cold. Now, in the long, pleated linen dress with her hair flowing loosely over her shoulders, she sat as relaxed as any wife and mother at home with her family.

Aware of his gaze, she turned suddenly. Not wishing to offend her, he averted his eyes. At that moment, the children collapsed in a heap, laughing and gasping. The King rose and giving a hand to each child, assisted them to their feet.

"Well, my sweet Phaedre, it's bedtime," he said. "You, too, little Nikos, it's time for your bath — say good night to your mother."

The boy ran to his mother, the Queen, and kissed her. The young girl, Phaedre, embraced her sister,

Princess Ariadne, smiled at the Queen, and said goodnight. Then, holding the King's hand and pulling her nephew, Nikos, with the other, she led them out of the salon. As they departed, Zaron stepped forward and presented the two visitors. Queen Kara received them with a charming smile and invited them to sit down.

"It's very kind of you to receive us, madam," Andreas said. "I hope you and the Princess are in excellent health." Dr Ahmed murmured a similar greeting as he sat near the Queen. Andreas bowed and remained standing. His eyes strayed for a moment towards the door through which the King had left.

Princess Ariadne beckoned to Zaron and patted the cushion beside her.

"Well, Uncle Zaron," she inquired, "did you back the winner of the Tournament?"

"Oh, goodness, no, Princess, I don't waste money on gambling!" he replied with a chuckle, sitting beside her.

"Ah! But if you had backed Theseus you would have won."

In some respects Ariadne resembled her brother, King Minos. She had the same large, dark eyes and proud bearing, but her retroussé nose and pointed chin gave her face an elfin charm. However, Ariadne was a creature of mood and her charm could vanish like the sun behind a cloud.

The Queen ordered her attendants to serve refreshments. Then she smiled courteously at Ariadne and asked if she would care to sing for the visitors. The princess struck a few notes on her lyre but then said abruptly that she was not in the mood. Andreas watched the scene with interest. The statesman in him calculated that Princess Ariadne was to be reckoned with. He bowed to her and said, "Good evening, Your Highness."

She acknowledged the greeting briefly, ignored Dr Ahmed and once more addressed Zaron. "Theseus excels in everything — the whole of Knossos applauds him in the Bull Ring."

Ariadne's enthusiasm for Theseus prompted Andreas to wonder if there was some truth in the rumours of a love affair between them. If so, Theseus might have access to confidential information — he might even be using the Princess to influence King Minos. The thought disturbed him. What was the Greek's real reason for coming to Crete?

Before Zaron could reply to the Princess the King returned to the salon. He was a tall man, of great presence, charming when he chose to be, at other times his reserve could create a chilling tension. Minos noticed his guests for the first time. No longer a genial father, he now appeared aloof and haughty. He glanced at his sister, seeking an explanation, Ariadne offered none but looked toward the Queen.

Her Majesty was aware of the unspoken intimacy between her husband and sister-in-law and spoke with quiet dignity. "Your Majesty, Uncle Zaron brought his friends at my invitation. Councillor Micalidos you know, of course, and this is the Egyptian physician, Dr Ahmed."

Andreas said they were honoured and delighted to be shown such a mark of favour. The King merely nodded. For a moment there was an atmosphere of restraint, which was heightened when the King and the Princess spoke together so quietly that the Queen and her visitors could not hear their conversation. They continued to talk as though there was no one present.

Embarrassed, Andreas felt that they should take their leave, having accomplished nothing. Endeavouring to ease the tension, Zaron asked for news of Old Madam, of whom he had an affectionate memory.

Queen Kara turned to Ahmed and inquired in Egyptian if he had news of his family. Delighted to hear his native tongue, Ahmed replied that he had heard from time to time and asked if she, too, had news from Egypt. A shadow passed over her face as she shook her head. He remembered the rumours of war between the two Kingdoms of Egypt. Kara was a Princess of Thebes and Ahmed knew that enmity between Thebes and Memphis would restrict communications. He had a sudden insight that she was lonely and unhappy.

"Did the Minister have some special purpose in this visit, Dr Ahmed?" she asked.

He told her that Andreas wished very urgently to speak with the King.

"The prospect does not seem promising," she said with a faint smile. The King suddenly abandoned his conversation with his sister and addressed the Queen abruptly, "Well, Madam, may we share your amusement, or is it a private joke?"

"It is neither private nor a joke, sir," she replied coolly. Ahmed thought he could detect a slight tremor of her hand, as she grasped a papyrus leaf fan, which rested on the bench between them. "Councillor Micalidos requests a private audience with Your Majesty," she continued.

"Then why does he not make the request himself?" asked the King looking coldly at Andreas.

"I awaited a favourable opportunity, Your Majesty," Andreas said, "I did not wish to interrupt your conversation with the Princess."

The King seemed to accept this explanation. He relaxed and placing his hand on his sister's arm, indicated with a smile that she should join the Queen. He then invited Andreas to sit by him. The others withdrew to the open court at the far end of the salon. Andreas was alone with the Priest-King of Knossos. In spite of many meetings in the Council and an acquaintance spanning the King's thirty years, Andreas had never felt close to Minos. Accustomed to following his instincts in judging men, and though by tradition and upbringing loyalty and respect for the Throne were second nature to him, Andreas had to admit that he did not trust the King. As he hesitated, Minos asked directly, "What is the purpose of your visit, Minister?"

"I regret calling on you at this hour without warning, Your Majesty, but I feel it is my duty to advise you of the great danger that I believe confronts us."

"Danger!" the King replied sharply, "please explain."

"Your Majesty, our main fleet is delayed in the south, leaving our coastline in the north virtually unprotected. The ships that are here, with a few exceptions, are unseaworthy. Sir, our main defences lie at sea, if we are invaded, this city could easily be overwhelmed. The Palace guards could do little against a seaborne invasion force."

Minós stared at Andreas, his eyes black and inscrutable. Andreas felt uneasy but held his own gaze steadily. The King said sternly, "You must be aware that my Council does not share your views." Andreas made an impatient gesture. Minos continued, "Have you discussed this with Minister Markos?"

"I called on him, sir, but he declined an invitation to dine with me."

Minos suddenly smiled and said reasonably, "Surely this is a matter for the full Council?"

"It is indeed, sir, but it must be discussed and dealt with promptly, not brushed aside on some pretext or other, as has happened previously."

"I must act within the law," Minos said.

"Your Majesty, where the safety of the country is concerned, all power is yours."

The King said nothing for a moment, and then replied, "We will give this matter our serious consideration, Minister." Exasperated, Andreas burst out, "There is no timber to repair the ships or lay the keels of galleys ordered last year. There are shortages of stores and materials vital to keep the ships in good order. These matters require immediate attention!"

"We have given you our assurance," the King said coldly. Andreas wished to continue; there was another matter he would have liked to have broached, but the

King rose, indicating that the interview had ended. Andreas stood too, bowed and began to thank Minos for his graciousness, but the King turned abruptly and was already on his way out of the apartment. Andreas stared after him and then crossed the salon to join the group sitting with the Queen.

Uncle Zaron was relating an anecdote about the late King who had shown great kindness to an acrobat. The man had injured himself on a slippery floor. The King had ordered a special sacrifice to be made to the Goddess for the man's recovery, and had provided for his wife and children until he was able to work again.

"That story is typical, Uncle Zaron," Princess Ariadne said, "it illustrates well how Minos, the King, is father and protector to all his people and helps those in need, and how Minos, the Priest, intercedes with the Goddess on our behalf and assures our spiritual welfare." She spoke as though she alone knew the mind and heart of the King, whether it be her father or brother. Ahmed wondered how this three-cornered relationship affected the Queen. She and the Princess behaved with outward civility. Were they, perhaps, a little too polite?

Andreas rose. He thanked the Queen for her assistance and Zaron most sincerely for his help. He and Ahmed then bowed to the Queen and Princess and took their leave. They made their way to the North Gate and the waiting chariot carried them home to the villa.

# CHAPTER 5

The following day Andreas did not feel at all well. Ahmed was not surprised. He diagnosed exhaustion and was thankful it was nothing worse. He prescribed a sedative, insisted on rest and would not leave for the surgery until he had a promise to that effect.

The interview with Minos had proved inconclusive, but Andreas took some comfort in the realization that he had, at least, aired some of the facts. He was confident that Markos, Minister for the Navy, spurred on by reports of his visits to the galleys and of his audience with the King, would hasten to investigate matters himself. And, when Markos discovered the deficiencies, he would remedy them.

The Minister for Supply, Xanthios, would have to be approached, and this would come better from Markos than from himself. He could not accept the thought that either minister could be a traitor. For the moment he had done everything he could. It occurred to him that perhaps he had exaggerated the problem, perhaps the disaster he dreaded was imaginary. The sedative Ahmed had prescribed probably contributed to his uncertainty. But, following the doctor's advice, he enjoyed two days of relaxation and peace of mind.

However, on the morning of the third day, his confidence was shattered. A clerk from his department brought a message advising him that his northern agent, Tarsis, had returned from Troy. He immediately ordered the chariot and directed the driver to the south viaduct. He took a chair up the steep pathway to the South Gate, from there it was a short walk to his office.

The Trade Department comprised a number of rooms in the East Palace near the South Gate. In the public office, the overseer's desk was on a central dais. The clerks sat below on narrow benches with clay tablets piled on tables in front of them. Messenger boys bustled about gathering up completed tablets for the overseer to check, ready for firing. All exports carried a bill of lading with the royal seal. Imports were recorded and receipt tablets given. On every transaction a tax was paid to Minos.

When Andreas entered, followed by his secretary, Senka, and the clerk, his staff rose and saluted him respectfully. The overseer, who was trying to remove a visitor, greeted him warmly.

"Tell them to sit down," Andreas said, and then noticing that the unwanted visitor was his wife's dinner guest, Grinkos, asked brusquely, "What are you doing here?"

Grinkos began a long explanation of his reorganization plans in the records department. "The boys are bringing too many baskets down, too many all at once, I need space to work in —"

Andreas cut him short. "Please stop wasting our time, get back to your work." Senka showed him firmly to the door. Turning to the overseer again Andreas asked, "Is that order for oil for Byblos ready?"

The overseer, reed pen behind his ear, began thumbing through a stack of papyrus rolls and found the appropriate one.

"Yes, sir, the last dozen jars were sent to Amnissos this morning," he said.

"Good. Everything else in order?"

"Yes, sir."

"Carry on then."

The overseer was very efficient. Andreas tried never to interfere with a man who knew his job. He beckoned to Senka, who followed him into his office.

"Senka, write a letter to Captain Dubal of the *Sea Wind* bound for Byblos. When he's sold the oil cargo, he's to load as much cedar wood as he can carry and return as soon as possible. Bring the message to me at once for my seal. I shall be in the Merchant's Court."

"Yes, sir."

The Merchant's Court was a long, narrow, tiled gallery which ran along the outer wall of the West Palace. It was, in fact, a bazaar or market-place which provided a wide range of goods for the people of Knossos, as well as serving the needs of the many residents of the Palace. Many shops and storerooms opened off the Merchant's Court. Huge, glazed storage jars for oil were set into channels in the floor and there were quantities of provisions, such as vegetables, cereals and preserved fish.

Foreign merchants offered their wares at public auctions — leather, furs, amber, bales of linen, silks and damasks were eagerly sought after. At other times there were goods from the Palace workshops — hand-painted china, carved bowls, woollen cloth, jewellery in gold, silver and bronze; also large quantities of oil from the Palace presses. All local and foreign agents paid a tax to Minos. Lead-lined vaults deep in the Treasury contained this wealth. Guards were ever present, but no one had ever dared to rob the Priest-King, with his sacred sign of the double axe on every pillar.

Andreas searched for the agent, Agidor of Phaestos, from whom Zanthope had purchased the zebra skins, but he could not be found. However, the agent Karkoran appeared, as usual breathing stale wine and garlic, and said in a low voice: "Tarsis is waiting for you, sir."

Andreas held up a length of embroidered silk as if they were discussing its value. "Anything to report?"

"I heard one of the sailors talking in the wine-shop at Amnissos," Karkoran replied, "he had a letter from his sister in Knossos. She was off to Phaestos for the rest of the summer to be near her husband — he's the bosun on the *Dolphin*. It's obvious the fleet's not coming north again this year."

"Anything else?"

"A fisherman, setting his lobster pots late at night, saw a foreign ship close inshore — she was taking soundings."

"Where was this ship from?"

"He didn't know."

"All right, keep at it."

A moment later Andreas found Senka at his elbow with the letter awaiting his seal. As he pressed the seal into the wax, Andreas ordered Senka to deliver the letter to Captain Dubal at Amnissos and return as soon as possible. He then walked slowly down the length of the Merchant's Court, stopping here and there to listen to an auction or examine some merchandise.

When he felt safe from observation, he entered the West Palace through a narrow door. Here, he was quite at home and threaded his way past shrines and through dimly lit courts and passages, then up a stairway and along an empty corridor. He took a key from a pocket in his belt.

The room was small and faintly illuminated by a light well. A thick carpet covered the floor and a feather bed stood in one corner. A man was sitting on a stone bench drinking from a wine-cup. When Andreas entered he rose immediately, and poured another cup. "I'm very glad to see you returned safely, Tarsis. I was beginning to worry."

"We had some delay, sir, on the journey home." The agent, Tarsis, was tall and thin. His swarthy skin was drawn tautly over a fine bone structure, the lines thread-like. It was a face that seemed to defy ageing, he could have been anywhere between forty and sixty.

His deep-set eyes were wary and intelligent, with the steady, unflinching gaze of one who is acquainted with danger. He had been many years at sea.

Andreas drank some wine and motioned the agent to sit beside him. "Well, Tarsis, what news have you?"

"It's not good news for Crete, sir, but I'll begin with Troy. There were rumours throughout the city of an alliance between Athens and Mycenae, and possibly Tiryns, too. It seems —"

"Did you learn the purpose of this alliance?"

"Not in Troy, sir, but there was talk in all the taverns of a big fleet of war galleys —"

"A fleet? Who's behind this? Go on, Tarsis, what more did you find out?"

"I couldn't discover anything definite in Troy, sir, but I learned a lot more on the journey home."

Tarsis refilled his goblet while Andreas contained his impatience with difficulty.

"We left Troy about two weeks ago," the agent continued, "there was a good following wind, but on the third night out it shifted to a sou'wester and freshened. We had to shorten sail and ran close-hauled. We passed by the island of Aegina and then, off the mainland coast, not many miles east of Mycenae, by my reckoning, we sprang a leak and began to list. We looked for a place to beach and towards evening we were lucky and found a narrow inlet with a sandy bottom. While the shipwrights got busy, I climbed a ridge to the south which overlooked a small bay. A number of galleys were moored there and several others were under construction on the beach. I couldn't get close in daylight without being seen, because they'd cleared the trees to build a camp, but when it was dark I went down into the bay and heard the foreman and his mate discussing the work schedule for the next day. The foreman said they'd have to get a move on to finish the other five ships by the end of the month. His mate said it couldn't be done — they needed more shipwrights. The first fellow said they were better off than the other camps, which had fewer men to meet the same quota. Then his mate asked why, in the name of Zeus, was there such a hurry, and the other replied that the ships must be ready by late summer before the ports close." Tarsis paused to drink.

"Go on," Andreas said grimly.

"Then I heard the foreman say that he thought it was a mad enterprise and could never succeed. His mate asked him what he meant and he replied, 'Crete is too powerful to invade'."

Andreas passed a hand over his brow. His worst fears were confirmed. "This is terrible news, Tarsis."

"I agree, sir, it's appalling."

"Our main fleet is still in Phaestos," Andreas continued.

"Phaestos!" Tarsis was incredulous.

"Yes, and it's to remain there, I understand. Someone is working against us. The naval yards have no timber, no supplies. Are the Trojans going to be involved?"

"They won't get much help there, sir. Troy's too concerned with its own affairs."

"They won't need help from Troy. But we need more evidence. Don't speak of this to anyone, Tarsis."

The two men remained silent for a moment. There had been a close bond between them since Andreas had rescued Tarsis from slavery in Cilicia, many years ago. As Andreas' agent he was now a free man.

After a moment Andreas said, "Do you think, Tarsis, it would be possible to get inside the fortress of Mycenae?"

Tarsis considered the question for a moment. "It would be difficult. We would need a small, light boat and probably two or three dependable men."

"I can arrange that. It's absolutely imperative that we discover when they mean to attack." His agent would be risking his life, but Andreas knew of no one else who could penetrate that citadel. "You've done well, Tarsis. Thank you. Stay here and rest for a few days. We'll discuss this again. I'll let you know when the boat and crew are ready." Andreas gave his agent some money. They shook hands and parted.

When Andreas returned to the Palace Courtyard, it was nearly midday. Many people were gathered for the noon sacrifice. Andreas saw his wife, Zanthope, some distance away with her admiring group of friends. A foppish young man was bowing to her in an exaggerated way and then said something which sent the group into peals of laughter. Doxa was there, with her companion Olivia and her husband, Grinkos. Nearby, Antonius was talking to Captain Senthios and his beautiful wife. With them was a tall, fat elderly man. There was no sign of Senka.

Watching these people, Andreas suddenly felt isolated and alone. His concern and anxiety for Crete weighed heavily on him. He caught sight of

Councillor Brecchius with a friendly arm around Councillor Markos' shoulder. Xanthios, the Minister for Supply was talking with them. Andreas felt sure they had seen and ignored him.

When a procession of priests and priestesses emerged from the main door of the West Palace, the crowd suddenly became quiet. The votaries wore long tunics from shoulder to ankle, belted at the waist. Two young women were bareheaded, their long, dark hair held by headbands. An older priestess wore a large turban. They carried tall, slender vessels which contained wine and oil for the sacrifice. Three priests followed them. Two were elderly, with shaven heads. The younger had long, dark hair and a handsome profile. But, when he turned, the narrowness of the facial bones gave him a sinister appearance. The eyes were set much too close, the lips were thin and bloodless. The priest Eburninos, for it was he, caught Andreas' eyes and instantly averted his gaze. A small boy walked beside him, leading a goat by a halter.

On reaching the altar at the north wall, one of the priestesses blew a single note on a conch horn. The citizens raised their fists to cover their eyes and shut out evil influences. The boy poured water into libation bowls for ritual cleansing. The goat was trussed, stunned, its throat cut and the blood drained. The elder priest intoned a prayer, imploring the Great Earth Mother to accept the sacrifice performed in her honour, to bless the harvest and protect the nation from the powers of the Underworld. One priest poured the steaming blood against a pillar. It ran down in a dark red stream. There was an acrid smell as part of the goat was burned. While the crowd watched silently, the wine and oil were offered. A final blast on the conch horn signalled completion of the sacrifice. The procession returned the way it had come.

The crowd moved away, talking and laughing. The solemn atmosphere was soon dissipated by street vendors coming in at the South Gate, shouting their wares — savoury meats, fish wrapped in vine leaves, fruit, nuts and honey cakes.

Andreas made his way back towards the department. He anticipated that Senka would be there. However, the crowd was so dense that he made only slow progress. Then, he heard a voice behind him.

"Father!"

"Antonius, my boy, how are you?"

"Well, thank you, father. Mother asked you not to forget the lamp brackets — for the villa at Mallia."

Andreas looked blank. He had forgotten about them.

"She wants you to order them at Phylon's workshop — it's only across in the East Palace," Antonius pleaded, seeing his father's unwillingness.

"Do you now where it is?"

"No, sir, but I can soon find out."

"Oh, don't bother, Antonius, I'll find the way. Look out for Senka will you? I want to see him urgently."

"Very well, Father, I'll send him to Phylon's workshop, and if not there, to your office."

"Thank you, Antonius."

Andreas turned wearily away. The young man stood for a moment, gazing after his father. He was accustomed to his short temper, but today he looked ill. Worn out. What's got into him he thought. If Andreas had known how much concern his son felt for him, he would not have felt so alone. He bought some food from a peasant girl dressed in a blue skirt and brightly embroidered apron. Her young breasts swayed prettily as she moved through the crowd with her tray of fruit and savouries. With some difficulty Andreas made his way towards the east side of the courtyard.

# CHAPTER 6

Phylon, the goldsmith, enjoyed a high reputation in Knossos. He conducted his business, supervised his staff of skilled craftsmen and trained his apprentices in several large, untidy rooms at the northern end of the East Palace. Here, he specialized in the production of ornamental gold and silver plate and jewellery.

Phylon was short in stature, with powerful arms and shoulders. His large head and thick, untidy hair made him seem even more ill-proportioned. His eyes were deep-set and of great intensity. Although his staff understood and appreciated his genius, he often exasperated his clients with his abrupt manner and absent-minded tardiness in filling orders.

As Andreas searched for the workshop through a maze of passages, he heard the faint bump and rattle of weaving looms and the noise of hammers and saws in carpenters' shops and armouries nearby. When he entered the workshop he was confronted by an extraordinary scene.

Phylon stood in the centre of the room with two beautiful young girls, scantily clad in cotton briefs. He had arranged two benches, side by side, and placed a stool on top of them, at one end. With many exaggerated gestures, he was endeavouring to show the girls that he wished them to leap and somersault over the improvised structure. When they indicated that this was unsafe, Phylon ordered several of his apprentices to crouch on the benches, while another sat on the stool with his head lowered and his arms curved upwards.

Andreas understood Phylon's intention. The lads on the benches represented a bull. He presumed the young girls were bull dancers — probably students in their first year and not yet dedicated to the Goddess. Their escort, two armed guards, stood unobtrusively near the doorway.

A large number of craftsmen and tradesmen from other workshops had crowded into the room to watch the entertainment. Phylon's comic appearance, as he demonstrated the poses he required, drew roars of laughter, but, when the two girls leaped and danced for him, their supple, athletic grace brought loud and enthusiastic applause. Absorbed in his project, Phylon made many quick sketches of the girls.

Andreas had no wish to interrupt the maestro. Leaning against a work bench, he began to eat his lunch while observing the scene. He guessed the young women were seventeen or eighteen years old. Both were blonde with fair complexions, which set them apart from the dark-haired islanders, the black Libyans and the swarthy Phoenicians. There, however, the similarity ended. The smaller girl had delicate bones and a youthful slenderness. Her eyes were brown and almond-shaped, and her golden hair framed her face in soft curls and was tied loosely at the back with a ribbon. Andreas was fascinated by her lissom beauty and unselfconscious charm. He had seen girls like her, in the slave markets of Troy, brought by merchants from distant places beyond Babylon. Her companion was taller and more sturdily built. She also reminded Andreas of the Troy market-place — not the smooth-tongued Babylonian slave-traders — but the gaunt, blonde northern men who travelled the amber route. Their women were often like this one, tall, strong and fine-featured. This girl had large blue eyes and ash-blonde hair which hung down her back in heavy plaits. Andreas considered that he had seldom seen two women better formed, each in her own way.

As they danced and posed for Phylon, they radiated grace, vitality and charm. They obviously appreciated their audience. Andreas had not enjoyed himself so much for a long time. He saw that the slighter girl's performance was more polished and professional and drew more applause. Approving, he watched her with intense interest.

Phylon was concentrating on a sketch of the taller dancer, while the other girl, free for a few minutes, stood aside. Conscious of Andreas' gaze, she walked over to him and stared at the food he held in the vine leaf.

"Would you like to share my lunch?" he asked.

"Yes, please, sir," she replied, smiling.

Jumping on to the work bench, she sat beside him cross-legged. He watched her while she ate hungrily, observing the delicate lines of her face, the cheek bones high but not too prominent, the chin firm and narrow, the mouth generous and the dark eyes set wide apart. Her face in repose had a haunting beauty. But this quality of a lost waif was instantly dispelled when she smiled, a broad grin that crinkled up her nose. Andreas enjoyed this brief moment and the proximity of her warm and vital youthfulness. He was sad, knowing she must soon depart.

She finished the food, licked her fingers, grinned and thanked him. He asked her name.

"Belia, mighty one."

"And your friend?"

"Freyna."

"Where do you come from?"

"Freyna or me, sir?"

"Both of you."

"Freyna from the north," she waved her hand vaguely in the air, "far away."

"And yourself?"

She burst out laughing.

"Don't know, so long ago, I forget!"

"How old are you?"

"I don't know," she said, "maybe seventeen — eighteen."

At that moment Phylon called her. She jumped off the bench and was over to him in one flowing movement. Andreas wondered what her former life had been. She was obviously highly trained. She had natural ability and an instinctive sense of timing. He thought this would be an advantage in the dangerous and difficult career which lay ahead of her in the Bull Ring.

After a few more poses Phylon was satisfied. While the goldsmith studied his sketches, Andreas noticed the two girls talking together and staring at him. He wondered what Belia was saying about him and hoped it was complimentary. But he was not a vain man. She had called him "mighty one" — he smiled, wondering how many other men had been given this title.

The two guards escorted the bull dancers from the workshop. As they passed through the doorway, a man made a vulgar comment about the bull's horns. In a flash Belia capped his joke with an equally suggestive remark. The workmen shouted with laughter.

Andreas joined in the laughter and, when he was almost out of the room, realized he had forgotten the purpose of his visit. He crossed back to Phylon, who was working on a sketch of Belia. It was an unusual pose of a bull dancer falling forward over a bull's head. To save herself she was clinging to the horns. Andreas asked if the design was for a wall panel. Phylon looked up and said brusquely: "Who might you be?"

"I am Andreas Micalidos of the King's Council." Phylon was not impressed. "What do you want?" he asked without interest.

"I want some bronze lamp-holders for a summer villa." The goldsmith shook his head.

"Not a hope, sir. We have orders up to here," he held his hand under his chin. "We can't touch anything until this is completed." His gesture included the sketches spread out on a work bench. Andreas noted that in addition to the sketches of the girls, there were some excellent drawings of wild bulls. He asked, "Those designs are very fine, who are they for?"

Phylon looked at him gravely.

"You said you were a member of the King's Council, sir."

"That's right."

"Then I'm surprised you should ask. I understood this project had been approved by the Council."

"Yes, indeed," Andreas replied, "but not spoken of elsewhere."

Phylon lowered his voice.

"These designs are for the golden cups," he paused, as though he expected Andreas to recollect. Andreas nodded, as if he understood.

"The votive offerings for the Sacred Pilgrimage!"

"How did you know about that?" Andreas asked softly.

Phylon was wary.

"Just a rumour," he said.

From ancient times, it had been the custom for the King to make the Sacred Pilgrimage to Mount Jukto every ninth year. Eight years ago, the late King had made the journey shortly before his death. Next year, the present King Minos would make the arduous climb to the summit of the mountain and spend a long month of prayer and fasting, alone in the darkness of the Sacred Cave — the birthplace of mighty Zeus, son of the Great Goddess, Earth Mother. It was believed that the prosperity, perhaps even the very existence, of the Cretan state, depended on the fulfilment of these rites. If the Goddess was displeased and withdrew her protection, nothing would save the Cretans — the fury of Earth Shaker would be felt throughout the land, as had occurred so many times in the past.

But to advance the ceremony by a whole year would break the tradition and Andreas could see no reason for the change. Such a step could not be taken without the consent of the Council. When the proposal was first mooted, the priests had offered sacrifices and sought an answer from the Goddess. The Council had sat through long hours of wearisome discussion, but the decision had been delayed. Andreas had been puzzled to know the origin of the idea. King Minos was no innovator. Why should he seek to change this long-standing tradition when he had performed his duties in small, relatively unimportant matters strictly according to custom.

Perplexed, Andreas took his leave of Phylon. "I know I don't need to warn you to be discreet about this matter?" he said as he left the workshop. The goldsmith merely nodded.

Deep in thought, Andreas returned to his office. He was concerned that Tarsis' report had made the situation more threatening. And now there was this strange business of the gold cups for the King's Pilgrimage. The information he had gained from Phylon required explanation.

At the last Council meeting, when the priest Eburninos had kept pressuring the Council to take a vote in favour of the early Pilgrimage, Andreas had not hesitated to oppose him. This was the incident Grinkos had referred to at the dinner table. Eburninos might hold the key to the mystery. Had he pre-empted the Council's decision and ordered the cups from Phylon? Andreas remembered Uncle Zaron's reference to Eburninos and his audience with the King — "over an hour", the old man had said. Perhaps there was a plan to induce the King to leave Knossos and travel to Mount Jukto, in order to leave the city leaderless and unprotected if an attack occurred.

Senka failed to report to the office. Displeased, Andreas returned home. He began to plan his tactics for the next Council meeting. He now realized this could be of decisive importance to his country.

# CHAPTER 7

Andreas' wife, Zanthope, was at the top of the stairs when he entered the villa. She did not see him as she moved quickly to her bedroom. Then he heard Timon crying loudly in the kitchen. Credon, the steward, looking anxious, came across the loggia.

"What in Zeus' name is going on?" Andreas demanded

"I don't know, sir," the steward replied.

They crossed the hallway and entered the kitchen; a long, low room with a red stone floor and lines of copper utensils hanging along the white walls. Two kitchen maids were busy preparing vegetables at a large table. A third girl was sobbing into her apron. Timon, Andreas' younger son, stood beside her, howling loudly, the tears running down his face.

When the girl saw Andreas, she stifled her sobs, but Timon was too distraught. He sobbed and gasped for breath.

"What on earth is going on?" Andreas demanded again.

Deva, the cook, stirring a large copper pot over the fire at the far end of the room, gesticulated with her free hand and answered: "You may well ask, sir."

"I am asking. Please explain."

Timon ran to his father and flung his arms around him. Andreas saw that the boy had been viciously beaten. There were ugly weals across the boys shoulders and lower down on his buttocks, beneath the thin, cotton loincloth. The skin was broken in several places.

"Who did this? Who beat you?" Andreas' voice was quiet.

No one dared to answer. Then Vita, the boldest of the kitchen girls, found courage to speak, "Young Madam did it, sir."

"Why did she do that?" Andreas asked Timon. The child bit his lip and hung his head. Andreas looked inquiringly at Vita.

"He upset a bowl of fruit on Young Madam's dress that was being ironed. The juice stained it, sir."

"Why was the dress being ironed in the kitchen? Surely the laundry was the proper place." The girl who had been crying now spoke up, "Madam wanted the dress in a hurry — it was quicker to heat the iron on the fire here."

"Well, it was an accident, wasn't it, Timon?" Andreas lifted his son's face up and smiled. "Better have a wash. We'll get some ointment for your back from Dr Ahmed." He sighed. Obviously this could not go on. His wife's behaviour angered and disgusted him. The boy would be better cared for at the farm. No one supervised him properly here. He was always getting into scrapes.

"And you got beaten, too?" Andreas asked the girl, who was sharing the bucket of water that Deva had given Timon to wash his face.

"Yes, sir," she replied, smiling ruefully.

"Did the dress get burned as well as stained?"

"No, sir. It wasn't Young Madam who beat me. It was Old Madam." Andreas was astonished. He had never known his mother to strike a servant.

"What did you do to deserve that?" The girl hesitated, drying her hands on her apron. Suddenly the other two burst out laughing. Timon, now recovered, joined in, saying:

"It was something she said to me — that, if I was naughty any more, King Minos would feed me to his bulls!"

"What a thing to say," Deva said, "as if our dear King isn't the kindest man and so fond of children."

It was a favourite threat of peasant mothers to discipline their children. Andreas was surprised that his mother should have paid any attention to the girl. But she was old-fashioned and had a great reverence for the King.

"Well, behave yourselves, and you won't get any more beatings," he said, patting Timon on the head.

"Father, take me for a chariot ride, please," the boy asked suddenly. Andreas was tired, but the child's eyes pleaded and he wanted to make up for that cruel beating. As if she hasn't a score of dresses, he thought angrily.

"All right, just a short drive." Timon clapped his hands and danced for joy.

"Run out to the stable and tell the groom to harness the brown mare in the small chariot." She was quiet and easy to handle if Timon wanted to take the reins. The boy ran off in great excitement and Andreas returned to the terrace. His wife came down the stairs dressed for dining out.

"Ah, the return of the stranger — welcome home, Andreas."

He ignored the sarcasm and asked her sharply if Senka had returned.

"He would hardly have reported to me."

"I think he might have done just that. Don't encourage him, Zanthope."

She pretended injured innocence.

"I really believe his interest lies elsewhere."

"Just as well — if he wishes to keep his position here."

She sat down in the high-backed chair that Old Madam favoured and watched him with indifference.

"And another thing," he continued, trying to keep his voice calm and even, "don't ever lay a hand on Timon again."

"That little monster!"

"Understand me, Zanthope, I will not tolerate violence in this house. If he does wrong, I will deal with it, and punish him if necessary."

She laughed scornfully. "I can just imagine — well, it's not important."

Andreas turned to leave. "Don't run away, Andreas. Have you come from the Palace?"

"Yes."

"Did you order the lamp brackets?"

Her face turned to him eagerly. She was wearing a pale green flounced skirt, embroidered with flowers, a white, sleeved jacket, laced beneath her breasts and an elaborate jade necklace. He gazed at her, angry that her beauty could still move him, angrier that she knew it and cared so little.

"Lamp brackets —" he said, trying to drag his tired mind away from her mouth, her breasts, her slender foot, now tapping impatiently.

"Yes, Andreas, surely you remembered the lamp brackets for Mallia. You were to order them from Phylon's workshop."

"Yes, of course. I did inquire about them, but as I warned you, the goldsmith was too busy. You'll have to get someone else to do it." Again he turned to go, but she jumped angrily to her feet.

"Are you not a Minister of the Crown, a member of the King's Council? Can't you give an order to a Palace craftsman and have it obeyed?"

"Zanthope, there's nothing I can do. He's too busy."

"You could use your position, you could insist on your orders being carried out — threaten him, bribe him — those kind of people are always greedy for money."

"I'm sure it would make no difference," he said quietly.

She began to pace up and down, becoming hysterical. "It's just because it's something for me, something I want! I've told everyone that Phylon is doing the lamp brackets for us, now I shall look a fool before all my friends. If it were something for Antonius or Timon, or your mother, or even that half-witted sister of yours, you'd have moved heaven and earth to get it done —"

"Zanthope, be quiet, the servants will hear you." Andreas hated scenes and he dreaded losing his temper and precipitating one of his painful attacks, but she would not be silenced.

"I know the villa at Mallia means nothing to you. If it were not for me, it would never have been finished. You haven't shown the slightest interest in it."

"I'm sorry," he said, and added ironically, "perhaps Antonius will help you get the lamp brackets."

The chair carriers had arrived and stood impassively waiting beside the palanquin. Zanthope stepped in and angrily ordered them to move off. As they departed, a horseman dismounted at the gate and walked quickly along the terrace. Senka looked guilty and embarrassed when he saw Andreas.

"It took you a long time to deliver that letter," Andreas growled.

"I searched for you in the Palace, sir."

"Well, now you can set off again."

For some time Andreas has suspected that Senka was entertaining one of his lady friends when he should have been at work. The two men climbed the short stairway to Andreas' rooms. He dictated a letter, ordering the boat and seamen which he had promised to have ready for Tarsis.

"Ride to Nirou-Khani and give this into Cibaros' hand. Bring me his answer immediately."

"Yes, sir."

Senka went out and stowed the letter in his saddle-bag. As he rode off, Timon came from the stables leading the mare and small chariot. Father and son climbed in and set off down the steep road to the city. It was cool in the shade of the tall houses, but the late afternoon sun was warm on their backs as they crossed the river and left the city behind. They travelled at a gentle, unhurried pace along a tree-lined road, winding their way through green meadows.

Timon held the fig-wood rail of the chariot to steady himself and gazed about him, taking in every detail of the road, the fields, the cattle and the mountains, rising in steep ridges to the south. Andreas leaned back against the seat, his feet braced on the foot rail. "Are you too sore to lean against me?" The child returned his smile and nodded vigorously. In a short time they turned off the paved road on to a grassy track towards the mountains, following a shallow stream, a tributary of the River Kairatos.

Presently, they came to a flat open space, where tall trees lined the water's edge and a low shoulder of rock blocked any further progress. This area had been a burial place for many years. Here and there, the tree bark was worn smooth where horses and chariots had been tethered. The rocky outcrop revealed many tombs cut in its face, sealed with bricks or stone blocks. Most, mossy with age, bore carved inscriptions. One had a stone parapet with steps leading down to a small, sunken shrine.

Andreas told Timon to tether the mare loosely, so she could crop the fresh grass. The boy did so and then raced off to explore around the water's edge. His father strolled across the grass, enjoying the scent of the wild herbs and fresh earth. It was peaceful here; the drowsy warmth, the soft murmur of the stream, the drone of a bee, the muffled plonk of a stone Timon threw into one of the swirling pools, soothed and comforted Andreas. He sat down on a tree-stump, smooth with age. It was possible, here in this quiet place, to consider his problems with some detachment.

A small, lace-winged insect hovered and fluttered in the air nearby. He watched it idly and then his gaze passed on toward the rock-face, where the newly laid stones, bare of moss, showed the sealed door of a more recent tomb. Enshrined in a glazed coffin lay the remains of his mistress, Timon's mother. He tried to remember the first time he met her, but he could not. She had drifted into his life almost without his noticing, and then, without fuss or commotion, she had drifted out again.

She had died while he was away on one of his rare visits to the pottery at Zakro in the east. Ahmed had accompanied him. They had journeyed back in a leisurely way, stopping for a few days at Mallia to visit his daughter and son-in-law, who were married some years ago and settled in the Palace there.

He could never forget the evening when he returned from Zakro. The house was quiet and still. He knew at once something was wrong. The servants stayed out of sight. His mother, pale and tired, greeted him sadly. When he asked her if all was well, she burst into tears. As he was trying to comfort her, Zanthope entered the room.

"You should have been home earlier," she said calmly. "Nassica, the sewing woman — your mistress — died two days ago." Shocked and bewildered, he stared at the two women in disbelief.

"Why didn't you send for me?"

"It all happened so quickly, and we didn't know where you were," Old Madam replied. "Poor Nassica, she had so much pain," the old lady pressed her hand to her right side, "she was burning with fever and quite out of her mind, Andreas. She didn't know what was happening. She was dead in a few hours." His mother paused to wipe away her tears.

"I'm sure you did everything you could for her," Andreas said.

"Oh, we did, Andreas, we did. If only Dr Ahmed had been here. Just before she died, she spoke your name. She said it quite clearly —" His mother broke off weeping again.

"Where is her body," he asked, "is she buried yet?"

Nassica's body, according to the ancient custom, was buried in a large urn and placed in the cellar, under the house. Andreas had a fine coffin made for her by the best craftsmen in Knossos, painted with blue and yellow butterflies, representing the souls of the dead. The funeral was held on a mild autumn day, before the winter gales began and while the countryside was still mellow with the warmth of late summer.

There were few mourners; the girls from the kitchen, Deva and Credon. Andreas rode on horseback with the boy on the saddle in front of him. It was only ten months ago, but it seemed longer.

As he sat on the tree-stump, he still felt a deep sense of loss. He remembered with gratitude Nassica's sweet tenderness and her loving care of Timon. When the boy was five-years-old, she had arranged for him to have school lessons with Crespin, a retired clerk from the Palace. He reflected that payment for the lessons was all she had asked of him. He would repay her love now, by cherishing her child. There would be no half measures. He had already legally acknowledged Timon as his son. But, there was still the problem of his education. Andreas knew that his wife hated Timon and he would not tolerate her treatment of him. Either he must engage a tutor, or he must send him to the farm where the manager and his wife had children of the same age. Timon would enjoy the summer up there.

Bored with throwing stones and unsuccessful attempts to trap fish, Timon ran to his father and sat on the grass at his feet. "Can I take the reins on the way home, Father?"

"Yes, my boy. Come along, we must go now."

As they travelled home, Timon was given a lesson in driving the horse and chariot. He was told to hold the reins very firmly for the mare knew the stable and her bucket of oats were waiting.

"Is this right, Father?" the boy asked.

"You're doing very well indeed, Timon," Andreas replied, smiling.

Andreas took the reins when they approached the city and, on reaching the house, he drove to the stables at the back. They handed the reins to the groom and crossed the courtyard.

Korynna came from the kitchen with a jug in one hand and a plate in the other.

"There you are, Andreas. We wondered where you both got to," she said.

"Good evening, Korynna..."

"Father let me drive the chariot, Aunt Korynna!"

"Did he, indeed? Open the door for me will you, please, dear?"

The boy skipped ahead of her to the snake room. He knew Aunt Korynna fed her pets at this hour with milk and honey cakes. "Father, come and watch the snakes eat their supper."

"I must get ready for dinner," he said, smiling, but he lingered in the doorway, watching his son's excitement as they waited for the snakes to appear.

"Don't make a noise, dear, it upsets them," Aunt Korynna whispered.

The snakes were very tame and indulged. They lived in large terracotta pipes and each had bowls for milk and food. They emerged, coiling lazily, their tongues flickering. Korynna began pouring the milk.

"You spoil Eleothi, Aunt Korynna, he gets more than the others," Timon said in a stage whisper.

"Shh! I don't think so," she answered as she broke the cakes into small pieces.

"You like him best, don't you?"

"Yes, of course — that's my good darling!" Korynna cooed.

Andreas smiled when he remembered that she believed her dead husband's spirit had returned to her as Eleothi, the pet snake. It was a common superstition. Korynna's days were now almost totally taken up by religious observance. She tended a room in the house dedicated to the Great Earth Mother, placing fresh flowers on the shrine each day. She regularly visited her friend, Sappena, the High Priestess of the Palace Shrine, where they spent happy hours discoursing on religious themes.

As Andreas turned toward the house, he saw his mother by the fountain. She was staring with deep concentration into the water. He thought she was probably upset by the row in the kitchen.

"Good evening, Mother," he said.

"Hello, my dear," she answered vaguely. Although Old Madam was small and frail, she had great dignity.

"I've just given Timon his first lesson in handling the chariot. He'll make a good driver one day."

"He's beginning to grow up," she replied.

"The scene in the kitchen must have been very unpleasant, Mother."

An expression of disgust crossed the old lady's face, but she said nothing. She refused ever to discuss her daughter-in-law and Andreas accepted her attitude.

"Well, I must wash the dust off myself. Please excuse me."

"Andreas!"

"Yes?" he paused, concerned. There was tension in his mother's voice, "what's troubling you?"

"There is a child missing," she said.

"What do you mean?"

"The laundry girl, Marika, told me. It's her brother, Luki. He's about the same age as Timon." She looked at him for the first time. He was surprised to see the fear and anxiety in her eyes. He returned and took her hand.

"You mustn't upset yourself like this. Come and sit down, my dear."

They sat on a stone bench that rested against the side of the house. The fountain gurgled softly a few feet away and they could hear Timon prattling away to Korynna in the snake room.

"Now, tell me why you're concerned."

"I should never have struck that girl in the kitchen. I shall have to ask her forgiveness tomorrow."

"Don't worry about her. I'm sure she deserved it."

"You see, Andreas, I was upset because of her thoughtlessness. She should not have spoken as she did, knowing that Marika's little brother has been missing for two days. The laundry girl was so upset I had to send her home."

"Has he parents?"

"Yes — his father is a metal worker at the Palace. The mother comes here to help with the oil pressing at harvest time."

"They've searched for him?"

"Yes."

"Where was he last seen?"

"Down by the river. He and Timon often play together. In fact, I think Timon was with him. He's been playing truant from his tutor. We should have told you."

Andreas turned his head toward the snake room and called, "Timon, come here a moment." When the boy stood before him, he said, "Do you know Marika's brother?"

"Yes, Father — that's Luki. We play together sometimes."

"When did you last see him?" The boy looked wary. Andreas said warningly, "No fibs, now. I know you've been missing your lessons, so you may as well own up. This is very important. Your friend Luki is lost and you may be able to help."

"How could I do that?" Timon looked at his feet.

"By trying to remember where he was the very last time you saw him. Or, if you saw someone talking with him — anything like that."

Timon considered for a moment, frowning and biting his lip in intense concentration. "Well," he began, "we went down by the river with a jar to see if we could catch some fish." He paused.

"Go on."

"We were going to keep the fishes and see if they would grow bigger."

"Yes, but what about Luki?" Andreas said.

"Well, I was near the bridge, and Luki went down toward the Sacred Grove. I was going to splash in the water and drive the fish down to him. Then a man came out from behind one of the trees and spoke to him and they went away."

"Which way did they go?"

"Through the Sacred Grove."

"Toward the Palace, you mean?"

"Yes," Timon said. He was tired and wanted his supper. "Please, can I go now, Father?"

"Just a moment. What did the man look like?"

The boy thought and then shook his head. "I wasn't close enough to see him."

"Did you see his clothes?" Old Madam asked. She had been listening so quietly that Andreas had almost forgotten she was there.

"I think they were sort of long," Timon said.

"A tunic, you mean, like the Shrine Priests wear?" Andreas spoke sharply.

"Yes, it had a belt, I think. Can I have my supper now?"

"Yes, run along, my boy."

Old Madam looked searchingly at her son. "What do you make of it, Andreas?"

"I don't know what to think," he replied. "I'll have to make enquiries."

Many small boys lived in the Palace, cleaning the altars and guarding the shrine lamps. Most were orphans or children bought from poor families. Sometimes parents, ashamed to admit to selling their children, pretended they were lost. But as Luki's father was a Palace craftsman, this was not the explanation.

At the villa, only a small group sat down to dinner: Andreas, his mother and sister and Dr Ahmed. After a few moments, Antonius came in, surprising his father and pleasing them all. But even his bantering and good humour could not raise their spirits. Korynna never had much to say and Ahmed preferred the role of observer. Old Madam was silent and preoccupied with the mystery of Luki's disappearance and similarly Andreas had much on his mind.

"It's very good to have your company, Antonius. We'd be a dull lot without you tonight," he said.

"Where's Senka this evening?" Antonius inquired.

"He'll be late," Andreas replied, "he had business in Nirou-Khani."

The tone of his father's voice warned Antonius not to pursue the subject. He began to tell them how Klonka's Club was attracting rogues these days. "You can't trust any of them! While they're drinking your wine at table, their servants are rifling your saddle-bags in the stable yard. It's true!" he cried, looking around the table with dark eyes flashing. "Thamion swears he lost a gold trinket he'd just bought for his girlfriend."

"Are you sure he didn't lose it on the cards?" his grandmother said, laughing.

After the meal, Ahmed and Old Madam settled into their gambling session. "Which of you is going to end up wealthy?" Antonius asked.

"Neither of us, my dear boy," Old Madam replied, tapping him playfully with her fan as he kissed her cheek.

"It's nice to see from whom I inherit my taste for cards and dice!" he exclaimed.

"You scamp," she protested, "we only play for fun, with counters. If I lose a bronze piece in the whole evening —"

"It's a disaster!" Antonius finished the sentence for her and dodged away quickly.

Korynna excused herself and retired. Outside, the full moon was rising, filling the night with cold brilliance and deep black shadows.

"Come out on the terrace, Antonius," Andreas said. They strolled for a few minutes in silence. Then Antonius raised his fist to his forehead and said quietly, "The Moon Goddess holds sway tonight. May she protect us always."

Andreas wondered if his son felt the same anxiety which troubled him.

"Antonius, are you acquainted with Captain Keridos?"

"Yes, Father, he commands the *Griffon* now, doesn't he?"

"How well do you know him?"

"Fairly well, we've played cards, dined together. I haven't seen him since he took up his new command."

"Would you say he was loyal?"

"Loyal?" Antonius stopped short in amazement. "To the King?"

"Yes," his father replied, studying his son's face.

"Of course he's loyal. He belongs to one of the oldest families in Knossos. Two of his aunts are married to members of the Council."

"What are their names?"

"The aunts — I'm not sure."

"No. Their husbands."

Antonius stifled a yawn. "I don't know. Xanthios is one of them, I think."

"And the other?"

"Markos, Minister for the Navy."

"Indeed." Andreas paused thoughtfully and then continued, "Keridos' father, was he a naval man?"

"Yes, but he died years ago, the mother too. The aunts brought Keridos up. Why are you so curious about him?"

"It's not curiosity, it's concern. The *Griffon* can't put to sea. Her planks are rotten."

Antonius looked puzzled. "What do you mean?"

"She's not seaworthy."

"Why doesn't Keridos complain?"

"Why indeed, my dear Antonius. That question has worried me for three days."

"Why don't you ask him yourself?"

"I did. I went on board. He was polite but evasive."

"Perhaps — he just thought..." Antonius hesitated.

"That it's none of my damned business!" his father said sardonically.

"He probably has reported it, Father."

"Then why doesn't his uncle Xanthios, Minister for Supply, take some action?"

"You know what the Palace is like ... always delays."

Antonius wished that his father would stick to commerce and leave the Navy alone, but he could not suggest this without giving offence. He was about to make an excuse to leave when his father said, "Antonius, I need to ask you a favour. It's very important."

"Of course, Father, I'll do anything to help."

"Ride to Phaestos tomorrow and find a merchant named Agidor. I'll give you a letter to give to him.

Then call at the naval yard and discover how much work is being done."

"Father, I've no authority to enter a naval shipyard."

"Invent an excuse — speak to the foreman. Find out if they have timber supplies. I can't be involved personally."

Antonius stared gloomily into the night, unwilling to go but unable to refuse. His face brightened. "What about Senka? He'd make a better job of it than I."

"No. I can't spare him," Andreas replied tersely. "This is urgent, Antonius. I have to make a statement to the Council in two days' time. I must have first-hand and reliable information."

"All right."

"Go early tomorrow morning. You should be back by evening and please don't mention this to anyone."

Antonius remained silent. He loved his father but feared that Andreas' interference would cause trouble. Andreas placed an arm around his son's shoulder.

"Come in and have a nightcap, my boy," he said.

They returned to the house where the doctor and Old Madam had finished their game.

"Did you win, Grandmother?" Antonius inquired.

"She certainly did," Ahmed replied, "I'm bankrupt!" They all laughed and kissed the old lady affectionately as she retired to bed.

The steward poured the wine and Andreas thanked him.

"Good night, Credon. That will be all."

"Good night, sir."

The three men sat on the terrace and enjoyed the wine before parting for the night. Soon after, as Antonius was drifting into sleep, he heard Senka's horse clatter into the stable yard and he wondered what business had taken the secretary to Nirou-Khani at this late hour.

# CHAPTER 8

Klonka's Club was a popular meeting place for the well-to-do young men of Knossos. The proprietor was bald, large and affable. He ran an exclusive establishment with excellent food, high stakes and beautiful girls.

The club's clientele included Army officers, the sons of Palace officials and wealthy merchants, and a few artists, writers and architects. Varkos, the champion wrestler, was often seen there, but, since his defeat by Theseus, the Greek, he had stayed away. Theseus himself never came. As a bull dancer he was forbidden to leave the Palace. This was no hardship. His purpose in coming to Crete lay within the Palace walls.

Klonka's Club was certainly no place for a penniless young man like Senka. Antonius had introduced him and his charm and good looks assured a welcome. His only problem, as usual, was money — or the lack of it. Antonius was generous in a careless way, but Senka was too proud to accept charity. He preferred to live on his wits, to watch for some rich idiot with poor judgement, who would lose on the cards and pay up promptly. Senka would then remember a pressing engagement and leave with his winnings. He hoped some day to catch the eye of a rich widow.

Senka's father was a shoemaker, who emigrated with his small family to Zakro, in eastern Crete, from Byblos. Senka was then three years old. All his early memories were of poverty and struggle. Eventually his parents acquired a small farm where his mother kept goats. Senka, the only surviving child, was idolised by his mother who realized he was clever and was ambitious for him. His parents arranged for him to board with a family in Palaikastro in order to receive an education.

The young man was soon captivated by city life and dreamed of a career in Knossos. He was lucky. A local official gave him an introduction to Andreas and he became the Councillor's secretary. Senka wrote to his parents telling them of his good fortune, but for reasons of his own did not mention his employer's name and address. That was two years ago and he had not written since.

In Knossos, he invented a sad, romantic fantasy — how his father, a Colonel, had fallen against the Hittites and his mother had died of a broken heart. The story brought sentimental tears of sympathy from the girls who admired his dark eyes, his aquiline nose and wide, sensitive mouth. He was a success.

One day, in the Palace Courtyard, he had just delivered a letter and was on his way to spend an hour with his mistress, when Antonius called to him, "Have you met Madam Senthios? Chryssa, this is Sharim Senekor, but we all call him Senka."

She had smiled vaguely in his direction and then turned away and resumed her conversation. From that moment Senka's life had changed. Chryssa's beauty captivated him. He would race through his work, ride like a maniac to deliver the letters and then spend as much time as possible in the Palace Courtyard, hoping to meet her.

Hardly a day passed without an opportunity to see her and exchange a few words. Chryssa would smile, teasing him with her dark eyes. She gave no indication of her own feelings and made no move to encourage him, almost as if she were considering whether or not he would be an amusing lover. This was painful for him as he had always been successful with women.

While Andreas and Antonius were at home, walking on the terrace in the moonlight, Senka sat alone at Klonka's Club drinking his wine. The club was not busy apart from a small group of gamblers absorbed in their game.

"Young Micalidos not here then?" Klonka asked.

"No . . . no he isn't."

"Give them a surprise at home, perhaps?"

"Perhaps."

Klonka, finding him dull company, joined the gamblers. Senka's mind was struggling to come to terms with the chaotic events of the day.

On returning to the Palace soon after the noon sacrifice, he had met Antonius in the Courtyard and learned that Andreas had gone to Phylon's workshop. In spite of being ordered to report immediately, he decided he would risk an hour's delay. Chryssa was close by, talking with her husband, Captain Senthios, and his father, and some of her friends and admirers. Senka heard her laugh and moved closer. A hand on his arm made him turn. He was surprised to find Zanthope standing beside him.

"She's very beautiful, I know," she murmured, her mouth close to his ear, "but she has so many admirers. Do you think you have a chance?" Senka flushed. Before he could answer she went on, "Don't worry — your secret's quite safe with me. But, if you don't want the whole world to know, you really shouldn't stare at her like that!" Zanthope smiled at him sympathetically. The crowd pushed around them and he felt her breast and thigh press against him. Her perfume, heavy, faintly musty, stirred his senses, but at the same time, there was something overpowering about her that made him wary. Her grey-green eyes held him spellbound.

"A friend of mine has a spare room. The apartment of Pashote, any of the Palace slaves will direct you." She pressed his arm with her hand and turned away before he could reply.

Chryssa Senthios had disappeared in the crowd but he soon found her again, accompanied by old Papa Senthios, near the West Palace entrance. Her husband, Dino, had gone on duty and her father-in-law was trying to persuade her to accompany him to the Merchant's Court to see the auctions.

"You might fancy something, sweetheart," he said.

"Be quiet," she replied sharply, but smiling at the same time, "someone might hear."

He saluted a friend, then said quietly to her, "No harm in buying my little love a present, now and then."

"No harm at all — but please be more discreet in public," she murmured. Seeking to escape, she caught Senka's eye. He came to her immediately, oblivious of everything but her smile.

"You run along to your old auction, Papa," she said to her father-in-law. "I promised to spend the afternoon with mother. Senka can walk me over there."

Papa Senthios shrugged his shoulders and did as he was told. He was a realist. If he desired her, so must others, and if she wanted to spend the afternoon rolling about on a bed with this young fellow, there was nothing he could do about it.

"Come along, Senka," she said.

Senka drained his cup at Klonka's Club and called for another flagon. He ordered some food, though he had little appetite.

Today he had attained his greatest desire but it had brought him only bitterness and disillusion. Confused by weariness and wine, he tried to sort out his emotions, but he gave up in despair. The memory of the afternoon tormented him.

When he and Chryssa reached her apartment, it was empty. She invited him in, locked the door and led him into her bedroom. Loosening her belt she came to him. Her breasts were released from the tight bodice and the skirt slipped to the floor, revealing the voluptuous contours of her body. Senka gazed at her in rapturous admiration.

He grasped her in his arms, but her body was tense and she held back. Her sharp fingernails pressed sadistically into the skin of his shoulders. He gasped and looked into her eyes. They were black, dark and hard as ebony.

"Not so fast, my friend. You must do something for me."

"What is it?" he said hoarsely.

"There is something you must bring me."

"What is it, what do you want?" It was maddening to hold her so close, to feel her breath on his cheek and her naked body in his arms.

"I want the necklace!" she said fiercely.

"Necklace?" he repeated, "what necklace?"

"Her necklace," she hissed between her teeth, "Zanthope's necklace. *I want it!*"

He understood her now. All Knossos knew that necklace. Old Madam had worn it, years ago, and others before her. Zanthope wore it now, on grand occasions, glowing crimson and gold on her white throat, enjoying the envious glances of other women.

"Why? You must be mad," he stammered, "you ... you could never wear it."

"I don't care. I want it. You live in the house. You get it for me."

"How can I?"

"Find a way."

He knew she would refuse him if he did not comply. He was lost as he watched her undress. If she had asked him to commit a more serious crime, he probably would have agreed.

"All right — I'll see what I can do. I'll get it somehow."

"You promise?"

"Yes, of course. I promise."

She relaxed in his arms. He carried her to the bed and their lovemaking was brief and violent. When their lust was satisfied, Senka stared unhappily at Chryssa. The joy of fulfilment was missing. He knew that the girls at Klonka's would have given him more pleasure.

"Chryssa, I truly love you," he began, "I didn't mean it to be like this..."

Chryssa stretched luxuriously. Yawning, she turned away.

"Close the door quietly as you go out," she murmured drowsily.

He departed, angry and unsatisfied. Chryssa had planned this. She cared nothing for him. All she wanted was that damned necklace.

Senka knew he should report for work, but he had no inclination to do so. The necklace drew his thoughts to Zanthope and he recalled her invitation in the Courtyard. A servant came out of an apartment, carrying a market basket. On an impulse he asked her the way to Pashote's apartment. She directed him with a sly smile. He hurried down the narrow passage and knocked on the door. A slave ushered him into a dimly lit room. There was a curtained archway facing him and, presently, the heavy curtains parted and Zanthope entered.

Although Senka was well aware of her sensual beauty, here, in this small, isolated room, he felt trapped and would have fled, if he had dared.

Zanthope was relaxed and charming. Her long, golden hair was piled high on her head and held with tortoiseshell combs. As she came towards him, she removed the combs so that her gleaming hair fell about her shoulders. She put her arms around his neck and kissed him passionately. He succumbed to the overpowering warmth and softness of her body and followed her blindly into the room beyond the archway. It contained nothing but a large bed.

Time ceased to exist. Zanthope's passion fired his own. He had never known anyone like her before. He cursed Chryssa for her coldness and yielded with eagerness to whatever Zanthope desired. At last they lay quietly together and he fell asleep. When he awoke, Zanthope had gone and the afternoon shadows lay across the Courtyard.

Senka hurried back to the villa. In spite of the prospect of missing the evening meal, he was glad when Andreas ordered him to ride to Nirou-Khani with the letter for Cibaros. It was preferable to sitting with him at the dinner table.

It was late when Senka returned to Knossos. He carried an answer from Cibaros in his saddle-bag and knew it should be delivered immediately. However he had not eaten and the thought of Klonka's was tempting — Antonius might be there to share a flagon of wine — so he turned his horse's head towards the city. But Antonius was not at the club.

With little enjoyment, Senka finished his meal and returned to the villa. When he looked in his saddlebag for the letter from Cibaros, he was shocked to find that it was gone. His first reaction was disbelief. He searched again in the bag, then in the pouch of his riding cloak, but it was not there.

A cold wave of physical and emotional exhaustion overcame him. He felt sick. The lost letter, the stupid promise to steal for that damn Chryssa, the hours spent with Zanthope — all added up to a recipe for disaster. His life, which had seemed so promising and agreeable, had taken on all the aspects of a nightmare. He remembered once, as a child, losing his way in the mountains on a misty evening. His mother had come searching with a lantern and taken him safely home. He needed someone like that now.

As he entered the houses all was quiet — everyone, apparently, had retired. But the light was still burning in Andreas' apartment. Senka knocked. His palms were damp. Expecting to be dismissed, he reported the loss of the letter. Andreas' calm was misleading.

"Think very carefully," he said, "don't answer in a hurry. If you're quite sure you didn't lose the letter, it must have been stolen. Did you stop anywhere on the way? Apart from Klonka's, I mean?"

"No, sir."

"What about the guard station on the Mallia road, you must have stopped there."

"Yes, sir, but I didn't dismount."

"Did anyone follow you?"

"I don't know — perhaps — I didn't notice anyone."

"Don't ever lie to me," Andreas' voice was quiet but threatening, "you know I could have you deported and sent back to Byblos."

Senka wished to protest, but no words came.

"Now, think clearly," Andreas continued, "did anyone follow you when you left the city?" The secretary tried to recall each moment of the journey, but his mind had been so confused at the time, he had no recollection.

"You're quite sure you did deliver the letter to Cibaros?" Andreas' sarcasm was not lost on Senka.

"I assure you, sir, I delivered the letter into Cibaros' hands."

"At his home or at a tavern?"

"He was home with his family. I sat in the courtyard of his house. One of his daughters gave me a cup of wine."

"The girls seemed to treat you kindly. Did you notice anyone in the street, when you set off?" Senka was about to say no, when he recalled seeing a man staring at him from a doorway.

"I think there was someone watching me in the street."

"You may have been followed then."

"Yes, sir, it's possible."

"Possible," Andreas snapped, "it seems the only explanation. Well there's nothing to be done about it tonight. You'll have to fetch Cibaros here in the morning. I must know what was in that letter."

Senka went to bed depressed and miserable, but he soon fell into a sound sleep. Andreas was not so fortunate. He regretted threatening Senka. It offended his sense of justice that he should take an unfair advantage of an employee, it played on his mind and he could only manage an uneasy sleep.

# CHAPTER 9

After the steep climb up the winding road from Knossos, Antonius dismounted and paused to rest his mare, Lorca. He stroked the black satin of her neck and breathed in the fresh mountain air. Gazing up at the glistening white peaks, his eye followed the line of the rugged mountains, through the belt of dark cypress down to the lower slopes, where olive groves and orchards were streaked with morning mist. The wide plain stretched eastward as far as one could see. Far below lay the Palace of Phaestos, the city and the busy port. Beyond, the Great Green Sea rolled on, as if forever, to spend itself on the distant shores of Africa.

Without enthusiasm Antonius remounted and began the descent. He disliked this mission and was irritated because he had been talked into it. The old man must be going off his head he thought, recalling their conversation on the terrace the previous night.

Passing through groves of gnarled, grey–green olive trees, after a few miles he overtook a long caravan of mules. As he passed the lead mule, an old man greeted him.

Antonius inquired if he knew Andreas' agent, Agidor.

"That I do, young sir," replied the old fellow, not interrupting the steady measure of his stride.

"Where can I find him?"

"Most likely on the dock, near the trader *South Wind*. She sails on the next tide. He has to check this lot aboard." He jerked his thumb back at the line of mules, each with its bulging cargo of laden baskets.

Antonius thanked him and set off more eagerly towards Phaestos. The sooner this business was concluded the better. Descending through orchards and vineyards he reached the outskirts of the city. Soon the traffic in the narrow streets obliged him to slow down as he threaded his way among carts and carrying chairs.

Unexpectedly, he heard his name called and recognized his two cousins, Gina and Talia Micalidos. Riding in a curtained palanquin they ordered the carriers to stop at once, without any regard for other travellers wishing to pass. Eager for news of Knossos, they both talked excitedly without pausing to hear an answer. Antonius escaped, promising to call on them when his business was completed. They were members of the southern Micalidos family, deserted by his grandfather years ago, when he fell in love with Old Madam. How provincial these people are,

Antonius thought contemptuously, how could this city ever have aspired to rival Knossos!

But, indeed it had, long ago. The struggle for power had swung north, south and north again. Fierce internecine wars finally ended under the first great Minos. Knossos had triumphed and affairs had settled down after the treaty. Phaestos had prospered and now teemed with immigrants. Syrian horse-dealers rubbed shoulders with shaved Egyptian priests and swarthy Libyans, whose clipped beards and dark skins singled them out from the clean-shaven Cretans. Antonius often wished that his father would not persist in wearing a beard, but reflected that it was typical of his stubborn independence.

A short ride through the city brought him to the port. As he searched for the *South Wind*, he noticed the galley *Dolphin* at the wharf taking on stores. He stood watching the loading party for a few minutes and then asked the foreman casually when the fleet would be returning north again. The man shrugged his shoulders.

"We sail when we get our orders," he said finally.

"Not before we get our back pay, I hope," grumbled one of the sailors.

"If we get paid, we may as well stay here," said another, "the girls are as good here as anywhere."

"And cheaper, too!" cried a third.

Antonius left them, arguing the relative merits of Phaestian and Knossian harlots.

Presently he caught sight of his father's ship, *South Wind*. She was lying between a sturdy Phoenician trader, unloading a cargo of dates and bulky papyrus rolls, and a Cretan ship, newly arrived from Libya. From this vessel, a cargo was unloading itself, under the watchful eyes of a slave trader.

A group of Nubian girls, frightened and exhausted from seasickness, stumbled tearfully off the ship to meet their fate in the slave market. Some might be lucky and be sold into a good home. Those less fortunate would go to one of the brothels in the city. One or two might, like the bull dancer M'Boola, find fame, wealth and honour in the Bull Ring of Knossos. Antonius eyed them with a mixture of pity and curiosity.

On the deck of the *South Wind* a tall, strongly built man was speaking to the bosun. On his broad shoulders spread a heavy collar of beaten copper. A belt with a snake's head clasp supported his loincloth of fine red leather. He turned when Antonius inquired after the agent, Agidor.

"Who wants me?" he growled. It was an unpleasant face, cold yet sensual. Antonius took the letter from his saddle bag. Agidor crossed to the rail, swept a lightning glance over the young man, noting in an instant the glossy hair and love-lock, the stylish clothes and well-made riding boots and the beautiful Arab mare, and spat. It missed the boots by a hair's breadth.

Antonius controlled himself. At that moment, he envied Captain Senthios, toughened by military training. No one would ever dare treat him with disrespect. Even the dandy, Keridos, had authority in his bearing.

I must look like a milksop, he thought, his face flushing. He maintained his dignity and handed over the letter.

"Councillor Micalidos to the agent, Agidor."

To calm himself, while the letter was being read, he dismounted and walked down the quay toward the bow of the ship. Andreas chose his captains carefully and paid them generously. The ship was trimly kept and ready for departure. Evidently they only awaited the mule caravan Antonius had passed on the mountain. He was admiring the carved figurehead of a ram, with great curling horns, when he heard a whimpering sound, like a child in pain. It seemed to come from the belly of the ship.

Antonius tied the mare's reins to the ship rail and climbed aboard. Peering down into the dark hold, he saw oil jars roped together, packed in straw. Half hidden, in a heap of straw nearby, lay three small boys. They appeared to be Cretan as they still wore the padded metal belts which mothers put on children to constrict their waists. Soldiers, athletes and dandies could throw out their chests as much as they wished, but, if they were to be thought elegant and fashionable, they must tighten their belts and look as narrow in the waist as a wasp! This was a fashion thought strange by foreign visitors.

In his concern for the children, forgetting his anger, Antonius went back amidships and asked for the Captain. Agidor had crossed to the wharf to look over the Nubians, and was pinching them and looking at their teeth as if they were cattle. Just then the Captain came down the jetty with two servants carrying his sea-chest.

"Is that cargo from Knossos loaded yet?" he barked at Agidor.

"No, it's late again," replied the agent, without interrupting his scrutiny of one of the black slaves. She was proud and beautiful. Her dark eyes were tragic, yet, while the rest drooped in misery, she held her head high and kept back the tears.

"Don't sell this one. I'll keep her," Agidor said to the trader.

Antonius longed to be away. The Captain came aboard and assuming he was a passenger, asked if his luggage was stowed.

"I'm not taking passage, Captain," Antonius replied, "there are three children captive on this ship. It's against the law to kidnap Cretan children."

"Children? Kidnap? I don't know what you're talking about. Who are you?"

"Antonius Micalidos, sir. The children are bound and hidden amongst the oil jars forward," Antonius persisted.

"Where's the bosun?" roared the Captain.

When the man appeared, he denied all knowledge of the children. Antonius had the sensation of being watched and turned around just as Agidor's gaze shifted away.

"Fetch 'em here, at once, bosun," the Captain continued, "I don't want any stowaway brats aboard my ship." The children were brought at once and dumped on the deck. "Who hid these brats on board without my permission?" bellowed the Captain angrily. No one answered.

"Cut them loose," Antonius said. A sailor took a knife from his belt and freed the three boys. They sat rubbing their swollen wrists and ankles.

"Get 'em off my ship," the Captain ordered abruptly, glancing at Antonius. "Bosun, cast off."

The crew moved to their stations, the children were bundled ashore and Antonius hastily untied the mare.

"Aren't you going to wait for the load from Knossos?" Agidor inquired as the crew were casting off.

"Too bloody late — they can send it on the *Southern Star,*" the Captain replied.

"His honour won't like that," sneered the agent.

When the children saw Agidor, they cowered behind Antonius.

"Where did these children come from?" he asked sternly.

"I know nothing about them," Agidor replied smoothly. Tapping the letter he went on, "Tell his honour, the Councillor, there's no news of the fleet returning north, only rumours and they change every day." He snapped his fingers and a slave waiting nearby took the bridle of Agidor's horse. The agent mounted and rode off with the slave running behind.

Antonius was left standing on the quay wondering what to do with three grubby urchins. Some bystanders offered vulgar advice. Antonius called to a chair-carrier dozing nearby. Giving him some money, he asked the man to take the boys to the house of

Grivas Micalidos. The carrier looked him over, bit the coin and beckoned to the children.

"Get in, yer brats," he croaked and the boys scrambled into the chair, chattering like monkeys.

Antonius rode directly to his uncle's house. As he banged on the heavy door, he recalled the visits they had made there as children — he and Miklos, and their young sister, Hyacinth, gamine and coltish. Now she was queening it in the Palace of Mallia and Miklos was dead.

When the slave opened the door and Antonius asked for Grivas Micalidos, the man shook his head. "He is not here, sir. You will find him at the Palace."

Antonius cursed. He had forgotten that his uncle had been appointed Chancellor and had moved to the Palace. He rode wearily up the steep, paved highway. Arriving at the imposing entrance, he sent a slave to look for the children.

Framed by the glistening peaks of Mount Ida, the Palace of Phaestos reflected in its brilliant architecture, its wide stairways and lavish decorations the opulence and prosperity of the city it dominated. Compared with the vast, rambling building at Knossos it seemed small. Poky and insignificant, the Knossians called it! The Phaestians would grind their teeth in fury at the arrogant snobs from over the mountain, but Antonius had to admit this Palace had a distinction all of its own. Perhaps it was the city's maritime character and the prevailing sea breezes. Whatever the reason, the brooding, sinister atmosphere of Knossos was absent here. The Palace had a carefree, happy-go-lucky atmosphere, which obliged him, biased though he was, to appreciate its ambience and charm.

When he presented himself at his uncle's apartment, his welcome could not have been warmer.

"Come in, my boy," Uncle Grivas clasped him to his breast in a bear hug, "my daughters told me they'd seen you in the city. You're just in time for lunch."

Antonius' aunt, Myrna Micalidos, was a pleasant, vivacious lady, eager for family news and gossip from Knossos. He related everything which he thought would interest her and, when she was satisfied, her daughter Gina took up the interrogation.

"Antonius, what is the latest fashion in necklaces and shoe buckles?" she inquired.

Uncle Grivas interrupted. "What does a man know of this nonsense? He is hungry, let him eat, let him eat!"

But the young women's enthusiasm for gossip could not be quenched so easily. Talia, with a wicked smile, asked, "What about the Princess Ariadne and the Athenian bull dancer — what's his name?"

"Theseus," Gina prompted.

"Is it true, he's a prince and the Princess wants to marry him?"

Uncle Grivas looked stern and snapped his fingers. He bellowed, "That's enough! Women's tongues — like so many scorpions!"

The afternoon was well advanced when he took Antonius aside to ask for news of Andreas and the true reason for his nephew's visit.

"Just a trading matter, Uncle," Antonius said. He related the events of the morning in some detail. "The Cretan children I rescued were probably intended for the Libyan slave market."

"They would fetch a high price there! I'll look into it, my boy. This pernicious crime must be stamped out."

Antonius said that he was sure the agent, Agidor, was involved in some way.

"Can you prove it?" his uncle enquired.

"No, unfortunately."

They were seated on a stone bench beside a large window. The oiled parchment screens were drawn back to let in the cool breeze. Below them stretched the city and port of Phaestos, a kaleidoscope of coloured rooftops and painted walls. Far out to sea they saw the white sails of Andreas' ship *South Wind*, as she bent her way on the long haul southward to Libya.

"What can be done about these children?" Antonius asked.

"Were they honestly paid for or stolen?" Grivas inquired.

"I don't know, sir."

"We must find out. If they were stolen, we can reunite them with their families, if not, we can find a place for them here, in the Palace. We always need messenger boys and they can help the priests."

"The fleet, sir, it's due to sail north quite soon, I suppose," Antonius said after a moment.

The sudden change of subject caught the older man by surprise. He's not as alert as my father, Antonius thought.

"The fleet? Ah, yes ... er, *Dolphin*, *Porpoise* and the rest of them," Grivas replied, "I've no doubt they'll be leaving soon. Why do you ask?"

"My father is concerned that the absence of the fleet leaves the north coast poorly guarded — if we were attacked, or threatened."

"Goodness me," Uncle Grivas said, "what strange ideas my brother has. He shouldn't be so smart — he thinks too much!" he chuckled. At that moment, a slave announced another visitor. When the man entered, Uncle Grivas welcomed him respectfully.

"We are indeed honoured, Major Ortis. Two Knossian visitors in one day! This is my nephew, Antonius Micalidos."

The officer bowed stiffly. His call was a formality. He wished to stay overnight in the Palace. Grivas gave the necessary orders to his staff and asked if he could assist in any other way.

"My business concerns the Bull Ring," Major Ortis said, "I am inquiring at the ports for suitable recruits. Have your slave markets any candidates?"

Antonius remembered the courageous Nubian slave. Surely, he thought, she would prefer to take her chance with the bull rather than suffer misery and humiliation at the hands of Agidor. With satisfaction, he foresaw the agent's anger and frustration at being deprived of the girl. Agidor could not deny Major Ortis, King Minos' emissary, and he informed Major Ortis about the girl's beauty, courage and proud bearing.

"But is she a virgin?" Major Ortis inquired.

"I don't know. If Agidor keeps her, she won't be by tomorrow morning."

Ortis decided to interview the Nubian. At the shrine of the Mother Goddess, he obtained the services of a priestess. There was no point in acquiring this girl unless she proved to be unsullied.

The Micalidos family would not hear of Antonius returning to Knossos that night. He spent a pleasant evening with them and slept in the guest room. Early next morning he left Phaestos, loaded with gifts and messages for the family in Knossos. He rode first to the naval repair yards. As Andreas had suspected, the shipyard was idle. The foreman admitted they had had no timber supplies since the Spring Festival. Antonius turned the mare's head for home, and both rider and mount were delighted to be returning to the familiar pleasures of Knossos.

Among the jostling crowds was another traveller. Antonius caught sight of the slim, dark figure of the Nubian slave. A night's rest had restored her spirits. She seemed to be enjoying the speed of Major Ortis' light chariot. Antonius patted the mare's neck.

"That woman is nearly as beautiful as you are," he whispered in her ear. He spurred the horse on, smiling in silent satisfaction as he visualized Agidor's fury and frustration. He had made a bad enemy.

# CHAPTER 10

While his son was away in Phaestos, Andreas recalled his conversation with Phylon and considered how he might test its truth. If a vote on the Sacred Pilgrimage was forced through at the next Council meeting and was made public, there could be no turning back. He knew he must act decisively to prevent this.

The King's attitude would be of vital importance. It occurred to Andreas that Ahmed might be able to help — he had observed a considerable rapport between the Queen and her reserved countryman and hoped this mutual attraction could be put to advantage. Her Majesty would surely know what the King was planning to do, and might be prevailed upon to influence him against making the Pilgrimage. Especially if she was convinced that the safety of the country was at stake — and her son's safety — that could be a point Ahmed could stress. The more

Andreas considered this plan, the better it seemed. He broached the matter as soon as the doctor returned home from the surgery.

Ahmed was tired. The first hot days of full summer usually brought an increase of stomach complaints and his surgery had been crowded all day. The Egyptian doctor had won the affection of the people with his kindness and patience and they came to him confident that his skill would heal them.

However, to make an appointment with the Queen, to go alone to the Palace and question her on a matter that was no concern of his! Nothing could be more distasteful to one of Ahmed's reserve. He was adamant in his refusal to agree to Andreas' request. But, after a bath, a good meal and an excellent wine, his resolve weakened. Andreas' argument that the security of the state was involved — and with it, that of the Queen herself — decided him. With some misgivings he agreed to see her.

Andreas ordered the crimson chariot at once, before the doctor could change his mind. Guided by a Palace slave, Ahmed was soon making his way through the labyrinth of corridors.

When Doctor Ahmed was announced by a member of the Palace staff, he found Queen Kara seated in her salon with her ladies-in-waiting. One was spinning yarn from a great bowl of goat's hair while the rest were laughing and gossiping as they bent over their embroidery.

The Queen looked up in surprise when Ahmed entered.

"Good evening, doctor. To what do we owe this pleasure?"

"Good evening, madam," he replied nervously.

She smiled encouragingly and asked her ladies to withdraw a little.

"Do sit down, doctor."

He did so, very much aware that he was on an extraordinarily difficult assignment.

"How is Councillor Micalidos? In good health, I trust."

"Yes ... yes, indeed, thank you, madam."

Ahmed paused but saw that finally he must come to the point.

"Your Majesty," he said quietly, "Councillor Micalidos is very disturbed by a rumour concerning His Majesty, King Minos," He paused again, choosing his words carefully. The Queen said nothing. She always seemed calm and self-possessed. He glanced at her and noticed the perfect immobility of her features. Her needle stabbed busily at the embroidery, then he heard a sudden intake of breath and saw the blood start where she had pricked her finger. She continued sewing without looking up.

"It concerns the fulfilment of the Sacred Pilgrimage," Ahmed went on, "rumour has it His Majesty may set off before the winter this year. If this is the case, Councillor Micalidos has very urgent reasons for wishing to dissuade the King from such a course. He hoped I might be able to enlist your help."

He gazed earnestly at the Queen.

"I hope you are not offended. I am not a diplomat, madam, but this matter is of the greatest importance to our state." To his surprise, she seemed relieved. She relaxed and smiled wanly.

"I'm afraid, my dear doctor, you are wasting your time. Unfortunately, I am not consulted on matters of state or of religious ritual. The Palace slaves know more than I do about His Majesty's plans. I know I can trust you. Please don't repeat what I've said."

"Madam, I could never betray your confidence," Ahmed said earnestly.

She laughed quietly. She thought him charming, so formal and old-fashioned. "There is one person who may be able to give you the information you seek — Princess Ariadne. She is very close to the King." She spoke without rancour or envy. They might have been discussing the weather. Ahmed remained silent. The Queen continued, still smiling gently, "But remember, anything you say to her will soon be repeated elsewhere."

The significance of this last remark was not lost on Ahmed. He rose to take his leave, bowed and said, "Madam, you have been most kind. Thank you."

"I'm sorry I couldn't be of more help, doctor."

He bowed again, and intending to leave the way he had come, opened a small door. But he was mistaken. He saw only a dark passage which turned at a sharp angle a short way ahead. Queen Kara stood up and walked over to him.

"Not that way, doctor. This is the way out," she said indicating the large double door by which he entered earlier. "That passage leads to His Majesty's private apartments. Sadly, he doesn't seem to use it these days."

Ahmed stood still for a moment, staring down the dark, empty passage. He had a sudden insight into her loneliness and isolation. She had nobility and a quiet heroism which aroused his compassion. Their eyes met, and for a brief instant she understood the depth of his emotion. At that very moment, the main door opened and King Minos entered.

"Good evening, madam — and Doctor Ahmed — what brings you to the East Palace?" His tone was cold and without expression. Queen Kara greeted him calmly, walked to a table where she picked up a small statuette of an Egyptian sphinx.

"Look, sir," she said in a cool, light voice, "His Excellency the Egyptian Ambassador, has sent me this charming gift. Dr Ahmed was kind enough to bring it."

She held up the statuette for the King to examine. He glanced at it briefly, then turned his back on them both. Joining the group of ladies-in-waiting, he began to laugh and joke with them. Turning to Ahmed, the Queen made a small gesture toward the door. Dr Ahmed thankfully made his escape and once outside the Palace, gratefully gulped in the night air. He wondered how the Queen could endure this situation and felt anxious for her. At the same time, he had to admit, she was very cool. Obviously, she could look after herself.

On returning to the villa, Ahmed found Andreas playing cards with Old Madam and her daughter.

Andreas excused himself at once and drew Ahmed aside.

"Goodness me," Old Madam said, "Andreas is like a dancing bear tonight. Now he's going to monopolise the doctor so I can't have my game of 'Storm the Castle'."

"I'm sorry, mother," Andreas said, "but I must speak with Ahmed." He ushered the doctor out onto the terrace.

"What's going on?" Old Madam asked peevishly, "Antonius dashing off to Phaestos. Nobody tells me anything."

"Shall *we* play 'Storm the Castle'? You know you'll enjoy beating me," Korynna said soothingly.

Old Madam smiled. Suddenly contrite, she replied, "I'm sorry. I think I'm tired and it's time for bed," and went upstairs, leaning on Korynna's arm.

Out on the terrace, Andreas listened to Ahmed's account of his interview with the Queen.

"So we didn't achieve much," he said, "well, never mind, we tried. Come and join me for a nightcap." They went to Andreas' apartment. As they drank the wine he told Ahmed of his plan to send his agent, Tarsis, into Mycenae and how the letter had been stolen from Senka's saddle-bag.

"Cibaros came today and assured me there was nothing particular in his reply which could endanger the venture. But I'm still not easy in my mind about Tarsis' safety."

"When do you expect his return?"

"Maybe two weeks — but there could be problems — the weather, difficulties inside the city."

They were silent for a while, savouring the wine. Ahmed recalled his visit to the Queen and was concerned that she might be in danger. The thought tormented him. He had not told Andreas about the final moments of his visit to her. Andreas was suddenly aware of his friend's tense expression.

"What troubles you?"

The wine helped to overcome Ahmed's reserve. He told Andreas of the King's sudden appearance in the Queen's salon.

"I am concerned about her. In my opinion, the King is a difficult, unpredictable man, even unstable. I'm wondering if her position at court is secure. She is undoubtedly very unhappy. I can't get her out of my mind." Ahmed spoke quietly. Watching him closely, Andreas said, "I don't see much hope for you as a lover, my friend."

Ahmed was shocked and was about to protest, but Andreas silenced him with a gesture. "She's a beautiful woman. You wouldn't be human if that prospect hadn't occurred to you. As to her safety, you've no need to worry on that score. She has a close friend in User-Amon, the Egyptian Ambassador. You know he's a wise and resourceful man. Besides, as a matter of policy, she and her son could never be harmed here in Knossos. Queen Kara may not be happy, my dear friend, but don't worry about her safety."

Ahmed's fears were not entirely relieved. However, he bid Andreas good night and suggested a sleeping draught.

"You measure it for me and I'll take it later," Andreas said. "Now I must finish writing my speech for the Council meeting tomorrow. It will probably stir up more trouble, but somebody must take the bull by the horns."

With this cryptic remark they parted for the night.

# CHAPTER 11

The great Palace of Knossos provided a home for thousands of Cretans, including the royal family, many distinguished government officials and their families, Ambassadors and Embassy staff, a host of civil servants, priests, soldiers, craftsmen and artisans and a large number of servants and slaves. Most of these people were free to come and go as they pleased or as they were ordered. However, within the Palace walls, there was a small and unique group of young people to whom the Palace was both a home and a prison — they were the Bull Dancers of Knossos. Celebrated and much admired by all Cretans, they lived for one purpose only — the fulfilment of their destiny as artists and athletes in the Bull Ring.

The Bull Halls were situated at the northern end of the East Palace. Approached by a narrow, circular stairway, the quarters ran below ground like a series of large cellars. Stone floors and walls were cold and cheerless in winter, but in midsummer, when the citizens sweltered in brick houses and heat shimmered in the street like molten glass, the dancers' quarters were a cool sanctuary.

The great metal-studded doors leading to the Bull Ring were closed and barred. In the Bull Halls the old hands disliked the midsummer break. The interruption of routine was upsetting. The novices were edgy and untried and some of the senior dancers were due for retirement. This was a time when close friendships and partnerships would be ended. It was rumoured that many of the bulls were to be sacrificed, except Tauron, a huge roan and white beast, whom the dancers favoured because he was slow. He was to be spared as he was popular with the audiences and was indeed too large to manage with dignity in the sacrificial ceremony. Bulls in the new season might be unpredictable and dangerous.

During the day, regular exercises continued in the practice hall, a large circular room with a domed roof and an opening, high up, which gave a glimpse of the blue sky. In the centre of the hall stood "Diddy", the practice bull, a strange timber monster, covered in hide, hollow in the middle, with a pair of blunt horns projecting from one end. These were connected to a swivel inside and the whole contraption was mounted on wheels. One of the men would crawl inside it and charge at the dancers, simulating the movements of the bull. Even the novices were well aware of the speed and cunning of the real bull and considered it a poor substitute.

The Chief Trainer, Naxos, had been one of the great vaulters of his day, until a bull gored his thigh. Without warning he would limp into training sessions to supervise the novices in a series of leaps and complicated dance patterns. When Naxos grunted and walked out, it was assumed he was satisfied. Repeated mistakes were punished by banishment to work as a slave. This rarely occurred in the last months of training as Naxos' dedication inspired the dancers to strive for perfection. Fear of the bull tempted some to seek failure as a way out, but pride made most of the dancers strive to succeed. A word of praise from Naxos was valued more than gifts thrown down by the spectators.

Outstanding athletes became "vaulters" — the most revered status for all dancers in the Bull Ring. Other dancers had responsibility as "catchers". The vaulter faced the bull and moved forward when every instinct was saying run away. They had to judge the height of the horns and then, head down and close to the flaring nostrils and bloodshot eyes, grasp the horns and somersault high on to the huge, swaying back. There they would reach for the catcher's outstretched arm and jump down, ready to vault again if the bull turned swiftly. An experienced vaulter could often stand and ride the bull. This always brought great roars from the crowd, who chanted the vaulter's name and threw flowers, jewels and money into the ring.

The practice hall was the only place where the men and women dancers could converse. In the dormitories, the baths and storerooms they were segregated and strictly watched. In the communal dining-room they sat at separate tables. But, of course, these restrictions did not prevent the young dancers from being attracted to one another.

As was their custom, some of the male dancers had remained in the dining-room after supper.

Paulius was the most senior of the dancers. Tall and well-built, he was a brilliant and fearless vaulter and an excellent leader. He proposed a toast. "Let's drink to our amiable old friend, Tauron, the bull!"

The dancers cheered and raised their glasses.

"I'll drink to that," Paulius' friend, Leander, said enthusiastically.

Leander, who came from the warlike city-state of Sparta, was tall, lean and handsome. He had been in the Bull Halls of Knossos for nearly four years. Both he and Paulius were great favourites with the spectators and were much admired by the people of Crete. Paulius was in love with one of the senior women vaulters, Asteria. It was rumoured that when they retired in two months' time they would marry. Leander was deeply in love too, but, believing the situation to be hopeless — she was a novice with five long years to serve — he chose not to reveal it.

Other dancers, led by Theseus the Greek, had retired to their quarters to play cards and gossip. This group of seven young men and seven girls had arrived earlier in the year. Naxos had organized their training through a Greek-speaking instructor. He had wanted to split the group, to allow them to learn from the experienced dancers. However, Theseus was adamant that his dancers must remain together as a team. The Greeks were so insistent that Naxos agreed.

Many Bull Dance fans believed Theseus was a Prince, the son of King Aegeus of Athens. But others dismissed this notion. Why would a King allow his son and heir to participate in this dangerous entertainment? The Greek dancers were not popular with their colleagues, who thought them conceited and avoided them.

"To Tauron!" Leander repeated, "May he live many years."

"Tauron! Tauron!" the dancers shouted cheerfully, enjoying the more generous supply of wine, which was rationed during the Bull Dance season.

To relieve their boredom, the Egyptian dancer, Ali-el-Berber, leapt on to the long table and began turning cartwheels. His friends applauded, but Sardi, the Cilician, yelled, "Watch out, Ali, you fool!" as the acrobat set the jugs rocking and overturned wine glasses.

Sardi was a tough, good-looking young man, black-eyed and black-haired. It was widely known that his friend, the irrepressible Ali, was the bastard son of an Egyptian merchant and a Nubian harlot. Ali was a small, agile comic genius, with a broad grin and large owl-like eyes. It was Ali's custom to vault the bull and at the same time shout impudent comments to high-born ladies in the audience. His antics provoked gales of laughter. Demands for less levity and threats of punishment from the trainers brought no response. Ali was unique and the crowd loved him. He somersaulted from the table and landed perfectly.

"I didn't spill a drop," he grinned.

"Only because the jugs are all empty," Sardi pointed out. He shouted to the slaves — "For Zeus sake, fill 'em up before we all die of thirst!"

Naxos was well aware that boredom could be a problem for his athletes during the summer break. He insisted on regular practice sessions and awarded prizes for wrestling bouts and tumbling contests to keep the dancers occupied.

Bruni and Dek, two young cousins from Delos, spent hours arm-wrestling, hands locked in combat, eyes popping, teeth clenched, to everyone's amusement. Nino, a lively and cheerful young man from Cyprus, was a compulsive gambler, who had blithely lost all his money on cards. These three novices needed no urging to practise. They would soon be dedicated to the Earth Mother and face the bull, the awesome Earth Shaker, in the ring. They looked forward to this moment with a mixture of excitement and terror.

In the women's quarters the girl dancers were enjoying an hour of relaxation before Vanna, their strict dormitory mistress, ordered lights out. Their room was long and narrow, its wooden ceiling darkened by smoke and dust. The faded colours of old frescoes gave the walls a mottled appearance and tiles of many colours covered the floor. It seemed as if any tiles left over from paving in the Palace had found their way into the Bull Halls. This odd patchwork appeared everywhere.

The senior dancers slept on a raised section at one end, conveniently near the baths. Their part of the room was made more attractive by wall hangings, carpet, soft bed coverings and bright oil lamps purchased with gifts won in the Bull Ring. Novices were located at the far end of the room where the lamps were few and dim, the floor bare, the beds straw mattresses on the ground and the coverings ragged cast-offs, handed down many times from those who had retired or died after accidents in the ring. Life for beginners was neither easy nor comfortable. They ran errands for the leading dancers, mended their clothes and brushed their hair.

The foreign dancers had a language problem. They had to learn enough Cretan to understand the commands of the trainers, to learn the rules and generally keep out of trouble.

The novice, Belia, was lucky. She had learned some Cretan from the priestess in the temple where she had served after being rescued from the sea. She was able to help newcomers, especially her blonde friend, Freyna, who came from the distant north. Both girls had attracted much attention since their arrival. Their unorthodox visit to Phylon's workshop, where they met Andreas, was still being discussed in the Palace workshops. Wagers were already being laid on their chances of success and survival in the coming season. They were unaware of this.

As they lay naked on their straw beds, Belia stretched her pale, slender limbs and yawned expansively. Freyna, in the next bed, was drowsy and relaxed. They had waited patiently for their baths while the seniors lingered, chattering and using all the hot water. Belia had charmed the slave to heat up a little more, just for them. They had soaked for a delicious half-hour and then rolled on the tiled floor, squealing with delight, while Asa, the little bath slave, threw buckets of cold water over them until Vanna scolded them and chased them off to the dormitory with a flick of her birch rod.

Vanna, it was said, had once been a fine bull dancer. Now she was old and stiff. It was difficult for Belia to believe that anyone so wrinkled and infirm could have been young, nimble and pretty enough to be a bull dancer.

"It just doesn't seem possible," she remarked to Freyna, "I hope I never live to be like that. I'd sooner die young."

"Don't talk like that!" Freyna said nervously. "The Gods will hear you!"

Belia gestured rudely. "That for them!" she cried.

Freyna was astonished. Her friend had no respect for anything or anyone.

The Corinthian Asteria, one of the senior dancers, overheard Belia's remark and muttered darkly, "Those who show no respect never last long."

"I respect those who are worthy of it," Belia said lightly.

Asteria, who was proud and quarrelsome, was not at all popular with the other girls. Although she knew Paulius loved her, she was of a jealous disposition nonetheless. He had shown too much interest in the newcomers and Belia made no secret of her admiration for him. Freyna was uneasy.

Asteria, her voice hard and strident, continued: "I deserve your respect. For five years I've danced in the ring, three as a leading vaulter. You are nothing here — nothing. I was chosen from fifty virgins in the Temple of Astarte in Corinth."

"From what I've heard of Corinth," Belia snapped, "I'm surprised they could find a virgin."

Asteria stuttered with rage, "You Cilician guttersnipes! I don't know how you managed to pass the tests."

"Cilicia!" Freyna cried. "I don't come from that barren place. My country is beautiful with forests, lakes and snowy mountains — far away in the north."

"Well, it's a pity you didn't stay there," Asteria shrieked.

"They only chose you for the Bull Ring because you were too ugly for the brothels! You'd have frightened the customers away!" Belia cried, defending her friend.

"I'll tear your eyes out!" Asteria snarled.

"Stop it you two," M'boola, the Libyan, drawled in her deep, rich voice. "We'll have old Vanna in here with her birch rod in a minute. We were fined last week because of your quarrelling. I can't afford it." M'boola was reputedly very rich and this brought general laughter and shouts of agreement from the other dancers. They did not care about Asteria but most of them couldn't afford another fine.

M'boola was a tall, handsome Negress with skin as black as ebony. She had a fine head of tousled hair, enormous black eyes and full lips. She was admired and respected for her courage, strength and dry sense of humour, which she often showed in moments of tension.

The inactivity of the summer break affected them all. M'boola and Asteria were soon to retire; they and Paulius were the only survivors of their original group. Soon their five years of service would be rewarded with money and freedom. Asteria, who intended to marry Paulius, was in a tense and nervous state, often close to hysteria.

It took all M'boola's calm and authority to maintain peace in the dormitory. She was occupied, too, in teaching the Cretan language to a newcomer, a dark girl like herself from Africa. She had been rescued, so she said, from a brutal slave trader in Phaestos. Her name was Shahali.

Close friendships were not encouraged in the bull dancers' small world. Apart from language difficulties, the system did not allow intimate friendships. The distress was too great when dancers were injured or died in the Bull Ring. A strict law, reiterated constantly during training, forbade anyone to intervene should the bull claim a victim. It was believed the unfortunate dancer had been honoured by the Bull of Minos, the awesome Earth Shaker, and should go willingly to his or her death. However, most of the dancers rejected this in their hearts, but they usually obeyed the strict demands of their instructors in the ring. Accidents were seldom discussed afterwards.

Belia and Freyna had arrived in Knossos and were brought to the Bull Halls in the same week about six months previously. Belia was independent, cheerful and not easily put down. On the other hand, Freyna was gentle, shy and lacked confidence. However, she performed the athletic routines with style and grace and the trainers acknowledged her talents. But she was often homesick and afraid. She dreaded failure and dismissal to work as a servant or a harlot in a brothel.

The friendship between the two dancers was at first tentative. Neither had reached the point of complete trust, mainly because both had recently been victims of deception.

Now, relaxed and comfortable, they talked in whispers when the lamps were doused. Belia spoke of her childhood spent as a nomad in the wild regions south of the Caspian Sea. She began to recount her most vivid memories and Freyna listened with eager attention.

"We lived a strange life, wandering from place to place — wherever there was good grass for the animals. I remember a tent with sheepskin rugs, very warm and cosy ... and my mother crooning lullabies to my baby brother. When we moved camp my father would carry me on the saddle of his horse, or, sometimes, I'd sit on a pile of tents on the baggage horse. It was a happy life," she paused, "but it all ended in disaster. Our camp was attacked by bandits..." Belia shuddered at the awful memory. "I heard my mother screaming, the men shouting, the horses neighing wildly, the clash of knives!"

"Belia, how terrible," Freyna murmured.

Tears glistened in the young dancer's eyes as she recalled her lost family. She had never spoken of these things before. Freyna took Belia's hand.

"What happened?" she asked.

"They were all murdered." Belia's voice broke. She remained silent but then went on bravely, "My mother saved me by hiding me under a pile of rugs. The next day some shepherds found me and I was taken to Babylon and sold in the slave market."

"I know what it's like to be sold as a slave!" Freyna said suddenly, "but go on, Belia."

"I was bought by a woman who owned a troupe of child acrobats. It wasn't a bad life — Fedora was hard and greedy, but she was fond of me — she never admitted it, but she always protected me and would never sell me."

Belia was indeed the most attractive and talented performer Madam Fedora had ever owned. Freyna's eyes opened wide as Belia spoke of her travels to Samarkand and later to Egypt. She made light of the hardships and spoke of the Great Pyramids and the palaces and temples of Thebes and Luxor.

"How I'd love to see those places, Belia."

"Perhaps you will one day."

After Egypt the troupe travelled north and performed in Byblos.

"We sailed for Troy," Belia continued, "we called at Cypress for provisions and after leaving the island there was a great storm — the ship pitched and rolled — everyone was ill. We prayed to Poseidon, crying out in fear, but the Sea God was angry! Great waves crashed against the ship and in the night she began to sink. We clung together, terrified." Belia paused, remembering the young people she had known. "Poor Madam Fedora and my friends, they must have been drowned. I never saw them again."

"But you survived, Belia, thank the Gods!"

"Yes, I clung to a spar and the next day some fishermen rescued me."

"Poseidon heard your prayers!"

The story was similar to that told by Senka at Andreas' dinner table some months ago. Belia was befriended by the islanders. But she soon found they could not be trusted. She had amused the villagers and the temple priestess with tumbling and balancing tricks and performed willingly to entertain a platoon of Cretan soldiers. When the Lieutenant ordered her hands tied and took her away, the villagers turned their backs — even the priestess averted her eyes.

"And they brought me here to Knossos."

"My story is very much like yours," Freyna began, "we lived far, far away in the north. The country was so beautiful in winter — the trees hung with snow and the rivers frozen. My father came south to sell furs and amber," her voice trembled, "oh, dearest father, how loving he was. I was his only child. I don't remember my mother, she died when I was a baby."

Freyna explained how a bitter quarrel had occurred between two families whose sons both wished to marry her. "That's why father took me with him, to protect me. How I wish I could let him know I'm safe and well." Freyna wept as she imagined her father's sorrow and despair.

Belia wondered which was more tragic; to have no family or to have a father who believed you were dead. She stroked Freyna's hair, not knowing what consolation to offer. Freyna wiped away her tears and continued her story.

"We travelled with other traders and adventurers through great forests and over high mountains." She paused thoughtfully. "Looking back, it seems I was only a child then. I knew nothing of love."

"Go on, Freyna," Belia said eagerly, imagining the dark forests, full of wild beasts.

"We came to Troy — a great city with wonderful markets," Freyna continued. "When our trading was completed, we crossed the narrow sea and set off for home. One evening I was very foolish. I wandered from the campsite looking for wild flowers. Some bandits captured me. They bound my hands and stuffed rags in my mouth. I suppose I was lucky they didn't rape me."

"They knew you'd bring a better price as a virgin," Belia said dryly.

"I was taken back to Troy and sold in the slave market," Freyna continued, "then I couldn't believe my luck! I was taken to the country estate of a rich Trojan family. They had a daughter named Galina, about the same age as myself — she had blonde hair and blue eyes like me. They were so good to me, Belia. They began to teach me their language and gave me dresses of silk. I was wondering how I could get a message sent to my father..." Freyna paused and the tears glistened in her eyes. She controlled herself and went on. "Soldiers came, Cretans, I learned later, seeking boys and girls to train for the Bull Ring. Galina was nowhere to be found. Her parents sent me instead with much pretence of grief. I really can't blame them," Freyna added philosophically, "it's the Cretans who are wrong, abducting boys and girls for the Bull Ring."

"They wouldn't get enough volunteers if they didn't," Belia said, "anyway, it's better than being a slave or a whore."

Freyna agreed. They both yawned.

"What a day, all morning that boring religious lecture. Did you understand it, Bee?"

"Not a word. I had to pinch myself to stay awake and all afternoon the dancing — those silly routines drive me mad — so mechanical."

"We'll get punished if we don't get them right," Freyna murmured. They yawned again and soon fell asleep. The long, dark dormitory lay silent, save for the measured breathing, the sighs and occasional disjointed muttering of the sleeping dancers.

Some hours later Belia awoke suddenly. Freyna was also awake and was leaning on her elbow listening intently.

"What is it?" Belia whispered.

"I don't know. Something woke me up."

"Me too."

At that moment, from far away, so deep down it seemed to come from the centre of the earth, they heard a low, rumbling sound. For an instant the whole mighty building trembled. Then there was silence again. An oil lamp in a wall niche nearby rocked back and forth. They clutched each other in terror.

"Sacred Mother!" Freyna said. "What was that?"

"An earth tremor," Belia replied, "it's over. Don't worry."

"What would we do if this place collapsed?" Freyna's voice trembled. "We're locked in and there's no way to get out!"

"Don't think about it," Belia said firmly, "there's nothing we can do."

Freyna began to weep quietly. "Belia, I'm such a coward."

"Nonsense, we're all scared. Even Asteria, in spite of all her bravado. You're no different from anyone else."

"But I am. I know I won't be able to face the bull. I tremble at the thought of it. I'll lose my nerve and that bull will know and he'll pick me out." She sobbed helplessly.

Belia waited until the tears began to subside and said, "Listen to me. Naxos told me the other day he would train me as a vaulter and that I was to pick out a catcher to work with me. I've chosen you. Together we will outwit any bull."

Freyna was overwhelmed by Belia's confidence. "You'd trust me?"

"Of course ... you won't let me down."

After a moment's silence Freyna said, "Belia, I love Leander ... I haven't spoken to him, but I think he cares for me." She paused a moment.

"Do you think he does?" Belia asked.

"I'm almost sure. He hasn't said anything. Anyway, if he does I shall persuade him to try to escape."

Belia interrupted her quickly. "Be quiet. Somebody may be listening. We'll talk again later. Not now, it's too late. Let's get some sleep."

At the other end of the dormitory, Asteria was awake, her eyes wide open staring into darkness. She too, had felt the earth tremble and heard that muffled bellowing roar. Far below, in the black Underworld, the Earth Shaker had stirred. Sweat lay on Asteria's brow, chill and damp. She pressed her clenched fists to her eyes and prayed.

"Holy Mother, if He needs a victim, let Him take someone else. Don't let it be *me*!"

# CHAPTER 12

In a small brick house, built against the south wall of the Palace, the lamp-maker, Aptaeon, was awakened by his wife.

"What is it, Nerida?"

"It's my back again. I can't move for the pain."

Nerida was very stout and complained constantly. Her husband got out of bed, lit the lamp and began to massage her.

"You should go and see the Egyptian, Dr Ahmed, as Iros suggests."

"He's a foreigner," she snorted, forgetting they were immigrants from Corinth themselves. "Why does our son want to work for a doctor?" she continued. "Why can't he be a lamp-maker like his father?"

"The boy is clever," Aptaeon replied proudly, panting a little with the effort of massaging his wife, "and he's done very well. He's in charge of the surgery when the doctor's away."

"It will come to no good, you mark my words," Nerida said gloomily, "do you know, they treat slaves free of charge."

"How can slaves pay them when they earn nothing?"

"Ach! You and your son are as foolish as each other."

Aptaeon paused to ease the ache in his own back. "How is that, Nerida? Is it better?"

"Try lower down, it catches me when I turn," she complained. He went on massaging.

"You worry too much, Nerida. Iros says it causes your bad back."

"Oh! men, men!" his wife groaned, sitting up with difficulty, "you know it began with childbirth! What anguish I suffered!"

"Yes, yes. Cover yourself up or you'll catch cold." He wrapped her in a woollen blanket. "Would you like some warm milk?"

But she would not be silenced and kept on about Iros and his opposition to slavery. "How could the world get along without slaves? It's all very well for the rich, they can afford to pay wages, but we cannot. There have always been slaves, they are useful creatures."

They owned one slave, a strong, half-witted boy Nerida had bought cheaply from a peasant woman. He did the rough work, chopped wood and milked the goat. He slept beside it on the floor in a lean-to shed in the small yard.

"What would that poor creature do with wages?" she said, waving her arm in the direction of the yard.

"He gets his food and clothing, what more does he need? If he had money he would throw it away on rubbish."

"Perhaps he should have the right to do that," Aptaeon said thoughtfully. His wife rolled her eyes to heaven in despair.

"If we were invaded," he went on, "Iros might be captured, and he could be made a slave. Could you approve of that?"

"What are you saying?" Nerida began to cry. "You must be mad! Why do I have such a fool for a husband?"

"I'm sorry my dear, don't upset yourself. I'll heat some milk. The stove is still warm."

He was reaching for the cups when they heard the low rumbling deep in the earth, which had, at that moment, so startled Freyna and Belia. A pot crashed down from the shelf. The lamp-maker's wife was wide-eyed with terror, her heart hammering, her teeth chattering.

Aptaeon went over to her and they clung together. He comforted her. "Come, come, it's an earth tremor. It will pass."

He poured the milk and brought it to her. She held the cup, warming her hands.

"How good you are to me," she said tearfully. "What would I do without you?"

"There, there, drink up your milk."

Suddenly she gripped his arm. "Aptaeon, look at the wall," she said.

He put down his cup, took the lamp and crossed the room. A jagged fissure split the stones from top to bottom. Aptaeon and his wife had watched that fracture in the wall for five years. It was wide enough in places to insert the flat of the hand. Many times Aptaeon had gazed down at the ground to where the break disappeared into the earth. He imagined it piercing right into the earth's heart — the Underworld where the mighty Earth Shaker, the Great Bull, was imprisoned. Aptaeon pictured the long, sharp curving horn caught in the rock-bed, twisting and turning angrily to escape, cracking the earth from end to end, up through this defenceless little house, till even the mighty stone blocks of the Palace had split apart. When he thought of the power and fury that could accomplish such a thing, Aptaeon was afraid.

"Is the crack wider?" his wife asked.

With his hand he measured in several places. It was certainly wider, but he told his wife it was the same.

"We should move away, out into the suburbs," she moaned when he came back to bed, "I don't like living under the Palace walls."

"They are blessed each day at the Noon Sacrifice," he replied, "we must surely gain protection from that. Besides, business is good here. If we move to the suburbs we could lose money."

As he began to fall asleep, his wife continued to nag. "You must warn Iros about consorting with slaves. We don't want our son mixed up in any trouble. He could go to prison."

"If a man cannot be himself, he carries his prison inside. He must keep to his principles."

"Principles!" she said scornfully. "Words, just words. What good are principles in prison?"

"Iros is a man. He must live his own life. Be quiet woman, and go to sleep." He snuffed out the lamp and closed his eyes.

# CHAPTER 13

Andreas rose at dawn. The garden was cool and sparkling in the fresh morning air. He looked forward to the return of his son from Phaestos, but knew he was being optimistic — the family in Phaestos would probably delay Antonius. His sleep had been disturbed briefly by the tremor which had shaken Knossos in the night. It occurred to him that he might refer to it in the speech he had prepared for the Council meeting.

At noon Andreas ordered the chariot and went to the Palace. He left instructions with Senka for his son, who was to send in a written report to him, if the meeting had already commenced.

The Council Chamber, part of a complex of shrines and ante-rooms occupying two floors of the vast Palace buildings, was approached from the Courtyard by a short flight of steps. It was a large, rectangular room, entered by a narrow door, finely carved and inlaid with bronze studs. The walls were decorated with red and green frescoes of lions with plumed birds' heads, amidst swaying reeds and grasses. The floor was of red tiles and the ceiling was decorated with an intricate spiral pattern in blue and white and gilded plaster rosettes. Stone benches lined the walls on three sides. At the centre of the long wall was a carved stone throne decorated with patterns of gold leaf.

Directly opposite the throne, across the narrow room, a flight of steps descended to a tiled area — a place reserved for sacred rituals — surrounded by huge pillars. A light well above illuminated the chamber.

The Council members assembled in a small ante-room. It was Andreas' intention to enlist the Chancellor's support in the motions he intended to put to the Council. As Chancellor Darien was one of the senior members, his opinion would influence others. The Chancellor's greeting was affable, but when Andreas attempted to draw him aside, he excused himself, and moving to the far side of the ante-room, began a conversation with his deputy.

Brecchius, who had dined at the villa only a week ago, gave him a brief greeting and turned his back. He and Xanthios made a great show of friendliness. Markos, who was with them, scowled in his direction. The other Ministers returned his greetings, but it was obvious there was a conspiracy to isolate him. This was not going to be an easy meeting.

At the appointed moment they all filed in to take their places on the left hand side of the throne. Andreas sat straight on the hard bench. The silk cushion gave some relief and he could lean back against the wall for support if he wished. There was, of course, the danger of falling asleep! And few were guiltless as the speeches were often long and boring. Today was different and he knew he must stay alert and miss nothing.

Each member had an opportunity to address the Council in turn. Before this, however, the Council priests held the floor. They entered from an adjacent shrine, dedicated to the Mother Goddess. Beyond this, up a short flight of stairs, was the King's private suite where he prayed and meditated before entering the Chamber.

When the Councillors were assembled, the Shrine Priests entered in their long, belted tunics and took their places to the right of the throne. A herald blew a note on a conch shell, the Councillors and priests rose as the Priest-King Minos entered.

In Andreas' opinion, whatever King Minos lacked in decisive judgement, he could find nothing amiss with his bearing. His mien was calm, dignified and noble. Ordained as the intermediary between the citizens of Crete and the Goddess, he isolated himself from the disputes of his Councillors and the day-to-day problems of the ordinary citizens.

He was dressed in a long cloak of fine silk, with wide cuffs and a high collar of leopard skin. On his head he wore a simple coronet of gold studded with gems. As a symbol of justice he carried a gold double-headed axe, which he laid across his knees when he sat on the Throne.

A priest walked behind him carrying, on a velvet cushion, the gold mask of a bull's head with magnificent curving horns, the symbol of the power of Knossos. This was placed on a small table in front of the throne.

The Chief Priest, Pasterion, who was ill, was carried in a chair and assisted to his place at the King's right hand. Pasterion was unable to sit upright and leaned heavily on a stick. His secretary, Eburninos, sat on a stool at his feet. The other priests objected to this, but the sick man had become dependent on Eburninos and no one dared object.

Pasterion's speech was slurred. Few could understand him. Frequently Eburninos took it upon himself to speak for the Chief Priest. It was said that he had insinuated himself into the King's confidence. Arcanos, the High Priest, was the most incensed. He saw a threat to his own authority.

The meeting, at first, followed the familiar pattern. Stewards entered with linen towels and ablution bowls into which priests and councillors dipped their hands in ritual cleansing. Each received a mark of holy oil on the forehead. Body and spirit were thus cleansed of evil before the work of the Council began.

The King signed to Arcanos to deputise for the Chief Priest and recite the opening prayer, petitioning His Majesty to declare the meeting open. Lamps were lit on small tables for the scribes, who wrote an account of the meeting for the Palace archives.

The King then invited Pasterion to speak. The sick man tried but, after a few garbled sentences, lapsed into silence. His trembling hand rested on Eburninos' shoulder.

It seemed to Andreas that the younger man was about to rise and speak. But Arcanos, who had been fidgeting nervously, forestalled him and rose to address the assembly. He was a poor speaker, long-winded and repetitive. He referred to signs of evil in the sacrificial blood and emphasised the need to be cautious and watchful, to build additional shrines, to say more prayers and perform more sacrifices.

The High Priest's monotonous voice stretched Andreas' patience to the limit. This pointless, time-wasting rhetoric had occurred so often in the past. He watched King Minos overtly, who sat motionless and without expression. Andreas' habit of yawning openly when speeches were too long, always offended those, like the High Priest, whose self-importance exceeded their ability. Today was no exception. He yawned loudly and irritably snapped his fingers. The meeting must come to grips with the real problem.

Arcanos' speech was followed by a Shrine Priest whose fervour for the Dove Goddess was unmatched by eloquence. Then Eburninos rose. Holding Pasterion's hand, the young priest addressed the meeting.

"Most noble and holy ruler, Minos, Priest-King of Crete, Sacred Priests of our Holy Shrines and Honourable Councillors. As a matter of great urgency, I ask you to put aside all other considerations and to decide now on the arrangements for the Sacred Pilgrimage. Our beloved Pasterion has convinced me that this matter must be expedited with all possible speed." He paused for a moment, as Pasterion made a pathetic attempt to speak. His head moved jerkily, but whether he was nodding or dissenting it was impossible to be sure. Eburninos continued quickly. "Unfortunately, many sacrificial signs point to impending disaster. We must not hesitate to take measures to offset these evil omens. All our senior priests are eager for His Majesty to make the Sacred Pilgrimage — the most significant and beneficial of all His Majesty's commitments — and you may be sure the people of Crete would wish him to carry out this sacred duty without delay. Honourable Councillors, I now call on you to support your priests in advising His Majesty to undertake this dangerous and difficult but vitally important journey as soon as possible."

In the silence which followed, Andreas watched the King. Minos remained so absolutely still he could have been a marble statue. Arcanos rose nervously and called for the vote. Andreas was suddenly aware that the meeting had been stage-managed.

This has gone far enough, he thought. He rose to his feet and addressed the Council:

"Your Majesty, Priest-King of Knossos, Shrine Priests, Honourable Councillors." Glancing at each man in turn, he noted with contempt that few of them would meet his eye. He continued, "I have listened to our young priest, Eburninos, with some astonishment. He says he speaks for our Chief Priest Pasterion. Senior members of this gathering will have vivid memories of the events eight years ago, when our present beloved King's honoured father undertook the harsh journey and rituals of the Sacred Pilgrimage. It is well-known that this ceremony is governed by strict traditions, and one of the most firmly established of these is that the Pilgrimage should take place every ninth year. Honourable Priests and Councillors, I should not have to remind you that the ninth year occurs next year, not this year."

Councillor Markos, Minister for the Navy, immediately leapt to his feet and angrily attacked Andreas.

"Councillor Micalidos is wasting our time. We are aware of these things. There is much to be done. We must plan now. I say we should vote as the priests suggest."

Most of the young priests chanted support for Markos, who was applauded by Brecchius and Xanthios. This did not surprise Andreas, who expected them to unite against him. However, other Councillors hesitated. General Imanos, Minister for the Army, had listened throughout with strained attention, turning his broad shoulders to face whoever was speaking, one hand cupped behind his ear. Imanos was an imposing man, with craggy features and hair speckled with grey. Accustomed to being obeyed, his sharp eyes glanced to right and left. As he rose to speak the protests and arguments immediately subsided.

"I deplore these interruptions," he began, "they are most unseemly. It is proper for each to speak in turn. For my part, I have been concerned for some time at the lack of rigorous training in our battalions. There is too much time spent on parades and festivities. Too many military duties are left to our

Libyan recruits — please, do not misunderstand me, I have no prejudice against the Libyans, they are fine soldiers. But, it would please me better to see more of our Cretan youth seeking a career in the Army."

"I agree with the General," Andreas said, hoping fervently that he would not talk for too long. The remark served to remind the General of his real purpose.

"Ah, Micalidos, I remember your father, a fine man, a man of integrity. Now, let us have no more interruptions. Let us hear what Micalidos has to say."

Grateful for the General's support, Andreas continued, "Priests and Honourable Councillors, I am aware the sacrificial signs portend disaster. These warnings have disturbed our sleep for months. Only last night an earth tremor shook the city!"

A murmur of agreement from several Councillors greeted this statement.

"However, to advise His Majesty on this course of action, without fully considering its implications, would be an act of gross folly. The timing of this pilgrimage demands careful thought and consultation. We all have the right to be heard. All I ask is that you hear me out." He paused. He had their attention.

"Many of you will recall the events of eight years ago. However, I shall refresh your memories and inform those who do not know." He glared in the direction of Eburninos, who sat at Pasterion's feet.

"The departure of our beloved King on the Sacred Pilgrimage is a momentous event. The whole of our religious and judicial life is embodied in him. Without

Minos, Knossos becomes an empty shell. Consider, too, the life of the people, as they become involved in the rituals that continue while His Majesty is absent in the mountains — accompanied by his Priests and attended by his Ministers — the normal life of our country is disrupted. The absence from the capital of those responsible for government leaves our city vulnerable and defenceless. Who shall make decisions in Knossos? Who will take command in the event of unforeseen emergencies?" The Chamber was silent now. Andreas paused, gathering strength and determination in order to win them over.

"Your Majesty, Councillors and Priests, the omens foretell that we face a very grave disaster. This great Palace, as you know, stands on the ruins of a former palace. Deep in the foundations lie the crypts and rubble of even earlier buildings destroyed by violent earthquakes. These disasters have affected the lives of generations of Cretans but we have overcome them. However, my friends, I am convinced that we now face another and even greater calamity. It is my duty to inform you that this city and island is now facing the gravest danger in its long history, a danger which involves the threat of invasion and bloody war!" There were cries of dissent and a sharp word of derision from Councillor Xanthios. Andreas sensed their antagonism but he ignored it and continued.

"For more than a thousand years our people have lived on this beautiful and prosperous island in peace and security. No hostile army has dared to land on our soil. And why? Because our warships sail unchallenged the length and breadth of the Great Green Sea! It is natural for our priests to believe that prayers and sacrifices keep us secure. Of course these things are vitally important. It is proper that we should follow the traditions of our forefathers. However, by the same rule, should we not, like them, look to the repair of our ships? Our ancestors built up our great trading empire and kept our nation secure with brave men fighting in well-found ships. Our navy is the bastion behind which we have lived and prospered for generations. Councillors, you should know that the fleet dallies in Phaestos while our northern coast lies unprotected! Shipyards are idle for want of timber. New vessels ordered last year are not even begun —"

Markos, Minister for the Navy, unable to contain his rage any longer, leaped to his feet. A heavy thickset man, his voice shook with anger:

"In the name of Zeus, what damn business is it of yours, Micalidos, to lecture us on matters concerning the Fleet? How dare you ... how dare you, sir, encroach on a sphere of government which does not concern you!"

"The safety of this country is my concern!" Andreas shouted, not wishing to lose the initiative he had struggled so hard to attain.

"Listen to me! I have reliable information of an enemy alliance against us. Mycenae — Tiryns and Athens are now, at this very moment, preparing to invade our country. They plan to destroy us!" Andreas' words created an uproar. Enraged priests and councillors shouted their protests. Markos shook his fist at Andreas and was restrained from attacking him.

At that moment a slave entered nervously, saw Andreas and handed him a letter. He broke the seal and read it quickly. It was from Antonius, brief and to the point: the shipyards at Phaestos, as at Amnissos, were idle and without supplies. The letter written in his son's hand reassured him. He was not so alone now.

As the shouting subsided, Markos continued his attack. "Your Majesty, High Priests, Councillors; Micalidos is a troublemaker! He is causing unnecessary alarm and anxiety by spreading false rumours of invasion and unjustly criticising the state of our country's defences. These are foul lies! Exaggerated nonsense! What proof has he of these fantasies?" Markos' voice trembled with rage. "Micalidos should stop interfering in matters outside his own jurisdiction and attend to his own responsibilities. In my opinion he is little more than a traitor and should be dismissed from this Council."

Markos' remarks were greeted with roars of approval. Xanthios, Minister for Supply, immediately took up the attack. A pale, neat man, his voice was cold and concise. He spoke in acid tones, censuring those "who, inadequate in their own department, saw fit to protect themselves by fault-finding in others". He made much of the falling off of trade with Egypt and laid the blame for this on "the appropriate Minister".

"Finally," Xanthios concluded icily, "the implied criticism of our sacred and worthy members of the priesthood — this we cannot permit. The priests are urging the most fitting remedy for the threatened danger, which comes, I am certain, from the oft-repeated warnings in the sacrificial omens not from some imaginary bogey in the north. I add my recommendations to the those of the Priests. Let His Majesty give earnest consideration to the immediate fulfilment of the Sacred Pilgrimage."

He sat down. The priests cried with one voice, "The Pilgrimage! The Pilgrimage!"

Andreas rose to his feet once more. He realized they were bent on removing him from the Council. He did not comprehend their reasons, but was not going to waste precious time defending himself. That could wait. All his strength must be put into one last effort. As the priests began to run out of breath, he spoke in a strong resonant voice.

"Your Majesty, Priests, Councillors, what you think of my motives and actions is of no importance. This letter —" he waved it at them, "confirms the presence of the fleet, delayed in Phaestos, instead of returning north as it should have done. This shows the same state of idleness and lack of supplies in the south that I, myself, witnessed here at Amnissos. These are facts, Councillors, not lies or exaggeration. And as for fantasies of invasion, Sacred Zeus, how I wish this were true! It is my duty as a Minister to inform you that my agent, Tarsis, an entirely reliable man, saw with his own eyes new warships in a coastal inlet near Mycenae. He heard the foreman speaking of many other ships under construction! This invasion force is planned to be ready in late summer — before the ports close for winter — you must believe me! Your Majesty, for the sake of our people and the survival of our country, I implore you to adopt the following measures:

"Do not make the Sacred Pilgrimage this year. Stay in Knossos. Order the fleet to return at once to guard and patrol the north coast. Let our ships be repaired and new ones built — the timber must be commandeered from the merchant Praxitor at Amnissos. Let the Army establish lookouts and defences on the north coast, recruit more battalions, double the Palace guard and increase our fortifications.

"These measures are vital and urgent. There is nothing to prevent an enemy landing here tomorrow, an invading army could land and march on Knossos in a few hours! We must take steps now to save ourselves, our families and our nation from this catastrophe!"

Andreas sat down. He was exhausted and trembling. Perspiration ran down his face. If they did not listen now, all was lost. He could do no more. He put his hands over his eyes. He heard a roaring noise and was not sure if it was the tumult of those in the Chamber or if it was inside his head. From a long way off he could hear General Imanos speaking.

"I will do my part. All Army reserves will be called up. Signal fires will be prepared along the northern coast and ... "

His voice trailed off and suddenly all was quiet. Andreas looked up and saw that King Minos had risen and was removing his coronet. The Priest-King lifted the golden bull mask with its great curving horns, and placed it on his head. Arcanos began to chant the opening lines of a hymn and the other priests joined in, singing in harmony. Grasping the double-headed axe, the King walked forward and slowly descended the stairs to the sunken shrine. As the singing ceased, the King's voice, clear and strong, enunciated the ancient prayers to the Mother Goddess, while all stood with fists covering their eyes.

"O Great and Powerful Goddess, Earth Mother, Goddess of Sky and Sea and Underworld. You alone have power to intercede for us, to avert the wrath of the all-destroying Earth Shaker. You alone give us your Son each year in the rebirth of Spring. You suffer his loss in the death of winter. You dwell in our trees, in our pillars. You bring us abundant crops and our rich harvests of oil and wine. O Mother of the Sacred Pillars, stabilize the earth and save our cities and palaces from the wrath of the Underworld."

Minos placed the golden Double-Axe in a wall socket, and stretching his arms out between the great pillars so that his hands touched one on either side, he cried in a loud voice:

"Earth Mother, protect us, save us, deliver us! We will perform great sacrifices to propitiate the Earth Shaker! Let these Sacred Pillars hold the earth secure forever!"

The singing began once more as King Minos returned to his throne. He removed the golden mask and laying it on the cushion, allowed Arcanos to replace the coronet on his head. When he was seated he signed for all to sit and spoke quietly but firmly.

"There will be twelve days of prayer throughout the kingdom. All public contests and entertainments will be suspended. I will remain here in the shrine in fasting and meditation, and I shall appear only at the Noon Sacrifice. Each day I will sacrifice a bull. At all Great Shrines throughout the land the High Priests will sacrifice at the same hour. After these rites are fulfilled, there will be a week of festivities and the Court will attend the opening of the new season of the Bull Dance."

He did not refer to the Sacred Pilgrimage and now that he had pronounced the period of fasting and sacrifice, no one, least of all the priests, could raise any objection.

I didn't give him credit for being so smart, Andreas thought. He felt quite certain now that for some reason the King did not want to leave Knossos.

Minos beckoned to Arcanos and spoke a few words in his ear. The High Priest then called for a vote of approval for the King's plans. This was passed immediately.

Andreas seized the opportunity. "May we vote on the measures I raised, Your Majesty?"

"Those in favour of Councillors Micalidos' proposals please raise your hands," Minos replied quietly.

General Imanos raised his hand at once. He was supported by a small group of Councillors. Then Arcanos became aware of the King's eyes fixed on him, with their peculiar luminous intensity. Without any words being spoken, he realized that Minos wished him to support Andreas. For a moment he doubted, raised his eyebrows and looked questioningly at the King, who gave the slightest nod. Arcanos raised his hand, and, turning to the priests, indicated that they should support him. They followed suit. Then, even Xanthios and Markos, against their will, raised their hands in a perfunctory manner. The scribes recorded a unanimous decision.

Arcanos recited a brief prayer to close the meeting. King Minos led the procession to the Shrine from whence they had entered, the priests followed and the Councillors returned to the ante-room.

Markos, Brecchius and Xanthios departed immediately without a glance in Andreas' direction. General Imanos congratulated him warmly on his success. "For my part," he said enthusiastically, "I shall lose no time in advancing plans for Army manoeuvres."

Darian, the Chancellor, cautioned him. "My dear General, you will have to await the completion of the Sacrificial Days of Prayer, won't you? It may take many weeks to provide an adequate supply of bulls — expeditions will have to be sent to the mountains. And then, of course, there is the paper work." Darian shook his head gravely, yet his eyes held a gleam of enthusiasm.

Andreas, who knew about bureaucratic delays replied dryly, "I understand what you mean, Chancellor."

As the General and Darian argued, he considered the events of the last hour and was astounded that he had, in a sense, triumphed. He knew that he had made enemies but did not care. All that mattered to him was the welfare of Crete. He was aware the King had cleverly manoeuvred the priests and had created a delay which could be extended. After the period of sacrifice was over, the new season of the Bull Ring would open and then it might not be possible to arrange the Sacred Pilgrimage so late in the year. With the onset of winter, the high passes would become blocked with snow, and the priests would find it difficult indeed to persuade the Councillors to leave the warmth and comfort of the Palace.

Andreas foresaw that winter would again bring heavy storms. The ports would close. The wild sea was their friend, providing the Cretans with a defence no enemy craft could overcome. Cretan sailors could haul their ships high above winter tide levels and repair them. They would also build new vessels. Andreas had a plan of his own, but this was not the moment to discuss it. He saw the King had proved himself no fool and for this he was grateful, but he was exhausted.

Chancellor Darian, seeing this, ordered a chair to take Andreas home.

# CHAPTER 14

Antonius and Senka were enjoying a mid-afternoon meal at Klonka's. Antonius' letter to his father had been delivered to the Council Chamber and he was relieved that his obligation was discharged. He yawned and stretched, replete with food and wine. One of Klonka's voluptuous girls winked at him, so they went upstairs, arms entwined. To the girl's chagrin, Antonius promptly fell sound asleep. He had sat half the night talking with the family at Phaestos.

Senka joined the card players but had no luck. He lost continually and became very drunk. He had to sign a promissory note on the last hand and then ordered another flagon of wine. Klonka hated two things — bad debts and shrewish women. He avoided one and sacked the others. However, he obliged Senka on account of his friendship with Antonius. Senka picked up a lute belonging to one of the musicians. He began to play and sing bawdy songs.

Sometimes Klonka let him pay off his wine bill like this, for he had a pleasant voice.

The card players stopped to listen, and, as the shadows lengthened outside, the clientele of early evening began to drift in. Soon shouts of laughter punctuated the songs, and Senka, who had the temperament that blossoms before an appreciative audience, grew bolder. He drank deeply, forgot his gloom at losing a month's pay at cards and taxed his memory for every risqué song in his repertoire.

Antonius awoke, heard the muffled laughter downstairs, saw the lamp lit, for it was now nearly dark, rose and walked out on to the landing. Looking down into the crowded salon, he stopped for a moment to blink the sleep from his eyes.

Senka now had a large audience. He launched into a composition of his own. With a few jaunty chords, reminiscent of a sea-shanty, he drained his wine-cup and began:

*There once was a man who sailed the sea,*
*A man of noble birth was he -*
*Hi, ho! the Great Green Sea!*
*And for a princess he did sigh,*
*Close by her side he hoped to lie!*
*But that's all Greek to me -*
*Hi, ho! the Great Green Sea!*
*O, he is fair and he is tall,*
*That stranger drinking in the hall.*
*He was led to her bed by a linen thread -*
*But that's all Greek to me,*
*Hi, ho! the Great Green Sea!*

Antonius had listened with mounting horror, for the song obviously referred to the rumoured love affair between Theseus, the Greek bull dancer, and the Royal Princess Ariadne.

Klonka looked angrily in Antonius' direction and indicated that he should remove Senka immediately from his club. As Antonius moved down the stairs, Senka was singing the third verse, too drunk to be aware of the changed mood of the audience.

> *Now they say all the whores*
> *are shutting their doors*
> *and putting their prices up higher!*
> *But it's no great loss*
> *if they don't come across*
> *to a princess we all can aspire!*

The reference to the Princess was now even more obvious. Senka ended with a flourish and stood up to bow, apparently unaware that there was no applause. Klonka angrily nodded to one of his "strong men" and Senka was unceremoniously thrown out. Antonius immediately followed him.

Inside the club the relaxed atmosphere was quickly re-established — the musicians played loudly, the wine-cups were filled and Klonka's girls soon had the crowd laughing again.

Senka was ready to create a scene in the street, and, not wishing to take him home in such a state, Antonius hired a chair and directed the carriers to a quiet tavern under the viaduct, near the Travellers'

Inn. They found an empty booth. Senka banged the table and demanded wine.

"You've had enough. You're drunk." Antonius ordered lime water.

"Wine — wine!" Senka shouted.

"All right," Antonius nodded at the waiter. "Just be quiet!" he said angrily to Senka.

"What yer drag me away for? I was terrific ..."

"You drunken idiot. Why did you sing that song?"

"...'s a damn good song — wrote it meself."

"You half-wit, people have been locked away for less!"

"They liked it — they shouted for more — why can't you keep still?"

Senka stared across the table at Antonius with owl-like eyes, his head wagging slowly from side to side. He looked ridiculous. Antonius smiled in spite of his annoyance.

"Lucky for you, Klonka's friendly, but you'd better stay away from the club for a few weeks." Senka suddenly laughed stupidly.

"I lost a month's pay — a whole month's pay," he gurgled.

"That'll teach you to play cards when you're drunk!"

The waiter poured wine into their cups. However Senka snatched the jug and drank from it, spilling it over himself and the table. Slamming the jug down he once again burst into song.

*Hi, ho! the Great Green Sea!*
*He was led to her bed ...*

"Shut up, Senka!" Antonius hissed, as the people in the bar began to stare at them. He threw his cup of wine in Senka's face. It had little effect. Senka sat for a moment as the wine dripped down from the end of his nose. He looked up as if it was raining and then mouthed stupidly — "but that's all Greek to me." Senka swayed gently forward until his head thumped the table. Antonius leaned over and shook him.

"For Zeus' sake don't pass out here. Come on, I'll take you home."

He tried to lift Senka to his feet but the secretary was a dead weight and would not move. Antonius sat down again, poured more wine and sipped it. It was harsh and strong. He grimaced and kicked Senka violently under the table.

"Wake up!"

Senka lifted his head and stared vaguely into space.

"How could she ask me to do such a thing? How could she?" he muttered.

"Stand up, Senka. Let's go."

"She took me to her place, damn 'er," his voice became louder. "Do you know wha' the bitch asked me to do?"

"Will you lower your voice!"

"That bitch, Chryssa Senthios!" Senka shouted.

People sitting in their booths raised their heads and stared in their direction. Antonius, for the second time in two days, flushed with embarrassment. He tried to cover up with feigned laughter, but his voice was urgent in its entreaty to Senka to be quiet.

"She wants me to steal ... how can I do that ... how could anybody ask anybody to do such a thing ... I mean I ask you ... what would you do?" His voice stumbled on, muttering and slurring.

"I'd go home and sleep it off," Antonius interjected.

"She wants me to steal the necklace..."

"What necklace?"

"Your mother's ruby necklace ... she made me promise ... I can't do it ... I can't do it ..."

"Do what?"

"Steal your mother's necklace!"

Antonius began to laugh. "You idiot, you stupid idiot! She's not serious — she's playing games! Chryssa's the worst tease in Knossos! For Zeus' sake let's go home and you can sleep it off." Antonius managed to drag the drunken secretary outside and steer him into a chair. When they reached the villa, Credon helped Antonius carry Senka to his bed where he collapsed without a word.

"Where is everyone?" Antonius asked. "Have they dined yet?"

"No, sir," Credon replied, "the master has gone to his room. He is tired and the doctor is attending him."

"My father's not ill?"

At that moment Ahmed came down the stairs from Andreas' apartment.

"You can ask the doctor yourself, sir," the steward said.

"He'll be all right after a good night's sleep," Ahmed remarked, "I'd rather you didn't disturb him now, Antonius. I gave him a sleeping draught."

"I'll see him in the morning then. How did the meeting go? Did he tell you?"

"No details. But I understand it went very well."

"Is that you, Antonius?" It was his grandmother's voice calling from the front loggia.

"Come here, dear boy, I want to ask you so many things about Phaestos. You rushed in and out this morning so quickly and promised to come back and talk to me. Where have you been all day?" Antonius went to her and kissed her and greeted Aunt Korynna.

"I'm sorry, Grandmother, I fell asleep after lunch."

"We'll have dinner here, Credon," Old Madam said, "so we need not move and Antonius can tell me absolutely everything that went on in Phaestos."

Antonius tried to remember all the family news that would interest her. While he spoke a small, sleepy head peeped round the door and Timon, in his white nightshirt, entered the room.

"What are you doing out of bed, you little monkey?" Old Madam said, but she allowed him to kiss her cheek. Then he curled up on the floor beside Antonius' chair. Seeing him there reminded Antonius of the young boys on the ship at Phaestos. He had not mentioned them in the letter to his father as it did not seem relevant. He was about to recount the story when Credon and the serving girls arrived with food and wine. The family realized suddenly they were very hungry and the meal was eaten and enjoyed in a picnic atmosphere.

"We should do this more often," Old Madam said laughing, "it's more fun than a formal dinner."

When the meal was cleared away Antonius had forgotten for the time being the mystery of the kidnapped children on the boat in Phaestos, so it was never mentioned. Aunt Korynna asked him if he were going to Mallia for the summer holiday.

"I thought it was all arranged — there's to be a ceremony to bless the new villa and a house-warming party afterwards," Antonius replied.

"I'm sure you'll have a good time, Antonius. I like the farm myself. It's so much cooler up in the mountains," his grandmother remarked.

"Can I go to Mallia?" Timon asked, with his mouth full of honey cake.

"It's not your kind of party," Antonius replied.

"I thought you wanted to come to the farm with us," Aunt Korynna said.

"Yes, I do. I want to come to the farm, too," Timon said grimacing with the intensity of the problem.

"Even you can't manage to be in two places at once," said his grandmother.

Antonius lifted Timon up by the arms and helped him to turn several somersaults on the mat. Then they started racing and romping up and down the terrace, till Old Madam called them in, for fear they might disturb Andreas.

"You'll have to make up your mind, Timon," she said, "it must be Mallia or the farm. It can't be both."

"I want to be with father," Timon panted, "so why can't he come to the farm, too?"

"I only wish he would," Old Madam replied, "perhaps you can persuade him — in the morning, when he's feeling better. But now it's getting late. I think it's time we all went to bed."

It was nearly midnight. They all agreed, except of course, Timon, who had to be bribed with another honey cake.

# CHAPTER 15

Zanthope's new and splendid villa, built in the garden of the old house at Mallia, looked oddly out of place. It was set among the gnarled, ancient trees that thrust up from the tangle of neglected field grass and flowering creepers running wild everywhere. The rectangular two-storeyed building was surrounded by a wide terrace. From here, at one end, a staircase led to the upper floor. Andreas disliked the place, but he acknowledged that he was prejudiced. Unaware of any incompatibility between the antique setting and the new house, Zanthope was delighted with it. She cared nothing for gardens anyway.

"Darling, what is the use of a garden?" she had remarked to her friend, Doxa. "One cannot wear it, eat it or sleep with it!" Today all her friends gathered for the house-warming celebrations. However, Andreas had not yet arrived. His absence had delayed the opening ceremony. The guests had run out of superlatives, the patience of Zanthope's most devoted admirers was dwindling rapidly and their hostess' charm became each moment more brittle. Finally she sank down on a sofa and Doxa's husband, Grinkos, pleased to have an excuse to relax, accepted the task of fanning her.

Zanthope, thinking that most of the guests would soon be intoxicated before the ceremonies could commence, had given orders that only a small quantity of wine be served. They can drink themselves silly when the dancing and feasting begin, she thought.

Young men and women, old people and children, in coloured dresses, jackets and festive ribbons were gathered beneath the terrace, near the steps to the main entrance.

"Who on earth are all those extraordinary people?" Doxa Grinkos said, leaning over the terrace and shading her eyes with a brightly painted fan. She spoke to a handsome young man beside her, who smiled in a superior way.

"Some of the local peasants, by the look of them," he replied.

Brachne's hair was elaborately curled, glossy with oil and perfumed like a woman's. Doxa stretched out her hand and playfully tugged his love-lock, the long strand of hair that snaked down over his face. In a teasing voice she asked him, "Isn't it true, Brachne, that you're a native of Mallia yourself?"

The young poet turned away. "Yes, I was born here," he admitted with a trace of annoyance.

"But your poems are recited at our best parties. You're almost a Knossian now. How does it feel to be so successful?"

"Sweet enough," he said indifferently. His eyes searched the crowds below. Doxa asked him what all these strange people were doing here, surely they were not invited to the party. His eyes focused on a tall peasant woman, standing a little apart from the others, leaning against the trunk of a tree.

"Doxa, that's Olykka, the dancer," Brachne said, "she draws big crowds wherever she performs. We shall have dancing after the ceremony." Olykka was combing her long, black hair, which flowed over her shoulders and down her back, below the waist.

"I hope they don't drag things out endlessly," Doxa said, "Andreas is so late we shall be waiting till midnight before supper is served."

Other guests came out on the terrace and soon the whole balustrade was lined with people gazing in the direction from which Andreas was expected.

"Zarkos!" Brachne called to a pale, emaciated young man nearby. Zarkos walked over to join his friend, the poet, who put an arm around his shoulders and introduced him to Doxa.

"You have an admirer in Madam Grinkos, she's fallen in love with your frescoes," Brachne said.

"Thank you," said the young artist, smiling with unfeigned pleasure. His work had only recently been appreciated. Unlike his friend, he had not yet become bored with success.

"Your paintings are most charming and original," Doxa said, "tell me, whatever gave you the notion to paint blue monkeys gathering yellow crocus?"

"I like the colours, that's the way I see them," Zarkos replied simply.

"Well, you must paint some for us in Knossos."

Olivia, Doxa's companion, had strolled along the terrace, exchanging greetings with Madam Brecchius and her younger daughter, Leda; with Antonius and his friend, Captain Senthios and the captain's beautiful wife, Chryssa.

"Whatever has become of Andreas?" Olivia remarked. "Poor Zanthope, her nerves are frayed to breaking point."

Doxa did not share her companion's concern for their hostess. "I'm sure she'll survive," she murmured.

Olivia was accustomed to difficult situations. They certainly occurred often in the Grinkos household where Doxa's imperious egotism affected everyone. Olivia was widowed, after she and her husband had squandered their money. She was left with no roof over her head, but an insatiable taste for the luxuries and entertainments of Knossos. Life on her family's estate in the country was intolerably boring, so she grasped the only alternative — a bare room at the top of Doxa's house, and apparent comfort and gaiety, for Doxa took her wherever she went. Olivia soon realized she had no life of her own. She was as much a slave as the laundry girls, at the mercy of Doxa's whims and bad temper. While she smiled and gossiped and flattered, she endured bitterness and schemed for the means to gain independence. Grinkos joined them, unsteady and drink-fuddled.

"If there's been another crisis at the Palace, Micalidos may not get here at all," he mumbled.

"Don't be a drunken idiot," Doxa said, "how could there be a crisis with the Court away at the summer palace? Life will be dreary for weeks with the Bull Ring closed and Zeus knows if there'll be enough bulls to reopen it when all these sacrifices are finished!"

Antonius spoke behind his hand to his friend, Captain Senthios.

"My father didn't really want to come!"

"I shouldn't be here myself," Senthios replied, "Torcas is standing in for me. I'll have to go back to Knossos tomorrow."

"Surely you could stay, Dino," Chryssa said without enthusiasm.

"There's no need for you to return, sweetheart," her husband continued cheerfully, "the country air will do you good."

"I hope you'll stay till the end of the month," Madam Brecchius said and looked fondly at her favourite daughter, "Madam Micalidos has asked Leda and me to stay on. It's so unfortunate my husband was unable to come," she added with a nervous glance at Antonius, "he was invited to go boar hunting in the mountains with Councillor Markos."

Antonius thought that his father would be delighted at Brecchius' absence, but of course did not say so.

A shout from someone in the crowd set off a burst of cheering. The waiting guests sighed with relief and Zanthope, hearing the commotion, stepped out on to the terrace, expecting to see her husband's chariot at the foot of the steps.

But it was a false alarm.

Walking over to her son, she asked irritably, "Antonius, how much longer do you think we should wait?"

"Relax, Mother. Father said he'd come, he'll be here. It's very pleasant here on the terrace." He directed the servants to fill up the wine-cups.

"If he doesn't show up soon, Micalidos will be as unpopular here as he is at the Palace," Brachne whispered to Zarkos.

At last they heard the sound of chariot wheels. The horses came in at a gallop, and reared to a halt. The local people pressed forward, cheering and jostling to get a closer look at the latecomers. The distinguished guests watched from the balustrade as Andreas, Dr Ahmed and Senka alighted from the chariot. As Andreas made his way through the throng of country people, a young woman ran down the steps and greeted him eagerly.

"Dearest Father, how happy I am to see you!" She flung her arms around his neck and kissed him.

"No one could be more pleased than I to see you, dear Hyacinth." Andreas smiled at his daughter and added in a stage whisper, "You are the only reason I came!"

She turned, laughing, to her husband. His son-in-law, the handsome young Prince Lerintos, greeted him as warmly as his daughter. It was generally conceded that he bore a striking resemblance to his cousin, the Priest-King Minos. Andreas had tried to refuse the match. Partly because he did not care to be closely linked to the Palace and also from some premonition he could not define. However, as the couple were so obviously in love, he had agreed. Now he was thankful they were settled in Mallia. They were both so innocent and loving — a pair of turtle doves who were no match for the gossips and troublemakers of Knossos.

The Head Priest, after a respectful greeting to Andreas, raised a sistrum and rattled it vigorously. A procession formed up, led by the priests and votaries. Olykka, the temple dancers and musicians followed, with their flutes and lyres. Then came Andreas and Zanthope, with Lerintos and Hyacinth and all the guests, the younger ones running down the steps eagerly, the elder people at a more sedate pace.

As the music began, the procession moved forward. They did not have far to go. The pebbled path led round the side of the house, through a grove of cypress and figs. Beyond this lay an open space where the long summer grass had been scythed, so the dancers could perform in comfort. Half buried in myrtle and oleander an old weather-worn shrine faced the sea. Many years of wind, rain and hot summer sun had bleached the statue of the Earth Mother.

The priest intoned a prayer to the Goddess, imploring her to be merciful, especially to those present. The votaries sacrificed three doves and made offerings of wine and oil. Once again the priest raised his voice, asking that the new house, the Villa Mallia, might never face misfortune or the wrath of the Earth Shaker. When the ceremony was over, the temple dancers took up their places and the musicians played a sweet, haunting melody. The guests and visitors sat on the grass in a wide circle to watch the dancing.

The famous temple dancer, Olykka, stepped forward and raised her arms to the sky. For a moment she stood perfectly still and every sound died away, until one could hear, very softly, the distant sea-surge on the rocks far below. Then she led the dancers to the accompaniment of low, soft notes on the flute. The performance was religious in theme, illustrating the different characteristics of the Great Goddess, the Earth Mother.

The dancers glided, swaying and moving their arms to imitate birds' wings. Olykka was the Dove Goddess, gentle and loving. As she danced the perfect line of her body was apparent and her face, dull in repose, became alive with happiness.

As the tempo of the music increased, the dance changed. The performers leaped high in the air, their arms became tree branches floating in the summer breeze or bending in a winter storm. They represented the Goddess of Trees and Pillars. As the music rose to a crescendo, the dancers knelt before the altar, their backs arched, their long hair trailing in the grass, their arms writhing. Olykka became the Snake Goddess, the guardian of the dead. Then, as the music ceased, the dancers lay prostrate before the shrine.

A moment's silence was a tribute to their artistry, then the tension was released in a loud burst of applause. The temple musicians retired and were replaced by a group who were to play for the popular dancing to follow.

The guests had dispersed, those who preferred food and wine returned at once to the villa, the others remained to dance. Soon the glade was full of colour and movement, as the young people danced and laughed beneath the trees. The women held hands and formed an inner circle, while the men formed an outer. They danced in opposite directions until the music ceased and when it resumed each accepted the partner who stood before them. After dancing together for a short time, the music changed once more, the circles reformed and the dance continued on in this pattern.

For Leda Brecchius the dance had its moment of bliss when Antonius stood before her. She smiled shyly and swayed for a few happy minutes in his arms. Senka danced first with Chryssa, her dark eyes mocking, and later with Zanthope. He was delighted when she whispered in his ear, "Come tonight."

Soon the music and dance form changed. Two long lines formed a figure of eight, hands clasping and unclasping, bodies swaying, everyone yielding to the pleasure of the music. Presently, there was a break and Zanthope, recollecting her duty as hostess, returned to the villa.

Leda, seeing Chryssa in Antonius' arms, felt a pang of jealousy. Why did Chryssa charm everyone? To her husband, Captain Senthios, the question if it occurred to him, posed no threat. Believing in her fidelity, he saw other men's admiration only as a tribute to his own good fortune.

At dusk, lamps were lit at the shrine and more hung in the trees. The older folk and young children watched from a low grassy bank, commanding a view of the glade on the far side.

Andreas and Dr Ahmed found a wooden bench nearby. Presently, two small boys, the sons of Hyacinth and Lerintos, came shyly to their grandfather. He lifted one to his lap and Ahmed held the other. They sat happily jigging and clapping to the music.

"Perhaps I should have brought Timon after all, instead of sending him to the farm," Andreas said. He surveyed the happy scene contentedly. The dancers were now in shadow, now in lamplight, the women's skirts swirled and billowed and their hair floated in the soft evening breeze. This is a memory to cherish, he thought, but could not banish the premonition of trouble. During a pause in the dance, Hyacinth and Lerintos ran to Andreas, breathless and laughing.

"How are you Father? Not too tired? Should I send the children to the house to sleep?" Her concern was endearing.

"Don't fuss, my dear," her father said, "enjoy yourselves. The boys are happy with us. Isn't that right, Petras?" He tickled the small, wriggling child on his lap, who collapsed in peals of laughter.

"It won't hurt these scamps to stay up late for once. We'll go up to the house soon and get some food," Andreas said.

Chryssa overheard his remark.

"Why don't we have the food brought here?" she said enthusiastically.

"Oh, yes, it would be lovely here, under the trees," Hyacinth agreed.

Senka was sent with orders for food and wine and beer for the musicians, too. Soon a long, torchlit procession of servants trooped from the house, carrying plates and steaming dishes of food. The young people settled on the grass in groups, eager for refreshment after their exertions.

"This is one of the most successful parties we've ever had," Antonius said, pouring wine for the guests, "you must admit the building of the villa has some merit, Father."

Andreas smiled and assented. He had no desire to sound a discordant note. The bills would come later. He had had so little interest in the project that he had left the design and construction and the ordering of the timber almost solely to the agent and his wife. From a brief inspection it was obvious that, if the timber was bought from Praxitor, the cost would be very high indeed ... but these were hardly thoughts to voice at a house-warming party.

Soon many of the guests departed in chariots and palanquins. The elderly people and families with young children also went home. As there was a large number of house guests, it was necessary for some rooms to be shared. Madam Brecchius and her two daughters occupied the room next to Zanthope, and Antonius, Senka and Captain Senthios shared a room further down the long corridor that divided the house. Olivia was put in with Deva, the cook, and the kitchen girls, an indignity she bitterly resented.

"Do try to be helpful, dear, under these very difficult circumstances," Doxa purred. However, as her husband slept snoring on a couch on the terrace, Doxa did not disturb him. She allowed Olivia to sleep in her room on a floor rug.

A small group was left on the terrace still drinking. Captain Senthios was not by nature a talkative man, but the wine and good company lightened his spirits. A junior officer in his company, Cadet Nimos, who was very drunk, began to propose a series of toasts — to the ladies, the house, the wine bottles — to a moth that fluttered round the lamp. Wine-cups were emptied jovially as each toast became more bizarre.

Captain Senthios was sure that the occasion needed a special oration. He began a pompous speech on the illustrious history of Crete and the achievements of the Army. His solemn, owlish expression was unconsciously comic and the speech drew laughter and loud acclaim. Chryssa noted that her husband was making a fool of himself. On these occasions she found him very boring. Stifling a yawn, she drew Senka aside and whispered into his ear, "Have you forgotten the promise you made me?" Senka remembered Antonius' comment that Chryssa was the worst tease in Knossos.

"Don't be ridiculous," he replied, "you don't expect me to take you seriously."

"Yes, I do," Chryssa's lips smiled but her voice and eyes were cold. "I meant what I said. I want that necklace and I expect you to honour that promise."

"It's out of the question. You're impossible. I could lose my job."

"You could lose it now," she said softly.

"What do you mean?"

"I know about you and Zanthope. You used Pashote's apartment for your fun and games. She's a friend of mine." Chryssa gave him a sly look. Senka would never forget that afternoon. He was suddenly afraid. "The necklace is here," she pressed, "earlier today Zanthope showed it to my mother. It shouldn't be beyond your skill to remove it from her room while she sleeps."

"You crazy bitch," he said and left her abruptly.

Antonius, growing weary of the loud carousing, strolled to the end of the terrace and gazed out into the misty darkness of the garden. A young girl came timidly out of the shadows.

"Antonius!"

He turned and Leda was beside him. Her face was pale in the shadowy moonlight.

"Why, Leda, I thought you'd gone to bed."

"I couldn't sleep."

"I'm not surprised," he said, glancing along the terrace, "I hope they aren't keeping the whole house awake."

"Did you enjoy the house-warming?" he asked after a moment's silence

"I'm not good at parties," she replied, "but I loved the dancing."

He turned away and she admired his handsome profile. She came to a decision and drew a deep breath.

"Dear Antonius, I'm so glad to find you here. I couldn't sleep. I wanted to talk to you."

He turned back to her and spoke in a brotherly tone. "Dear Leda, I always enjoy talking to you." Shyly she hesitated. He took her hand and said gently, "How can I help?"

"Antonius, I must say what is in my heart."

He did not reply and she hurried on. "We've been friends for a long while, but we don't see each other very often and I may never have another chance. Antonius, I love you. I've loved you very much for a long time..."

"Leda..."

"Could you love me too?"

When he did not reply, she repeated her question. "Could you love me, Antonius?"

Antonius sighed. "Dearest Leda, I can't answer you. Tell me what love is?" He shrugged his shoulders and smiled.

"I care so much for you," she pressed his hand, her voice low and intense.

"Sweet Leda, I'm not worthy of your love. Wait for someone else — someone who can love you as you deserve."

Tears ran down her face as he looked into her eyes. She paused for a moment, turned and moved quickly away down the dark terrace.

Raucous shouts from the revellers made him turn. He saw Chryssa coming towards him and watched her, leaning against the balustrade with his arms folded. She came close to him, closer than was necessary. He saw the dark line of her long, curling eyelashes, the curve of her throat, the outline of her breasts.

"Was that my little sister talking to you?" Chryssa asked, her eyes cat-like and watchful. "What could she want at this time of night?"

"Nothing," he replied quietly, "she couldn't sleep, so she came down here. It's really time we all went to bed."

Chryssa agreed, stretching her arms wide and yawning luxuriously. He moved away and rejoined his guests. The party was now breaking up. Some had fallen asleep, sprawled on couches or on the floor. Those sober enough to manage the stairs with much laughter, finally made the upper floor, where Antonius guided them to their rooms. Soon the house slept with an absolute quiet. Some hours passed. From a doorway a figure emerged, crept silently down the corridor to Zanthope's room and stealthily opened the door. A night-lamp burned on the dressing-table. Zanthope was asleep, half-naked, breathing deeply. The intruder stepped carefully around some garments on the floor, inspected the dressing-table and then moved to the bedside cabinet on which stood an embossed silver jewel casket. The thief stood for a moment watching the sleeping woman, then carefully tested the casket lid. Finding it locked, a search began first in the cabinet drawers, then back to the dressing-table, where an embroidered bag lay among strewn ornaments, hair combs and perfume bottles. The search was unsuccessful.

Without warning, Zanthope stirred, muttering. She turned to face the thief, who stood motionless, paralysed with fear. As the sleeping woman sighed and showed no sign of waking, the intruder crept nearer to examine the golden pendant which hung around Zanthope's neck, and a bracelet on her wrist. But there was no key for the casket.

In a last desperate attempt, the thief, constantly watching the sleeping woman's face, slowly and gently slid a hand beneath the pillow. After a few moments' search, the hand encountered a hard metal object and carefully withdrew a gold key attached to a chain. In a moment the casket was unlocked, a heavy piece of jewellery removed, the casket quietly relocked and the key replaced. The thief then moved silently from the room.

Zanthope did not discover the loss of her ruby necklace until she returned to Knossos.

# CHAPTER 16

Andreas awoke early in a guest chamber of the Palace of Mallia. The previous evening Hyacinth and Lerintos had bid Zanthope good night and returned home with their two sons. Andreas had been pleased to accompany them, thankful to avoid any further involvement with his wife and her friends at the villa.

To his surprise he had slept soundly. The room prepared for him by his daughter had an air of charm and comfort which she managed to impart to everything she touched. He realized it was too early to expect breakfast and walked out into the paved court which led through colonnades to a terrace. He strolled along its full length, breathing the cool sea air and watching some fishing boats far below which bobbed like toys on the misty sea.

The Palace of Mallia was nearly as large as that of Knossos, but as it lacked the power and politics of its mighty neighbour, the atmosphere here was more friendly and harmonious.

His reverie was interrupted by his grandchildren. With whoops of joy they descended on him and, as always, he lifted them up one at a time for a hug and a kiss. They wanted piggyback rides, but Hyacinth, hearing the noise, came laughing to the rescue and led them off to breakfast. Hyacinth was not as beautiful as her mother, but when she smiled the sympathy and sweetness of her character shone from within her. She had inherited her father's brown eyes and many Cretans admired her chestnut hair. Andreas loved her more sincerely than anyone he had ever known.

After the meal Hyacinth suggested they should walk through the vineyard while the morning was still cool. They strolled up the sandy path, escorted by the two young grandsons, who scampered back and forth with the exuberant energy of puppies. The tiny granddaughter placed her hand in his to "help him up the hill". They paused for breath at each turn in the path as it wound amongst the terraced vines. Some women were working nearby. One of them brought a bunch of grapes that had ripened early.

"The crops are wonderful this year," Hyacinth remarked, "the Great Lady is good to us. She's given us double rations to make up for the poor harvest last year and the bad winter."

Presently they came to an open meadow where sheep and goats were grazing. Here they sat on a small hillock, admiring the wide sweep of the northern coast with its bays and headlands stretching into the distance on either side. The sun was high now. This was a favourite spot of Hyacinth's. When she had a problem, she always came here to think it out in her clear, sober way. There was a small shrine nearby and she and the children would bring wallflowers or a bunch of sweet-smelling herbs to place on the altar. Sometimes they would bring a coloured pebble or shell they had found on one of their seaside walks.

While they sat together she watched her father thoughtfully. There had been no opportunity to question Dr Ahmed about his health. She was concerned to see the lines of tiredness and strain on his face. She began to talk about the children and the funny things they said. Petras had inquired, "What is the full moon full of?"

Andreas laughed when she told him how her small daughter, Lara, had asked why she did not have a little spout like her two brothers.

"I seem to remember her mother asking much the same question at the same age!" he said. This reminded him of Antonius and he began to tell her of their differences.

"I don't want to force your brother to any course against his will. If there was anything he was interested in, I'd spare nothing to help him. It's his damned indifference that irritates me. I think he's wasting his time, his youth — and my money. But that concerns me least of all!" he added with a laugh.

Hyacinth took his hand and said seriously, "I think Antonius is really very clever and sensible. I believe he's unhappy."

"Unhappy?" Andreas was surprised. "He has everything he wants."

"Perhaps he's in love."

"Well, most young men are. That's no great tragedy. He's handsome enough. Why doesn't he marry her or buy her if she's the other kind."

"Perhaps she's already married."

Andreas frowned. He considered the problem but could not resolve it.

"Perhaps I have been too hard on him," he replied thoughtfully.

While they were talking some of the village women came up with pails to milk the goats. One of them lagged behind. She was young and pretty, but her face was pale and tragic. Andreas pointed her out to Hyacinth and asked if the young woman had been sick or widowed. Hyacinth nodded.

"She was widowed some years ago, poor girl, but now she has lost her only son as well."

Hyacinth briefly related the woman's story. The boy, Kiros, was seven-years-old. He loved to go climbing in the hills with his friends. When he did not return some weeks ago, his mother became worried and anxious. The whole village joined in to search for the boy. When darkness fell they went out with lanterns and torches. They searched the hills and gorges and beaches for two days, but found no trace of him.

"The villagers tell me she comes to work each day but never speaks. The poor woman seems beyond comfort. Perhaps Kiros fell into the sea and drowned."

Andreas was reminded of the strange disappearance of Timon's friend, Luki. Inquiries after him at the Palace had yielded nothing. A sudden thought struck Andreas. "You never let your children play without supervision, do you?"

"There's always someone with them," she replied, puzzled.

"I'm concerned because a friend of Timon's disappeared some weeks ago in Knossos."

"I'm sure no one in Mallia would harm our children," she said. They watched the children playing for some moments without speaking.

"Timon is up at the farm with your grandmother and aunt. I hope he's behaving himself. He's always in mischief at home, the servants spoil him."

"You can send him to us, if it will help," she said with a smile.

"It will be cool in the Courtyard of the Palace," Hyacinth assured him, as much to encourage herself as him, for they had sat overlong and the sun was now very hot.

"I must return to Knossos soon," her father said. But she would not hear of his going until he had rested a few more days.

Time at Mallia drifted slowly by. A child's shrill laugh, the muted voice of the nurse, the note of a distant cowbell were often the only sounds to break the spell of summer days. A heat-haze hung over the vines and pastures. The Palace Courtyards provided welcome relief, with their cool tiled floors and walls painted in soft colours which rested the eyes from the glare outside. The easy rhythm of life restored Andreas' spirits. Lerintos and Hyacinth noted with pleasure how much better he looked every day.

One afternoon Prince Lerintos and Andreas were alone in a shady corner of the Courtyard. Andreas briefly described to his son-in-law the events of the last Council meeting and also the reports from his agents, particularly Tarsis, from whom he hoped soon to have intelligence from within the fortress of Mycenae.

Prince Lerintos was incredulous. "If this is true, sir, why isn't the nation mobilized?"

"Why indeed, my boy! It's been damned nearly impossible to convince anyone in Knossos of the danger we face! I'm afraid I can't stay here any longer. I must return to the city soon."

"Hyacinth will be upset."

"You must make her understand, but try not to worry her."

Lerintos looked perplexed. "If the King should decide to make the pilgrimage —"

"I'm sure he doesn't intend to," Andreas interjected.

"But if he should," Lerintos persisted, "who will be in authority in the Palace? Would it help if I offered to come and live there in the King's absence?"

Andreas fervently hoped that Lerintos would not do so. He would be a conscientious ruler, but could not deal with the priests. Besides, Andreas did not want Hyacinth in Knossos, where he was sure she would be unhappy. If the King died and the Queen's delicate son did not survive, Lerintos would become Priest-King of Knossos. Sacred Zeus, Andreas prayed, don't let that come to pass! Then there was the problem of Ariadne.

"I'll keep your suggestion in mind, Lerintos," Andreas said quietly, "but it is rumoured, you know, that Princess Ariadne wishes to rule in her brother's absence."

"What are you saying about the Princess?"

Hyacinth had come looking for them. She kissed them both and sitting at Lerintos' feet, asked with a mischievous look in her eye, "Is it really true that she wants to *marry* a Greek bull dancer?"

"I don't know, my dear." Andreas replied. "Zeus knows what follies women will commit in the name of love," he added dryly. She was silent for a moment. She understood the rift between her parents. Now there was gossip about the secretary, Senka.

"I met two beautiful young bull dancers a month ago," Andreas said, steering the conversation back to a more cheerful level.

"Really? Nothing exciting like that ever happens here. What were they like?" she asked.

"Well, they were still in training and not yet performers." Andreas told them in some detail about his visit to Phylon's workshop and his encounter with Belia and Freyna.

"It must be a strange life," Hyacinth said, "were they happy?"

"I don't know. They were very cheerful, eager to do whatever was wanted of them. I've thought about them a good deal since then, especially the younger one Belia ... beautiful ... fascinating. Little more than a child, yet so assured and independent."

"She obviously made a great impression on you!"

Andreas frowned and abruptly changed the subject. He had said more than he intended and was unprepared for his daughter's sudden insight. "I must return to Knossos soon, my dears. There is much to do."

"Father, just a few more days," she pleaded, "we see so little of you."

"I don't think so," he said, "I really should go."

Hyacinth suddenly burst into tears. Lerintos put his arm around his wife and took her to a couch nearby.

"Come, my dearest, and rest. This heat is tiring you," he said soothingly.

The Prince signed to Andreas not to worry.

"We think there's another child on the way, sir."

"That's wonderful news. Congratulations, my dears."

Andreas decided that his self-imposed duties in Knossos could well wait for one more week.

# CHAPTER 17

Despite Andreas' late arrival, the house-warming party was considered a success and Zanthope was pleased. However, in the ensuing days, though she hoped to capture a holiday mood, the atmosphere was often strained. There were too many undercurrents. Doxa Grinkos was anxious to leave at once and was only persuaded to remain by the combined efforts of their hostess, and Grinkos, who was loath to leave because the wine was of better quality and quantity than his wife's economies allowed at home. Olivia, too, appreciated the plentiful food and leisure.

Doxa herself had to weigh up the saving on housekeeping against the annoyance of not always having her own way. She and Zanthope waged a subtle and continuous battle to organize the day to suit their own particular whim. If Zanthope chose to spend the morning with the hairdresser, Doxa wished to go on a chariot drive to the mountains. If Zanthope suggested a picnic by the waterfall at Nirou-Tarsa, Doxa would have a headache and need to lie in a darkened room. The guests tried to pander to two egos in conflict.

Madam Brecchius talked a great deal to all who would listen. One day she struck a chord of sympathy with Doxa on the subject of slaves. The two women, with Zanthope and Olivia, were lying on sofas on the shady terrace as the servants fanned them with woven matting suspended from the ceiling. Others hovered near the door, ready to bring cool drinks from the cellar at the mistress' signal. In the garden the ilex and oleander groves were limp in the noonday heat and in the distance the sea and sky merged in a heat-haze.

"Don't talk to me about slaves," Doxa said sharply, "lazy good-for-nothing creatures, eating their heads off and doing as little work as possible in return!"

"My dear Doxa, you should think yourself lucky to own them," Zanthope stretched luxuriously, "Andreas insists on employing servants for wages, which I regard as an extravagant waste of money. He says the owning of slaves is ..." she yawned in an effort to recall his words, "ah, yes, 'an insult to human dignity'."

The women burst into peals of laughter.

"Well, I must admit you have some cause for complaint," Doxa agreed, "at least I don't have to find wages. But one must keep a constant watch — if they're not thieving food or money, then they're daydreaming — or worse, making love!" She and Zanthope laughed again.

"Well, I suppose they are human," Madam Brecchius said coyly.

"Hardly," Doxa replied contemptuously. "You cannot allow such a thing. It takes their mind off their work. And worse — the girls get pregnant and you have to sell them at a loss and train new ones. You have to be on guard night and day."

"But if there are babies, you have an extra slave at no extra cost," Olivia suggested.

"Olivia, what an impractical fool you are!" Doxa exclaimed. "When pregnant, the girls pretend to be sick every morning; they steal extra food, because they always want to eat like horses, and when they get big, they want to sit down all the time. After the brat's born, it's worse — they're forever sneaking off to suckle it. Then it has to be fed for four or five years, before it's capable of any useful work. Far better to sell the girl before it shows, that way you get a better price."

"I couldn't agree more," Zanthope drawled. She related how Andreas intended to acknowledge Timon, the servant's child. "Disinheriting Antonius! His legal son, born of his legal wife, in favour of a servant's bastard! Can you imagine anything more disgraceful?"

"But surely Antonius will get his share?" Madam Brecchius inquired tactlessly.

"His share!" Zanthope sat up, her eyes glinting. She snapped her fingers at the serving girls. "Where are the cool drinks? Do we have to wait all day?"

The girls scurried nervously away.

"You don't know what I have to put up with from Andreas," Zanthope continued, "my wishes are the last thing to be considered. I'll never forgive him for being so late for the dedication party."

"I'm sure that was unintentional," Madam Brecchius ventured, "Councillor Micalidos is a very busy man."

Zanthope laughed. "He'd be very angry if he knew where the timber for this villa came from."

"Aha ... I know the answer to that." Grinkos, throaty and snuffling from his afternoon nap at the far end of the terrace, coughed and spat over the balustrade. Madam Brecchius put her hand to her mouth in disgust. "Yes ..." Grinkos continued, "I thought to myself when I first saw this place, he wouldn't get this kind of timber anywhere but the royal timber yards."

"How smart of you," Zanthope said coolly, annoyed that he had spoiled her story, "as a matter of fact, Andreas had nothing to do with it."

"How much did it cost?" Doxa demanded.

"Not as much as on the open market," Zanthope replied, "but of course I had to bribe Agidor. Without his help the villa would never have been finished."

"Agidor is a treasure," Doxa said.

"He's a monster!" Zanthope replied, "but he deals in everything. I doubt if there's anything you could possibly want that he couldn't get. At a price, of course."

"Does he buy as well as sell?" Olivia asked.

"You stupid numbskull," Doxa snapped, "of course he buys. How could he sell at a profit if he didn't buy first?"

"He could steal," Olivia said quietly.

That evening, in one of their rare moments alone together, Doxa said to her husband, "What a hypocrite Micalidos is. After all his strictures on other people filching timber from the Palace, he allows his wife to get it through one of his agents." They had bathed and dismissed the servants and were about to go down to dinner.

"Zanthope said he didn't know," Grinkos murmured.

"That's a likely story. He probably told her to say that if it leaked out. These high and mighty people are all the same."

Grinkos turned to his wife. "You've no call to slander Micalidos," he said, "we've dined at his home..."

"He can afford it, so don't sympathize with Micalidos. If they drag him down, they'll drag you down with him. Why face ruin for a man who doesn't respect you?"

"He's the best man in the Council. Let's go down to dinner. I need a glass of wine," Grinkos muttered.

"You drink too much. We must leave for home in the morning — Olivia can stay in Knossos and collect the rents — and then we must go up the mountain and inspect the olive crop. That damned manager cheated us last year."

"Well, he's entitled to something," Grinkos said.

"Oh, you're hopeless," she replied, putting on her rings and admiring herself in the mirror, "if I didn't manage things we'd be bankrupt in six months."

"Yes, my dear, I'm sure you're right." And with that they went down to join the company at table.

The holiday at the new villa in Mallia had not been particularly enjoyable for Andreas' secretary, Senka. He was caught between his desire for Chryssa and Zanthope's insatiable demands. The older woman's passion was cloying and he found himself drained and exhausted. Chryssa had the fascination of a beautiful animal — a tigress, he thought. When he was close to her, she lost no opportunity to tease and torment him. But they were never alone and she made no attempt to renew their lovemaking. She had pressured him constantly to steal the necklace and accused him of cowardice.

"All you need is a little courage, my friend," she whispered in his ear.

"It's not so simple as that," he replied, flushing angrily. "It offends my code of honour."

She laughed loudly, so that her mother and Olivia, strolling nearby, asked to share the joke.

"Just nonsense, Mother. Senka was telling me about a song he wrote," and turning back to him she went on in an undertone. "How is it you can steal his wife and not feel ashamed?"

"It's not the same thing. How could you give yourself to me?" he parried.

"I gave you nothing," she said contemptuously.

"And what about your husband?" he snapped, stung by her tone.

"What about him?"

"Aren't you afraid he'll find out?"

"I can manage him. I always have."

"What are you two chattering about?" Zanthope said, approaching them quietly from the far end of the terrace in order to overhear their conversation.

"I was quizzing him about his love affairs," Chryssa said smiling at her hostess.

"I'm sure yours would make a longer story," Zanthope replied sweetly. He left them. Chryssa was right, he did not have the courage to steal the necklace. Although the casket was at Zanthope's bedside and he knew the key was under the pillow, yet, as she lay asleep, limp and love-weary, he did not dare unlock it.

Senka knew that mutilation was the punishment for theft and shuddered at the prospect. He thought it would be wiser to steal the necklace when they returned to Knossos, where some local thief would be suspected. Here in Mallia they were too isolated. He came to no definite decision.

Antonius, moody and irritable, spent the week at the villa boar-hunting in the hills with the young officers who had accompanied Captain Senthios. When they returned to duty in Knossos, he had only Senka for company. They took mules one day and rode on the narrow tracks in the bracken-covered mountains. The hillsides slanted beneath them, green and precipitous, the villages small and neat as children's toys. They spoke little. Since the night at Klonka's their friendship had cooled.

A few days later, Antonius went into the garden early where he found Leda filling a basket with iris and roses. She smiled and asked him if he was enjoying his holiday.

"My life is one long holiday. Each day I must find some reason for not being bored," he said laconically.

She wandered through the long, dewy grass in her search for flowers.

"Don't walk there," he called to her, "come here, where the grass is scythed. The long grass is a favourite place for puff adders."

"Oh," she looked about fearfully, "I heard something rustling but I thought it was only a mouse."

He offered her his hand as she stepped over a fallen log. They crossed the field where Olykka had danced and sat under an ancient yew. Leda leaned against the trunk.

"I'm sorry I was so silly the other night. I probably had too much wine."

"You weren't the only one," he replied and they both laughed. After a few moments she spoke with some hesitation. "I couldn't help overhearing — when you were talking with Madam Micalidos, you said you were thinking of joining the Army. Is it true?"

"I'm thinking about it," he replied.

"I heard a rumour before we left Knossos that the Palace guard is to be increased. Would you be in Captain Senthios' company?" When Leda asked the question she was hoping it might be true, for he would then be quartered in the Palace and she would see him more often.

"I think I'd rather serve in the east or at one of the guard stations in the mountains."

"Surely not! It's so far from all your friends and family and the mountains are so wild and lonely!"

"I think they're very beautiful," he said.

She pointed to a steep cliff face overlooking the sea.

"Do you see that cliff, Antonius? Your mother told us that a young girl threw herself down from there because her lover deserted her."

"Silly girl," he said, "no one is worth that."

"But if she didn't want to live?"

"She should have had more sense. Life is to be lived, each day as it comes, good or bad. Only cowards reject it."

"I did not mean that I approved, but I found the story very sad and romantic."

"Surely you don't think it right that a young girl should throw her life away for nothing?"

"The sentiment is beautiful," she ventured.

"Sentiment! What nonsense!" he said scornfully.

Chryssa's voice shattered their intimacy.

"Hello! What are you two doing out here so early in the morning?" She walked towards them, fresh and vibrant, in a brilliant saffron dress and with her dark hair held by a yellow band.

"I came to gather flowers before the sun wilted them," Leda said, showing her basket. She set off for the house, followed by her sister and Antonius.

"O Sacred Mother, it's going to be hot again today," Chryssa complained, shading her eyes. The sun was already fierce although it was still early.

"Think of poor Dino in Knossos," said her sister, "here at least we have a cool breeze."

"It's entirely his own fault — he should have stayed here. He's much too conscientious. One has to pay for virtue in this world," Chryssa said, laughing.

"You're a cynic!" Antonius observed.

On reaching the house, they found Senka speaking to a messenger on the terrace. "Councillor Micalidos has sent for me," Senka said. He ordered the man to saddle a horse at once.

"I'll ride with you, Senka," Antonius said, "tell the groom to saddle my horse too."

"You're not leaving us?" Chryssa asked.

"I must see my father," Antonius said. He went up the stairway without looking back.

Leda went to the kitchen to find a vase for her flowers. and Chryssa and Senka were left alone on the terrace.

"Well, he certainly doesn't waste words," she said, looking after Antonius. She turned to Senka with her teasing voice. "You may escape me for the time being, dear one ..." she wound a lock of his hair around her finger and pulled it till he winced, "nevertheless, I shall find a way of making you do what I want."

To please Hyacinth, Andreas remained longer than he intended at the Palace of Mallia. Her tears proved more persuasive than any argument. During the second week of his stay he sent for Senka to join them and was delighted when Antonius came too.

The days had passed happily with rides in the early morning, when the mountain air was cool and refreshing. The evenings were lively with music, laughter and singing. Occasionally the villagers danced in the big courtyard, accompanied by lyres and flutes, with tambourines banging out the rhythm and the whole gathering clapping and stamping. Andreas found it difficult to leave.

However, he could not banish from his mind the thought that in spite of his apparent success at the Council meeting, nothing constructive had yet been accomplished. It was one thing to get a vote passed; quite another to have it put into effect. In addition to the normal delays of a ponderous bureaucracy, there could be deliberate hindrance by those who wished to frustrate his plans. It really did not matter to Andreas whether their motives were personal or treasonable, the end result could be disastrous for Crete. He would have no peace of mind until he was sure that his recommendations had been carried out.

Andreas, Antonius and Prince Lerintos found themselves together one evening after the other guests had retired.

"I suppose you will soon be joining the Army, Antonius," the Prince remarked.

Antonius replied that he was considering it.

"For my part," the Prince continued, "I intend to train every able-bodied man on my estates and I shall conduct the exercises myself."

Antonius was surprised. He liked and respected his brother-in-law, who obviously supported Andreas' concern for the country. The idea that his father had assessed the situation correctly had not occurred to Antonius. Prince Lerintos then suggested to Andreas that a fort should be built, above the inlet at Nirou-Khani, to protect Mallia and the inland towns nearby.

"I've no doubt it would have some deterrent value, Lerintos," Andreas replied, "but we would need to build forts at every inlet on the northern coast, and this would be a formidable task! No, my boy, if an invader lands in great force, I doubt if we can hold out. I believe our only real defence lies at sea, with the fleet."

# CHAPTER 18

Early next evening, at sunset, the chariot was harnessed and Andreas bid farewell to his much loved family. Dr Ahmed sat beside him. Senka had ridden ahead in the morning to advise Credon of their return. Antonius remained with Lerintos and Hyacinth as they were loath to part with him.

Andreas had two main projects. The first was to ensure that the shipyards were supplied with timber. The second was to organize a meeting with people he could trust — General Imanos, Captain Keridos and his young lieutenants, the Chancellor, of course, and perhaps Captain Senthios. He intended to discuss all this with Chancellor Darian on his return. This meeting could plan to improve the country's defences and its success would be greatly enhanced by the presence of his agent, Tarsis, who could give a first-hand report of the situation in Mycenae.

The recollection of the letter stolen from Senka's saddle-bag troubled him, in spite of Cibaros' assurances that it contained nothing to betray the enterprise. Andreas was also concerned about Senka himself. Was he to be trusted? The loss of the letter was almost certainly an act of gross carelessness, but Andreas hoped it could be nothing more sinister. In the past, Senka had been the perfect secretary — efficient, cheerful and eager to please. He could not condemn him for one incident and gave him the benefit of the doubt.

Dr Ahmed went to his surgery on the morning after their return to Knossos. He was pleased to find that his assistant, the Corinthian Dr Iros, had experienced no problems in Ahmed's absence. The Corinthian doctor was a tall, good-looking young man of fair complexion. He was generous in his vocation to care for the sick among the working people of Knossos. If there was a flaw in his character it was this bias in favour of the poor and low-born. Ahmed would sometimes point out to him, with a gentle smile, that the rich and noble could suffer pain and ill health too.

Iros embraced Ahmed. The staff and patients welcomed the Egyptian doctor warmly. Ahmed's surgery, once used as an oil store, was long and narrow. Windows cut along the upper wall were shielded in wet weather by glazed parchment. The waiting-room and dispensary were certainly not cheerless, the patients sat on long benches round the walls and there was an atmosphere of warmth and friendliness. Relatives came and went and street traders sold hot food and fresh milk at the door. An area was railed off for those on stretchers. Those with no families were cared for on the upper floor by nursing assistants whom Ahmed had trained.

When all the patients had departed, the two doctors relaxed. Much as he loved the well-to-do Micalidos family, Ahmed had a special feeling for his work in this surgery. The patients were his real family, and Iros, who shared his aims, was as dear to him as if he were his own son. They discussed some matters relating to the surgery, then Ahmed turned the conversation to his friend.

"You must take your holiday now, Iros. I can manage without you and the apprentices will benefit from more responsibility."

"Damon and Althion deserve a holiday as much as I do. They have both worked hard."

"They must wait their turn," Ahmed said firmly, "I can spare you now. Councillor Micalidos is much rested after his holiday." They were sitting in the small courtyard which connected the surgery building to the house where Iros and the nursing staff lived. He hesitated a moment before speaking.

"While you were away, Dr Ahmed, I had to make a decision."

Ahmed was puzzled. "Do you want to leave us?"

"No! Certainly not. It's something quite different." Iros hesitated again, then added, "Perhaps if I let the people concerned speak to you, it will be the best way." He rose and entered the house. Presently two young people came slowly into the courtyard. The girl was very pale and the young man had a protecting arm around her.

Iros spoke gravely. "These two slaves have run away from the Grinkos house. I have given them shelter." Ahmed sighed and shook his head.

"This may cause trouble for our patron, Councillor Micalidos, you know. I could not approve of that."

The young girl threw herself at this feet, pleading that he show mercy and not hand them over to the authorities.

"I can't make any promises," Ahmed said and added more kindly, "tell me what this is all about."

The two young slaves sat down at his feet and began to tell him the story of their escape from slavery.

He gazed in perplexity at the two young people. Tyra, thin, waif-like, shyly returned his gaze. Her lover, Arkos, held her hand. Prompted by Dr Iros, she began the tale of their escape.

"Sir, we are both slaves of the Grinkos household. Madam Grinkos returned from Mallia in a very bad mood. She found fault with everyone and even accused us of breaking into the storeroom."

"As if we were thieves!" the young man interjected heatedly, "when the cook pointed out that Madam Grinkos had not given the steward the key before going away and there was no food for anyone, Madam slapped her face."

"Madam's ring cut the cook's face and she burst into tears," Tyra added.

Ahmed said nothing, but listened intently as the young people's tale unfolded.

Arkos related how, the following day, Madam Grinkos had ordered two carrying chairs to transport her husband and herself to inspect their olive grove on the mountain. Arkos and three other slaves were to carry the heavy chairs. Tyra was to walk, with Trebus, the elderly steward, who carried reed pens and papyrus in a satchel to tally the olive crop when they arrived.

"We hoped to leave early, before the day grew hot," Arkos said, "however, Madam Grinkos kept the hairdresser till after midday, so when we set off the heat was stifling."

"They were all right in the shade of the chair canopies," Tyra continued the story, "but we had to walk in the blazing sun. Poor Trebus was panting and wheezing even before we left the paved road. It was much more difficult when we reached the mountain track. Madam Grinkos kept urging the men to go faster, flicking them with her leather whip."

"She told Grinkos to do the same," Arkos said, "only he was asleep and didn't hear her. She wouldn't allow us to have a drink. She said it 'would teach us slovenly mules to make better time'!"

Suddenly Arkos laughed. "Looking back, I can see the funny side of it, I don't know exactly what happened — I may have been blinded by the glare of the sun — I tripped on a loose stone and fell. Grinkos, peacefully nursing his wine bottle, was flung out of the chair on top of me!"

"I ran to Arkos to help him up, but he couldn't walk, his ankle was badly sprained," Tyra continued. "Madam Grinkos was furious. She shouted 'here we are delayed because a clumsy lout can't stay on his feet' and she ordered Trebus to take Arkos' place." Tyra paused. Then she began to weep. "Doctor, she made that frail old man carry the heavy chair up the mountain. We've since heard that when they arrived at the house, he collapsed and died."

"Doxa Grinkos is a cruel, vicious woman," Arkos said bitterly.

Ahmed sighed. He pitied all those condemned to slavery.

"When Tyra was bandaging my ankle," Arkos continued, "Madam Grinkos ordered her to continue the journey, but Tyra refused."

"She said Arkos could crawl home without help," Tyra said indignantly, "then when she saw I was determined not to leave him, she flew into a rage and leapt from the chair. She hit me in the face with her whip."

"We left her," Arkos said, "and as we went off down the mountain track, she shrieked after us, 'You disobedient wretch, Tyra! Tomorrow I'll sell you to a brothel!'" Arkos paused for a moment, then continued. "On the way down the mountain, we discussed what we should do. We decided to run away. We'd heard about your surgery, doctor — that you help the poor without payment. We came here to throw ourselves on your mercy. Tyra carries my child and I'm sure Doxa Grinkos will sell her when she finds out. We shall be parted and that would be worse than death."

The two young slaves were silent. Iros spoke impulsively. "Sir, please don't hand them back to this woman. You've told me that our patron, Councillor

Micalidos, disapproves of slavery." Ahmed nodded. He felt great sympathy for the two young lovers.

"You must remain hidden here for the time being," he said, "these people, Grinkos and his wife — I've met them. They dine at the villa sometimes and are friends of Madam Micalidos, I believe. Well, stay here for now and help Dr Iros all you can."

Iros told him that the two young slaves had stood night duty in the ward and Tyra had helped in the dispensary.

"Don't let the out-patients see you," Ahmed warned, "someone might recognize you. Now I must return to the villa. We'll see what can be done."

# CHAPTER 19

When Andreas arrived at the Chancellor's office in the West Palace, he was shown into an ante-room. Chancellor Darian had a visitor. The office was familiar to Andreas. The lack of furnishings and ornaments made it depressingly bleak. A few small pieces of bronze statuary stood in niches and green tiles covered the floor. The place had an air of impeccable taste, but to Andreas it seemed cold and impersonal. He reflected that the office of Chancellor required a certain detachment. Not a job for me he thought with a wry smile.

Presently the Chancellor entered, accompanied by a tall man, dressed in white pleated linen, who approached Andreas and bowed.

"I owe my good fortune to you, sir," he said.

Andreas recognized him as one of the Egyptians he had employed in the shipyard at Nirou-Khani. He had subsequently recommended him to the Egyptian Ambassador.

Shep-Anep was a clever and personable man. As he spoke Cretan well, the Ambassador, User-Amon, had employed him as an interpreter. Shep was now in such favour that His Excellency found him indispensable.

"Councillor Micalidos, please do not hesitate to contact me if I can be of service to you," Shep said enthusiastically.

"Thank you, Shep. I'll remember your offer," Andreas replied. Shep bowed to both Councillors and left the room and Andreas remarked to Darian on the meteoric rise of his former shipwright.

"Yes, indeed, he has done well," Darian agreed. "It's a tribute to his character that he hasn't been spoiled by his good fortune."

"What did he want with you?" Andreas asked bluntly.

For a moment Darian did not reply but stared out over the Courtyard. He then turned to Andreas with a sigh and remarked that it seemed impossible to keep anything a secret in Knossos.

"What do you mean?" Andreas asked.

"His Excellency, the Egyptian Ambassador, has heard a rumour of an invasion from the north. Of course I've assured him there's no truth in it and that he should give no credence to it." Darian noted Andreas' reaction and hurried on. "The Egyptian Ambassador is so concerned by the threat that he has ordered a ship loaded with stores to lie ready in Phaestos harbour to evacuate his people. He offered to escort the Queen and her son back to Egypt. Dr Ahmed, an acquaintance of yours, I believe, is to be invited to accompany Her Majesty. In my view all this hysteria is quite unnecessary."

"I don't know anything about this. Dr Ahmed has been in my employ for twelve years," Andreas said sharply.

"I'm sure it will come to nothing, Micalidos. I hope Her Majesty will not leave Knossos. It may start a panic."

"She would never dream of going," Andreas replied. "She wouldn't leave the King."

"But she might be alarmed for the Prince's safety."

"Then we must reassure her. Ahmed can speak to her."

"I'm pleased to hear you say so, Micalidos. Pleased and grateful."

Andreas judged the moment was right to disclose the reason for his visit, but, as he began to outline his plan for a proposed defence meeting, Darian strongly disapproved.

"No, Micalidos, I can't be involved in anything like that. It's absolutely out of the question. If you intend to go ahead with this idea, of course I can't stop you. But I have no wish to be told of it ... officially, you understand? I don't wish to know the meeting place or the date."

Andreas' expression made Darian avert his eyes. He went on in an apologetic tone, "I have to consider my position, Micalidos. I can't afford to take sides. And another thing, if this plan of yours should become known, His Majesty would be deeply offended. For my part, I shall not breathe a word, but I am almost certain somehow it would leak out. I think the other ministers would object, too. Micalidos, you are making a mistake. I strongly advise against it and I definitely could not be a party to it."

Andreas accepted this setback with equanimity. Darian, more cautious and diplomatic than he, was probably right. It would give offence. He would have to be circumspect.

"Could you tell me if the requisition order for the timber has been signed?"

The Chancellor was taken aback at the abrupt question. "I doubt if it is even drawn up. You surely must remember the final decision of the last Council meeting?" As Andreas did not reply, he went on. "The Days of Sacrifice must be given first priority. I thought you would have realized that, Micalidos. It is the reason I returned from my villa to this sweltering city."

Andreas made a great effort to keep calm. "I would have preferred to remain longer with my family. Chancellor, I appreciate your views, but I, too, have obligations. The defence of this land is a matter that transcends all others in importance. I trust you understand me, Darian."

"Of course, my dear Micalidos, you must follow your duty, as you see it, and I mine."

The interview ended and Andreas withdrew. He descended to the deserted Courtyard. The elation he had felt after the last Council meeting was dissipated in this arid and empty place. He was halfway to the North Gate when he paused. An idea had suddenly occurred to him. A plan that could solve the island's timber problem, but might put himself and his family at some risk.

He thought there was a way by which he could perhaps discover if the King had signed the timber requisition order for the Navy. Andreas' father-in-law, Aeschyton, now retired, had worked at the Palace as Custodian of the Records Office.

Hiring a chair at the North Gate, it was not long before Andreas alighted outside his father-in-law's dilapidated house. Passing through an archway, he knocked on the door at the rear of the building. He saw that a peach tree growing nearby was laden with ripening fruit.

Aeschyton greeted him affectionately. The old man was tall and very thin, but had great dignity. He asked Andreas to be seated and inquired politely after the family without mentioning his daughter. The proud old man believed that Zanthope's conduct had disgraced him. He offered Andreas a cup of wine and poured one for himself.

The room was sparsely furnished but clean and neat. Aeschyton had always declined assistance from his rich son-in-law — neither money, nor gift, nor favour. He managed on his small government pension. When both were seated, Aeschyton inquired as to the reason for his son-in-law's most welcome visit.

"I need your help, Father," Andreas said seriously. He spoke without reserve of his fears and concern for the safety of the country and his acute anxiety over the unpreparedness of the Navy.

"Our ships must be the first and perhaps our only secure line of defence, Father."

Aeschyton nodded. He had followed Andreas' argument with great attention.

"I understand your problem, my son, but how can I be of help?"

"Well, sir, documents — including requisition orders for timber — are stored, I believe, in the Palace Records Office?"

"Yes, indeed they are," Aeschyton replied.

"There must be security arrangements?"

"In my time all important documents awaiting signature were stored in a large chest in the inner room of the office. I doubt if the system would have changed. Why do you ask?"

"I need the key to enter the office and open that chest, Father. The safety of our island may depend on that requisition order. I must know if the King has signed it."

"Well, how can I help you?" Aeschyton asked again.

"Father, would you still possess your keys to the department — to the office and the chest?"

"I really can't remember, my son. I doubt it."

The old man rose, crossed to his cupboard and began to remove the contents. His possessions were few — winter clothes and blankets, boots for wet weather, reading and writing materials. After some moments' search he found a linen bag tied at the top. He opened it and spread the contents on the table. Most were momentos of his dead wife: a few trinkets, a hair comb, a locket with a strand of golden hair. A shadow passed over the old man's face.

"There doesn't seem to be anything here, my boy." he said.

He shook the bag vigorously. Other souvenirs tumbled out: a string of faience beads, a fan, some scrolls with faded writing. They all fell to the stone floor, and with them a number of keys attached to a copper ring. Stooping, Aeschyton picked them up.

"Zeus! Andreas, how extraordinary, I had completely forgotten about these!" He selected two of the larger keys and showed them to his son-in-law. "They may well be the keys of the Records Office. I don't think anyone would have changed the locks."

Andreas could scarcely believe his luck.

"May I borrow them?" he asked.

"Of course, my son. They are of no use to me."

Aeschyton began to gather up the momentos of his wife. Andreas thanked him sincerely for his help. He felt, as always, great affection for the old man, along with some pity and exasperation.

"Please let me know if you need anything, Father."

Aeschyton nodded. When Andreas left him the old man was staring out of the door at the peach tree his wife had planted many years ago.

Back at the Palace, Andreas considered what he would say if he were challenged. He entered through the office of his own department and thence through the Merchant's Courtyard into the West Palace. His own keys served for this. It was the noon siesta. The place was quiet and deserted ... so far, so good.

The High Priests and the Court had followed the King to the Summer Palace. The few officials, priests and guards who remained on duty were like sleepwalkers awaiting a trumpet call from the Gods to bring them all back to reality. An old priest dozed before a shrine, his prayers half said. At another, two altar boys were absorbed in a game of tiddly-winks with ivory discs. As Andreas walked by, they did not even turn their heads.

The archives and records were stored in a long, low-ceilinged chamber which was entered by a door down a short flight of steps. Andreas tried the keys. One of them fitted. The place was dark and musty. He found a lamp and lit it. Clay tablets were stacked against the walls and on narrow tables. Papyrus scrolls filled the shelves almost to the ceiling and overflowed onto the floor.

There was an inner room, beyond the light well. Aeschyton's keys again gave him access and here Andreas found what he was looking for — a large, heavy wooden chest, decorated with gold leaf and inlays of mother-of-pearl and chrysoprase. He tried the largest key and it fitted. Then he sat down to examine the documents.

There were copies of letters relating to the forthcoming ceremonies and lists of shrines to which they had been sent. There were many other documents, some recent, some years old, but nothing concerning the orders for timber or any of the other measures he had spoken of. His suspicions were confirmed. He searched on shelves and in other chests which lay open. Before leaving, he noticed a locked wall cupboard. None of his keys would open it. He looked about for some means of forcing the door. Finally, angry and determined, he returned to the first room and began to break clay tablets until he had one with a sharp enough edge to prise open the cupboard door.

Inside he found the scribes' accounts of the last Council meeting. He sat down and read them carefully. They gave an accurate record of the meeting and contained all the measures the Council had approved. However, a line had been drawn through the minutes of the meeting and across them, written boldly in another hand, was the word: DEFERRED.

Cursing, Andreas took the scrolls and left the Palace. Now he knew what he must do.

# CHAPTER 20

The hottest days of summer hung over Knossos and the nights brought little relief. Andreas lay sleepless for hours, thoughts, plans and anxieties spinning around in his head till he felt he would go mad. He had dictated letters to General Imanos and to Captain Keridos of the Navy, and Senthios, Captain of the Palace Guard, sounding them out as to their willingness to meet with him. There was still no news from his agent, Tarsis.

General Imanos had answered promptly and enthusiastically although his frankness would have betrayed the project had his letter been intercepted. Keridos declined the invitation, but suggested that Lieutenant Rekkyn might represent him. Andreas smiled. He felt sure that Antonius could talk Keridos round when Tarsis returned. Captain Senthios replied swiftly that he would be honoured to speak with Councillor Micalidos at any time that did not conflict with his duties.

Andreas drew up an agenda for the meeting. This he would normally have dictated to Senka. However, he did not confide in his secretary. Senka had become a problem. 'If I dismiss him', he thought, 'people will say it's because he's my wife's lover — but I have no proof of that.'

Andreas knew Zanthope too well. Seduction came naturally to her. He didn't care a damn what she did, if she was discreet. 'Even if he is her lover, people will be less likely to believe it, if I keep him on,' he thought.

He dismissed these melancholy thoughts and invented a few trivial tasks for his secretary.

Returning from one of his errands, Senka discovered he was free for the afternoon. The young women he knew were away, at the sea or the mountains. Chryssa and Zanthope were still at Mallia. Klonka, the club proprietor, had retired with his nymphs to a summer villa. Senka felt sorry for himself and lonely. Then he remembered a woman he had not visited for some time. Vasca, a harlot, who lived in The Narrows, a dark, sunless alley beneath the viaduct near the Travellers' Inn. He counted the houses. Hers was the seventh, he remembered, and went in.

Vasca overlooked his past neglect and welcomed him warmly. Without artifice, but with a conscious instinct for effect, she suddenly loosed her voluminous robe. Her sturdy peasant body was warm and voluptuous. Her figure reminded him of a clay statuette he had once seen from an ancient shrine in Zakro — the clay had been modelled firmly into breasts, belly and thighs, but the statuette was faceless, with no concern for individual personality. It was the universal embodiment of the Earth Mother.

Vasca, however, had a beautiful face and her hair was thick and soft. She was warm, animal and desirable. "How's my Senekor?" she cooed in his ear, her voice melodious and gentle, "You are all the more welcome for your long absence."

When he was satisfied, he rose and dressed. He wanted to leave at once. She, however, wanted to talk. "Senka, my fine little bantam cock," she began, "I've heard tales about you. You're on a dangerous path, they say. Aren't you aiming a little high? Remember what they say, the higher you climb, the further you fall!"

"I don't know what you're talking about," Senka snarled.

She laughed and her breasts heaved. "My friend, we know most men's secrets, and you, my young stallion, are running a dangerous course."

"Mind your own business," he said angrily, moving toward the door.

She took his chin in her hand and ruffled his hair with the other in a gesture that reminded him of his mother. "Why don't you find yourself a rich widow?" she rattled on. "Any woman over thirty would give anything for a handsome young fellow like you."

Her flattery soothed him. His anger turned in on himself for being thus disarmed.

"Now, what about that friend of Doxa Grinkos," Vasca went on, "what's her name — Olivia something or other. She'd have you, I've no doubt."

"Olivia!" he said scornfully, "she hasn't a penny, and she doesn't care for men."

"Your wrong. She has got money. She's going to live in the Palace, in her own apartment. We hear things. *We* know what's going on."

"I'm going," he said.

She smiled, but he did not want to touch her again. He paid her and left. In the street, she called after him, "Mind where you sleep, sonny, this town is full of holes for the unwary!"

Thankful to escape, Senka walked down the southern highway and crossed into the Street of Doves, ignoring the chair carriers who pestered him for employment. The summer break was bad for them with so many customers out of town. Senka preferred to walk and consider what Vasca had told him about Olivia going to live in the Palace.

As he went, someone called to him. Thinking it was a beggar he paid no attention. His name was called again. He turned and was surprised and embarrassed to see his father.

The old man was more bent than Senka remembered, his hair was now nearly grey, but his eyes were still bright and alert. He held open his arms and embraced his son. Senka saw his father's eyes fill with tears. He was moved himself, but he silently thanked the Gods that all his friends were out of town. He took his father to drink a glass of wine at a nearby tavern.

Senekor was oblivious of everything but his son's face. He plied him with a dozen questions and before they were properly answered a dozen more.

"Are you still working, father," Senka asked.

"Oh yes, my boy, shoemaking is a good steady trade," the old man replied.

Then, Senka inquired after his mother. For the first time his father's eyes reproached him.

"Why did you not write, my son?"

When he could not reply, his father went on, "Your mother breaks her heart for you. Senka, we don't want to intrude in your life. We realize you must make your way amongst people who are —" he lifted his hands, "rich, better educated than us. That's what we wanted for you — a better life than ours. But, Senka, my son, you should write to her. Sacred Gods! It would involve no great effort."

"I'm sorry, father," Senka protested, and at that moment he was. "I'll write in future every —"

His father grasped his arm. "Not every anything, Senka. Just now and then. Let us know you are well. That's all we want — your health and happiness, and one day, perhaps some grandchildren!"

The old man's face was wreathed in smiles. Senka was conscious of his own shortcomings. He contemplated introducing his father to Andreas at the Villa. But a glance at his coarse clothes and his work-worn hands settled that. He knew Andreas would not care, but the servants would talk. Zanthope and Chryssa might find out. He could not face their teasing, after all his silly lies about his father being a Colonel. He would be a joke in Knossos. He could not endure that. Senka hoped his father would soon leave for Zakro and inquired where he was staying. As if reading his thoughts, the old man hastened to assure him that he was comfortable at the Travellers' Inn and would leave early in the morning.

"What brought you to Knossos?" Senka asked.

His father looked hard at him. "Your mother gave me no peace for months, and — I had some business on the way."

Senka knew that something had been left unsaid. His father embraced him and said good-bye. "I shall give your love to your mother, Senka."

Senka nodded and watched his father set off on foot for the Travellers' Inn. Senka himself took a chair and drew the curtains to hide from the empty street.

# CHAPTER 21

Andreas was almost drunk. "Open another bottle, Credon. This is a night to remember." Andreas, Ahmed and Senka had dined in the quiet house and were now sitting on the terrace enjoying the best vintage in the cellar. The air was soft and fragrant. The lights of the city lay below them, warm and friendly.

"Have some yourself, Credon," Andreas said, as the old steward refilled their wine cups.

"Thank you, sir."

They had much to celebrate. Ten days of hectic activity had accomplished what seemed, in retrospect, almost a miracle. Andreas suddenly roared with laughter. "I don't know why I should be getting drunk and feeling so damned happy!" He laughed again. Ahmed, usually serious, and Senka, moody and depressed, laughed with him.

"I'm almost penniless," Andreas remarked, wiping

the tears from his eyes, "you'll both have to wait for your money till the olive harvest is sold!"

It was true. In order to buy the entire stock of timber from the merchant, Praxitor at Amnissos, Andreas had mortgaged everything to old Senthios, the merchant and money-lender — his villas, the galleys, the repair yard, the farm, the olive grove, the pottery. Andreas would only keep this year's olive harvest. That, and a sum he had in gold, would pay his employees. The loan was to be repaid in four months, by which time Andreas was confident the King and Council would ratify the vote to purchase the timber and he would be reimbursed from the royal exchequer.

Andreas' agent, Karkoran, had bargained for nearly two days with Praxitor, the timber merchant. Both were rogues, but finally, the price was barely in excess of Andreas' estimate. He was delighted and the release from tension made him light-headed.

Dr Ahmed and Senka accompanied Andreas to the merchant Senthios' apartment to witness the final contract. Senthios was very pleased to have Andreas in his debt. Dr Ahmed was anxious and concerned. In his opinion, Senthios was as trustworthy as a cobra. Andreas, however, was beyond caution. He knew that if the Council delayed repayment, the goodwill of his business enterprises and even the family heirlooms, including Zanthope's ruby necklace, could provide ample security for the loan.

When the agreement was finalised, a convoy of mules, escorted by Captain Senthios and a guard of Nubian soldiers, carried the gold to Amnissos.

Senka was sent to the *Griffon* to inform Captain Keridos of the arrangements to service the fleet. The young Captain was impressed with Andreas' plans. Loyalty to his uncles on the Council had made him wary and suspicious, now, however, he was prepared to place his ability and energy at Andreas' disposal.

The return of the agent, Tarsis, from his secret mission at Mycenae prompted Andreas to call a defence meeting at the Villa. Captain Keridos attended, with his Lieutenants Rekkyn and Dessios, also General Imanos and Captain Senthios.

Keridos agreed to organise work at the shipyard. He ordered Rekkyn and Dessios with gangs of men, to transport the timber from Amnissos. Senka and Karkoran were to scour the northern towns for more shipwrights and carpenters. The men would be rostered on day and night shifts to lay the keels of six galleys.

One of Andreas' trading galleys had recently returned laden with cedar. This shipment Andreas held in reserve. Rope and sailcloth were to be purchased, so that nothing could impede the commissioning of the new ships.

Tarsis' report to the meeting from the citadel of Mycenae was laconic and encouraging. His contacts there revealed that the enemy, also, had supply problems and, as yet, no date had been set for the invasion of Crete. According to Tarsis, the Mycenaean War Lords had demanded that their Generals be in command. The Athenians disagreed. They said, as this was to be primarily a naval battle, their Sea Lords should lead the attack.

Andreas smiled. He asked Tarsis to return to Mycenae. There he was to recruit agitators and to incite disputes and arguments in taverns and gaming houses.

"Let them kill each other!" Andreas said grimly.

General Imanos tabled a number of moves to improve Crete's land defences. Andreas was grateful for his support, however, he was adamant that the warships in Phaestos should return north immediately.

To this end, Captain Keridos agreed to go to Silamos, where his uncle, Councillor Markos, the Navy Minister, was on holiday at his estate.

Andreas warned Keridos not to broach the subject in front of anyone else. "Don't mention my name, either! Get your uncle alone and make him agree with us."

Keridos understood. He had his own arguments to put forward. He was aware that foreign ships had been taking soundings off the northern coast.

Andreas' optimism was not unfounded. Keridos returned in two days with the signed order to bring the Phaestos fleet north again. Lieutenant Rekkyn had ridden south at once to deliver it.

"All praise to you, Moon Goddess!" Andreas said, raising his wine-cup and saluting the full moon as it rose above the Cretan mountains. Ahmed and Senka followed suit. The three men were relaxed and content. Andreas was free now to holiday in the mountains.

"We'll leave for the farm first thing in the morning. Credon, order the large carriage. You can drive, Senka."

They finished their wine, said goodnight and went to bed.

Early next morning, they set out. The road to the farm climbed slowly up the mountain, winding between fields and orchards. Cherries were ripening and the scent of orange groves filled the air. Soon they left the valley behind and, as they ascended, they could look back on the city far below, the vast bulk of the Palace throwing its shadow westward as the sun rose. A pair of eagles glided below them, turning in lazy, majestic circles, dark shapes against the emerald green of summer. Above them, the peaks of Mount Ida rose serenely in the clear, transparent light of the early morning sky.

"How good it will be to see them all again," Andreas remarked. Turning to Ahmed he wagered, "I'll bet you a silver piece that Timon will have grown at least an inch!"

"You'll probably win!" the doctor laughed.

They passed under the white stone archway and into the inner courtyard. It was a charming old house, cool and gracious, with dark cedar floors and white-washed walls.

There were two magnificent yew trees in the courtyard. Seated under one of them, Old Madam and Korynna were enjoying a bowl of sweet, mountain strawberries. Their joy at seeing Andreas overflowed in tears and laughter. They embraced him and Dr Ahmed and Senka were welcomed warmly.

"Come and share our strawberries," Old Madam said, "they are quite fresh and delicious."

Andreas looked about smiling. "Well, where is he? Don't tell me the young scamp is playing truant up here too!"

Old Madam looked puzzled. "What do you mean, Andreas — where is he?"

"Timon, of course. I hope he's been behaving himself."

Old Madam turned pale and Korynna put a protective arm around her.

"Andreas," his sister said quietly, "Timon is not here. We thought he had gone to Mallia with you."

Old Madam began to weep and wring her hands.

"Oh, hush up, Mother!" Andreas said tersely, and turning to Korynna went on, "Surely the arrangement was for him to come here with you?"

"Yes," Korynna replied, "but when we were ready to leave he was nowhere to be found. We told Deva to send him up with the baggage cart."

"When Dorcas arrived with the baggage," Old Madam said tearfully, "we asked him — where Timon was and he said he had left him with Deva."

"Naturally," Korynna added with an air of finality, "we assumed he had gone to Mallia with you."

Andreas stood silent for a moment unable to comprehend the seriousness of the situation. He struck his brow with his hand.

"Holy Zeus! That's nearly a month ago, where can he be? What can have happened?" His voice was tense and strained. "I must return to Knossos at once."

"You cannot go back without a night's rest, sir," Ahmed interposed firmly.

"Cannot," Andreas snapped, "who says I cannot!"

"You're pushing yourself too hard, sir." The doctor said and looked anxiously at Andreas, who suddenly staggered and would have pitched forward on the hard, pebbled courtyard, if Ahmed and Senka had not supported him. They helped him to a couch inside the house as his mother began to weep afresh at this new and unforeseen disaster. Andreas lay gasping for breath.

"I ... should ... send ... letters." His voice, so weak and faint, frightened them all.

"Senka should fetch Antonius," Old Madam said, finding strength in her fear for her son, "you will feel stronger, Andreas my dear, with Antonius here."

Andreas nodded. A fresh horse was brought for Senka, who was soon on his way to Mallia. The family sat staring at each other silently as the hoofbeats faded away. The sun's oppressive heat beat down on them in the small farmhouse and the heaviness of the air further depressed their spirits with its promise of a storm to come.

# CHAPTER 22

When Senka arrived with his unwelcome news about Timon, Andreas' daughter, Hyacinth, and her family were having their midday meal. At first they were incredulous.

"Do you mean to tell us that all the time we were dancing and enjoying ourselves here and at the villa, young Timon was lost?" Hyacinth exclaimed and began to weep. They had their own troubles: she was pregnant and not very well, the children were sick with summer fever and she was exhausted from caring for them. She wanted to leave with Antonius at once to see her father.

"My dear girl, it's out of the question," Lerintos said firmly, "I won't hear of you going anywhere."

Later, as Antonius was drawing on his riding boots, Lerintos remarked, "I cannot go with you at this time, Antonius."

"Sir, there's no cause for either of you to come,"

Antonius protested. "Please don't worry. I'm sure we shall find Timon safe in Knossos. He often played truant and probably went to one of this friends' houses or to his tutor, or ..." he was about to say "Luki's house". Then he remembered that Luki was also missing and immediately recalled seeing the young boys on the boat in Phaestos. He did not want to add to his sister's anxiety, so he said nothing of this.

"Don't upset yourself, Hyacinth. I'm sure it will turn out all right." Antonius decided also not to mention the report from Senka that Andreas had collapsed. Hyacinth became calmer and drank some wine, which Lerintos poured for her. But she remembered the peasant woman's child, and the conversation with her father. She had not thought about it since that day they had walked in the vineyard.

Prince Lerintos agreed with Antonius that Timon would be found unharmed. Nevertheless he was surprised that there should be all this fuss over a servant's child and annoyed that his wife should be upset over such a trivial matter. He was also engrossed with his military preparations, which he had commenced as soon as Andreas departed for Knossos. As Antonius was leaving, he suggested quietly to Lerintos that a reward might be posted locally for the boy. The Prince was surprised.

"Why should he be here?" he asked.

"He knew his father was going to Mallia," Antonius explained, "he may have tried to walk here and become lost."

"Very well, I'll send one of my stewards to inquire in the district. But I don't want my wife upset."

Antonius, feeling he was in no way responsible for the situation, was annoyed at the reproach in his host's voice.

"I've no wish for my sister to be upset either," he said.

Some hours later he and Senka arrived at the farm, hot, tired and dusty. Andreas was in bed propped up by large pillows. His face was drawn and there was no welcome in his eyes. Antonius was ill-prepared for the coldness of this reception. He was hurt and puzzled. To be ignored was something Antonius had seldom, if ever, experienced. After a few minutes he and Dr Ahmed walked out into the courtyard.

"What in Zeus' name has got into him?" Antonius said when they were out of earshot.

"He's had a terrible shock — we all have," Ahmed replied.

"I only want to help. Why does he refuse to welcome me?"

"He is very ill. He must have absolute rest," the doctor looked anxiously toward the house, "there are many things you can do. First, ride to Knossos and warn Credon of our return. Then order two litters, one for your father and the other for Old Madam. I am worried about her, too."

"Surely Senka could do that?"

"I need him to help move your father. He's a heavy man," the doctor tried to be patient. "I want your father kept calm. Senka can write any necessary letters, he's accustomed to it."

Antonius set off for Knossos shortly afterwards. Ahmed was still doubtful about undertaking the journey when the litters arrived. But Andreas was fretting continually to get back to Knossos to organize the search for Timon so the doctor thought it best to humour him. He and Korynna drove back in the chariot.

Old Madam complained of giddiness, worried continually about Timon and insisted on taking the blame for his disappearance. Credon helped her out in the morning to a daybed in a shady place on the terrace and back to her room at night. It was pitiful to see her growing weaker each day. Her mind, always so lively, began to wander. Occasionally she would call to Andreas "not to climb too high in the trees or he would fall and hurt himself..." as she had done many years ago, or she would mistake Credon for her long dead husband.

On the day of their return to Knossos, Andreas had Senka post notices throughout the city with Timon's description and offering a large reward for his safe return. Letters were sent to the agents to watch the ports and make inquiries in their regions. Captain Senthios was sent for. He came, surprised but obliging, and was asked to search the Palace which was an exceedingly difficult task, considering its size and labyrinthine character.

Andreas remained in his own apartment and was watched over by Ahmed day and night. He was seriously ill and could see no one. After some weeks his physical condition improved but he remained gloomy and morose. He would not rouse himself to eat properly or speak with anyone. A poor, fitful sleep came to him only with the help of drugs.

Ahmed was in despair as he could find no reason for this malaise. He reflected that it was strange that the absence of one small child should cause such disruption. The doctor had his own private concerns, including the presence of the two escaped slaves in the surgery, which nagged incessantly at his mind. Doxa Grinkos had posted a large reward for information leading to their recapture. It would have been cheaper to replace them, but she sought revenge and was prepared to pay for it. With so many poor people attending the surgery and street traders daily at the door, it seemed likely that when their presence was known, someone would be tempted by the reward.

Ahmed decided not to worry Andreas with this particular problem. He warned his assistant, Iros, to be careful, hoping that some means could be found to send Tyra and Arkos away from Knossos as soon as possible.

Antonius, accustomed to a life of pleasure and activity, found this strange, changed household almost unbearable. His grandmother either did not recognize him, or his presence reminded her of Timon's disappearance. She was then so distressed that Korynna gently suggested that Antonius should not come near her. His mother, whom he loved dearly, was still at Mallia and Andreas had ordered her and the staff not to return. So there were no servant girls to quiz and no Deva to tease and tickle. Life in Knossos was dull and he hated it.

He rode to Phaestos to confer with Uncle Grivas and to make sure that Agidor had indeed posted the notices and reward for Timon. The agent had been assiduous, but his manner did not disguise his malice and Antonius found him more revolting than ever. He next visited Mallia. His mother was bored and irritable and delighted to hear that Timon had disappeared.

"You can post rewards from me for anyone who doesn't find him," she said.

Then he rode to the Palace of Mallia to see Hyacinth, whose health, much to his relief had improved. She told him she hoped to persuade Lerintos to let her visit Andreas soon. The Prince was polite but did not invite him to stay and Antonius went home feeling sorry for himself. He wondered when Klonka's Club would reopen and swore, remembering the Days of Sacrifice which would delay the start of the new season.

The only member of the family who seemed to be able to remain calm was Aunt Korynna. With surprisingly good sense she shared the management of the household with the steward, Credon. She asked him to engage temporary kitchen help, nursed her mother and helped to bathe and dress Andreas every day. She took the evening meal in her mother's room.

As Senka sat each night with Andreas and read to him while he dined, Ahmed and Antonius usually dined together at the long table.

"Why does my father give way like this?" Antonius said one evening and poured himself some more wine. "It could ease his mind to talk. We might even hit on the solution to the mystery of Timon's disappearance."

Weary of Antonius' complaints, Ahmed sighed and did not reply.

Antonius, with some of his father's arrogance, banged the table.

"By Zeus! We might do better with another doctor!"

"Of course, you may call in anyone you please," Ahmed replied quietly. Antonius, nettled by the doctor's reply, continued in an angry tone.

"Why don't you tell him to speak to me? Are you trying to turn him against me?"

"Don't be ridiculous, Antonius!" Ahmed flushed angrily but maintained a dignified manner. "I told you before, my only concern is your father's health. If he doesn't wish to speak to you, I'm not going to be the one to upset him."

These arguments usually ended in Antonius storming out of the house to go to a tavern. On this particular occasion he was about to leave when he recollected that he had no money. He apologized, paused in the doorway and asked Dr Ahmed for a loan.

"Let's go out on the terrace, Antonius, I want to talk to you," replied Ahmed rising from his chair.

They strolled up and down, always turning before approaching Andreas' apartments. Ahmed told Antonius about the huge loan his father had raised from the family properties, and Senthios, the merchant, to buy the timber from Praxitor.

"Mortgaged everything we own?" Antonius could hardly believe this.

"Everything," Ahmed replied nodding.

"He must be mad. What are we going to do? Does my mother know?"

"I don't think so. As to what we should do — there's nothing we can do — except, perhaps, not run up bills!" He glanced quizzically at Antonius, who smiled.

"Well, there's plenty of wine in the cellar. I shall have to resign myself to drinking at home."

"Of course, your father has the Council's warrant to acquire the timber, so the money will be repaid eventually."

"Heaven knows when," Antonius said gloomily, "this house is like a morgue, there's no life in it any more." They leaned over the stone balustrade. It was dusk. The city was quiet and peaceful. The light from the setting sun glowed behind the jagged range of mountains.

"I should have told you before, doctor," Antonius began and then related how he had rescued the small boys in Phaestos and had not mentioned it in the report to his father because it did not then seem relevant. The diversion of the visit to Mallia had since put it out of his mind.

"It would have been wise to mention it," the doctor said, "your father will have to be told, but we must choose the right moment. What a difficult situation this is. Are you quite sure, Antonius, that your uncle has put a stop to this trade?"

"Yes indeed. I made inquiries when I returned to Phaestos last week. Uncle Grivas told me the children were stolen and have since been returned to their families. They were from small villages in the neighbourhood and all of them had a similar tale. They were enticed away — one with a bogus message from his mother, another with the promise of a bowl of figs to take home, and so on. They were bound and gagged, kept in a warehouse near the docks and smuggled on board the ship at night."

"Can't they identify this man, Agidor?"

"He was too clever. The children were blindfolded and the man who kidnapped them wasn't employed on the dock. It has the appearance of a well-planned scheme. Uncle Grivas questioned the crew — he even had the bosun flogged — but, they were all too scared to talk."

"This island seems prosperous and happy, but there's so much cruelty and tension beneath the surface," Ahmed mused. He briefly recounted how the fugitive slaves, Tyra and her lover, Arkos, took refuge in his surgery.

"I'm very concerned that they should not be discovered there, both for their own sakes and because it could cause trouble for your father. We must find a way to get these young people out of Knossos."

"Hyacinth would take them," Antonius said after a moment. "Dorcas could drive them to Mallia in the vegetable cart."

Doctor Ahmed shook his head wearily. "It won't do, Antonius. Firstly, Prince Lerintos would not allow it and secondly, it would still involve your father. No one would believe he had not arranged it." Antonius stared at the dark silhouette of the mountains.

"I have many friends. I'm sure between us we can arrange something."

"Tell as few people as possible about this," Ahmed warned.

"Of course I'll be careful," Antonius replied impatiently.

The Doctor was uneasy. Not a superstitious man beneath the calm he affected as a professional habit he had his misgivings. He sincerely hoped there would be no more problems for the Micalidos family.

# CHAPTER 23

After practice in the gymnasium, Belia went to the lamp-room for some oil. It was a dark, musty place cluttered with chipped lamps, cracked oil jars and an accumulation of dusty odds and ends left over by generations of bull dancers. As she prepared to fill the lamp, a scratching sound from a dark corner caught her attention. When she pulled an old cupboard away from the wall, a rat scuttled through a stone grating, part of the vast ventilation system throughout the Palace. The gratings were usually fixed firmly, but without much effort she was able to remove this one. She peered into a dark narrow shaft located inside the wall.

This discovery was a challenge to Belia's inquisitive nature. Without hesitation, she lit her lamp, and pushing it ahead of her, found she could, with some difficulty, squeeze through the narrow opening. On hands and knees she crawled along the dark passage.

The tunnel led past other, similar openings, closed by the same gratings. She passed the empty dining-hall and the dark kitchen, full of cooking odours. The shaft then turned sharply to the left and ahead was a faint glimmer of light. Ignoring her discomfort, Belia crept forward, shading the lamp with one hand. To her surprise, she found that she was above the men's quarters. She could faintly hear two men arguing and drew back. Suddenly, both snatched up towels and raced for the baths. At once she thrust the lamp forward and, in the dim light, could see an opening ahead, where the shaft ended abruptly. She moved forward and looked down into a small, empty room.

A ledge ran along the wall and there, thick with dust, was another lamp, the wick rotten but the oil still present. A dusty flint lighter lay nearby. Someone had used this room once. Belia wondered who it was and under what circumstances it had been used.

It was not difficult to climb down into the room and holding the lamp high she examined it. The walls seemed very old indeed, made of large blocks of rough cut stone and rough-hewn timber beams supported the ceiling. She was about to dismiss the place as a dead end, when the lamp flickered in the draught. She then discovered a narrow doorway, concealed by a stone partition and passing through, stood in a passageway. The blackness extended in every direction. It seemed tangible and claustrophobic. The small circle of light from the lamp made little impact on this wall of darkness.

She began to walk down the passage, one hand feeling the rough surface of the wall but stopping now and then to shield the lamp flame, constantly threatened by wayward currents of air. It was cold and damp. With faltering steps she crept forward. She paused a moment to look over her shoulder and discovered that the opening, leading back to safety, was no longer visible. Despite this, she forced herself to go on, step by step. Then the lamp spluttered and went out. She stood in the darkness, her throat dry, her heart pounding in terror.

Turning about and placing her other hand against the wall, she began to retrace her steps. At last, after what seemed an eternity, she found the opening leading into the small room and made her way back through the shaft to the lamp-room. Evidently no one had noticed her absence.

This incident made Belia very curious to explore the Palace further. The brief visit which she and Freyna had made to Phylon's workshop had shown that the Bull Halls were only a small part of the huge and complex building. Belia suspected there might be a vast network of passages, ventilation shafts, cellars and storerooms beneath the Palace and it occurred to her that these could lead to a way of escape. But she did not tell Freyna of her discovery, not wishing to disappoint her if the passages led nowhere.

She also realized that she would need more light if she was to explore further. In the lamp-room she found an old lantern with a wind shield, some candles and an empty wine bottle, which she filled with oil. These things she hid inside the ventilation shaft, replacing the cupboard to conceal the broken grating. Belia looked forward eagerly to the time when she would slip away unnoticed and continue her exploration of the Labyrinth beneath the Palace of Knossos.

# CHAPTER 24

Hyacinth visited her father surrounded by children and nursemaids. Her husband, Lerintos, had not wanted her to go. It became their first serious disagreement.

"How is my father?" she asked as Dr Ahmed came forward to help her from the chariot.

"He's doing very well, Princess."

In spite of this reassurance, she detected a note of doubt in his voice. Meanwhile, the children were jumping from the chariot, laughing and chattering. She turned to remind them that poor grandfather was not well and must not be disturbed.

As they walked along the terrace, they stopped to greet Old Madam, lying on her couch. She smiled vaguely at them and murmured "...the child will get his feet wet and catch cold". Hyacinth kissed her as Korynna appeared and welcomed them all.

"Come along," she said to the children, "I've something nice in the kitchen for you." Hyacinth nodded to the nurses to follow her aunt. "If they get too much for you, send them into the garden," she said.

When they were alone, Dr Ahmed spoke hesitantly.

"Princess, before you see your father, there are some matters I would like to discuss."

"Of course, doctor."

They walked into the loggia and sat down in the long, cool room. She looked expectantly at him. He paused a moment, as though trying to work out a problem.

"Your father has made great progress — in a physical sense. His pulse and breathing are normal, he has no fever, no pain, as far as I can ascertain — yet..." he paused again.

"Please go on, doctor. What is wrong with him?"

"It's the state of his mind that concerns me, Princess. After all these years, I thought I understood him very well and yet at the moment he just isn't the man I know. He's had problems and anxieties and tragedies in his life before this, but he's always been able to cope with them. Now — for some reason I don't understand — it's as though he's almost given up, almost lost hope. He's in a state of melancholy from which I don't seem to be able to rouse him. At first he needed absolute rest and quiet — he was fighting for his life. That crisis has passed, thank the Gods, he's out of danger, convalescent. Now, there are things that need to be discussed. He should be eating and sleeping well, but he isn't. He is still in a state of acute mental suffering."

"Well, surely, the loss of the child ..." Hyacinth could imagine nothing worse.

"Timon is not to be presumed dead," Ahmed interrupted. "We must be optimistic. No, it's something worse than that. He has a grievance against Antonius which none of us can understand. Your brother is naturally very distressed about it. When you see your father, Princess, please encourage him to talk. Try, without upsetting him, to break down this self-imposed barrier. We're so thankful that you've come." He smiled at her with such gentle, genuine affection, that Hyacinth, who was easily moved, reached out and clasped his hand in hers. Her eyes filled with tears.

"Thank you for all you've done for us, Dr Ahmed," she murmured, "what would we have done without you?"

Ahmed then told her about the kidnapped boys Antonius had rescued from the ship at Phaestos. In turn, she told him about the child lost in Mallia. Then, they discussed the disappearance of Timon's friend, Luki.

"There could be a pattern in all this," Ahmed said finally. "I haven't told your father about the children in Phaestos, but of course, he will have to be told, eventually. If there's an opportunity, you might tell him yourself. Make him talk, Princess, that must be your first objective."

"I'll do my best, doctor."

Hyacinth found her father sitting in his big chair, which had been moved to the edge of the open court so that he could enjoy the fresh air. His appearance shocked her. He was very pale and had lost weight. For an instant he stared without recognizing her. Then, when he realized who she was, joy brought light to his eyes and colour to his gaunt face. They embraced and then she drew up a low stool and sat beside him. When he inquired if the children were with her she told him they were in the kitchen, eating honey cakes with Aunt Korynna.

"She's running the house," he said bluntly. "I never thought she had much sense. Now I know I was wrong."

"What a bad time you are having, Father dear. And poor grandmother, I don't think she knew who I was."

"It's a dreadful business." Andreas looked at his daughter, then away, sighed and fell silent. She tried to maintain the conversation.

"What do you plan to do, Father?"

He looked surprised for a moment but remained silent. Then he began to speak, at first hesitantly, and then more fluently.

"I don't know, I just don't know what to do. I feel so helpless just sitting here. I can't get about. I'd like to see the King — but he's away in the Summer Palace — and when he returns next week, he'll be incommunicado — in retreat for the Days of Sacrifice."

"Yes, our local priests are all involved, too. One can't get any attention from them. Father, we've posted notices in Mallia and for miles around, about Timon. Lerintos has had men search all the villages in our district."

"That's very good of him. Give him my thanks, my most sincere thanks." Andreas did not look at her and seemed defensive. He clearly wanted to avoid discussing Timon.

"And Antonius has searched everywhere," Hyacinth went on. "He's ridden to Phaestos to alert Uncle Grivas and he went to all the smaller ports on the south coast." She paused, but he remained silent. She noted with dismay the hard, bitter set of his mouth, the sudden clench of his fist.

"Father, don't be so hard on Antonius," she pleaded, "he loved Timon, I'm sure of it."

Inadvertently she had used the past tense and could have bitten off her tongue.

Andreas covered his face with his hands. He wept quietly as she clung to him, pressing his head against her breast. Her tears, too, flooded out. After some moments she smiled at him through her tears. He put his arm around her and poured out his misery, the anguish that had so long tormented him, the ghastly suspicion that Antonius and his mother may have been responsible for Timon's disappearance.

"Why should they do such a terrible thing?" she asked.

"I have adopted Timon legally. He will — was — to share the inheritance with you and your brother."

"Father, I'd stake my life, my love for Lerintos, our children, everything I have, that Antonius could never commit this terrible crime. It's not in his nature to do such a thing."

"And your mother?"

She returned his gaze steadily. They had always avoided the subject, but now she knew she must speak of it.

"Father, I know she's not been a good wife — she's hurt you beyond measure. She has many faults and she's always disliked Timon, but she's not a wicked woman. She wouldn't deliberately harm him. It's not in *her* nature to do that."

Andreas knew that it was not in Hyacinth's nature to think ill of anyone, least of all her own mother. But he was happy to grasp at any straw that offered comfort. Now that his fears had been expressed he was somewhat more at ease.

"May the Gods prove you right, my dearest girl," he said simply.

Now she felt able to speak without reserve and felt confident enough to repeat all that Ahmed had told her.

"Why in Zeus' name didn't Antonius tell me all this before?"

"I think he meant to tell you but so many things intervened — the Council meeting and the party at Mallia — then, I suppose he forgot. And while you were ill, Dr Ahmed wouldn't allow anyone to disturb you. Antonius had told Uncle Grivas that he thought Timon was quite safe at that time. Immediately Antonius knew he was lost he rode back to Phaestos to speak with Uncle Grivas again. I'm sure you'll be glad to know all those boys are returned safely to their families. Captain Dahl and your other captains are keeping a sharp watch on all the ships now."

"I don't think they'd take children from the north to Phaestos," Andreas said, "it would be too risky. I'm convinced the answer lies here in the Palace. That's where we must concentrate our search."

"Why should you think Timon is in the Palace?"

"I've no real evidence, just something Timon said when I asked him about the day Luki went missing. He said he saw him talking to a man in a long robe."

"A priest? That's very strange."

Hyacinth began to talk of homely, simple things, soothing her father's spirit with her gentleness and sympathy. When she left him to rest, he was more at peace than he had been for weeks.

A few hours later Ahmed was delighted to find his patient in a happier frame of mind. Andreas deeply regretted his treatment of Antonius. The next day, with Hyacinth's help, the doctor was able to effect a reconciliation. Antonius then told his father that he had decided to enlist. He would join Captain Senthios' company in a few days as a cadet officer and after two months' training he would be granted a commission.

"I'm in luck, General Imanos has ordered the Palace Guard doubled and they're eager to have Cretan officers. I've led such a soft life, I hope I can survive the training!"

"You'll do well, my boy," Andreas said, proud and thankful that his son had, at last, made the decision.

Another cause for satisfaction came from a visit by Shep-Anep, the Egyptian Ambassador's interpreter. He had seen the notices about Timon's disappearance and expressed his and the Ambassador's regret and sympathy. However, Andreas' pleasure at Shep's visit was soon dispelled by what the interpreter had to say. When pressed for information that could throw light on the mystery, the Egyptian hesitated.

"Please, Shep, any thoughts you have might be helpful," Andreas implored.

"They are only rumours, you understand, garbled and probably wrong..."

"Well?"

"Other children have disappeared, a metal worker's boy..."

"Yes, Luki, we know about that," Andreas said impatiently.

"There are others, girls too, but mainly boys. These children have simply disappeared." Shep paused. "I'm afraid I'm not bringing you much comfort."

"Who are the people named in these rumours?"

"There is one name that seems to recur — the priest, Eburninos. We've tried to set a watch on him, but it's difficult. You know what the Palace is like."

"Yes," Andreas said grimly, "as soon as I see His Majesty, I intend to settle with Eburninos."

Shep's silence had a curious intensity. When he spoke he chose his words carefully. "Councillor, if I had the right to advise you, it would be to tread carefully. They say this priest is very close to the King."

"What are you trying to tell me?" Andreas' voice was cold.

"The city is full of rumours ... many parents are anxious and concerned. Without proof I have no right to accuse anyone." Shep was ill at ease. As an embassy official he was aware that he should not repeat scandalous gossip. He had been generously treated in Crete and to criticise their popular King seemed ungrateful and churlish. Andreas understood Shep's reluctance but swept it angrily aside.

"Do these rumours suggest that Eburninos procures boys? That Minos is a pervert — that he lusts after children?"

"I wish I could contradict you, sir," Shep replied with quiet dignity.

For some moments Andreas was silent, endeavouring to control the intensity of his emotion. He now understood why these tragic children were never seen again. He thanked Shep for coming and ordered the chariot to take him back to the Palace.

On the following day, Hyacinth returned home as she did not wish to annoy Lerintos further nor burden Korynna with a second family to look after. She had brought light and hope into the stricken house and, much to Ahmed's relief, Andreas' health improved and he slept more soundly. However, the doctor was not pleased when Andreas asked him to go to the Palace when the Queen returned to tell her of Timon's disappearance.

"What has it to do with her?" he asked. "I don't wish to embarrass her, and the King would object."

"Let him," Andreas said bluntly, "if my son is alive, I believe he's in the Palace. But where? This awful question goes round in my head like a rat in a barrel."

"I don't see how the Queen could help," Ahmed said quietly. But he knew he would go if Andreas insisted and, in his heart, he looked forward to seeing Her Majesty again.

"We must try every channel, even the most unlikely," Andreas persisted, "after all, Queen Kara lives in the Palace. The servants gossip. She may have heard something from one of her ladies."

"Very well then, I will see her when she returns," Ahmed said.

However, they were both to be disappointed. When the Queen returned from the Summer Palace, she would see no one. Her steward announced that Her Majesty would be in retreat until the Days of Sacrifice were completed. He added that the people would have the joy and honour of seeing both His Royal Majesty and His Gracious Consort at the Grand Opening Ceremony of the Bull Dance in twelve days' time.

# CHAPTER 25

Belia eagerly awaited an opportunity to make a further expedition into the underground tunnels. On the evening that Freyna went to bed early with a headache and the other bull dancers began a noisy game of cards, she judged she could slip away quietly without her absence being noticed. She went to the lamp-room and crawled silently through the shaft, praying to the Earth Mother to keep the rats away. She crept past the dining-hall, where the men were drinking and then crawled silently on to the small dusty room. Here she lit her lantern. She carried a knife, candles and a flint lighter in a cloth bag attached to her belt.

Once more, tense with nervous excitement, she stood in the dark, draughty passage. Holding the lantern high, she saw that the walls on either side were solid and there was no immediate danger of becoming lost. She scratched a mark beside the opening and set off. She identified the place where her lamp had previously gone out. As she moved on, the passage began to curve to the right and seemed to become narrower. The lantern cast weird shadows all about her and she imagined the walls were closing in on her. The floor became uneven. She stubbed her toe painfully and cursed.

Fortunately, Belia paused for a moment, leaning against the wall. Looking down, she noticed that without warning the level of the passage dropped sharply. The possibility of falling had not occurred to her. It was a sobering thought and she moved on more slowly.

The passage was indeed becoming narrower and soon her shoulders touched the walls on either side of her. This was unpleasant and she began to feel a claustrophobic panic, an almost hysterical desire to turn back. In the dim light ahead, the passage ended in a block of masonry. It seemed that her expedition had failed. However, when she reached the obstruction, the narrow passage turned sharply, almost at right angles. It widened a little and once more the floor level sloped downwards.

The solid stone walls ended abruptly. The whole character of the Labyrinth had changed. It appeared to be the ruin of a house filled with rubble and Belia could no longer walk upright. Doorways tilted at crazy angles choked with dust and debris. The air smelled damp and musty. She dreaded to become lost and tore strips off her cotton jacket to mark the way. She raised her lantern and saw a fragment of mural depicting reeds and field flowers and felt sadness at this relic of a once-happy home.

Belia longed for the daylight and the voices of the living. Something gleamed in the dust. She bent down and picked up a china vase, perfect but for a broken lip; the beautiful design of tall tiger lilies and brilliant colours fascinated her. She began to lose heart. It seemed a waste of time and effort to try and penetrate this labyrinth of ruins. Holding her lamp high, she pushed through a shattered doorway and with great difficulty crawled on, moving bricks and china shards aside. Suddenly she froze in terror — a face glared at her! But then she laughed with relief. It was a painting of a young man and it was wedged in a window frame. The portrait had curiously remained undamaged though the building it once graced was gone. Belia touched the features gently — a handsome young face — the son of the house, perhaps?

She crawled a short distance and was confronted by a huge beam which had fallen diagonally and blocked further progress. Belia sighed in frustration believing she must now abandon her search. However, she observed that though rubble was crushed beneath the beam, above it the debris was more loosely packed. She reached up and removed a length of timber. Then some rubble clattered down, leaving a space large enough to peer through. To her surprise, she looked down on a narrow passage running at right angles about six feet below her. She cleared more rubble and was soon able to climb down.

The lower passage was smooth, level and free of obstruction. Leading off into the darkness, it appeared to have been recently cleared. The sides of the passage were of stone, part of the foundations of an ancient building.

Belia was beginning to tire and was concerned that she would be missed. She hesitated, uncertain what to do. On her left a large stone offered a place to rest and she sat down. As she placed the lantern on the ground, she saw a length of cord half buried in the dust. When she lifted it, she was surprised to find that it ran some distance into the darkness to her left and apparently further still in the opposite direction.

Intrigued, she stood up, removed her red headband, which she had worn at vaulting practice, and used it to mark the place where she had climbed down. Then, grasping the lantern in one hand and the cord in the other, she followed the passage to her left. It wound this way and that, dividing several times and without the cord she would have become completely lost. Intensely curious and excited, she forgot time and caution and hurried on.

A tunnel led off on her right. She passed it then stopped and quickly retraced her steps. She believed she had seen a flicker of light. She listened intently, ready to flee but then saw the light again. It was faint and stationary.

Placing the lantern on the ground beside the linen cord, she lit a candle from the lamp flame. Shielding the light with her hand, Belia crept down the side passage. It was soon blocked by a low wall. She heard the murmur of voices and waited, her heart pounding.

Two people were arguing. She listened and was startled to hear a name mentioned — Micalidos! She recalled the visit to Phylon's workshop. Micalidos was the name of the man who had shared his lunch with her — Councillor Micalidos. His charm and friendliness had impressed her.

She placed her candle close to the ground and standing on tiptoe, slowly raised her head above the wall. Some distance away, two people were seated facing each other across a table. The man wore a broad collar of beaten copper, which reflected an occasional flash of orange light from the lamp on the table before him. He leaned against a stone pillar, with his hands cushioning the back of his head. Opposite him sat a dark-haired woman, leaning forward with her elbows on the table. She was speaking with quiet intensity.

"There must be a market for them somewhere — the gems are large and perfect."

"That's what I mean, woman. Even if the necklace was broken up, they'd be recognized. Those jewels can't be sold in Crete."

"They would sell in Egypt or Troy. There's always a market there."

"Who's going to take them there — you?"

"Of course not. I wouldn't know how to set about it. You have contacts, you could arrange it."

"I can't," the man snapped angrily, "I'm watched and I can't take any more boys, not until things quieten down. Selling those kids in Libya was a real money-spinner. That project is ruined, now, thanks to that son of a whore, Antonius Micalidos and his half-witted uncle."

The voice was cold and sinister.

"Well," the woman replied, "if you dislike the Micalidos family so much, you should be pleased that I brought his son, Timon, for Eburninos. We keep the pretty ones for Minos. The Councillor was very fond of that child."

The man leaned forward, his face close to hers. "Have you considered, Madam, what Micalidos will do to get the boy back?"

"What can he do?" she replied scornfully.

"He'll suspect me, for a start."

"You could accuse Zanthope," the woman said tartly, "she was furious because Timon is to share the inheritance with Antonius. They certainly have a motive for getting rid of the boy."

"Maybe so," Agidor replied thoughtfully, "but that won't stop Micalidos from tearing this city apart to find him, and he's got the King's ear. If Minos orders it —"

"But he won't, my friend," she interrupted, "because by that time he will have ..." she dropped her voice and Belia was unable to hear what was said, "and afterwards," the woman raised her voice and sitting back, she stretched and ran her fingers through her long, dark hair.

"Afterwards?" Agidor snapped.

"Eburninos knows what to do. The boy will never leave the Palace alive."

"Pity it wasn't Antonius. We'll have to think of something very special for him." The venom in Agidor's voice made Belia shiver. Who were these people plotting evil against the Councillor and his family? The woman spoke again with finality.

"Find me a market for the necklace. What about the merchant Senthios? I want an apartment in the Palace. He could fix that, couldn't he?"

"How will you live there without money?"

"I can live on my wits," the woman laughed. "I've had plenty of practice," she added bitterly. "I want to hear from you soon, Agidor."

She picked up the lantern and Belia heard them leave the room together. Exhausted and confused she returned to the main passage. Who were these people, Agidor and the dark woman? Who was Timon and where was he hidden in the Palace? The Labyrinth had revealed a sinister character.

But next time, she said to herself with determination, I shall find out where this cord leads.

The way back to the Bull Halls seemed interminable. When she crept into the dormitory, the lights were out and everyone was asleep, except Freyna.

"Where've you been? I've been so worried," she whispered.

"I'll tell you," Belia said, unrolling her bedding, which Freyna had arranged to conceal her friend's absence. Belia told her amazing story as briefly as possible. Freyna was astonished and gripped Belia's arm in excitement.

"If those people were there, there must be a way in and out!"

"Obviously."

"And that cord must lead somewhere. Bee, do you think we should tell Leander?"

"You seem very sure that he feels as you do."

"I just know he loves me," Freyna said quietly.

"Well, I hope you're right," Belia replied, yawning, "I'm very tired. I must go to sleep. Good night, Freyna."

Belia stretched out and was asleep almost at once. Freyna, too, lay down and thinking of Belia's wonderful news, soon fell asleep.

She dreamed she was walking in a lemon grove with Leander, arms entwined, with the scent of lemon blossoms heavy in the air. Then they were sailing in a boat, far away over the Great Green Sea. The boat was full of people who were friendly and hopeful. She kept looking for Belia. She knew in her dream that her friend was there, but she could not see her. She awoke, feeling uneasy. Belia lay beside her, warm and safe. Reassured, she relaxed and sank once more into peaceful slumber.

When the Court returned to Knossos after the summer break, Chancellor Darian was angry and frustrated. He had wasted days in the Summer Palace waiting on the King's pleasure. His Majesty however, was in no mood for business. He had spent most of his time listening to the Princess playing her lute, challenging his courtiers on the new gaming board and riding his favourite horse.

Darian then consulted the High Priests, who couldn't agree among themselves about the ceremonies for the Days of Sacrifice. Uncertainty pervaded the air. It began in the Council Chamber, spread through the offices and apartments to the great Courtyard, fed by rumour and conflicting opinions until everyone felt anxious and vaguely uneasy.

Uncertainty even penetrated the barred doors of the Bull Halls. The instructors, accustomed to a month's lay-by, were faced with a further twelve days of inactivity. They were expected to attend religious ceremonies, yet the dates for these had not been announced. The priests and priestesses who instructed the students were absent on duties in the West Palace, so their advice was unavailable.

The Bull Dancers were unexpectedly free from the rigorous supervision to which they were accustomed and Belia grasped this opportunity.

"Freyna," she said, "now would be a good time to speak to Leander. I'm going down into the tunnels again."

"You must be careful, Belia," Freyna was afraid for her friend, "should I go with you?"

"No," Belia said, "I need you to answer for me in case I'm missed. You must speak to Leander today. It may be the last practice session we have with the seniors present."

Their dormitory mistress, Vanna, had advised them to pray and meditate.

"Your dedication to the Earth Mother is a serious matter. It is not to be entered into with sensual thoughts or a frivolous mind." She fixed them with her hawk-like glance. Freyna feared for a moment that Vanna had discovered her secret.

She was nervous at the thought of approaching Leander, but it was Belia who found the opportunity. During a short break at practice, he and Paulius had given an impromptu display of vaulting. The trainers enjoyed it as much as the dancers and relaxed their vigilance. In his final leap, Leander landed close to Belia. During the applause which followed, she sized the opportunity.

"Freyna wishes to speak with you, Leander," she whispered.

He flushed, betraying his feelings.

"In the lamp-room after practice," she said, moving quickly away. When she told Freyna, her friend's eyes lit up with pleasure.

"But what shall we do about Vanna?" she said.

"Don't worry, we'll take our lamps to the lamp-room for oil, as we always do. When Leander comes, I'll keep watch outside."

They had cooled off in the baths after practice and Freyna began to brush her long, blonde hair.

"Don't spend too long making yourself beautiful, or he'll think you're not coming and go away," Belia said.

Freyna was in a panic. "There's no time to plait my hair, and look at my clothes, Bee!" Freyna had only faded cotton shorts.

"Wait here," Belia said and ran off. She returned a few minutes later with a green silk skirt, a white cotton jacket and a long, blue scarf.

"Here, I told M'boola we were play-acting and needed some props."

"Thank you, Bee," Freyna said, delighted.

She used the scarf as a belt, letting the ends trail across the skirt and combed her hair over one shoulder, revealing the graceful line of her face and throat.

"You look stunning!" Belia said. "Come on."

They went together to the lamp-room. Leander was waiting there. The lovers' eyes met and they said nothing but stared intently at each other. Belia left them together, closed the door and took up her post.

Freyna stood quite still and watched Leander as he walked slowly towards her. She held out her hands to him and her eyes told him of her love without the need for words. They embraced, shyly at first and then passionately.

"You don't know how many times I've wanted to do that," he said.

"I too," she murmured.

Leander kissed her again, on her eyes, her neck, her breast. Then, suddenly, with an effort, he drew away and held her at arm's length.

"What is it?" she asked.

"We must be sensible," he said quietly.

"Don't you love me?" she asked and her eyes expressed doubt and sadness.

"Of course I love you," Leander said eagerly, "of course I want you! How can you doubt it?"

Freyna would have yielded to him without question, without thought of the consequences. It made this first meeting more difficult. While Leander had loved her in secret, it was the thought of the trouble his passion might cause which gave him the strength to conceal it. Now, her childlike innocence filled him with tenderness and weakened his resolve. He kissed her again and held her close. Then he went on, his voice tense with emotion.

"These Cretans are merciless — we are their puppets. Don't be misled by their applause," his voice became hard and bitter, "they only approve of us while we entertain them."

"Have you thought of escaping, Leander?"

"How can we escape?" He held up his arm with the bull dancer's identity bracelet locked to his wrist.

"We would need friends outside, food, money, a ship. It's a vain hope, Freyna, forget it!"

Then she told him of Belia's discoveries and showed him the grating behind the cupboard.

"Has she found a way out of the Palace?"

"Not yet, but she will, I know she will."

He bent down and inspected the grating and the narrow shaft.

"No good for me, I doubt even if your shoulders would pass through there. She must be very slim."

"She is. What can we do?" Freyna asked despairingly.

"I hoped that when I finish, in a year's time, I could help you to escape."

"A year is a long time," she said sadly.

They stood in silence. There was nothing to say. They were roused by Belia's warning voice at the door.

"I must go," he said.

"You'll come again?"

"Of course."

"Soon ... soon!"

They embraced once more and he went quickly from the room. Belia came in at once.

"Sorry to interrupt. I heard Vanna nearby. You look sad, what's the matter?"

"Leander says we cannot escape without money, friends outside and a ship," Freyna replied. "I'm still a virgin."

"Poor thing, what a disaster," Belia said, laughing. Freyna laughed too.

"But I was right — he *does* love me!"

"Hush. Come on, let's go."

They took their lamps and returned to the quarters.

Later that evening, when they returned the borrowed clothes to M'boola, she offered them a glass of wine. She was sitting on her bed, her broad shoulders and her fine head, with its mass of black hair, leaning comfortably against large, green cushions.

"Sit down, dears," she said affably, with an expansive gesture. She had been giving the new Libyan girl, Shahali, a language lesson. Chloe, a fourth-year dancer, occupied the bed next to M'boola. Chloe was a slender, gazelle-like girl from the Phoenician coast and had been catcher for M'boola for two years. Opposite, on a bed resplendent with a red and blue coverlet, sat Asteria. She was combing her thick auburn hair, teasing the ends around her finger to form ringlets. Glancing coldly at Belia and Freyna, she accepted M'boola's offer of wine as though she were conferring a favour.

"How was the play-acting?" M'boola drawled, as they sipped their wine. She grinned and raised one eyebrow. Freyna blushed. Belia replied that the play had gone well, just as they had planned it.

"What play is this?" Asteria said sharply. "When shall we see it?"

"Not just yet," Belia replied, "we still have a few lines to tidy up."

She changed the subject quickly by asking M'boola how Shahali was getting on with her language lessons.

"She's learning slowly," M'boola replied.

Shahali sat up straight and said with a thick accent, "Goo morning, how do you been, goo nigh."

"Good ... good night," M'boola shouted, opening her large mouth and demonstrating the "t" and "d" with her tongue to Shahali at the end of the words. They all joined in, except Asteria, laughing and clicking their tongues. When the laughter subsided, Chloe asked, "Are you both prepared for your dedication?"

The air seemed suddenly chill.

"As much as we ever will be," Belia replied.

"What happens at the ceremony?" Freyna asked nervously.

"Nothing much," Chloe answered. "Just prayers and more prayers and then you all recite the oath —"

"And the priest marks you with the sacrificial blood," M'boola broke in, "on the forehead, the breast and the hands —"

"And then a few more prayers and that's it," Chloe finished, "nothing to worry about."

"That comes later," Freyna said in a low voice.

"You'll be all right," M'boola assured them cheerfully, "you won't have much to do in the first few weeks."

They drank their wine in silence. It had occurred to Belia that although the dancers were well trained in acrobatic skills, they were not so well informed about the behaviour of the bulls. Nor did they have much opportunity to discuss this with senior dancers. Novices spoke when spoken to and this was seldom. Belia wondered sometimes if there was a sinister reason for this lack of information.

The popular success of the Bull Dance was due mainly to the exploits of leading dancers. It was inevitable the God should have a victim now and then. For obvious reasons the trainers preferred to lose a beginner and the death of a well loved and admired dancer was a cause for great public grief. The death of a novice was soon forgotten.

The wine and M'boola's jovial mood encouraged Belia. She began hesitantly. "M'boola, you, Asteria and Chloe have had so much experience. Tell us, truly, what to expect in the ring? How do you know what the bull is going to do? Why are some bulls easier to handle than others?" Belia blushed, self-conscious for once at asking these questions. M'boola raised her eyebrows and rolled her dark eyes. She stared at the five dancers, so diverse in colour and features.

"Look, the bulls vary as much as we do," she said, "they vary in colour, size, speed, stamina; in the length of their horns, in their intelligence and, of course, in age. Now, a young bull of, say, three-years-old, may look very large and powerful, but he is not yet fully-grown. He lacks the staying power of a four-year-old. And the wisdom. Bulls, like people, learn from experience, and the smarter they are, the quicker they learn. This makes the old ones much more dangerous. Some bulls are cowards! They put on a great show to intimidate you, pawing the ground, bellowing, sweeping the air with their horns, but you can never be sure what they will do, whether they will charge or not. You must be alert all the time — and never get near the side of the head — a blow from the flat of the horn can be fatal. Not at once though, but later, because the wound bleeds inside. You must remember always that the bull is fast and very strong. He can turn on the spot like a mountain cat — and he can throw a grown man across the ring easier than you would throw an apple core! And you must never forget that a bull can be 'left-horned' or 'right-horned', as a man is left- or right-handed. He often twitches the ear on the side of the favoured horn. Now the most important thing to remember is that a very brave bull makes no threats, he just fixes the eye on the one he marks, twitches the ear and charges like a thunderbolt!"

M'boola, eager to be helpful, had forgotten the sensibilities of her listeners. Asteria was secretly terrified; Chloe, though brave and steady in the ring, was always sick with nervousness before facing the bull; Belia and Freyna were spellbound and the latter horror-struck at this sudden flood of information. They were all silent for a moment. Then, Belia whistled softly, licked her lips and said quietly, "Holy Zeus! There's a lot to learn."

Freyna stared gloomily. M'boola sensed she may have said too much. She tried to make amends.

"Fill up your cups," she boomed, pouring the wine, "don't worry, all will go well. Look at us," she pointed to Asteria, now manicuring her nails, "five years and we're still leading dancers!"

"Don't boast," Asteria said, "don't tempt fate!"

"I'm not boasting, I'm just stating a fact."

"Thank you, M'boola," Freyna said. She realized they could only accept whatever lay ahead. Changing the subject abruptly, Chloe asked, "M'boola, what will you do when you retire?"

The Libyan's dark eyes flashed with anticipation and pleasure.

"I'm going back to Africa to invest my money in a circus."

"A circus?"

"Yes, can't you see me?" M'boola said, flinging her arms wide, as though she were already greeting her audience. "I shall have lions, elephants, horses, camels ... acrobats and jugglers and a band of musicians to parade through the streets!"

"Oh! M'boola," Belia said laughing, "I can just see you as a lion tamer in a wonderful spangled costume!"

"Yes indeed. I shall take my circus on the road through Libya and into Egypt, we might even go to Babylon. You and Ali could join me, Chloe, when you retire next year."

"Maybe I'll just get married and have a baby," Chloe said with a smile.

"You lucky thing, with only one more year to serve," Freyna said, "we have five years to face. It seems like a lifetime."

It was late. The wine was finished. Belia knew they should say good night, but there was still one question that troubled her.

"Tell me," she said, "do you know of anyone here who got —" she made the shape of a big belly with her hands, "with child?"

There was a moment's silence. "I only heard tell of it. M'boola, do you remember a girl who finished the year I came? Drusa or Drusilla, I think her name was," Chloe answered.

"No. I don't remember her."

"Well, anyway, I heard Drusa speak of someone in *her* first year, well, that's going back nine years."

"What happened?" Freyna asked.

"She just disappeared," Chloe replied.

"Was nothing said?" Belia inquired.

"The girl was taken away in the night, and she was crying. Later, when someone asked for her, Vanna said there was no such person."

"I wonder what happened to her," Freyna said quietly.

"The punishment is death," Asteria's voice was hard, cold and final. With this sobering thought playing on their minds they thanked M'boola for her hospitality and went to bed.

# CHAPTER 26

The news that Antonius Micalidos had joined the Palace Guard delighted Leda Brecchius. Marriage seemed unlikely after she learned he did not love her, but she still hoped that somehow a miracle would happen.

Now she had bad news. Her father returned from boar-hunting on Councillor Markos' estate with an arrangement for her to marry the Navy Minister's son. Her mother was pleased, and, as she could not see any special qualities to recommend her second daughter, she told Leda she was a very lucky girl.

Both parents were surprised when Leda showed neither eagerness nor gratitude. She pleaded against the match. Her father raged and bullied, her mother nagged and cajoled.

Leda would have agreed if she could have liked and respected the young man. But she knew Vaden Markos was a dissolute and swaggering braggart.

However, as her father was determined, the family arrangements went ahead.

"I don't know what's got into her," Madam Brecchius complained to Chryssa, who had returned from Silamos with her father. (She had left Mallia shortly after Senka and Antonius had departed.) "He's rich and handsome," her mother continued, "what more could she want?"

"Don't you know, Mother," Chryssa said in a bored voice, "she's mooning after Antonius Micalidos."

"Oh," Madam Brecchius said, surprised, "why didn't you say so before?" They were seated by the light well in Madam Brecchius' garden court. Chryssa was trying out a new hair style and her mother was holding the mirror.

"Higher, please Mother," she said impatiently. "There was no point in telling you. She's not Antonius' type — too dull. He likes someone more lively."

"Like you, you mean?"

"Perhaps. He's dining with us tonight. My dear Dino is delighted that he has enrolled in his company. They've been friends for so long."

"Yes, of course," Chryssa's mother went on slowly and thoughtfully. "I might speak to your father. Councillor Micalidos is a Minister. It would be a good marriage and I do want Leda to be happy."

"My dear Mother." Chryssa paused to adjust a strand of hair. "Father hasn't spoken to Councillor Micalidos for months, not since you dined at the villa in the early summer. They've quarrelled. Something about his interference in the shipyards. Besides, haven't you heard the rumours?"

"What do you mean, what rumours?" Madam Brecchius' eyes narrowed.

"They've lost all their money," Chryssa said and carefully arranged a curl on her left temple, "you wouldn't want Leda marrying into a family of paupers?"

"Oh! dear me, no indeed!"

The charm of Chryssa's elegant apartment was enhanced by walls decorated with panels of white lilies on a dark red background and woven rugs in red, black and white which were scattered over the floor tiles. Expensive ornaments and vases, a bronze statuette of a bull dancer and a small ebony cabinet, inlaid with lapis and pearl shell, gifts from Papa Senthios, added to the atmosphere of sophistication. Her gown matched the amethyst and crystal necklace which sparkled between her breasts and the flounced skirt shimmered when she moved. Gazing across the room at her, Captain Senthios felt, as always, amazement at his good fortune in marrying a woman as beautiful and gifted as his Chryssa. Tonight, Senthios was in genial mood. The enlargement of the Palace Guard had increased his responsibilities. Life seemed especially good at present. The room was rapidly filling with guests and his reverie was disturbed by the arrival of Antonius and Senka. He greeted them cordially.

"Have the singers arrived yet?" Senka asked.

At that moment two sophisticated young women entered, followed by two foppish young men, whose curls and love-locks glistened with pomade. Their host welcomed them.

"Good evening, Lieutenants and my dear Alida and Serina. You all know my guests Cadet Micalidos and Sharim Senakor."

Alida darted forward and slipped her arm through Senka's. "Are you to accompany us this evening, Senka?" she asked.

"Of course," he replied, "I hope you're both in good voice."

"Indeed we are, never better," Serina assured him.

"Come and tell me your programme."

Senka led them away across the salon. Antonius smiled and remarked that Senka would be in his element with music and two admiring young women.

Senthios agreed and then said in a sincere and serious way, "Only a few more weeks, my dear Antonius, and I shall be able to welcome you as a brother officer."

"Thank you, Dino. I should like to do a stint in the provinces, when I get my commission," Antonius replied, "you could fix that for me?"

Senthios was surprised. "Don't be ridiculous. I need you here, Antonius. I must have someone I can trust, particularly at the North Gate." The Captain nodded towards the effeminate young men who had come with the singers and lowered his voice.

"Too many like these — great fellows to drink with but no talent for command. Why do you want to bury yourself in the provinces?"

"I'm no soldier. I need to toughen up."

At that moment, Senka struck a chord on his lyre and the hubbub of conversation subsided. Alida announced their first song, a duet entitled "Spring in the Mountains".

"Don't think of leaving Knossos, Antonius," the Captain said earnestly once they were seated.

The voices blended perfectly, the programme was excellent and the applause generous. Senka had tried to excuse himself when Antonius brought the invitation, claiming he always read for Councillor Micalidos in the evening. Chryssa was the last person he wanted to see. But Andreas was in an amiable mood and patted his secretary on the back.

"Go out and enjoy yourself, my boy. Have an evening off, you've earned it."

Senka had to go. The applause and the wine now gave him a feeling of well-being. He began to enjoy himself. But he was not to be let off so easily. Chryssa played the perfect hostess, charming each of her guests in turn. When an opportunity came, she drew Senka aside, her dark eyes hard and resolute.

"I wanted you here for a special reason."

"For the music?"

"No." She smiled as though they were making small talk. "You made a bargain with me. You've not kept it. Bring me that necklace or..."

"Or what?" he said contemptuously. She kept smiling sweetly.

"I have some information. Something you would prefer not to be made public." Senka was uneasy.

"I shall need to order some new shoes for the coming season. Can you recommend a good shoemaker?" she said and laughed. He pretended not to understand, but she went on softly, "You always told us your father was a Colonel. How Knossos will laugh when they know he mends shoes!"

Anger exploded in him and he gripped her wrist. She kept quite still.

"How did you find out, you bitch!" he growled, his voice choked with fury.

"Servants have boy friends who wait at table in cheap wine shops. Really, Senka, you should have taken your father to a better place." She broke free from his grasp.

"You have one week," she hissed.

"Zanthope's still at Mallia, I can't," he said desperately.

"Well, maybe that can wait," she replied calmly, "bring me something else." He was relieved. He looked about the room, hoping no one had noticed his momentary loss of control.

"What is it you want now?"

"Let me have copies of all the letters you carry for Micalidos," she said and moved abruptly across the room to farewell some guests who were leaving. Senka stared after her. He could not comprehend this new demand. By the Gods, he thought, I'd clear out, if only I had some money.

More guests were leaving. He found Antonius at his elbow.

"I'm meeting Brachne and his friend Zarkos at the Green Cat — like to come?" Antonius asked.

"I'm broke," Senka replied.

"So am I," Antonius said and took his arm. "What were you and Chryssa arguing about?" The question seemed casual but the grip on his arm was not.

"She wants me to play at parties for her friends. I'm not a slave!"

"Good for you," Antonius laughed.

They bid their host and hostess good night and set off. When they arrived at the Green Cat, Antonius' friends were waiting. Brachne welcomed them and called for more wine. The tavern had a clientele of Palace craftsmen, local traders and many young artists and writers not yet successful enough to afford the prices at Klonka's. They came to drink, discuss their work, their money problems and the unpredictability of patrons. Brachne and Zarkos were less frequent visitors since fame and success had come their way.

From the wall above the wide fireplace, a mosaic depicting a large green cat winked a malevolent yellow eye at the company. The tables were of scrubbed wood, the floor of stone blocks.

"This place isn't bad — cheaper than Klonka's," Brachne remarked.

"When does the club reopen? He'll lose custom if he doesn't look out," Antonius commented, drinking his wine.

"Klonka's having a gala evening on the opening night of the Bull Dance season. I hear he has some special new attraction," Zarkos said.

"A two-headed monkey, perhaps," Senka suggested, amidst laughter.

"How was the party?" Brachne inquired, "Madam Chryssa in good form?" A curious silence followed. Senka said nothing. "Chryssa'll never change," Antonius said after a moment with a shrug.

He looked about him in a conspiratorial way. A small group of men were drinking and arguing near the door, otherwise the tavern was empty.

Nailed in a prominent place a large notice offered a reward for the capture alive of two escaped slaves named Arkos and Tyra; their description followed with the name of their owner — Doxa Grinkos. Antonius directed Brachne's attention to the notice. "Do you see that? I know where they are. We need help to get them out of Knossos," Antonius said in a lowered voice.

Brachne whistled softly. "Antonius, what are you getting mixed up in?"

Antonius related in some detail the story Ahmed had told him of Doxa's cruelty and the lovers' escape.

"So, you see," he went on, "we must get them out of Knossos. My idea is to dress them as peasants and hide them in our cart — the one that brings vegetables from the farm. But the problem is where to hide them."

Brachne stared thoughtfully into his wine-cup.

"I have some clothing — cloaks and jackets — you're welcome to them," Zarkos said quietly.

Brachne drained his glass and looked across the table at Antonius. "I might be able to help you," he paused and held out his wine-cup for Zarkos to refill.

Antonius listened intently.

"Do you remember the dancer who performed at the house-warming party at Mallia?"

"Yes — Olykka, a fine dancer. Why doesn't she perform in Knossos?" Antonius said enthusiastically.

"She won't come," Brachne replied, "she doesn't care about money. She's studying to be a priestess at the shrine in Mallia." For Brachne the conversation had become a confession. He did not find it easy. "Olykka is my half-sister. Her mother was a peasant my father lived with before he married. After mother died, Olykka came to live at the farm. I resented her but she was always kind. I'll get a message to my sister. She hates slavery and I'm sure she'll help you."

"Thank you, Brachne. Senka will take a letter," Antonius said.

"If Councillor Micalidos does not object," Senka replied, annoyed to be used as a messenger.

"Of course my father won't object. He'll be thankful to have them away from the surgery."

"He hasn't been told about them yet. What excuse can I make for riding to Mallia?" Senka persisted.

"You'll think of something," Antonius replied, "you've never been short of an excuse before."

Presently two young officers came in and, seeing Antonius, greeted him, and joined the group at the table. One, Lieutenant Sartis, a loutish young man whom Antonius disliked, suggested cards. The other officer was enthusiastic. He and Sartis made a practice of playing together and cheating.

They all agreed to play but after an hour Antonius lost far more than he could afford. He was forced to write an I.O.U. which Sartis accepted off-handedly. "It's not so easy when you're short of cash, is it?" Senka whispered maliciously.

Antonius disguised his anger, excused himself and walked back to the barracks alone. The game broke up and Brachne and Zarkos said good night and went home.

Senka stayed with the two officers, finishing the wine. Lieutenant Sartis walked over to the notice on the wall and read it.

"Phew!" he said, "some reward. Seen any escaped slaves lately?"

He gave an unpleasant laugh and returned to the table. He took Antonius' I.O.U. out of his pocket.

"Will he pay up?" he eyed Senka coldly.

"Why shouldn't he?"

"I heard there was money trouble."

Senka shrugged. He went to the notice and studied it thoughtfully.

"Know where they are?" Sartis asked.

"I wouldn't tell you if I did."

"What's so special about these two? Why so much?"

"I don't know. She's a vindictive woman, Doxa Grinkos. Well, it's late. I'm off. Good night."

Senka left the Green Cat and walked slowly home, his footsteps echoing in the quiet streets. It was indeed late, even the chair carriers had despaired of custom and had gone home. Senka considered the reward money for the slaves. He did not relish the idea of betraying them, however, he reasoned, they were bound to be caught. He desperately needed money to leave the city and escape from Chryssa. Why did she want copies of Andreas' letters? If I tell Doxa her slaves are in the surgery, they'll be arrested there and Councillor Micalidos will be involved, he thought to himself. Antonius will suspect me and I'll lose my job. Then, if that mean bitch Doxa doesn't pay up, I'll be in real trouble.

He considered these things but reached no conclusion.

When he entered the house, he ascended quietly by the back stairway and, crossing the hall, noticed a light under the doorway of Zanthope's room. He tapped lightly and heard her voice bid him enter. She lay on the bed, gazing into a small hand mirror.

"Come here, you monster," she said softly, "why did you desert me in Mallia?"

He sat beside her. She stroked the back of this head and ran her hands across his shoulders. Then she lightly touched his forehead with her fingertips.

"Why so worried? Have you missed me?"

"Of course."

She smiled the smile he knew so well and drew him close to her. This was the first time they had made love at the villa. He was afraid of being discovered and realized that this added spice to an act which for him had become rather tedious.

When Zanthope was satisfied, she soon fell asleep. The jewel casket was, as always, beside her bed. Summoning all his courage, Senka felt under her pillow and found a key. He unlocked the casket and saw, to his consternation, that the ruby necklace was gone! Quickly relocking it and replacing the key, he went quietly to his own room.

# CHAPTER 27

Shortly after Freyna and Leander had their first meeting alone, Belia set off again into the Labyrinth with the single aim of finding a way out of the Palace. She had vivid memories of being brought, under guard, from Amnissos to the North Gate. The great bas-relief of the charging bull had filled her with fear and excitement. The guards had hustled her past the sentries and down steep stairs to the empty Bull Ring, then through a narrow door into the Bull Halls. There was no escape route there. The trainers' quarters were close by and the outer door was always locked and barred.

Freyna accompanied Belia to the lamp-room, to replace the cupboard over the grating. Staff coming for lamp oil would not be suspicious.

"We should have thought of that before," Belia whispered, checking her oil-filled lantern, the flint lighter, candles and knife.

"Belia, take care," said her friend anxiously, "don't take any risks. How long will you be?"

"Some hours, probably," Belia said and crawled into the shaft.

"I'll pray for you, dearest friend," Freyna said.

Belia followed the route she had marked on the previous visit. She was considering which direction she should take in the passage which contained the mysterious cord. The left hand passage seemed to lead deeper under the Palace foundations. There was no rational proof of this, but instinct persuaded her that the right hand passage might lead eventually to the outside world. Having made that decision, the task seemed easier.

She climbed down, hung her headband on a piece of broken timber, searched in the dust and found the cord. Holding her lantern before her, she turned right and began to walk ahead carefully. The wall on the right had few breaks, but on the left there were many, most choked with debris. After walking some distance, she saw a passage which had obviously been cleared. Judging by the firm surface, the path must have been used quite frequently.

Curious, she paused, but then firmly held to her purpose and went on, following the cord. After a few yards, a huge mass of stonework jutted out. The path turned abruptly around it, almost at right angles. Further on, it turned again at right angles. The stonework of the wall was reminiscent of an ancient fortification. Although Belia did not know it, this was the foundation of the North Keep, the oldest part of the Palace of Knossos. The path continued on for some ten yards. At this point there was a break in the wall, where a dark archway led to a flight of spiral stairs. Stone steps led down from a small landing. Another flight led upwards into the darkness.

Belia was elated. The upper stairway could lead to a way out of the Labyrinth! However, to her great disappointment, the cord passed beyond the archway and continued in a left hand direction, winding off into the darkness. This time, Belia did not resist the impulse to investigate and dropping the cord, she carefully climbed the dusty stairs. The surface was worn and uneven and after spiralling a short distance, the steps ended abruptly at a solid wooden door. She pushed and pulled, but it was immovable, almost as if it had been bricked up on the other side. Disappointed again, she retraced her steps. The lower stairway did not seem to offer much chance of escape, but the temptation to explore was too strong.

She descended slowly. The air seemed to become colder. Moisture dripped from the walls and she shivered when she thought she heard a rat squeak. At the bottom of the stairway, she found a short passage leading off it, with several doorways on either side. The heavy doors had a spyhole cut near the top and were secured with large bronze bolts. Belia suspected these were probably prison cells.

Her first instinct was to leave this sinister place immediately. But she hesitated, still curious. The lantern light wavered in the silent darkness and it revealed that only two cells were locked, the rest were open and empty.

Placing the lantern on the ground, Belia withdrew the bolt from one of the locked cells and with some difficulty pulled open the heavy, creaking door.

Something was lying in the dust in the corner of the cell. She moved closer. It was a skeleton, the lantern light revealed the white skull with its dark, hollow eye sockets.

Belia shivered. The skeleton was small, hardly bigger than her own would be. It was not a fully-grown man, a youth, perhaps, or a woman. Gazing down at it, she was puzzled by the awkward position of the left arm. It was curved close to the body as though holding something. She knelt and brushed away the dust, which lay thickly over the bones. Then her fingers discovered the skull of a small baby. This had been a woman and her child. Belia shrank back in horror. Was this the young dancer that Chloe had spoken of? She saw now only too clearly the danger of Freyna's love for Leander. She pictured the desolation of that poor girl, alone in the dark with her baby, and said a brief prayer to the Earth Mother for their souls. She was about to leave when she noticed with surprise a small opening in the wall to the next cell. Holding the lantern up, she looked through but could see nothing. She left the place thankfully, but something made her pause and draw the bolts from the second door.

The lamplight revealed another skeleton beneath the wall opening. The remains of what appeared to be a tall man. She stifled a scream and ran from the cell and up the stairway. In her haste she missed her footing and fell. The lantern clattered down the stairs, spluttered and went out.

Belia felt sick. Her knees were bleeding and the strap of her sandal was broken. After a moment, she calmed herself and crawled about, searching for the lantern. It was broken. She felt the spilled oil on the stairs and swore. Now, she knew, the time for exploration was seriously reduced. Thankfully, she found a candle and flint in the bag attached to her belt and soon had light.

As she mended her sandal thong she recalled Asteria's gloomy words — "the punishment is death" — a horrible and lingering death. She felt rage and hatred for the heartless and cruel Cretan laws they were forced to obey. It was even more urgent, now, to find a way to escape.

She began to ascend the stairs carefully. When she reached the landing, she saw a glimmer of light, which flickered on the wall opposite the archway. Then she heard the sound of muffled footsteps. Quickly she put out her candle and shrank back in the shadows, her heart pounding with fear. As the light increased, she saw with astonishment the cord lift out of the dust! A man passed by, only three feet away, walking fast and confidently. Obviously the way was familiar. Belia nearly gasped aloud in astonishment — it was Theseus, the Greek bull dancer! She recognized his tawny hair and the set of his shoulders. As soon as he was out of sight, she picked up the cord and followed him, one hand against the wall. In this way she could walk without a light and not be discovered. Now and then, as the path straightened, his light bobbed in the darkness ahead. When he turned a corner, darkness returned, but the cord was her talisman, safe and secure.

It was a long path and many questions raced through her mind. How did Theseus enter the Labyrinth? There must be a way in from the Bull Halls, a way which Freyna and Leander could use. She had only to follow Theseus when he returned to discover it. Belia soon judged they were long past the point where she overheard the man and woman plotting against Councillor Micalidos.

Presently she saw another, brighter light ahead and heard a woman's voice, shrill, chiding, sobbing.

"How can you treat me like this, Theseus! After all these weeks, you don't know how I've suffered away in the Summer Palace, and it's so difficult for me to get here, even now. It's beyond bearing to be so humiliated." The woman sobbed violently. When she paused for breath, Theseus spoke. His voice was hard and impatient. "Stop your damn noise! I can't always get away when it suits me. I'm here now, isn't that enough?"

"I'm sorry. I've sat here alone for hours. I thought you would never come, my dearest love," the woman replied softly, her anger spent.

It seemed to Belia that now they must have embraced, for there was silence. She looked about her. The light came from a doorway a few feet down a side passage. The cord, attached to a spool, was wedged in a wall niche. Belia could not pass the lighted doorway. The main passage continued, no longer cleared of rubble. Not wishing to trip over some obstacle in the dark, she relit her candle and crept some way on.

The lovers' embrace, if indeed it took place, was brief. Belia soon heard the low murmur of voices again. There were several gaps in the wall, large enough to see into the room where Theseus and the unknown woman were talking. But Belia had no wish to spy on this bizarre love scene. She put her ear to the wall and heard Theseus speaking in a casual, offhand manner.

"Is that all you have to tell me? I might have saved myself the trouble of coming down here."

"How dare you!" the woman screamed "Did you come here only to know what Minos is planning? What a fool I am. Did you not come at all for me — for our love? After all this time, when I long for you day and night..."

"Ariadne, you know my feeling for you — I've shown you often enough." His voice was strong and vibrant. "And I know *you* — once we start lovemaking you'll forget everything else. Business first, dear Princess, and after that we can please ourselves."

Belia then looked into the room. She almost exclaimed aloud. Neither care nor money had been spared to make it beautifully luxurious. The walls were hung with strips of rose coloured silk mounted on batons. The dust and irregularity of the ceiling was concealed by a dark blue damask, fastened at the centre and draped to the corners, like the canopy of a tent. There was a large divan against the wall opposite, with cushions embroidered in bright colours and a covering of fleeces. On the floor were a number of fur rugs. The room was brightly lit with lanterns on brackets either side of the doorway and a bowl lamp, a wine jug and two silver goblets stood on a small table.

Theseus was sprawled comfortably across the divan, leaning back against the cushions. Princess Ariadne was seated in a high-backed chair, angled away from Belia. She could only see a slim hand on the chair arm, the fingers fidgeting restlessly, and a sandalled foot tapped impatiently on the floor.

"Well, what is it you want to know," the Princess asked in a low voice.

Theseus stretched and settled more comfortably. "You know what I want to know," he continued. "Is he going on the Pilgrimage? And have you told him of our marriage plans?"

"The answer to both is 'no'," she replied tersely.

Belia saw his face clearly. She noticed a stiffening of his jaw muscle, a tension around the eyes, but he stared stonily ahead and said nothing. The Princess continued, hysteria threatening as her speech gathered momentum.

"I don't think my brother wants to go on the Pilgrimage, not this year, not ever! Truly I think he'd go mad, shut up in that cave for a month. He hates the dark — he always has."

"You should offer to go with him."

"That isn't part of our plan! It's not my fault, Theseus — Eburninos and I almost had him persuaded. Andreas Micalidos ruined everything at the Council meeting. He influenced the King to stay in Knossos." She paused for a moment, then, as he remained silent, she went on.

"As for our marriage, truly Theseus, I tried to speak of it but there always seemed to be someone there, so many visitors, Princess Phaedre, that Egyptian woman and her sickly son ..."

"I've heard Queen Kara is very beautiful, very much in command of herself," he said at last, drawing out the words.

Stung by his tone, she went on quickly, her voice restrained.

"Whatever you may have heard, Theseus, I did my best for you." She paused again and, as he still said nothing, continued pleading, "Theseus, there's nothing I would not do for you. Why do you delight in tormenting me? You know how much I love you, how can you waste precious time in argument?" Without looking at her, he stretched out his right hand. "Come here," he said.

She rose from the chair and Belia saw Ariadne for the first time. She had a charming profile, the nose delicately tip-tilted, creamy skin and soft dark hair that gleamed as she moved across the room. She wore a crimson gown embroidered in gold and amethyst, laced tightly under her breasts. She went to him eagerly. In one swift movement he loosened his belt and removed his loincloth. Belia saw his nakedness, but she had no desire to witness their intimacy.

There was no choice but to wait and she sat down, hoping it would not be for too long. Leaning back against the wall, she placed her candle in a china shard and tried to relax. Ariadne sighed and moaned with pleasure. Belia felt pity for this beautiful Princess, for any woman enslaved to passion. She put her fingers in her ears and waited.

Time passed and still the lamps burned. Belia was exhausted and soon her eyelids became heavy. She fought against it, but finally, without realizing it, she dozed.

She awoke with a start. At first, she thought that only a few moments had passed. She was now in total darkness. When she reached for the candle, she found only a pool of wax. She had missed the opportunity to follow Theseus and Ariadne and reproached herself bitterly. Lighting the last candle, she began the return journey. She passed and recognized the now familiar landmarks, the stone where she had sat, the red headband hanging from the broken beam, as the candle-light wavered and flickered against the walls.

Soon she expected to pass the archway and shuddered at the memory of the dungeons. The candle was rapidly growing smaller and the hot wax burnt her fingers.

Suddenly she was stopped by a strange wailing cry. Trembling with fear, she cautiously moved forward and realized the sound had come from the narrow cleared path she had noted before. The sound came again, this time unmistakably a child's voice crying out, "No, no, don't, don't!".

The crying ceased as if a hand closed over a child's mouth. She recalled the dark woman's threat. "Eburninos knows what to do, Timon will never leave the Palace alive!"

She remembered, too, that the Princess had mentioned Eburninos ... and Andreas Micalidos! While these thoughts raced through her mind, she had dropped the cord and turned down the unknown passage from which had come the child's cry of despair.

To her dismay, the passage divided after a short distance. She foresaw the danger of becoming lost. Taking the left-hand fork, she went on, listening intently. Then she heard the sound of sibilant whispering, which seemed to come from everywhere and nowhere, indistinct, as though an echo was bounding from wall to wall. She remained in an agony of indecision, almost incapable of making a reasoned judgement. Holding up the candle, she made a mark halfway down it with her thumbnail. She decided that when it was burnt to that mark, she would turn back.

Presently, she descended four stone steps. Blocks of hand-hewn granite seemed to be massive stone walls but she soon realized they were in fact pillars surmounted by cross-beams of stone.

She paused to trace with her hand an incision in the stonework, the shape of an axe with a central haft and two heads lying flat on either side. The wavering candlelight illuminated the word "LABRYS". She wondered what the letters meant. Moving between the great pillars she came to another short flight of steps leading down to a crypt with a broad stone alter. An oil lamp stood on a shelf near the altar. A bit of luck, at last! Belia thought, lighting the lamp from her candle. The crypt was suddenly illuminated.

Then she noticed a dark stain at one end of the altar and bent to examine it more closely. A narrow groove in the stone ran down the side. The dark stain continued down this groove and disappeared into the ground.

Belia had seen sacrificial altars in many countries she had visited as a child. The sacrifice of doves, goats and bulls was not unusual. Yet who would bring animals for sacrifice down here in this dark and remote place?

At that moment she was terrified by the sudden booming of a man's deep voice. Although amplified by some trick of reverberation, the sound was distorted and meaningless.

She ran quickly up the steps of the crypt and darted behind a pillar, uncertain whether or not to douse her new found light. She had no idea from which direction the sound had come. Muffled footsteps approached and the voice was closer and more distinct. Lamplight flickered among the pillars. Belia quickly pinched the wick of her own light and moved into the shadows. Suddenly the light was very bright and she heard a voice.

"Is everything ready? Have you lit the lamp in the crypt?" a voice hissed.

"It's not there, master," another voice answered.

"Then fetch it, you fool!"

The footsteps retreated and Belia peered out. There was no one in sight. A bright light shone some distance down the passageway, making the darkness around her more intense. While she was staring down the passage, she was suddenly transfixed with horror. A low, muttering sound reverberated dully among the pillars. Then, silhouetted against the wall, she saw the shadow of the horns of a huge bull!

Stifling a scream, she ran desperately between the pillars, searching for the stairway. She found herself in another dark passage, certainly not the one by which she had entered the crypt. After a few moments, she crouched down in the darkness, trembling with shock and weariness, her heart thumping with terror. She longed to relight the lamp, but dared not. She waited tensely as minutes dragged by. Was a bull really pursuing her? But there was no sound, no pursuit. This was a nightmare. Who were these men? What strange rites were being enacted down here? She could find no answer but surely, for one thing, a bull would not be running loose in this Labyrinth.

Leaning back against the wall, she tried to be calm and rational. She had taken risks to come to this sinister place for one purpose only — to find a way out of the Palace. Everything which had occurred seemed to deflect her from her purpose. The conflicts, intrigues and threats she had overheard were of no concern to her. She had to get out of this place. Belia relit her lamp. Dreading to go back toward the crypt, she went on a short way, hoping she might find the main tunnel by this new route.

She was disappointed. The passage ended in a small, low room. Holding her lamp high, she inspected it. It was, apparently, a storeroom. A row of empty jars, about three feet high, stood along one wall. Others were placed on the other side of the room. She saw they were filled with sawdust, as though ready packed — or waiting to be unpacked. One jar stood alone in the centre of the room, beside it a heap of sawdust and a shovel. Belia wondered who would be packing merchandise here. There was nothing to pack and nothing had been unpacked.

She reflected, with some uneasiness, that the room was a dead end. If anyone followed her, she would be trapped. She realized she must return by the way she came.

Yet, those jars, filled to the brim with sawdust, intrigued her. It suggested something breakable, like china-ware. She had to satisfy her curiosity.

Belia put the lamp down and going over to one of the jars, delved into the sawdust with both hands. The next moment, her whole body stiffened. Unable, in her petrified state, to cry out, she groaned and fainted. She soon revived, but lay still with a cold sweat on her brow. Her stomach heaved and she vomited till her ribs ached and the tears ran from her eyes. Her fingers, searching in the sawdust, had closed on the small, cold feet of a dead child.

She counted the sawdust-filled urns — sixteen. Clenching her fists she beat the ground. What bloody fiends! What monsters! She saw the empty jars stacked along the wall, waiting for their gruesome cargo and felt weak with nausea and impotent rage.

A memory of Councillor Micalidos came to her — his kind, quizzical eyes, his friendliness and generosity in sharing his lunch with her. She gazed with renewed horror at the jars. Was his child, Timon, in one of these?

Then the solitary jar caught her eye, standing beside a pile of waiting sawdust.

"Holy Earth Mother! Sacred Zeus!" she uttered the words in a horrified whisper. Did the cry she had heard come from a child in its death agonies? Would he, or she, presently be carried lifeless to this empty urn?

Whatever the risk, she knew she must go back. She had to discover the secret of this terrible place. Perhaps the child, whoever he was, might still be alive. She got to her feet, fighting to overcome her nausea, and went back to the pillar crypt. It was still in darkness, the slave had apparently not found another lamp.

Belia took a few tentative steps down the passage from where she had seen the shadow of the bull's horns. It was dark and silent. Nervously, she returned to the steps above the crypt and stood for a moment, leaning against a pillar. Her head ached and she pressed her hand to her forehead. She was tempted to escape while there was still a chance.

Then, from within the crypt, she heard a whimpering sound. She moved quickly down the steps, and there on the floor was a small, skinny child. He was gagged and bound with ropes. Setting the lamp down, she reached for her knife to cut him loose. His eyes dilated with fear.

"I'm your friend — I want to help you," she reassured him. "We must go quickly before those men come back. Are you Timon Micalidos?"

He stared at her and nodded once. She cut the ropes which bound his legs and hands. When he was free, he pulled the gag from his mouth.

"Come quickly. Don't make a sound," she whispered.

Belia picked up the lamp and taking the child's hand, led him up the steps. He tried to follow her, but his legs were weak and he tripped. Wondering how long he had been tied up, she pulled him along behind her, desperately searching among the pillars for the steps by which she had first entered the crypt. To her relief she found them and moved as fast as she could down the narrow passage.

Timon's feet stumbled and dragging him after her, she continually urged him to hurry. I must find the cord quickly — then we'll be safe, she thought.

Although she was tired, she grew more confident with every step. At last they reached the main passage. She bent and felt in the dust for the cord. With a sigh of relief she found it.

"Come on, Timon, we'll be safe soon," she urged.

"I'm so tired," he murmured and leaned against her.

She put her arm around him to assist him to move faster. Looking anxiously ahead, she hoped at every bend to see the red headband, which indicated where they should climb out of the passage. No one will follow us there, she thought.

Belia was perspiring and breathing heavily. It was awkward holding the lamp and the cord and helping the tired boy. Suddenly her foot twisted on a rough patch and she nearly fell. She paused for a moment while the pain throbbed in her ankle. She must be careful, she thought to herself and slowed her pace.

"Don't worry, Timon, it won't be much further." But her optimism was cut short. From behind her came the sound of footsteps and angry, distorted voices. Looking back, she saw the flickering of another light. "Sacred Gods! What can we do?" she muttered.

She lurched on, searching desperately for a sight of the broken beam with the red headband hanging from it. The shouting grew louder, echoing violently as their pursuers came closer. Belia was gasping. If I fall, she thought, were finished!

She rounded a bend and way ahead, down a long straight stretch, she could just see the headband. But she realized they could never reach it. Her legs ached, as if they could no longer support her. Timon stumbled and nearly fell. There was one last hope — to find a place to hide.

Not far ahead was a narrow recess, partly blocked by debris. She pushed the boy into this and put out the lamp. They crouched down a few feet from the main passage. Placing her hand over Timon's mouth, the bull dancer and Andreas' son clung together in the darkness.

Two men hurried by, the first carrying a lantern, the second cursing and shouting at his heels.

"Incompetent fool! Why didn't you tie him up properly?" he snarled.

"But I did, master," wailed the other.

The sound of their footsteps soon died away. It was dark again and Belia quickly got to her feet.

"Come on, Timon, hurry. They may come back." She lifted him up. "Keep still. I'll light the lamp."

She tried, but the lamp would not light. In her haste to hide, it had tipped over and the oil was spilled. She threw it down in disgust. Holding Timon by the right hand, she began to walk with her other hand on the left-hand wall. She guessed the headband would be about thirty paces down the passage.

After twenty-five paces she reached up and felt for the headband, without success. Thirty-five paces, and she still had not found it. Each moment she dreaded to see their pursuers' light returning. On a count of forty paces, she was in despair. They had missed the headband in the dark — or worse, it was not there at all.

Then, she began to retrace her steps, feeling higher up on the wall.

"Merciful Gods be thanked!" Belia said fervently, the headband was found.

"Timon, you must climb through a gap in the wall here, and down a little way on the other side. Don't be afraid. I shall be behind you."

She supported him while he felt in the darkness for the opening in the broken wall. They heard footsteps again and the light came flickering back. The faint light did, in fact, aid Timon, for it revealed the place through which he had to climb. Belia pushed him, leapt up herself and quickly followed him. They lay in a breathless heap on the other side.

"Be quiet!" she whispered.

The murmur of voices grew near, then passed and faded away. Belia experienced a feeling of great relief, with an almost overpowering weariness, a desperate need to sleep. But she knew she must go on. There was still the maze of ruins to negotiate and the cloth markers she had placed earlier could not be seen in the dark.

Then, she remembered the small stump of candle she had nursed along the way to the pillar crypt, before she took the lamp from the altar! It was there, in the cloth bag with the flint lighter. She lit it immediately and led Timon through the Labyrinth of damaged rooms. The way seemed endless, but they reached the safety of the ventilator shaft just as the candle spluttered out.

Freyna found them there soon after. She had come many times in the night to listen for Belia's return. It was early morning now. Freyna was amazed to see Timon.

"Who is he?" she asked.

"This is Timon Micalidos — the Councillor's son. The man we met that day in Phylon's workshop, d'you remember?"

"Of course," Freyna said and stared at Timon.

"Where can we hide him from Vanna?" Belia asked wearily.

"Don't worry, Leander will help us," Freyna assured her, aware of Belia's exhaustion, "they have slave boys in the men's quarters. Usually a bit bigger than him." She gazed at the dishevelled boy. "Poor Timon, you must be hungry," she added.

"Me too," Belia said, "but I need to sleep."

"Stay here," Freyna suggested, "no one will come for oil before breakfast. I'll signal Leander to meet us here. Then you must tell me everything." She hurried away. Belia knew there was much that she would not tell her impressionable friend!

# CHAPTER 28

It was a perfect autumn day, warm and mild. Old Madam was on the terrace, resting on a couch, enjoying the soft breeze. Andreas was seated beside her. The old lady smiled at him, but her eyes were vacant.

"Why isn't Timon home for his tea, Andreas?"

"He'll be home soon, Mother."

Andreas sighed and took her hand in his.

"This autumn sunshine is very pleasant," he went on, trying to raise her spirits and lead her thoughts away from the child.

"The summer is gone now," she murmured, her voice trailing away on a note of finality.

It was true. Heavy cloudbanks drifted over the mountains and the nights were cooler. Almost every evening there was sheet lightning and distant thunder heralded the equinox. The threat of storms hung in the air as the city waited breathlessly for the autumn rains.

Andreas looked forward impatiently for the winter gales which would close the ports. He had been so occupied with affairs of state, with anxiety over his son's disappearance and his own recent illness, that he had had little opportunity to consider his personal life. He accepted that he was no longer a young man, but he was too honest not to have regrets. During the last week, with returning health, he had felt restless and depressed.

It was over three months now since he had been to Phylon's workshop to order the lamp brackets for Zanthope. He often recalled the two young bull dancers he had met there — especially Belia, with whom he had shared his lunch. He smiled ruefully when he remembered her blonde hair, her lithe figure and her youthful sense of fun. Perhaps I'm getting to the age when old men chase after young girls! I've committed many follies in my life, but to be infatuated with a bull dancer who is almost young enough to be my granddaughter, he thought gloomily, would be a great folly. And then, she was soon to be dedicated to five years' service to the Mother Goddess and virginity, and she might not survive that service.

Gently releasing his mother's hand, for she had fallen asleep, he sighed deeply. His sister, Korynna, came out on the terrace.

"Andreas, are you all right?" she asked. She was concerned for him. "I'm well, thank you, Korynna," he said with a smile.

"How is mother?"

"Much the same."

They gazed at the old lady, childlike in her sleep.

"Andreas ... I wonder if you could manage without me for half a day tomorrow, if it would not be inconvenient," Korynna said diffidently after a few moments.

"Of course we can, my dear, there's no need to ask."

"Thank you, Andreas, it's a very special opportunity. You know — or at least, I believe you know — that I'm honoured by the friendship of the High Priestess Sappena? Of the Shrine of the Dove Goddess in the Palace?"

Andreas did not know or care about High Priestesses, but he inclined his head politely.

"Well," Korynna continued, with nervous excitement, "she has invited me to witness a dedication ceremony at the shrine attached to the Bull Halls. Two bull girls and three bull boys, I understand, are to make their vows. I'm so looking forward to it. I've never seen this ceremony before."

His sister was a tall, angular woman, kind and generous. Andreas reflected that her interest in religion filled a life, that otherwise, widowed and childless, might have been bleak. She and Andreas had lived for years in the same house without ever really knowing each other. In their present troubles, she had been a real source of strength and comfort and he felt guilty because he had previously valued her so little. Now that he wanted to speak from the heart, he found it difficult.

"I ... er ... we're all very grateful for your help, Korynna, my dear. We couldn't have managed without you."

"Andreas, I'm so sorry this trouble has come to you," Korynna said, blushing. "But I've been glad to repay your kindness, since the death of my dear husband."

"Korynna, it's been a pleasure to have you here, and mother has always appreciated your companionship."

"Not more than we have both appreciated you, Andreas!" Korynna said sincerely.

He was embarrassed.

"My word, we're a mutual admiration society this morning!" he quipped, "go along to your ceremony tomorrow and enjoy it."

Old Senthios, the merchant, reclined on a large, red, silk-covered sofa in his apartment in the East Palace, drinking wine leisurely from a silver goblet. Papa Senthios was a huge man, with iron-grey hair and thick eyebrows. Had he not been so grossly fat, he might have been considered handsome. He had fine eyes, almond shaped, the iris black as polished obsidian, but without variation of expression. His countenance was hard and unyielding. He seldom smiled. He was watching his daughter-in-law, Chryssa, with a steady gaze which she found disconcerting. However, she returned his gaze with equal candour, sipped her wine and remarked on its excellence.

"I thought you would like it," Senthios said, without shifting his gaze, "I chose it especially for today." He spoke with meaningful emphasis.

"What's so special about today?" she asked with raised eyebrows.

"That depends on you."

She did not reply and dropped her gaze as she placed her wine-cup on a small table by the couch. She was dressed in a quiet colour, a flounced skirt in shades of dark blue, with a long-sleeved jacket heavily embroidered in silver thread, laced beneath her breasts. She wore a tight silver belt and around her neck, a silver chain with a blue, enamelled pendant. The dress set off her ivory skin to perfection. She leaned back and picked up a small fan.

"I suppose you are going to tell me why you invited me here," she said at last.

He stretched out his hand and grasped a red silk cord which hung down from what appeared to be an easel, covered by red curtains. Watching Chryssa with some intensity, he pulled the cord and drew the curtains apart. Chryssa was unprepared for what she saw. She gasped in amazement, her eyes glowed, excitement flushed her pale face. Old Senthios thought he had never seen her look more beautiful.

He had given much thought to this display of the ruby necklace. To surprise her, he had had a frame built, lined with a pure white fleece. He noted with satisfaction that she was impressed. It amused him to think how easily he had acquired the necklace, for a ridiculous sum — considering its value — and an additional gift of a small Palace apartment. That had cost him nothing. It had been simple to turn out one of his relatives, an elderly aunt, he couldn't remember her name. His steward had found a cottage for the old girl in the suburbs, a damp, dark place full of cockroaches and too isolated for her to benefit from the small, neighbourly gifts of food and fuel which had helped her through past winters in the Palace. This winter would be her last. Senthios' aunt would die, cold, hungry and alone.

Also, Senthios reflected with satisfaction, there was the embarrassment the loss of the necklace might cause Councillor Micalidos. Yes, all in all, things were working out splendidly.

Chryssa, once the first moment of astonishment was over, turned away from the necklace and stared at Senthios. She began to understand what he intended. Until now their relationship had been a contest of will. She had played with him, allowing only so much licence and no more. More, however, than a decent wife should, particularly a daughter-in-law. But she had always stopped short of that total surrender which Senthios desired so passionately. She pretended — perhaps even to herself — that it was out of loyalty to her husband, Dino. In truth, she did not fancy the fat old man. Now, however, with the necklace within her grasp, she might change her mind. She tried to bargain with him,

"I have some letters that you asked for," she said, "there will be more."

"What letters?"

"From Andreas Micalidos."

Gazing steadily at her, he shrugged his shoulders.

"Don't you want to put the necklace on?"

She hesitated, hoping he would take the jewels from the frame and place them around her neck. He remained inert. In spite of her obsession to possess the necklace, she was afraid.

"How did you come by it?" she asked.

Senthios did not reply. His eyes devoured her. He sensed that the prospect of handling the jewels excited her.

"I could always sell it," Senthios murmured.

"You wouldn't!" Her reaction made him smile, the rapacious gleam in her eyes assured him of success.

"Take it," he said without moving.

She could not reach it without leaning across him. As her fingers closed on the jewels, his hand closed on her wrist. He drew her on to his lap and taking the necklace from her, placed it around her neck.

"It's marvellous!" she said, her eyes gleaming.

"Now I shall have my reward," he said, his large, fat fingers stroking the silky skin of her arm.

"Of course," she said eagerly, "oh, soon, soon. We must arrange something. But not just now. Dino went to Silamos recruiting today, but he'll be home directly and I must go. I shouldn't have stayed so long."

She tried to move away, but he held her firmly. The arm beneath the fat was exceedingly strong and was covered, she noticed distastefully, with long, black hairs.

"No, my dear," he said gently, "your Captain won't be back today. He will stay in Silamos."

"How do you know?"

"I arranged for him to go there. He will not return for two days."

"I can't stay here all night," she said, trying to conceal her dismay.

"If you want the necklace, you must stay with me for two nights, my dear."

"My family, my friends ... I will be missed."

"We'll tell them you are ... visiting," he said with a smile.

"You are a wicked old monster!" Chryssa laughed. She saw his smile disappear. His eyes were black and hard.

"You'd better make it worth my while. You've made me wait long enough." His voice was soft, but it threatened. Suddenly, she felt afraid. Sacred Zeus! Two nights — but the jewels! Her hand went to her breast, she felt the gems smooth and warm against her skin. She lifted them up, the light glowed within them, liquid red fire, rich, luminous, infinitely desirable. She would submit gracefully. She sighed and surrendered herself to her husband's father.

Micalidos' secretary, Senka, could reach no decision about the betrayal of the escaped slaves, Arkos and Tyra. He distrusted Doxa Grinkos and she was well-known for meanness. Would she pay up promptly if he informed against them? He doubted it. He rode to Mallia with a letter from Brachne to his sister, Olykka. Inquiring at the farm, he was told she was not there. A peasant farmer, a relative of Olykka's dead mother, was managing the property.

"You'll find her at the Temple at Mallia," he said, "the Pillar Shrine, that's where she's serving now."

Senka then rode back to Mallia and, to his annoyance, was kept waiting in the ante-room at the Temple for over an hour. When Olykka appeared, impressive in her long priestess' gown and with an air of calm, unassailable dignity, she received the letter without a word, waving him to be seated while she read it. Olykka then sat for a few moments in thought.

"How will they travel?" she asked.

"In a farm cart."

"Whose?"

"My employer's, Councillor Micalidos."

"Does he approve?"

"He doesn't know about it yet. His son, Antonius, is arranging everything. He's a friend of your brother."

"Yes, I remember Brachne speaking of him. I should feel happier, though, if Councillor Micalidos was aware of these arrangements."

"The Councillor is recovering from a serious illness and his doctor said he was not to be worried. Antonius does not want to involve him."

"Councillor Micalidos would be involved if this plan failed."

Senka became bored with the interview and wished to end it.

"Shall I tell them you're not agreeable to the plan?" he asked.

"Of course I'll help these people," she spoke quietly but her eyes smouldered. "I strongly object to Councillor Micalidos not being informed of this project. Will you please convey my opinion to Antonius?"

"As you wish," Senka replied. He left Olykka and rode back to Knossos.

As Senka approached the city, two carts blocked the narrow roadway and he had to rein in his horse. As he waited impatiently, he saw a beggar on the footway. The old man did not call out for alms but stared at him so intently that Senka wondered if he was one of Chryssa's spies. That bitch! he thought. As he rode on, he recollected their recent meeting. He had taken her copies of three of Andreas' letters — business correspondence, very dull. It had occurred to Senka that if there was anything in the letters which might cause trouble for his employer, he might alter the copies. But Chryssa had demanded the originals.

"You can't break the seal!" he protested, but she eased it open with a heated knife. When she was satisfied that the copy was correct, she returned the original.

"Now what am I supposed to do?" he said angrily. "I can't deliver letters with the seal broken."

"You'll have to stick them down again. Try glue. And don't bring me useless rubbish like this. You know the kind of letters I want."

"What kind?"

"Anything political."

While these thoughts rankled in his mind, the horse turned up the narrow path leading to Andreas' villa. Senka reined in. Antonius was sometimes difficult to contact, now that he lived in the barracks. It would be simpler to go directly to the surgery and report how matters were progressing.

When Senka arrived there, Dr Ahmed had just finished examining a patient. He was relieved to know that Olykka was willing to shelter the runaway slaves at her farm.

"They must leave as soon as possible," he said, "every moment's delay is dangerous."

They did not notice that during this conversation an old beggar limped into the surgery and sat down.

When the surgery was busy, Dr Iros allowed Tyra to help dispense the medicines. He had arranged a workbench for her, behind a screen, with pestle and mortar, bottles and jars. As the weeks passed, the young slave became relaxed and happy. She enjoyed the dispensing work, her health improved and the prospect of bearing Arkos' child filled her with joy. On evenings like this she would forget caution and come to the door of the surgery to distribute the medicines. Tyra was tired today and was glad when the last patient stood waiting for his prescription — a jar of ointment for sores on the feet. Though others had come after him, he had waited until they had gone. He thanked her effusively and looked so sharply at her that she felt a stab of anxiety.

At that moment, Arkos entered the courtyard and called to her. She turned to silence him, to warn him, but it was too late. He had heard from Ahmed that they would be leaving soon and had come to tell her. He put his arms around her and blurted it out before she could stop him. She looked to see if the beggar had heard, but he was gone.

Arkos laughed when she told him her fears.

"We shall soon be safe in the country, surely no one will look for us at Olykka's farm. And, in the spring, Dr Ahmed will find us a ship for Egypt! Take courage, dearest Tyra."

She clung to Arkos, trying to share his confidence. But she was afraid.

On the day before the opening of the Bull Dance season, the novices, Belia and Freyna, and the three young men, Nino, Bruni and Dek, made their dedication to the Earth Mother.

Korynna attended the ceremony in the afternoon. She returned home and went first to her mother's room to satisfy herself that all was well. Then she went downstairs and crossed toward Andreas' apartment. She met the steward, Credon, carrying a bowl of fruit.

"How is the Councillor? Is he resting?" she inquired.

"The master has been resting," Credon replied, "but he asked for some fruit a few minutes ago."

"I must speak to him at once," Korynna said urgently.

Credon opened the door and stood aside as she entered.

"Korynna, my dear, how did the ceremony go?" Andreas asked.

He was seated in his high-backed chair, reading a book of poetry by Brachne and others, given to him recently by Antonius.

"Thank you, Credon," he added as the steward placed the bowl of peaches, grapes and figs beside him and withdrew.

"Andreas, the ceremony was most absorbing, indeed very moving."

"I'm glad," he said, hoping she would not stay too long. Then, as she hesitated, he knew he should ask her to sit down. "Have some fruit, Korynna," he said, helping himself.

His sister hovered nervously and then sat down.

"Not just now, thank you, Andreas. Those two girl dancers are so beautiful. The young men are handsome, too. Sappena told me one of them came from Cypress and another two from Delos. They were all very sincere. Of course it was a most significant moment in their lives." She paused, sitting on the edge of the chair, twisting her veil in her hands.

"Andreas, I had a strange experience..."

"What's the problem, Korynna," he asked encouragingly, fearing she was about to describe one of her religious revelations.

"The shrine in the Bull Halls is not large," she continued, "and I was very close to the young dancers. The younger girl — just a slip of a child, really — spoke to one of the votaries and pointed at me. I'm sure she asked who I was and I heard the priestess say 'Councillor Micalidos' sister'."

Andreas had surreptitiously returned to his book but now he looked up.

"Well, what of it?" he said sharply.

"This young girl looked straight at me and beckoned!" She paused again and Andreas began to lose patience.

"For Zeus' sake, Korynna, come to the point."

"Andreas, I'm not sure what the point is. I went closer and while the priest was reading the last prayer, the girl leaned over to me and whispered..."

"Yes?"

"I *think* she said ... oh! Andreas, I can't understand it, but I'm sure she said 'Timon is safe'!"

Until that moment Andreas had been having difficulty paying attention to his sister. Now he looked at her in amazement and disbelief.

"Safe! How would she know? Tell me again exactly what she said." In his agitation he almost shouted and Korynna was near to tears.

"Andreas, you're upsetting me. I didn't hear the first thing she said — it might have been 'Tell the Councillor' — but I'm absolutely certain she said 'Timon is safe'."

"Then where is he? Why didn't you question the girl and find out where Timon is?"

"Andreas, the High Priestess, Sappena, reprimanded her for speaking to me. She stood between us. I had no opportunity to question the girl and when the ceremony was over the dancers were marched out with the guards."

Andreas was silent for a few moments.

"When does the Bull Dance season open?"

"Tomorrow, I believe." She feared she had given Andreas false hope for his son's safety.

"Korynna, we must contact this girl as soon as possible." His sister reminded him that no one could enter the Bull Halls.

"There must be messengers — go-betweens. The men have women admirers."

"An admiring public, perhaps," Korynna replied primly, "but they are *all* pure like the priests."

"Some men never deny themselves!" he growled.

"Andreas, I know you're not religious, but you should respect the priesthood."

"Damn all the priests!"

Korynna drew herself up.

"Andreas, I will not stay if you continue like this."

He was contrite at once.

"I'm sorry, Korynna. Innocence of mind is so rare, I'm apt to forget it exists." He continued quickly. "We must find this girl at once and talk to her. You say the Bull Dance season opens tomorrow?"

She nodded.

"Then we shall go," he said decisively.

"I would prefer not to go. I don't care for the Bull Dance. Zanthope will go with you."

"I've no doubt she'll go — she always does. But it's you whom this girl will recognize. She may not remember me."

"How can we make contact with her?"

"We must arrive early and find seats in the front row. Senka could lean over the barricades and attract her attention and hopefully she will see you and then it's up to her. Please, Korynna," Andreas implored suddenly, with great simplicity, "we must make every effort to find that child before they harm him."

"Of course, Andreas, my dear, I'll do anything I can to help you."

"Thank you, Korynna. Tomorrow, please the Gods, we shall find my son."

# CHAPTER 29

Public auctions of local and imported goods were held twice a week in the Merchant's Court and were usually attended by large crowds. Palace guards were always present to keep order and discourage pilfering.

Antonius was due to take command of the squad at noon. He had to report first at the Guard Room near the South Gate. In order to escape the delays occasioned by the crowds and his many friends in the Courtyard, Antonius regularly used the narrow passageways of the West Palace. As he went swiftly along, a man suddenly stepped out from the shadows of a doorway and asked the way to the Egyptian Ambassador's suite.

"You can go up these stairs," Antonius said, turning to point in that direction. As he did so, without warning, the man took a wooden club from beneath his cloak and struck Antonius a violent blow on the head. Taken off guard, he had no opportunity to defend himself and the force of the blow made him stagger and fall. Two other men appeared out of the shadows. All three men began beating and kicking him viciously. Remembering the sentries on duty at the Council Chamber, he tried to call for help as he struggled with his assailants.

However help did not come. The Palace walls and passages swallowed up the sound of his voice. He tried to stand up and draw his sword, but, in the confined space, this was impossible. He hit out and kicked wildly as repeated blows fell upon his head and back.

Then, two of the men grabbed his legs and dragged him along the narrow corridor, while the third continued to batter his head and shoulders with the club.

Antonius kept shouting loudly for help. His cheek was split open and he tasted the salty warmth of his blood. One of the men placed a knee on his chest, while another opened a nearby door which revealed a gloomy stairway descending into darkness. He began to despair. His helmet had rolled off when a kick to the head half stunned him.

"Down you go, soldier, you won't see daylight again!"

The voice was familiar, harsh, mocking and sadistic. Antonius twisted and wedged his body across the doorway to try and avoid capture. He took a painful breath. He thought he might have a cracked rib and yelled a last, desperate cry for help.

Then there was noise everywhere, the thud of blows, grunts and curses. Someone kicked the breath out of him and he lost consciousness. When he recovered, he was lying on his back against the wall. His attackers had disappeared. A tall, dark-haired man in a long robe of pleated white linen was bending over him, staring anxiously into his face.

"Are you feeling better, sir?" he inquired politely. His voice had a trace of foreign accent.

Antonius struggled to his feet.

"Thank you, I'm all right." He took a step, staggered and clutched at the door for support. Then he noticed several men in short tunics — guards or servants, he supposed, by the deference they showed the tall man at his side.

"I believe you have saved my life — thank you," Antonius said, gasping in pain, "what is your name?"

"I am Shep-Anep," replied the stranger, "I am Chief Steward to His Excellency, User-Amon, the Egyptian Ambassador."

"And I am Cadet-Lieutenant Antonius Micalidos," said the young man weakly, offering his hand to Shep, "I owe you a great debt of gratitude."

The steward's reaction surprised him.

"Ah! You are the son of Councillor Micalidos?"

When Antonius nodded, Shep continued.

"Your father is my great benefactor! I am very pleased to be able to help his son." The Ambassador's steward invited Antonius to rest and refresh himself in the Ambassador's apartment but Antonius declined.

"I'm already late on duty."

"But you need medical attention."

"I shall report for duty first. Then I shall see Dr Ahmed."

"Ah! Ahmed, I know him well. Have you any idea who attacked you?"

"No," Antonius replied, "would you and your servants please not mention this incident to anyone? I don't want my father to hear of this."

"I understand," Shep answered, "how is Councillor Micalidos' health?"

"He is recovering, but he needs rest."

Antonius wiped the blood from his face.

"I was very distressed to learn of the disappearance of your brother, Timon," Shep said, "has he been found yet?"

"Not yet."

"I'm sorry to hear that," the Egyptian said, "I hope you will call on me as soon as you are able."

Shep ordered three of his men to accompany the lieutenant to the South Gate. Antonius would have preferred to say nothing of the attack. But when he saw that Major Ortis, a disciplinarian, was duty officer, he explained briefly what had happened.

"I want this matter kept quiet, sir," he concluded.

"Have you a witness to corroborate this?" Major Ortis asked.

"The Egyptian Ambassador's Chief Steward saw the attack and helped me."

"Who were these men — robbers?"

"I don't think so, sir."

"You obviously have an enemy then," Ortis said, without concern, "I'll have to make an official report on this matter — it will be confidential, of course.

Clean yourself up and to your post, then, lieutenant."

The Merchants' Court was already crowded as the Noon Sacrifice was long over.

"B-by the Gods, your face needs s-stitching up," young Cadet Nimos stuttered, "didn't that b-bastard give you leave to s-see a doctor?"

"Not him," Antonius growled.

"What happened?"

"Fell off my horse — Nimos, keep your eye out for pickpockets."

The afternoon seemed endless. Antonius' ribs ached and his head throbbed. His duties obliged him to move around in the crowd, which added to his discomfort. The hours dragged on. He exchanged a few words now and then with Cadet Nimos, who stammered his complaints at the boredom, the heat and stuffiness of the long court, now jammed with damned sweat hogs! Antonius agreed. He had a great thirst and went to a drinking fountain nearby — a trickle of water from a clay pipe. No sooner was he back than thirst tormented him again.

To distract his mind, he searched for any incident or misconduct on his part which might have caused this assault. Was it chance — robbers needing money — or was it, as Ortis suggested, a deliberate attack? He recalled that he still owed Lieutenant Sartis for cards, but this was a trivial matter.

Then he recollected the harsh voice of the man who had spoken — it reminded him of someone — the agent, Agidor! And then he remembered his visit to Phaestos and his rescue of the young boys Agidor had hoped to sell at great profit in Libya. Was this attack then an act of revenge? Perhaps Agidor blames me, he thought, for the loss of the beautiful Nubian slave whom Ortis had taken from the agent to become a bull dancer. Maybe this was the explanation. Antonius suspected that Agidor could provide an answer to Timon's disappearance. He began to feel nauseous.

"You l-look all in," Nimos said sympathetically.

The sun was setting and the crowds began returning home. Storekeepers and merchants were packing up.

"You go, sir, I'll s-see to the locking up."

"No, it's my job," Antonius said, "you bolt the doors at the northern end and those into the West Palace."

"Right, sir."

When the last trader had retired and the doors were bolted, Antonius returned the keys to the Guard Room. Major Ortis had gone to dinner and the night officer had taken over.

"You'd better see a doctor," he said when he saw Antonius' face.

The young soldier left by the South Gate, walking unsteadily down the long, sloping roadway. The cool air revived him somewhat. He engaged a chair and sank back exhausted as the carriers set off for the villa.

When they arrived, he paid the men and walked slowly into the silent house. He stood for a moment, uncertain, fumbling with the strap of his helmet. Presently Credon came out into the loggia.

"Good evening, young master, we did not expect you ... What's this? You've been hurt!"

"It's nothing. Where's everybody? Is Dr Ahmed here?"

"They're attending the Bull Dance, sir. The new season opened today."

"Zeus, I forgot."

"Except Young Madam, she ..."

At that moment Antonius fainted. Credon called to the other servants. They carried the young man to his room as the servant girls ran ahead to prepare the bed.

"Fetch hot water and clean towels," Credon ordered, and turning to the groom he continued, "Saddle up and go and look for young Dr Iros. If he's not at the surgery try his father's house — Aptaeon, the lamp-maker. He lives by the Palace wall, near the South Gate, you'll see his sign outside the house."

Credon asked Antonius if he would like some wine.

"No thank you — just water, cool water."

One of the girls was sent to fetch a pitcher from the cistern under the house. He drank deeply and thankfully and was soon bathed and made comfortable.

"If you want anything, call me. I shall be close by," Credon said, and with that they left Antonius to rest.

# CHAPTER 30

The official opening of the Bull Dance season was the most important event of the year. It was always followed by an evening reception in King Minos' Palace. The queues for seats at the Bull Ring began at dawn and the festive atmosphere increased as the hours passed and the day grew warmer. Street musicians and jugglers entertained the waiting crowds and vendors of hot snacks and cool drinks attracted many customers.

Preparations had gone on for weeks. Workmen raked and levelled loads of sand and sawdust till the ring was as smooth as a tidal beach. For this occasion, the barricades were newly painted and flagpoles hung with streamers and coloured pennants. The tiers of stone benches allocated to the priests, leading citizens and the public were now crowded with excited people. A feeling of expectancy possessed the audience as they anticipated the entertainment and pleasure to come.

His Majesty King Minos had been in retreat for the Days of Sacrifice, appearing only briefly at noon in the Palace Courtyard. His arrival with Queen Kara and Court officials was expected shortly, and the citizens watched the royal enclosure with noisy curiosity. The entrance of each Court official was greeted with applause and encouraging whistles and when, at last, the Court musicians took their place in the gallery facing the audience — above the great doors from which the dancers would soon emerge — there was a burst of prolonged cheering. Children clapped and shouted excitedly as the musicians began to play a popular tune.

The muffled bellowing of bulls from the holding yards behind the far end of the arena increased the tension in the crowd. The dancers, gathered in their ante-room on the other side of the great doors, also heard the noise of the bulls. The bright afternoon sunlight streamed through a high metal grille set along the wall overlooking the Bull Ring. While beneath the grille the five young novices stood on a bench and stared out into the arena.

"Have a good look now," Paulius said, "there'll be no chance later."

As if they needed to be told! How often had they stood here before, studying the skill of the experienced dancers. Today marked a great change in their lives; in a short time, they would themselves face the bull.

"Will we be all right, Nino?" Belia asked. She stared intently at the rows of people as if searching for someone she knew.

"We'll be fine," Nino replied confidently.

"It's Freyna I'm worried about," she whispered, "she's so afraid."

"We'll have to look after her, won't we?" he said, smiling, "don't worry, Bee, she'll be all right. Waiting makes us all nervous."

Time dragged endlessly for the dancers and they longed to begin. Recollecting the events of the last twenty-four hours, Freyna shivered.

After discovering, during the dedication ceremony, that their visitor was Councillor Micalidos' sister and therefore Timon's aunt, a less pleasant surprise had awaited them. At the completion of the ceremony Belia was reprimanded for speaking to Korynna. Scarron then led the five young novices to his quarters nearby. Closing the door, he took a double-headed axe from a small shrine in the wall. He then ordered the dancers to place their right hand on it.

"You must now swear never to reveal to an uninitiated person what you are about to experience."

They did so.

"You enter the Bull Ring to serve the Goddess, but never forget that you are there to entertain the public. No bull dancer must ever lose control. If you, or one of your comrades, are honoured by the God, you must accept your fate with dignity, as befits the traditions of our art. This final instruction in your training is called submission."

He stared coldly at each of them.

"Blindfold yourselves."

They did so, using their headbands. When he was

satisfied they could see nothing, he said, "Whatever occurs, you are not to cry out."

Then followed an unpleasant half-hour. They sensed that more people were now in the room and for a few moments all was silent. Their nerves grew taut. The sudden crash of cymbals made them gasp.

"Be silent. Remain still!" Scarron hissed.

The dancers were then struck painfully on the shin, the knee and ankle-bone and startled by shouts and slaps in the face. They were momentarily stifled by a cord pulled tightly around the throat. Their heads were jerked back when their hair was pulled from behind. They had to accept these trials without a sound.

After what seemed an eternity Scarron told them they could remove their blindfolds. The room was now empty and he pointed to a bucket of sawdust.

"Fill your mouths," he said.

After some hesitation, distastefully they did so. He picked up a pair of bull's horns. Thankfully they saw that the points were sawn off. He then walked around each of the five dancers in turn, jabbing them hard in the thigh, the back, the ribs, the breast.

"Remember — if the bull gets you down, do not scream. Fill your mouths with sawdust and remain silent."

They clenched their teeth. Soon it was all over. There was fresh water to rinse their mouths and wine to revive their spirits.

"I wouldn't mind so much," Belia whispered, rubbing her bruises, "if I wasn't so sure that bastard enjoyed doing it!"

Now that they were trained, dedicated and initiated, Naxos glanced at his new bull dancers with some pride.

Now they are ready, he thought, I can do no more.

In the bull dancers' ante-room the mounting din of the audience could now be plainly heard. Freyna peered through the grille at the dark archway through which the bulls entered the ring. Soon she and her friends would be confronting them. She went to the fountain for some water.

"How are you?" Leander said.

"All right," she answered, thinking how much she loved him and how handsome he was.

All the dancers were a sight to behold, young and beautiful, their fine athletic physiques enhanced by their scanty costumes. The women were bare-breasted, their curving hips covered only by embroidered silk shorts, cut away to the waist. The men, too, wore the briefest shorts. Their hair was washed, oiled and bound by embroidered headbands. Belia and Freyna had new costumes, gifts from the leading dancer, M'boola, resplendent herself in saffron yellow silk. She had stitched a pearl necklace, an admirer's gift, into the headband which restrained her mop of thick, black hair. Freyna wore blue, and Belia sea-green. Many of the dancers wore tight-fitting armlets. The catchers' costumes were less gaudy than the vaulters, who wore vibrant colours, sparkling with silver and gilt metal discs which attracted the bull.

The dancers stood in a group, making desultory conversation and complimenting one another on their appearance. The tension, even for the most experienced of them, was very great.

"You look wonderful, Freyna," Leander said quietly.

"So do you," she replied.

"I'll scream if it doesn't start soon!" Belia cried.

"It will all begin soon enough," Asteria said coldly, "and it won't finish soon enough," she muttered to herself. Asteria was afraid and would have refused to go on, if she had had the courage to do so.

"The King is late," Paulius said to M'boola in a low voice, "I hate this waiting."

As leader he felt concern for the whole group, but for Asteria in particular. He had come to know her well over the years. Her nerve was gone and that made her a danger to herself and the troupe. However, he understood her pride. She would never forgive him if he sent her back to the quarters. He loved her more than he could say and looked forward to their retirement together.

The Egyptian vaulter, Ali-el-Berber, was a comic. But despite his buffoonery and pranks, his main concern was survival, and money. Ali liked and respected Paulius but he thought him a fool to love Asteria and resolved to stay clear of her. If that bitch cracks up today, he thought, I won't go down with her!

"Now, listen everyone — no heroics," Paulius spoke quietly. "Just take it easy to begin with. That means you, too!" he said to Ali, who rolled his eyes in mock reverence and bowed.

The rest of the group waited patiently: Chloe, gentle and nervous, but lithe and quick enough to take care of herself; the Cilician, Sardi, a tough young man, who, barring misfortune, would probably survive; and Catalene and Rhina, two third-year bull girls from Attica, who both were good catchers. Lastly, of course, there were the five who were newly dedicated — Belia, Freyna, Nino, Bruni and Dek. This was the team of fourteen dancers Naxos had chosen to open the season. He did not generally put five novices in the ring at once, but he wished to give them some experience as there would shortly be three retirements from the troupe. He knew Paulius would help to protect them.

Theseus, the Athenian Prince, was angry. He complained bitterly because he considered he and his Greek dancers should have opened the season.

"Her Royal Highness Ariadne will not be pleased!" Ali had said with an impudent grin.

But Naxos stood firm. The honour was for Paulius, M'boola and Asteria, who, after five years, deserved this recognition. He also wished them to receive the material benefit — patrons were always generous at the opening ceremony.

Silence in the arena caught the dancers' attention. The audience was quiet and the music ceased. Then came the blare of trumpets and the sonorous blowing of conch horns. King Minos and his Court had arrived.

The young dancers leaped onto the bench to look through the grille while the experienced dancers affected indifference. They smiled indulgently when Belia and Nino made excited comments to no one in particular.

"Just look at that head-dress! Jewels and peacock feathers!"

"Magnificent! Who's the tall lady?"

"Must be Queen Kara..."

"And the other, the younger one near the King?"

"That's Princess Ariadne."

Belia's statement, so assured, surprised Nino.

"How do you know?" he asked.

Belia was saved from answering by a loud and enthusiastic burst of applause from the audience as the King and his party took their places.

Belia beckoned to Freyna who was standing beside Leander.

"Come here, Freyna," she called.

Freyna climbed on the bench once more.

"I can't pick him out in this huge crowd, you look," Belia whispered.

"Look for who? What do you mean?"

"The Councillor, Councillor Micalidos."

Freyna scanned the vast crowd through the grille.

"I can't remember what he looks like," she said, "it's so long since we saw him."

Andreas, entitled to a place among the King's Councillors, had nevertheless planned to bring his party early with the intention of sitting close to the barricades. However, just as they were about to set off from the Villa, they were startled by a scream.

Zanthope came from her bedroom half-dressed, her hair dishevelled. She stood at the top of the stairway.

"My jewels! They're gone! Holy Zeus — my necklace has been stolen!"

They stared at her in amazement.

"Andreas! I've been robbed" she screamed again.

"Be quiet, Zanthope," he said, "you'll disturb mother."

"By the Sacred Gods! Is that all you can say?"

Without a word Andreas climbed the stairs to his wife's bedroom. The room was in disorder. She had emptied every chest, every cupboard. Clothing was scattered about.

"You've searched everywhere?"

"Of course I have."

"Where do you keep the necklace?"

"In the casket by my bed. I took it to Mallia."

"Did you wear any of the jewels there?"

"No, but I showed them to Madam Brecchius."

"And they were safe when you returned here?"

"I believe so, yes, I'm sure. The casket was locked." Zanthope began to weep.

"We must search for them later," Andreas said. "you'll have to wear something else."

"I will not appear at Court without my rubies!" she screamed.

"Who could have taken them?"

Zanthope could not reply. She stood in the middle of the room, angry and afraid. She could not look at her husband. She suspected Senka of stealing the necklace but dared not say so.

"Say I'm not well, I'll stay at home," she said.

"Don't be ridiculous," Andreas replied irritably, "you probably left the necklace at Mallia."

He left the room and rejoined Korynna, Dr Ahmed and Senka who were waiting below in the loggia.

Then there was further delay. The noise had awakened and frightened Old Madam and Korynna would not leave until her mother had taken a sleeping draught.

Some time later, when Andreas and his party finally arrived at the Bull Ring, the auditorium was full and the King and his Court were taking their seats. Andreas was fuming because his plan to arrive early had been frustrated.

"What damnable luck!" he remarked to Ahmed as they were wedged uncomfortably into the back row. Korynna and Senka had seats in front of them.

"Later on, Korynna, you and Senka will have to go down the walkway to the barricades," he said urgently to his sister.

"That's impossible, Andreas," she protested, "there are people sitting on the stairs and you know I hate crowds. I wish I had not come. I do not care for the Bull Dance."

"We must somehow attract that girl's attention."

He made a great effort to control his irritation. Ahmed did not like the Bull Dance either. Senka was the only member of the party likely to enjoy the spectacle.

Now the music had begun again. This sequence was the cue for the dancers. An expectant murmur came from the big crowd. It sounded, Korynna thought, like a huge swarm of bees, an uneasy, threatening noise.

Naxos had seen the King arrive and sit down.

"Line up!" he snapped.

The dancers quickly took their places. But Freyna sat down again on the bench, her head between her knees. Belia knelt by her at once.

"Are you ill?" she asked.

"My legs are shaking — I — I can't face it."

Freyna was very pale and her hand, when Belia took it, was ice cold and trembling. She tried to reassure her friend.

"You'll be all right. Paulius won't ask us to do anything difficult. Just the dance routines and we know them backwards. Don't look at the old bull, just watch Paulius."

Freyna took her place between Belia and Nino. Then Naxos gave the order to the slaves to open the heavy, wooden doors to the arena. The music rose to a crescendo as Paulius and M'boola ran forward, leading the dancers into the ring.

A thunderous roar greeted their entrance and a snowstorm of flowers was thrown over the barricades. The performers faced King Minos and Queen Kara, bowed and took their places. The orchestra played the savage, ancient theme which introduced the age-old ritual of the Bull Dance, while shouts of admiration and applause echoed around the arena.

The opening dance, based on religious symbolism, had a barbaric intensity. The line of scantily-clad young men and women moved in asymmetric patterns difficult to imitate and requiring absolute discipline and concentration. For the Cretans every step was familiar. These celebrations had been witnessed since early childhood. This first dance sequence was a thrilling prelude to the life and death drama which was to follow.

As they danced and the crowd cheered, Belia felt such nervous excitement that it took all her determination to remember the defined order of the steps. Freyna, on the other hand, was terrified by the tumult and uproar. Her heart pounded and her legs trembled as she forced her mind to concentrate on the dance. The image of the bull tormented her. For the novices Nino, Bruni and Dek, this was a great moment and a chance to prove themselves after their arduous training. Although the older dancers were more accustomed to this experience, they too were elated by the ecstatic reception.

Andreas, from his seat in the back row, forgot his discomfort and frustration. He recognized Belia and Freyna — they were so different from the other dancers with their golden hair and fair skin — and he was once again full of admiration for their grace and beauty. Indeed, he found it hard to take his eyes from Belia.

The music now changed its character and the dancers formed three sides of a square. They faced the dark archway at the far end of the arena. Their arms and bodies swayed in sinuous movements to the tempo of the music which became gradually softer and then faded away. A drummer began to beat slow, solemn notes.

The Cretan audience now became silent and tense. Suddenly, they heard the sound of hoof-beats and a black bull charged through the archway into the arena. The crowd roared their welcome as the bull advanced toward the dancers. The athletes waited silently, their eyes riveted on the animal.

The bull was young, lean and powerful. It halted abruptly and stood, head erect, taking in the new and unfamiliar environment. The crowd murmured its admiration and approval. Slowly the bull began to move forward and the afternoon sunlight gleamed on its long curved horns and rippling muscles. Paulius and Leander exchanged glances. They saw that this was a dangerous bull. They would have to tire him out.

Paulius, as leader of the group, was to make the first vault, always difficult with a young, strong bull. No one could predict its reactions.

Quickly Paulius advanced toward the animal with Catalene, his catcher, on one side and Ali's catcher, Rhina, on the other. Now the arena was absolutely quiet. Every spectator held his breath.

The bull rushed at Paulius suddenly. The lowered horns were angled sharply and the experienced vaulter wisely left them alone. He leapt forward, placing both hands on the great arch of the neck. He somersaulted quickly on to the bull's back and then leaped to the ground where he was steadied by Catalene. The crowd cheered and shouted compliments, but Paulius did not hear. He spun around as the bull turned with amazing speed and charged again. Paulius vaulted over the horns once more. The bull tossed its head angrily and he was flung some distance, but Catalene was there to steady him.

Those first passes had taken only a few seconds and a great roar of appreciation came from the crowd. Money and some jewels showered into the ring and the coin boys, nimble as mice, darted out with their baskets to gather them.

Paulius vaulted again, trying to vary the direction and distance of his leap. Leander saw that their leader should have immediate support. He signed to the other vaulters, M'boola, Ali and Asteria to move in on either side of the bull, with their catchers close behind.

They did so, whirling and spinning. This new approach distracted the bull and it could not decide which dancer to attack first. The contest became a battle of wits. Each vaulter in turn somersaulted over the curving horns. When the vault was completed and the bull rushed to charge again, another dancer leapt forward to confront him. They hoped in this way to take the edge off the bull's apparently inexhaustible energy.

The five novices watched with admiration. Paulius, his chest heaving, signalled to them to withdraw slowly towards the outer edge of the ring. They did so most thankfully. For a moment it seemed as if Asteria, one of the leading vaulters, would accompany them. But pride saved her. However, she did not vault herself and gave no support to the other dancers. Seeing her in this mood, Paulius did not call on her. Later, she bitterly accused him of ignoring her and giving her no opportunity to vault.

The wild music from the orchestra, the whirling figures and the spectacle of barbaric excitement and colour had the audience stamping, clapping and shouting with delight. Connoisseurs applauded Paulius' clever manipulation of a situation that had looked dangerous and unpromising. This indeed was a difficult bull. It seemed tireless and determined to do damage but would not permit the vaulters to shape the dance to their own design. They could not demonstrate their particular style or impress the spectators with their individual skills.

The crowd rose to its feet when Leander was flung violently over, missed his footing on the edge of the bull's shoulder and fell. Freyna gasped with terror, but her lover recovered and was up instantly, grasping Sardi's outstretched hand.

To distract the bull, Ali quickly leapt on its back. Before he could attempt to ride it, the animal began a wild, circular convulsion, twisting and bucking until Ali was pitched off. He leaped sideways as the bull turned, viciously sweeping its horns in an effort to bring him down.

Naxos watched the progress of the Bull Dance with critical eyes. There was a policy to be adhered to in this business. Above all, the crowd had to be entertained. However, he knew the dancers should be eased back into harness after the longer than usual six week lay-off and the novices had to acquire experience. But not with this bull! Naxos wished to avoid mishaps at the opening of the season. It seemed to him now, that the crowd had had its fill and this bull was vicious and difficult. Naxos made his decision. He ordered the keepers to remove it from the ring. A more tractable animal was to be sent in as soon as possible.

When he saw the keepers enter the ring, Paulius realized Naxos' intention. He and the other dancers began to work the bull toward the exit archway but when the bull saw the keepers it fiercely pawed the ground. As Ali leaped once more on its back, it began another spasm of ferocious plunges. In throes of fury it rushed toward the archway and, as Ali leapt, or rather, was thrown violently off its back, the keepers were able to surround it. The bull tossed its head defiantly and galloped from the ring and the crowd cheered enthusiastically at this show of independence.

In the interval the musicians began a lively tune and the dancers spread out in two lines facing each other across the ring. They gave a brief and brilliant display of acrobatic tumbling, leaping and cartwheeling, the two lines passing each other as the dancers crossed and recrossed the ring several times. Then they took up their positions to face the next bull.

To their delight it was their favourite, the great brown and white bull, Tauron. He came proudly on, holding his huge head high. The auditorium resounded with shouts of welcome and the dancers joined in. From that moment the performance reached spectacular heights. Their fear and tension gone, the dancers relaxed and flung themselves into a superb exhibition.

Tauron, a personality in his own right, became one of the performers. He lumbered back and forth, lowered his head obligingly for the vaulters or let the catchers hold his horns, curved under their armpits, as the great artist, Kotos, had depicted in one of his popular frescoes. The dancers leapt on and off his back, showing off all the acrobatic skills, the double somersaults, the triple twists, the jack-knife splits which they had practiced so assiduously. The performance was a triumph and the crowd continued to cheer and stamp wildly.

For Asteria, however, the opening of the Bull Dance season was a failure. She vaulted once on the horns, but mistimed her leap and fell off Tauron's shoulder. The bull stepped aside to avoid her. When Chloe assisted her she was humiliated and angry. Try as he would, Paulius could not persuade her to vault again. Her nerve was gone. She found yet another reason for jealous resentment. At Paulius' nod, Belia stepped forward and with the grace and poise of an expert vaulter, grasped Tauron's horns and somersaulted onto his broad back. Turning around, she rode almost the full circuit of the ring, arms curving high as she had seen the senior vaulters do. The crowd went wild when they saw this beautiful young girl riding the bull with her blonde hair streaming out behind her. Money, trinkets and jewels showered into the ring. Freyna rejoiced in her friend's success and was sure she would remember this moment for the rest of her life. Each of the young dancers displayed their skills, Nino, Bruni and Dek leaping and somersaulting over the bull, and Freyna turning cartwheels alongside as if she had been a bull dancer all her life.

Soon it was all over. As Tauron galloped off, the applause echoed again and again around the arena. The musicians played the final theme for the dancers to salute King Minos and make their exit. The audience began to disperse, tired and satisfied, and the opening of the Bull Dance season was hailed as a great success.

In the Bull Halls the mood was one of exhilaration. Naxos was proud of his troupe and congratulated them. They congratulated each other. They had splendid appetites for the festive meal that awaited them. Freyna was ecstatic in the belief that she had conquered fear and would never be afraid again. Leander watched her gravely. He knew she had much to learn.

But for now, the five novices, Freyna, Belia, Nino and the two island boys, Bruni and Dek, were justified in their happiness. They had been tested and they had triumphed. During the meal, Naxos knocked on the serving table for silence. He spoke in his solemn voice.

"The following dancers have been honoured with a command to attend the royal reception in the Throne Room this evening." He then read out the names from a roll of papyrus. "Prince Theseus, Paulius, Leander, Ali-el-Berber, M'boola, Chloe, Belia and Freyna."

When he left the room, conversation resumed, but in a lower key. Those who were not chosen were disappointed. Asteria, pale and thin-lipped, left the dining-hall at once. Had her name been on the list, Naxos would have struck it off. In his view she did not deserve that honour.

Belia excitedly grasped her friend's arm.

"Freyna, we may see Councillor Micalidos — Timon's father!"

"Yes, Belia, he would surely be there."

Andreas usually avoided royal receptions. But when, after the King and Queen had departed, it was announced that a group of dancers were invited to attend, Andreas decided he would go to the reception himself.

"Senka, escort my sister home, please. Thank you, Korynna, for coming to the Bull Dance with me."

"I enjoyed the second half, Andreas," she replied, "once that horrible black creature disappeared."

"Yes," he agreed, "but you were right — we had no chance to speak to that young woman. My word, she was brilliant."

They all agreed enthusiastically.

"We might have better luck at the reception. Will you accompany me?" Andreas asked Ahmed.

Ahmed agreed politely, bowing to the inevitable. Royal receptions were not to his taste either. Queen Kara would be there, of course. He sighed, for he doubted there would be an opportunity to speak to her.

# CHAPTER 31

The familiarity of Antonius' room at the villa was comforting after the attack on him at the Palace. He recalled with gratitude Shep-Anep's timely assistance.

The throbbing in his head had eased but he was exhausted. The house was quiet again after his unexpected arrival. He dozed.

Suddenly, he heard his name.

"Antonius, what are you doing here?"

Zanthope stood in the doorway. She was drunk and her speech was slurred.

"Mother, why aren't you at the Bull Dance?"

She gave a strange cry, half sob, half shriek. Antonius stared at her in some surprise.

Zanthope walked unsteadily to his bedside and sat down. Antonius had never been aware that his mother was aging. She always seemed young and beautiful. Now, looking at her drunken, tear-stained face, he noticed for the first time the sallowness of her skin and the lines around her mouth and eyes.

"Mother, what's the matter?" he asked.

"I've been robbed!" she cried hysterically, "robbed, Antonius!" She began to weep, moaning and beating her hands in a foolish ineffectual way.

"What do you mean, robbed?"

She gripped his arm and shook him violently. The pain in his body was excruciating.

"He robbed me — that's how he rewarded our kindness — robbed me of my jewels, d'you hear?"

"Who robbed you?"

"That Phoenician gutter-rat your father brought here — Senka!" she screamed in his ear.

"Mother, please control yourself."

"You encouraged him! Making a friend of him, taking him everywhere, treating him like one of the family."

"I didn't take him to bed."

"How dare you!" she shrieked and struck him across the face. Antonius cried out in pain.

She was contrite at once.

"Forgive me, Antonius, I'm half out of my mind. I shouldn't have struck you. Oh, dearest boy, forgive me!"

"It's all right, Mother. I shouldn't have said what I did." He wanted her to go away, but her contrition was as relentless as her anger.

"Poor boy, what's happened to you — your face is cut. It needs stitching. Where's that damned Ahmed? What happened, you look so ill."

"It's nothing, Mother. I had a fall. Please go to bed."

"How can I go to bed? I can't sleep. I can't sit still." She jumped up and began to pace the room, weeping and wringing her hands.

"My ruby necklace — it's gone! Your father is so angry. Oh, that swine, Senka, that monster, I'll have him flayed alive!"

"Why should Senka take your jewels?"

"Are you taking his side? That ungrateful wretch, this is how he repays our trust!"

"Are you sure? Perhaps someone else took them?"

"Who? Who would dare? You're not suggesting one of my guests stole them?"

"Did you know that father has mortgaged this house, everything in fact?"

"Mortgaged? What are you talking about?" Her voice, shrill and angry, battered him. He put his hands to his head.

"Mother, he borrowed money for timber to repair the fleet. Ahmed told me. Perhaps he needed the jewels for security."

"He took my jewels? Is he mad?" she screamed.

"I don't know. I said perhaps ..." Antonius groaned. She was silent. He looked past her and saw the tall, blonde figure of Dr Iros in the doorway.

"Good evening, madam," Iros said gravely, "may I see Antonius alone, please."

The doctor stood aside for Zanthope to pass but she remained swaying drunkenly. Then she moved towards the young man, her loose wrap showing more of her body than it concealed.

"I don't think we have met before," she said

coyly. She came close to Iros as Credon hovered embarrassed in the background. Iros drew back.

"Madam, please go to your room while I attend to your son."

"Don't you order me about, you damned foreigner!" she screamed and tried to strike Iros. Credon nervously urged one of the girls to help Zanthope to her room. Zanthope struck the girl but Iros gripped her wrist and marched her out of the room.

"Where is her bedroom?"

The maid showed him. He thrust Zanthope in and locked the door. At once she began hammering on the door and shouting obscenities.

Dr Iros returned to Antonius' room and closed the door. He asked for water and washed his hands and then examined Antonius' wounds.

"You're lucky," he said at last, "it could have been much worse. There's extensive bruising — there might be a cracked rib. The wound on your face will soon heal. There'll be a scar. How did it happen?"

Antonius told him briefly and then asked Dr Iros and Credon to tell no one about the attack.

"Councillor Micalidos has enough to worry about without this," he added.

Iros stitched the wound and promised to send a potion to ease the pain.

"The groom will go with you and bring it back," Credon said.

"Very well. Drink plenty, Antonius — fruit juice, milk — no wine for a few days."

Antonius raised himself on one elbow. He felt shame and embarrassment.

"Thank you for coming, doctor. My mother's unwell and upset —"

"It's already forgotten. By the way, you remember those two friends of ours," he paused, "those who wanted to visit Mallia?" Iros was referring to the escaped slaves, Arkos and Tyra.

"Yes, doctor, I remember."

"It has all been arranged, but we need transport," Iros said.

"Don't worry, I'll see to that tomorrow," Antonius assured him, "good night and thank you, doctor."

# CHAPTER 32

When Andreas and Ahmed arrived at the King's reception in the East Palace the great staircase was already crowded with guests. They slowly descended the four flights of marble stairs, which were supported by massive red cedar columns, wide at the top and tapering toward the base in the characteristic Minoan design.

Andreas paused occasionally to exchange greetings with acquaintances, many of whom expressed surprise and pleasure at seeing him. In the babble of conversation the Bull Dance was, of course, the most predominant subject.

"How truly magnificent Paulius was! And no one makes me laugh more than Ali-el-Berber."

Recognizing the voice, Andreas looked down over the marble balustrade and saw Chryssa Senthios with her husband and old Papa Senthios. She was wearing a crimson gown with a gold embroidered jacket.

Then, as she turned to greet a friend, Andreas saw that she was wearing a magnificent necklace. For an instant he was puzzled. Surely he had seen those rubies before? His first reaction was disbelief followed by great anger when he realized that Chryssa was wearing his wife's necklace. He was about to draw Ahmed's attention to the woman and the jewels when Chancellor Darian greeted him, presented his wife and began a long conversation as they continued to descend the stairs.

It was impossible to confront Chryssa. While Andreas was pretending interest as Darian rambled on, he was asking himself who could have had access to the necklace and how it had been removed from his wife's jewel casket.

They had now reached the bottom of the stairway. The small court, so deserted when they had met Uncle Zaron there three months ago, was crowded with guests, laughing and talking as they moved toward the reception hall.

Wooden panels, which separated the Hall of the Double Axes from the King's apartments, were folded back in recesses in the large pillars. This created a magnificently spacious salon in which the reception was to be held. The huge pillars cast black shadows on the dazzling white walls; lamplight shone on brilliantly coloured frescoes and the golden word LABRYS — and the sign of the Double Axe — gleamed on pillars and walls throughout the long reception hall.

There was little room to move. Andreas found himself near Doxa Grinkos.

"Whatever was the matter with Asteria?" she demanded in her bored voice, "I've never seen a more lacklustre performance."

Her companions agreed.

"But that new dancer," Doxa continued, "the little blonde creature, what was her peculiar name?"

"Belia," Andreas grunted as he pushed past.

"Councillor Micalidos, we don't often see you here at Palace receptions."

"You don't often come here yourself," he retorted. He wondered what this harpy would make of his wife's necklace being worn by Chryssa. Obviously Doxa had not noticed it yet. She and Grinkos — who was intent on having his wine-cup refilled as often as possible — were indebted to Olivia for their seats at the Bull Dance and for their invitation to this reception. Doxa bitterly resented the change in Olivia's fortunes.

The mystery tantalized her as she had always considered Olivia a fool. When she tried to find out how her companion had achieved this metamorphosis from penniless lodger to an affluent resident of the Palace, Olivia's enigmatic smile and her reply, "a small piece of good fortune, my dear", only stimulated Doxa's curiosity.

Andreas and Ahmed moved slowly through the cheerful, animated throng. As they approached the King, the conversation and laughter became more subdued out of respect for His Majesty.

King Minos was enthroned on a dais at the northern end of the long hall, surrounded by High Priests, Councillors, handsome young men and a fawning group of people who pressed respectfully forward, eager to greet and flatter him. Minos wore a magnificent crown, decorated with jewels and peacock feathers; a gold chest-piece, studded with emeralds and a flowing robe of shimmering silk.

The King was in an affable mood, but Ahmed observed he was tense and nervous.

"He is insecure and unhappy," the doctor diagnosed.

The elegant Cretan ladies wore long, flounced skirts richly embroidered with gold or silver thread and sewn with jewels. Many wore close-fitting jackets designed to reveal naked breasts made more prominent by tight lacing beneath. Their hair was elaborately dressed and bound with ribbons, jewels or coloured beads and their faces were heavily made up.

Palace society had always irritated Andreas. These slim, highly-strung women with their mannered, affected voices and wanton looks repelled him. Observing them, his thoughts strayed to the brilliant young dancer, Belia. Would she come with the Bull Dancers to this reception? He fervently hoped so. He compared her with these sophisticated women. Would she retain the fresh simplicity he remembered at their first meeting in Phylon's workshop? Probably not, he thought sadly, looking about him. The men were no less fashion-conscious than the women, with their glossy, oiled curls and love-locks — a style he had never admired. In the elderly and grossly fat, like Papa Senthios, it was especially grotesque.

Andreas saw Councillor Brecchius and Councillor

Markos with Vaden, his arrogant, ill-mannered son. Councillor Xanthios was there, too, cold and thin-lipped as he edged nearer the throne.

Andreas and Ahmed moved forward and made their dutiful obeisance to the King. Minos welcomed them politely but without warmth and they soon withdrew.

Dr Ahmed, whose stature made him feel conspicuous in public, stood beside a pillar from where he could observe the royal dais and the two women seated on either side of the King. On Minos' right was his sister, Princess Ariadne, radiant and excited and anticipating the arrival of Prince Theseus. And, on the King's left were his wife and the former Princess of Egypt, Queen Kara, whose beauty and sweet personality so appealed to Ahmed. The doctor was distressed to see that she was being ignored. She was dressed in the Cretan style, the vivid skirt elaborately embroidered, and the jacket laced beneath her breasts, which were modestly covered. Ahmed thought he had never seen a woman with such classic beauty and simple dignity. To many observers Queen Kara seemed aloof, but not to Ahmed. He knew she would have a smile for those who greeted her. He wished he could step forward himself, but his shyness prevented that.

As Ahmed watched, he saw the Egyptian Ambassador approach the Queen. User-Amon was a big man with an aquiline nose and piercing black eyes. As the Ambassador and the Queen conversed, Ahmed noticed several other foreigners standing nearby, endeavouring not to appear bored. These diplomats represented the governments of neighbouring powers — Cyprus, Anatolia, Troy and Phoenicia.

From the moment he had seen her, Andreas had determined to challenge Chryssa for wearing his wife's necklace. However, it was not easy to approach the Senthios family in the crowded reception hall. It was almost impossible to move from one part of the salon to another. So Andreas, like Princess Ariadne, but for quite different reasons, could do little but watch and wait for the arrival of Theseus and the bull dancers.

They did not have long to wait. The sound of cheering came from the grand staircase and almost immediately the bull dancers, with an escort of soldiers, made their entrance. When they appeared, a great burst of applause filled the huge salon and continued unabated as the group approached the throne to pay homage.

From that moment Andreas put aside thoughts of the necklace. He found himself pushed and shoved on every side as excited people, mostly society women he noted with annoyance, struggled to get closer to the young dancers.

Prince Theseus led them into the reception hall. Though he had not danced in the ring today, he had been invited by Princess Ariadne. As heir to the Greek throne, he strode with assurance to the dais, his copper hair gleaming, a half-smile barely concealing his arrogance. Paulius came next with M'boola at his side. Behind them came Leander and Ali, occasionally rolling his eyes and winking at the guests. The three young girls, Chloe, Freyna and Belia, came last, their eyes shining with pleasure and excitement. However, Belia and Freyna were very surprised by the behaviour of some of their admirers. The dancing girls' blonde hair was of great interest to the dark-complexioned Cretan ladies who touched and pulled the girls' golden tresses to discover if they were genuine or if they were wearing wigs! Belia and Freyna accepted these attentions with good humour.

Andreas saw at once that some determination was necessary if he was to approach Belia. He pushed and shoved with the others and was delighted when Belia recognized him. He was still some distance from her, trying to avoid two over-excited ladies who were blowing kisses to Leander, when a young man pushed him aside. Almost knocking the ladies off their feet, the young man grasped Belia around the waist and pulled her to him.

Andreas, at first, thought that this bold young man must be a friend of Belia's. Then he noticed, with surprise, that it was Vaden Markos, the Navy Minister's son. A moment later, as the impertinent young man attempted an even more intimate embrace, Andreas saw Belia's face. Her eyes flashed with fury and her knee jerked up sharply. Vaden howled, released his hold on the girl and, doubling up in agony, collapsed on the floor. People nearby were surprised by this unseemly behaviour so close to the throne.

Andreas, now beside Belia, saw that young Markos was recovering. He was drunk and swearing and obviously about to make trouble. In a sudden decision Andreas took Belia by the hand.

"Follow me, this way," he whispered.

He pushed through the throng with Belia close behind and soon reached the outer court. The great staircase was now almost empty and Andreas saw that the guards were busy eating and drinking in the ante-room.

"Belia, are you all right? That fool was drunk," he said.

Her look amused him. It said everything. Young Markos had been dealt with. He was unimportant and forgotten.

"There is a place we can talk without interruption," he suggested. She nodded and followed him across the deserted courtyard. He led her to his apartment in the West Palace, unlocked the door and ushered her in.

"Let's sit over by the light well," he said. He lit a lamp and set it near her so that he could see her face.

Timon's disappearance had obsessed Andreas and he had been in a state of constant anxiety for many weeks. Korynna's strange message had brought some hope and here before him was its source. He was eager to question Belia, but stood watching her without speaking. She had changed in those few months since he had first met her in Phylon's workshop. The young girl, the urchin, was gone. She was still boyishly slender but there was now a more sensuous curve to her breasts and thighs. Andreas saw that she had become a beautiful woman.

"Now Belia, my sister tells me that you know something about my son's disappearance."

Belia assured Andreas that his son was safe, living in the men's quarters of the Bull Halls and in the care of Leander.

Andreas gazed at her in astonishment.

"Belia, I'm so relieved, I don't know what to say ..."

"I suppose you are wondering how this came about," she asked, smiling.

"Indeed I am," he replied, sitting beside her.

"It's quite a long story. I wanted to let you know sooner. I tried to make your sister understand."

He nodded encouragingly and she recounted how she had first discovered and then explored the tunnels and the rooms of the Labyrinth under the Palace of Knossos.

"Many people use those passages, Councillor Micalidos. People I do not know — except one — Theseus, the bull dancer." Belia related how she discovered the prison cells and the mysterious cord leading to the room where Theseus and the Princess had their rendezvous. She told Andreas of their argument about Minos' pilgrimage and how upset Ariadne was because Andreas had influenced the King against it.

As Belia spoke, Andreas understood who had instigated the intrigue which had concerned him for so long. It was the Greek Prince, Theseus.

Then Belia recounted the conversation between the unknown man and woman in the Labyrinth who said Timon would not leave the Palace alive and also threatened harm to Antonius. From her description of them, Andreas was confident he could identify his agent, Agidor and Zanthope's friend, Olivia. He felt a cold rage against these two who had betrayed his family's trust in their greed for money.

Finally, Belia told Andreas how, on her last visit into the Labyrinth, she had found his young son bound and gagged in the Pillar crypt and had taken him safely back to the Bull Halls.

Andreas was overcome with gratitude and admiration for the resourceful and courageous bull dancer.

"Dearest Belia! How can I ever thank you? The Goddess has smiled on us! Timon is safe and I am forever in your debt."

"I am so glad I was in time to save your boy," she said. Belia told Andreas sadly of the dead child's body in the burial urn and of the other urns, some containing children's bodies, others empty and waiting. "Those vicious murderers! How could they?" Belia murmured.

The sound of her voice, soft and musical, gave him intense pleasure. He had listened without interruption as her extraordinary tale unfolded. The death of the other children increased his thankfulness and relief at Timon's escape. But the sinister evil behind these events horrified and disturbed him. He wondered how he could prevent further hideous crimes.

Belia reminded him of the threat against Antonius.

"And you must be careful," she warned, "Theseus and Ariadne are your enemies."

"I will warn Antonius, but we can look after ourselves," Andreas replied grimly, then with a change of tone, he continued, "Now, we must arrange to bring Timon home. Can this friend of yours, Leander, take care of him until tomorrow?"

"Of course. He will be safe with us."

"How can I get a message to you, Belia?"

"The guards will take messages for the bull boys. They do it all the time."

"Good."

He hated to let her go.

"Belia, I've thought of you often since that day in Phylon's workshop," Andreas said tenderly.

"I too have remembered it," she answered shyly.

Then he remembered he had not praised her performance in the Bull Ring.

"You did so well this afternoon. You will be famous one day."

"It was wonderful — after being so nervous," she said with a laugh.

"You weren't frightened?"

"Of the black bull, yes! But not of old Tauron. We love him and believe he loves us."

"I can understand how Tauron feels," Andreas said with a smile.

As he watched Belia in this small, dimly lit room, he realized that his feelings for her were far deeper than admiration of her beauty and courage and even gratitude for the life of his son. He deeply regretted the discrepancy in their ages and compared himself, sober and middle-aged, with the handsome, virile young athletes by whom she was surrounded in the Bull Halls.

You bloody old fool! he thought, longing to stroke her blonde hair, gleaming in the flickering lamplight, to touch the soft smoothness of her skin.

"You are a very beautiful and brave young lady," he said softly, "I am deeply indebted to you."

"It was nothing — almost an accident," she replied simply.

Andreas still did not understand why Belia had first ventured into the Labyrinth.

"Was it curiosity, Belia, that led you to explore these passages?" he asked.

"No, Councillor, not curiosity," she answered quickly, "I had a purpose. There is a favour I would ask of you, only because I do not know whether we will ever be able to meet again."

She looked anxiously into his face.

"What is it?" he said quietly.

"My friends in the Bull Halls — Freyna and Leander — I'm very worried about them." She told Andreas of their love for each other, how disastrous discovery would be and how she planned to help them escape through the tunnels under the Palace.

"They must have a hiding place outside the Palace and a boat to leave Crete."

He stared at her, wondering if she was only using him to help her friends. Her innocent gaze reassured him. And then, of course, he owed Belia and the bull dancers a great debt.

"You know the ports will be closed in a few weeks? No Captain will risk his ship when the autumn gales begin."

"Yes, I understand," she replied, "but if Freyna gets with child — the punishments for bull dancers are horrible."

"I see." Andreas paused. "There is one man in the Palace I can trust," he said thoughtfully, "The Egyptian Ambassador's steward, Shep-Anep. If you need help, ask Leander to send one of the messengers to the Egyptian Embassy. I will do all I can to help. Does that ease your anxiety?"

"Yes, Councillor, I am so grateful," she said, and quite spontaneously embraced him.

Andreas held her in his arms, intoxicated by the warmth and perfume of her body. But still he hesitated, believing her embrace was merely gratitude and drew back from her a little. "This Freyna you speak of, is she the young woman who was with you in Phylon's workshop?" he asked.

"Yes, that's right."

"And she loves Leander?"

Belia nodded.

"Do you love someone in the Bull Halls, Belia?" he asked, surprised at himself, for it was no business of his. But he wanted to end this madness before he made a fool of himself.

"No, Councillor," she replied, smiling, "Paulius is our leader and we all love and respect him. He is going to marry the vaulter, Asteria, soon."

"Then whom do you love, Belia?" he persisted. One of the brave and good-looking young men in the Bull Halls must have pleased her.

"I think I could love you, Councillor," she said seriously.

He gazed into her eyes, his heart pounding. At that moment she seemed more mature than her seventeen years and he almost believed that she meant what she said. Andreas felt as if he were a young man again, in love for the first time. He struggled to be wise and fatherly.

"My dear girl, you are very young and beautiful and sweet, but..."

"May I call you Andreas?" she asked.

"Of course, my dear."

"Andreas," she said again and kissed him on the mouth.

He returned her kisses as she clung to him and wondered how he could have deserved such joy.

"I wish I could be warm and safe with you forever," she said softly.

Andreas realized that she would soon be out of reach in the Bull Halls and this might be the only time he would ever hold her like this. Even if she escaped with her friends, they would have to leave Crete. And if she remained for five years as a bull dancer, there was a worse possibility, which he could not bear to consider. It was hopeless. He saw that clearly. But this moment was very precious and he tried to memorize every detail of her face, her eyes, her voice and her slender, exquisite body.

She drew back suddenly, her eyes shining.

"Andreas, if you can find a way into the Labyrinth from the Palace, we could meet there."

"No, Belia," he said firmly, "it's too dangerous. You must never go there again."

"But there must be a way in from the Bull Halls that Theseus uses," she said eagerly.

Andreas took her face in his hands.

"Let Leander find it. Belia, promise me you will not go into those passages again."

She looked into his eyes and saw that he loved her.

"I promise, Andreas," she said.

Then he kissed her gently on the brow, the eyelids and the mouth. They looked at each other for a moment without speaking and she shivered.

"I must go," she said, "there will be trouble if I am missed."

They returned to the reception in the East Palace and not a moment too soon, for the dancers were about to be escorted back to the Bull Halls. Fortunately the guards were drunk and Belia was able to slip between Chloe and Freyna without her absence being noticed.

"Thank the Gods you came back," Freyna said, "we were wondering what we would say."

"How did you get on?" Belia asked as they walked along. "Did that fool make trouble?"

Chloe giggled.

"I thought Leander might kill him!" Freyna replied. "He pulled Chloe's hair first and then started on me! Fortunately the guards intervened. Did you arrange anything for Timon?"

Belia explained briefly and asked Freyna to tell Leander. Then they were back at the Bull Halls and all that Freyna and her lover could do was exchange a look as they said good night and parted. They had returned to reality, so much more painful after the brief taste of freedom they enjoyed at the reception.

When Andreas looked for Chryssa Senthios, she and her menfolk were gone. He and Ahmed returned home.

Credon had waited up for them and in spite of Antonius' admonition he told Andreas of his son's unexpected return, his injuries, and that Dr Iros had been called.

"What did Iros say? Is it serious?" Andreas asked, shocked.

Credon repeated the doctor's opinion.

"You did well, Credon. How is Antonius now?"

"The doctor prescribed a potion and he's sleeping comfortably, sir."

"Then we'll not disturb him. Good night, Credon, don't wait up."

"Thank you, sir. Good night."

When the steward was gone, Andreas and Ahmed sat for some time discussing what action might be taken to recover the stolen jewels. Andreas then related what Belia had told him of Timon's rescue.

"We have much to be thankful for, Councillor," Ahmed remarked, "this bull dancer must be a very remarkable young woman."

"Yes, indeed," Andreas said and abruptly changed the subject. "Ahmed, you must examine Antonius yourself in the morning. We shall learn more from him about this damn business."

Andreas passed his hand wearily over his eyes.

"Thank the Gods Antonius and Timon are safe."

Ahmed agreed but he too was tired. He had wished for some time to speak of the escaped slaves, Arkos and Tyra, who were still at the surgery, but this was not the moment. Andreas was near exhaustion and Ahmed knew that arrangements were progressing well. The runaway slaves would soon be safe at Olykka's farm near Mallia. The doctor decided to say nothing about them.

"Good night, sir, may you sleep soundly," he said.

"You too, Ahmed. Good night, good night."

# CHAPTER 33

The first autumn rain fell in torrents, mist hung over the mountain tops and the wind gusted violently, sending swollen clouds across the grey sky.

During a sleepless night, Andreas tried to sort out the web of intrigue and enmity, as dark and threatening as the oncoming storm, which now surrounded his family. Timon's abduction, the theft of his wife's jewels, the attack on Antonius, and the ostracism of his colleagues all pointed to a conspiracy — but by whom and why? What harm have I done to anyone? he asked himself, I tried to do my duty and place the safety of Crete first.

The rain pelted down, drumming on the roof for hours. He stood on the edge of the garden court and held out his hands as the rain splashed on his face and ran through his hair, cool and refreshing. He laughed. He had been a thorn in their sides, they had no reason to love him. But my sons, why my sons? he asked. He shook his head and returned to the room. His colleagues in the Council might dislike him and resent his interference, but they would not harm his sons, of that he felt sure. There was a more sinister thread in this enigma. He decided that he must approach each of these vicious assaults individually.

This morning he had wanted to question Antonius more fully but Ahmed was against it. He agreed with Dr Iros that there might be a cracked rib and there was extensive bruising. Ahmed was adamant that Antonius should have rest and a month off duty.

"I shall be well in a few days," Antonius protested, but his haggard face belied this.

"We'll see," Ahmed said diplomatically.

"Meanwhile," Andreas continued grimly, "there is much to do. You say that Agidor was responsible for this outrage, Antonius?"

"I think I recognized his voice," his son replied wearily.

"But you didn't see him?"

"It was too dark, I couldn't be sure."

After a signal from Ahmed, Andreas had let the matter drop. He left his son's room telling him not to worry and to get well.

Andreas wanted to bring Timon home at once. He was impatient to set off for the Palace, but the storm became more violent. He did not care about his own comfort, but was greatly concerned for the boy's health. Frustrated and irritable, he waited for the storm to pass.

Ahmed was eager to visit the surgery and was most anxious to complete the arrangements for the departure of the slaves, Arkos and Tyra, for Mallia.

When Andreas left the room, Antonius sent one of the maids to fetch Dorcas, the cart driver. He came, cap in hand, wet and moving awkwardly from one foot to the other. He was good-natured and willing enough. It only remained to agree on a time for him to convey Arkos and Tyra to Mallia.

"Should it be tonight?" Antonius asked.

The doctor glanced anxiously out of the window.

"What if the storm persists? They could become lost in the dark. Tyra is in her seventh month. Early tomorrow morning would be better if the weather clears."

So it was agreed. Ahmed sighed. He was uneasy because Andreas had no knowledge of these arrangements. However, he did not wish to burden him further. The prospect of the slaves' departure was almost as welcome as that of Timon's return.

Andreas sent for Dr Ahmed to join him for the midday meal. A small brazier burned in the apartment and they were glad of its warmth. The storm had brought the end of summer and a foretaste of winter. Senka, the secretary, joined them. When the meal was over and Credon had withdrawn, Andreas confronted Senka.

"Can you cast any light on the theft of my wife's jewels?"

The directness of Andreas' question shocked Senka, but he kept his nerve. His eyes met Andreas as he sought desperately for an answer that would sound both truthful and helpful without involving himself.

"I believe they were stolen in Mallia," he said at last.

"Why?"

"There were many strangers and visitors there — so much coming and going. There was plenty of opportunity for someone to enter a room unnoticed."

"How did you know the jewels were in Mallia?"

Senka paused.

"Chryssa told me that Young Madam had shown them to her mother, Madam Brecchius."

"You're on first name terms with Madam Senthios, then?" Senka did not reply.

"Did Chryssa steal them?"

"She could have."

"But did she?"

Andreas glared at his secretary as if he intended to drag the truth from him by force.

"By the Gods, sir, I do not know."

They were silent as Andreas stared into the fire. Again he looked sharply at the young man.

"Senka, you must go to Captain Senthios and demand the return of our property."

Senka averted his eyes.

"Very well, sir."

"I shall lay charges against the agent, Agidor, for assaulting my son," Andreas continued.

"What if Agidor can't be identified?" Ahmed said.

"A charge may deter him from attacking again."

"Perhaps the Egyptian steward, Shep-Anep, can identify him."

Andreas slapped his knee.

"Of course, Ahmed! Why didn't I think of that?" Andreas paced about the room. "I can't stay here. I must go to the Palace and thank Shep personally for helping Antonius to escape from those bastards. Senka, tell Credon to order the carriage at once and then return here. I'm going to dictate some letters."

Senka left the room thankful to escape further scrutiny. When he returned, Andreas' first letter was to the bull dancer, Leander, informing him that they would wait for Timon at the entrance to the Bull Halls near the North Gate.

"I want this letter written immediately," Andreas said to his secretary, "you can write the second in my absence. I'll sign it when I return."

This second letter was to Andreas' brother, Grivas Micalidos at the Palace of Phaestos, informing him of the attack on Antonius and instructing him to arrest the agent, Agidor, immediately.

When the letter for Leander was ready, Andreas and Ahmed set off. Dr Ahmed would have preferred to go to his surgery, but Andreas was pleased when the doctor offered to accompany him to the Palace. At the Egyptian Embassy they inquired after Shep-Anep. He was delighted to see Andreas and the three men walked together across the Courtyard to the East Palace where a narrow stairway led down to the Bull Halls.

They handed the letter for Leander to a guard at the door and waited impatiently for more than an hour. The passage was dark, draughty and cold and the tension was painful. Andreas stamped his feet to relieve his impatience. Each man began to fear that the venture to rescue Timon would fail. While they waited, Shep gave a full account of the attack on Antonius.

"Could you identify these criminals, Shep?" Andreas asked.

"None of them were known to me, sir, as soon as we arrived they raced down the stairway and disappeared."

"I can never thank you enough, Shep."

"I am happy to serve you in any way I can, sir."

This remark prompted Andreas to ask Shep if he would go with Senka to Captain Senthios and demand the return of Zanthope's necklace. After Andreas had explained the circumstances, Shep agreed.

The locked door remained obstinately closed. They discovered later that the delay was due to Timon's refusal to leave Leander. The boy was so terrified that at last the bull dancer persuaded Naxos to let him pass through the trainers' quarters, normally out of bounds, to deliver Timon himself.

On seeing the tall young man and the child holding his hand, Andreas stepped forward.

"Timon!"

"Is that your father?" Leander asked.

"Yes."

The boy ran into his father's arms. Andreas kissed him tenderly, the tears welling up in his eyes. As the door began to close he called out, "Thank you, Leander. Thank you, with all my heart."

The young dancer nodded and smiled.

"Is Belia all right? There was no trouble last night, I hope?"

"Everything's all right, sir, no trouble."

Leander raised a hand in farewell and the heavy door closed. Andreas, his son and his friends went out into the fresh air. The three men parted, Shep to his Embassy, the doctor to his surgery and Andreas, with the boy clutching his hand, home in the waiting carriage.

Aunt Korynna wept with joy to see Timon returned safely. Later that evening, the doctor examined him and although Timon was still upset and whimpered as he clung to Andreas, they could find no injuries, only the marks on his wrists and ankles. That night, Andreas and Ahmed discussed the boy's abduction and imprisonment in the Labyrinth beneath the Palace.

"Timon is in a state of shock," Ahmed said, "it would be wrong, even dangerous to question him at this time."

"We can encourage him to talk when he recovers," Andreas replied.

A few days later, however, when Korynna tried to persuade Timon to talk of his experiences the boy immediately became hysterical and was sick. After this he sometimes awoke at night, screaming. Ahmed counselled patience and loving care.

Plans for the marriage of Vaden Markos and Leda Brecchius were progressing in spite of her reluctance when fate intervened. Madam Brecchius became seriously ill and Councillor Brecchius saw the necessity of keeping Leda at home. Young Markos was in no hurry, so the wedding was postponed, awaiting Madam Brecchius' recovery. The two Councillors were content that for the time being, the engagement should seal the bond between the families.

Leda nursed her mother with selfless devotion, preparing dainty meals to tempt her meagre appetite, bearing with her querulous complaints and supporting her in the hours of pain, which gradually became more frequent.

Chryssa came once to visit her mother. She did not stay long because she disliked anything to do with sickness and death. Urging her mother to "get well soon, dearest", she hurried away with a scarf over her nose. As Chryssa departed, she remarked casually to Leda that Antonius was looking very well.

"I'm glad to hear it," Leda replied calmly.

She had not seen him since their visit to Mallia. She still loved him and in her quiet, constant way would always love him. Now, however, hope had given way to resignation. Antonius was not for her and acceptance of this had brought some peace of mind.

"He's engaged, I'm told, to a girl in Mallia," Chryssa continued, watching her sister sharply to gauge the effect of her words. Leda looked blank. If Chryssa had hoped for tears or distress, she was disappointed. The engagement was, in fact, based on rumour. An idea of Hyacinth's which had come to nothing.

"If you need anything, just send for me," was Chryssa's parting remark. Leda did not reply but smiled faintly.

Councillor Brecchius paid his wife short courtesy visits. Escaping thankfully from one of these, he spat down a light well as he made his way through the winding corridors toward the central Courtyard. He deeply resented his wife's illness. Why could she not recover — or else die — rather than linger between life and death, inconveniencing everybody and delaying the wedding.

Leda's quiet courage reproached Brecchius and her transparent pallor bothered him. What if she too became ill? How tiresome that would be. His thoughts turned to her projected marriage. It was most advantageous. Markos had wealth and land and that idiot son would get it all. Of course, he had an unsavoury reputation — raping a peasant girl, they said — but this was of no real consequence. The Markos family needed this marriage to gain respectability. But what if they heard that Leda might not be robust enough to bear a child? They might try to stop the marriage. Brecchius relished the idea that both his daughters would inherit wealth — Captain Senthios was also an only son — but he had another reason for advancing this union with the Markos family. Greedy and extravagant himself, he had, for a price, agreed to a scheme which old Papa Senthios had devised. The plan needed Markos' support and, though he did not know it yet, this marriage was a way of drawing him into the conspiracy.

Brecchius reached the Courtyard and caught sight of Xanthios. They greeted each other with toothy smiles and the Minister for Supply inquired after

Madam Brecchius. He gauged from the evasive reply that she was no better.

"How sad the wedding had to be put off, such a disappointment," he said, smiling. Xanthios' small, sharp eyes probed for signs of despair. He had a young daughter himself, almost of a marrying age and some rather pressing debts. Brecchius knew this and laughed.

"It's only temporary, a short postponement." He could afford to be affable. When old Papa Senthios was ready to move, Councillor Xanthios would do as he was told.

In the narrow alley beside the surgery building, a small cart, half-filled with vegetables, waited unobtrusively.

The early morning air was chill, the driver shivered and drew down the earflaps of his woollen cap.

Presently a tall figure came out of the surgery, listened, peered up and down the dark street and returned inside. Then two young people came out, the woman wearing a cloak, the other with his arm around her. They hurried into the alley, mounted the cart and sat among the vegetables. The driver, Dorcas, urged the horse to move. It baulked. He alighted and, taking the rein, led the animal from the lane into the street.

He was about to remount the cart when two men ran from a doorway and pushed him roughly aside. One held the horse's bridle. A third man, in officer's cloak and helmet, appeared and in a harsh voice ordered the two people in the cart to get down.

"In the name of the King and Council, I arrest you, Arkos and Tyra. You are escaped slaves and I will claim the reward for your return to Madam Grinkos!"

Tyra screamed in terror. She jumped from the cart and ran down the street. Arkos raced after her, pursued by the two soldiers. The driver, left to himself, for Lieutenant Sartis was now concentrating on the runaways, grasped the reins, urged the horse to a gallop and with a great clattering, disappeared down the cobbled street.

The slaves were unlucky. Tyra tripped and fell heavily. The two soldiers caught her and dragged her roughly to her feet. She began to weep and scream hysterically. Arkos tried to free Tyra, but he was no match for the two burly soldiers. Lieutenant Sartis reached them, held a dagger to Tyra's throat and ordered his men to bind their hands. Tyra screamed and fainted. Arkos rushed at Sartis and tried to throttle him, but the officer threw him off and drawing his sword, struck the slave a blow on the head.

Arkos staggered, blood pouring down his face. He fell heavily, hitting his head on a stone step and lay unconscious. As Tyra wept piteously, an old woman came out of a hovel in the street and knelt to comfort her.

Dr Iros, who had watched the drama from the surgery, was horrified that their plans had miscarried. He rushed down the street and accused Lieutenant Sartis of brutality.

"And I'll have you arrested for harbouring escaped slaves," Sartis retorted.

Iros controlled himself with difficulty.

"I am a doctor and this girl is my patient. She is pregnant and needs attention."

He knelt and felt Tyra's pulse. It was strong and racing. He was concerned she might abort.

Without warning, Sartis kicked Dr Iros.

"Clear out, you Greek vermin!"

Iros was speechless with rage but he was unarmed. Sartis shouted at the soldiers.

"Pick up these two and get a move on. We'll go to the Grinkos house in the Street of Doves."

One of the men hoisted Arkos on his shoulders. The other found Tyra awkward to lift with her swollen belly. He tried to drag her up by the arms, dropped her and she lay on the footpath moaning with pain.

"Poor little girl," muttered the old woman, "you men should have some pity, your mothers suffered to bring you forth."

"She's in labour. She must return to the hospital at once," Iros shouted vehemently, "I'll fetch a litter. You don't want her to give birth in the street!"

"I don't care where she whelps," Sartis snarled, "she can have it in the gutter as far as I'm concerned. Fetch the litter. You can help my men carry it to the Grinkos place."

Iros wanted to be near at hand to help Tyra and Arkos as much as possible. He swallowed his rage and pride.

"Stay with her," he said to the old woman and ran back to the surgery and called to his assistants.

"Sacred Gods. Everything's gone wrong! Damon, get a litter and blanket and come with me. Altheon, run at once and fetch Dr Ahmed. Tell him ... tell him there's trouble and ask him to meet us at the Grinkos house on the Street of Doves."

Iros and Damon returned with the litter and placed Tyra gently on it. They set off, followed by the two soldiers carrying Arkos.

Dawn was now breaking, bleak and chill and the cold wind was gusting down the narrow streets. Iros shivered. He blamed himself for being a fool as they trudged along. He had wanted to help them both, but now?

It was nearly daylight when they reached the Street of Doves. The litter was put down and the still unconscious Arkos placed beside it. Tyra sat up and tried to draw Arkos closer, weeping and whispering tender words to him but he did not answer.

Lieutenant Sartis knocked loudly at the Grinkos' door. The slaves were terrified as no one dared wake their mistress at this early hour. Sartis did not care. He continued to beat and kick furiously on the door, calling on Madam Grinkos to show herself immediately and make good her promise of payment for the return of her slaves.

The clamour disturbed the whole street and soon people leaned out of windows and others came into the street to watch the commotion at Doxa's door.

She came at last, wrapped in a blanket, her hair tousled and her eyes blinking with sleep. She was in an unpleasant mood. When she heard Sartis' demand for money, she looked distastefully at her injured slaves.

"Take courage and lie still," Iros whispered to Tyra, who was in great pain.

Doxa poked gingerly at Arkos with one foot.

"Money for this!" she cried. "Money for a corpse, you must be mad!"

Sartis and Doxa glared at one another.

"You advertised money for the return of these slaves. I claim that reward." His voice was cold and hard. In his hand he still grasped the sword with Arkos' blood drying on it but Doxa was not easily frightened.

"They are no use to me. Am I to nurse my own slaves? Bring them back in good health if you expect a reward." She turned to go but Sartis grasped her arm.

"The woman is conscious — she'll drop her child in an hour or two. Tomorrow she can wait at table."

"And what use is she if she dies? I might pay half the reward if she's still alive and healthy next week."

"I want all the reward now," Sartis shouted.

"I'm not going to pay you," Doxa screamed back.

"You miserable cheat!" he snarled and continued to abuse her as a large crowd gathered to watch the spectacle.

Dr Iros did what he could to comfort Tyra and was thankful, while Doxa and Sartis brawled, to see the alarmed faces of Dr Ahmed and Antonius emerge from the crowd.

"We came as soon as we had your message," Ahmed said. "How are you, Tyra?" he inquired anxiously. He knelt down, feeling for her pulse. She gripped his hand and began to weep afresh.

"They've killed Arkos! He can't speak to me!"

"Now, you stay calm," the doctor replied soothingly. "We must get them off the street and back to the surgery," he said to Iros.

Sartis and Doxa were almost ready to tear each other to pieces. He would not let her go back into the house and she began to scream for help from Grinkos and her slaves.

The two soldiers, fed up with the whole business, stood by uncomfortably.

"What are you two men doing away from barracks?" Antonius said sternly.

"He ordered ..." began one of them.

"Go back to your duties at once."

The two soldiers hesitated but then left, thankful to escape.

Gently the surgery assistants placed Arkos beside Tyra on the litter. Ahmed and Antonius led the way back toward the surgery as the sound of Sartis' and Doxa's violent altercation grew fainter with each step.

"Sartis will look for them in the surgery," Antonius said when they paused to rest.

"We can't prevent him taking them by force," Damon said sadly.

Ahmed sighed. He could not deal with violence.

"I'll take them to my father's house. They'll be safe there for a few hours. We can move them somewhere else after the baby is born," Iros said.

"Councillor Micalidos will have to be told at once," Ahmed replied.

It was agreed and they parted.

When Dr Iros and Damon walked in under the lamp-maker's sign, Aptaeon and his wife stared at them in surprise.

"Mother, a young woman is having her first child. She needs your help."

Iros' mother smiled kindly at Tyra. "My dear, you are welcome in our house. Do not fear — there will be some pain — but then, a son."

Iros gently bathed Arkos' wound and although the sword cut was not deep, the doctor was concerned about the young man's condition. He believed his skull could have been fractured in the fall after Sartis struck him.

Iros' mother, Nerida, tended Tyra all day, soothing and encouraging her when she became anxious. Arkos lay on a pallet close to her. She held his hand and talked to him, though he never moved or opened his eyes.

Iros delivered the stillborn boy shortly after midnight. Tyra, too weak to cry, lay with her head pressed against her lover's shoulder. Arkos never regained consciousness and a few hours later Tyra died. They lay together, hands clasped.

Nerida wept.

"Hush, Mother," Iros said, "tears will not change anything. We did our best."

"They were so young. They seemed scarcely more than children. Why did the boy die?"

"Arkos? He was knocked down and broke his skull, I believe," Iros said.

He and his parents sat gloomily by the embers of the fire until dawn.

"You've eaten nothing for so long," Nerida said, offering her son some warmed broth. "Don't grieve, my son."

"What had they done to deserve this?" he asked bitterly. His parents were silent, staring into the fire but after some time his mother asked what they would do with the bodies.

"I'll see to it, Mother, in an hour or two. Damon and Altheon will help me. We will bury them together."

The lamp-maker sighed. "Try to rest for a little while, my son. It is the will of the Gods."

"What a disaster!" Andreas said when he learned of the morning's events. "It's very sad. The slaves should have left Knossos immediately."

"So much happened all at once," Ahmed sighed, "I feel responsible. I delayed too long."

"Don't blame yourself. Doxa Grinkos must be an evil woman. Do you need help with the funeral expenses?" Andreas offered.

"No, thank you, sir. Iros and I and the people at the surgery would like to do that for them."

Some weeks later, when Antonius had recovered from his injuries, he met Senka in the city. Antonius believed the secretary had been avoiding him.

"Come and have a drink," he said.

The invitation was genial enough and the Lieutenant led the way to the Green Cat. Senka hesitated a moment when he saw the sign with the cat's malevolent yellow eye.

"Remind you of something?" Antonius asked.

"The card game. You lost quite a lot."

"I wasn't thinking of that. Two people died not long ago. Remember?" Antonius poured the wine.

He glanced toward the doorpost. The tattered notice about Arkos and Tyra still hung there.

"Sacred Gods!" Senka said. "How sad that was."

"Did you give them away?"

Senka looked shocked.

"I? Of course not. Why should I?"

"For the reward, of course. How did Sartis know where to find them?"

The secretary did not reply and seemed deep in thought.

"You stayed on with Sartis, after I left that night."

"So did Brachne and Zarkos. We talked and finished the wine. Sartis read the notice. He was interested."

"How is it he was waiting for them?"

"By all the Gods, I don't know."

Senka saw that Antonius did not believe him and stared into his wine.

"Do you think Sartis will make trouble? I've heard the Grinkos woman wouldn't pay him," he said after a pause.

"Yes. He's out of pocket," Antonius gave a contemptuous laugh, "that's the only good thing to come out of this rotten business. Right now, he's looking for the man who gave him the information."

Antonius watched Senka steadily, searching his face for some reaction. They drank their wine in silence.

"Do you think Sartis could make trouble for your — for Councillor Micalidos? The surgery is his property," Senka persisted.

"It would be hard to prove that my father knew they were there."

"Yes, of course."

They were silent again. Senka drained his cup and prepared to leave. Antonius grasped Senka's arm.

"You once told me that Chryssa asked you to steal my mother's necklace."

"I was very drunk."

"Did you take the necklace?"

"No, I did not! I've already told your father, I know nothing about it."

"Did *she* take it, in Mallia?"

"Who?"

"Chryssa Senthios, of course."

"She might have. I don't know."

"Do you know how she acquired it?"

"I've told you, I don't know."

"I can't believe she's a thief," Antonius said quietly.

He put his wine-cup down and left without another word.

# CHAPTER 34

The day came for Paulius, Asteria and M'boola to make their last appearance with the bulls of Knossos before their retirement. It was a triumphant finale for three outstanding performers. The younger dancers, still in bondage, felt some envy, but the departure of Paulius and M'boola, who were greatly loved, was sincerely regretted. Asteria would not be missed.

Before the Bull Dance commenced, there was a brief ceremony in the Bull Hall Shrine. The High Priest Arcanos thanked the three dancers for their dedicated service and gave them his blessing. After the performance Naxos was to address them all at a farewell banquet where there would be gifts, commendations and the presentation of money held in trust. The kitchen staff had worked since early morning preparing the feast.

The festive spirit had already taken hold. The new

dancers realized they were no longer novices and showed confidence born of success. Since the opening of the season, Paulius and his group had alternated with Theseus and his Greeks without mishap.

As they waited behind the great doors to the Bull Ring, Paulius drew Asteria aside. Pale and tense, she showed neither excitement nor pleasure at the prospect of their final performance. Paulius tried to raise her spirits, urging her to show courage and cheerfulness.

"How lucky they are," Freyna said in a low voice to Belia.

"They deserve it, one day it will be us!" Belia replied cheerfully. She and Nino were teasing Ali, who retaliated. Amidst hilarious giggles, Nino tripped and fell against the bench. This brought a reprimand from the trainer, Scarron.

Leander came close to Freyna and whispered, "Good luck, darling."

"You too, my love. Take care," she replied.

The other dancers were grouped around the African vaulter, M'boola, resplendent in a brilliant costume of scarlet, gold and peacock blue. The bull girls and novices had spent hours plaiting her hair in dozens of fine plaits, threaded with gold discs and coloured beads. Her black eyes glowed with excitement and they all agreed she was a magnificent sight.

The performance, organized as a benefit, was likely to prove the most successful of the season. The auditorium was packed, even the aisles were full and spectators crowded around the barricades.

Fanfares and the sound of conch horns announced the imminent arrival of King Minos and his Court and the dancers became silent, awaiting the order to line up.

Naxos disliked this kind of audience. Often the occasion was made an excuse for coarseness and ribaldry which the King apparently enjoyed. Naxos, a dedicated man, held the Bull Dance to be a sacred ritual and it disgusted him that a Priest-King could applaud vulgarity and laugh at obscene jokes.

As the applause for the King subsided, Naxos gave the order and the great gates to the Bull Ring swung slowly open. The audience shouted a welcome, cheering, throwing flowers and chanting the names of their favourites.

Naxos had planned an acrobatic display to open the performance to give the audience time to settle down. The leaps, cartwheels and aerial somersaults brought prolonged applause. Then, when the tallest men danced with Belia, Chloe, Rhina and Catalene on their shoulders and the others turned cartwheels nearby, the excitement rose to a high pitch.

Finally, the musicians played a dramatic theme, drums thundered and the audience became quiet as the dancers took their stations to face the bull.

In a moment of tense silence, the bull charged into the arena. He was black with a white flash on the forehead. He hesitated in the centre of the ring as if searching for a way of escape. Finding none, the animal began a great show of aggression, bellowing, pawing the ground and shaking his head. The audience yelled with delight.

Paulius judged the beast to be immature, perhaps three years old and of uncertain courage. As he advanced, with his group, Paulius signalled to Leander and M'boola to bring their groups forward on either side. The bull stood his ground.

This was a difficult situation. Paulius knew how dangerous and unpredictable a cowardly bull could be. If he came too close and the bull charged suddenly, he would be unable to time his leap.

However, the audience was becoming restless and some sort of action was imperative. Paulius decided to pirouette within a few feet of the bull's horns. Few spectators realized the risk he was taking. Then the bull backed away and lowered his head and in an instant Paulius leaped with a somersault on to the bull's back. The animal swerved to dislodge him. Paulius jumped down and Rhina steadied him.

The crowd roared its approval and shouted for more. The bull now faced M'boola who prepared to vault but once again the animal remained motionless, confused and afraid. The brilliant colours, the music and the yells of the spectators failed to encourage him. The vaulters were angry to see the bull run one way and then another, never holding direction long enough to give them the opportunity to show their skill. Paulius directed the dancers to spread out in a wide circle toward the edge of the ring but this device failed too. The bull ran in a circle, shook his head and bellowed but did not charge.

The audience, who were there to be entertained, yelled their dissatisfaction at a performance they were finding dull and lifeless. Naxos, who shared their resentment, had already sent a message to the stables demanding another bull.

Paulius brought the dancers whirling into the centre of the arena and they turned the bull toward the exit. When the animal caught sight of the gate he galloped off to the sound of jeers and catcalls.

The musicians played another lively tune as the dancers crossed and recrossed the arena in a further display of acrobatics and dancing. Then they took up their positions to face the next bull. The audience became quiet and expectant. When the bull charged through the open gate the dancers saw with some relief that it was Tauron. The audience greeted their favourite enthusiastically for they knew the Bull Dance would now go splendidly.

Ali vaulted first. A handstand onto Tauron's broad back and a leap off with a double somersault. Catalene caught for him, but he was steady as a rock and touched her hand as a courteous gesture. Paulius then invited Asteria to vault because in order to share in the benefit she had at least to perform one vault. There was really nothing to fear with Tauron. Freyna believed even *she* could vault on him!

Asteria stepped forward. Obediently, Tauron lowered his great head and thundered towards her. She moved forward to vault but at the last moment lost her nerve and stepped aside. The big roan and white bull was confused and charged straight at Chloe who waited to catch for Asteria. Being unprepared, she vaulted inexpertly and Asteria failed even to catch for Chloe, who fell, twisting her ankle. She was in pain and limped for the rest of the performance.

The spectators were unimpressed. Meanwhile, Tauron had turned and came lumbering back towards Paulius. He leaped astride the animal's back, first kneeling and then standing, and rode the bull around the ring. It was early in the performance, but the crowd always enjoyed this moment and Paulius was anxious to please them.

He succeeded. As the great animal galloped round the ring with Paulius triumphant on his back and the other dancers somersaulting and cartwheeling about him, the applause was thunderous. Flowers, gifts and money showered into the arena.

Naxos smiled with love and admiration for his dancers. Paulius, M'boola, Leander and Ali — he could even forgive Asteria! They were a great team and this benefit was likely to be one of the best.

Then the performers faced another setback. Tauron, instead of completing a circuit of the ring, suddenly galloped toward the exit. Paulius was forced to dismount quickly and to the consternation of the dancers, the great roan bull galloped from the arena.

The audience became frustrated and some members began to shout that they hadn't paid good money to watch rubbish and that a good bull should be sent in. They jeered, stamped their feet and began a slow clap.

Paulius stood for a moment, silent and embarrassed. He was not a deeply superstitious man, yet this ill-omened beginning to his last performance shocked him and wounded his professional pride.

For months afterwards, the cause of the bull's retreat was argued in the taverns and salons throughout the city. Some experts said Tauron was upset by Asteria's behaviour; others that he was too old and slow and weary of performing. However, many were adamant that the God had commanded it. And, in view of what followed, most people held to this opinion.

Paulius took control once more and signed to the musicians to play and the athletes to dance. Presently, the sound of hoof-beats warned them of the approach of another bull. They took their places to face him and saw with dismay that it was the wild, black animal they had danced with on the opening night of the season. He was so savage and hostile that he had not been sent into the ring again.

Even Paulius experienced a moment's uncertainty which was unusual and the dancers sensed it. Fear, so catching and debilitating, affected them all.

Realizing this, Paulius stepped forward to confront the bull. The vaulters remembered that the left horn was somewhat lower than the right and angled awkwardly. This made every vault both difficult and dangerous.

Paulius took the first leap and the crowd applauded enthusiastically. Leander was equally successful. Naxos, the Chief Trainer, watching from his vantage point, nodded in approval. When Paulius retired, the group would have a worthy leader in this young Spartan. Sardi stood as catcher, firm as a rock. Leander thanked him with a slight pressure of the hand. They dared not take their eyes off the wild bull whose strength was matched only by his unpredictability.

Supported by their catchers, Paulius, Leander, Ali and M'boola all vaulted again and again but no one attempted anything spectacular. They were thankful to vault and be secure on their feet and they all hoped the bull would tire quickly, but their hopes were in vain. The powerful animal wasted no energy on show. Favouring the left horn, he came at them fast in a deliberate and terrifying charge. This bull had killed before. Of that they felt sure. And he would do so again. As she watched, Freyna was overcome by nausea.

The bull was a superb animal of vicious temperament and tireless strength. The dancers saw this creature hated them. He lowered his head with its enormous dagger-sharp horns and charged again and again. They could only watch and leap; the vaulters over his back, the rest out of his way. They realized that this bull could wear them down and if they tired or missed their footing there could be only one result.

The five novices, at Paulius' direction, stood motionless. The crowd was hysterical, shouting and roaring, lusting for blood. The situation was desperate because Chloe was lame and Asteria was afraid and useless.

With a gesture, Paulius sent Chloe to join the novices and directed Nino to take her place. He came forward near to Sardi.

"Catch for me, Nino," gasped the young Cilician as the bull charged toward them. Sardi vaulted and the young novice stretched up his hand as the dancer balanced precariously on the bull's flank. Sardi was grateful for that hand. Hardly had his feet touched the ground when the bull pivoted instantly and came at them again.

"Watch out!" Sardi shouted.

The bull thundered towards Nino who, to the hysterical delight of the crowd, turned and ran and was butted in the behind. Nino leaped in the air and ran again. The applause was tremendous. Someone shouted an obscene joke. Naxos stamped in annoyance at the gross stupidity of this audience. Paulius, grateful for the opportunity to catch his breath, was disappointed that this last performance was so lacking in finesse.

Then, when Nino was knocked down, the raucous laughter died instantly. All eyes were on him. He managed to somersault and regained his feet but the bull followed, menacing him again. Nino did not dare to vault. His indecision was cut short when, quite suddenly, Asteria panicked. Leaving her position with the dancers, she ran away toward the group of novices. Her sudden movement distracted the bull, which turned and charged towards her. In terror she darted behind Freyna.

Panic began to affect all the dancers. They were afraid the God of the Underworld was demanding a victim. Their training forbade them to intervene to save Asteria and Freyna. However, Leander, seeing the bull threatening the woman he loved, reacted immediately. He raced towards her.

Later, experts agreed that it was probably sheer terror which saved Freyna. She stood pale and motionless, paralysed with fear. Asteria kept running and the bull swerved in her direction. Leander was, by now, between Freyna and the bull. Without hesitation, before the enraged animal could turn and gore him, the young Spartan reached forward with all his strength and grasped the base of the right horn with one hand, locking his arm around the other. He lay across the withers and gripped the bull's right ear in his teeth.

The crowd yelled with wild excitement as the infuriated beast thundered across the ring, bucking and heaving in a frantic effort to dislodge the young bull dancer. Leander hung on desperately, his face pressed against the rough bristles of the bull's neck.

Freyna revived instantly, crying out her lover's name but her screams were drowned by the roar of the spectators. Here was danger, sport and entertainment. At last the crowd was getting its money's worth.

Nino, no doubt grateful for his reprieve and realizing that Leander could not stop the bull alone, raced forward and grasped the bull by the tail. The animal galloped the full circuit of the arena, showing its immense strength, shaking Leander and dragging Nino through the sand and sawdust of the Bull Ring. The crowd yelled, clapped and stamped enthusiastically.

The great animal bucked violently and Nino lost his grip. Leander felt he would soon fall to this death beneath the pounding hooves. Then Paulius, concerned for his friend's safety, rushed forward and he too grabbed the bull's tail and was dragged halfway around the ring. At last the bull began to slow down. Leander could hold on no longer. As he released his hold, he threw himself sideways and rolled over to regain his feet. His legs trembled, his arms felt numb and at the same time, Paulius let go of the bull's tail and leaped aside, avoiding a vicious kick from its hind legs.

Then to everyone's surprise, the bull suddenly stood perfectly still, snorting and foaming at the mouth. It seemed the animal was exhausted. The crowd cheered and stamped its approval. The bull dancers had triumphed over the Underworld. Perhaps the God would now be satisfied.

Paulius knew better. With a bull of that calibre this was only the beginning. He would not charge at anything that moved, but would save his strength, aim carefully and no doubt choose only one victim. Now he was more dangerous than ever.

As leader, Paulius would have liked nothing better than to send this vicious animal off. But Naxos gave no signal. Perhaps he, too, thought the bull was beaten, that presently he would lower his great head and return meekly to his stall. What a triumph for the dancers that would be! They would earn the greatest benefit on record.

Paulius rallied the dancers who reformed in three groups. The musicians took their cue and the athletes began to dance, slowly, warily, never taking their eyes from the great animal.

The bull watched them, nostrils flaring, eyes bright, as if choosing which of the dancers he would attack. Without warning, the bull came for Ali, like a black thunderbolt. The speed and suddenness of the attack made the dancer's heart miss a beat but he grasped the horns and vaulted with superb timing. Rhina bravely stepped forward to catch him, but the bull jerked its head back and Ali was tossed some yards behind its haunches. He made a tumbling landing and regained his feet. The spectators shouted and cheered.

Fortunately for Rhina, the bull still concentrated on Ali. Turning with cat-like agility the huge animal almost knocked Rhina over as it charged again toward him. The dark Egyptian had anticipated this and he quickly joined M'boola's group. She knew that he was fighting for his life and did not blame him for drawing the bull towards them.

The bull was now confronted with five brightly-coloured dancers. He hesitated a moment and this slowed him down. But he still came at Ali who was standing between Chloe and Dek, one of the new bull boys from Delos. As Ali prepared to vault again, Dek stood on one side to catch for him and Chloe began to limp out to assist on the other side.

"Go to Paulius' line," M'boola shouted to Chloe, who lost no time in obeying her. Rhina was then left stranded alone in the centre and moved across the ring and joined Leander's group. Each dancer dreaded to be left alone and singled out as a victim.

As Ali vaulted and jumped off the bull's shoulder, he and Dek, his catcher, also joined Leander's group. M'boola was now the solitary dancer in the centre of the ring. Fortunately for her, the bull persisted in his search for Ali and she was able to join Paulius in the other line.

The dancers were now in two lines facing each other and Paulius called to Leander to make more space between them. They knew they had to wear their enemy down.

Once more the bull paused as though assessing the situation. He saw the two lines of brilliant, sparkling figures on either side, facing each other across the wide expanse of the ring.

Into this space the bull ran and took his stand. The great animal remained proud and motionless in the centre of the Bull Ring, flanks heaving, head held high. His neck arched magnificently and his red eyes gleamed. The spectators saw that this bull was a truly noble animal and applauded him enthusiastically.

"Hail, great Cretan bull!"

"Hail, bull of Minos!"

Many cheered and waved to the King and His Majesty responded by bowing and saluting. The entire audience was uplifted by this wave of religious patriotism. Here was the living manifestation of the God of the Underworld, awesome and terrible. This bull was a God of power and savage beauty.

In the centre of the ring the bull waited, immobile but alert and the two lines of dancers watched him. The experienced dancers noted the bull's throat remained closed and his tongue was never visible. This was the sign of a very courageous animal, one who would never admit defeat. Paulius saw that they would need every ounce of strength to outwit this adversary and survive.

The bull waited and the dancers watched in silence. As tension mounted, a few people began to scream advice, urging the dancers to take greater risks.

"They should try it themselves," Belia whispered to Freyna.

"How much longer?" Freyna gasped.

"Zeus only knows," muttered Leander, who was standing near her.

"I'm so thirsty," Freyna said.

They were all parched and nearing exhaustion. Paulius knew this was the most dangerous dance they had ever performed and prayed it would not be a dance of death. But the bull dancers could not stand still forever. The audience now screamed for action. The musicians were flagging. They would begin a tune and then stop, certain that they could not be heard above the yelling mob.

Abruptly, Paulius ordered all the dancers to link arms and dance in their lines, six steps sideways and then six back. The musicians quickly followed their rhythm. As they began to move, the bull stiffened, paused a moment and turned to face Paulius' group. In an instant, without warning, he lowered his head and charged straight at the African vaulter, M'boola.

M'boola was standing between Chloe and Asteria. The line spread out at once as she called for a catcher. Chloe began to limp out of the line, but Catalene called to her to stand aside. M'boola vaulted successfully and Catalene caught for her. The audience cheered and applauded M'boola who was a great favourite. She and Catalene stood ready as the bull pivoted quickly and charged again. This time, when the tall Libyan grasped the horns, the bull violently threw back its head, tossing the girl back into the line of dancers. M'boola landed heavily and, as she struggled to regain her balance, the bull charged again. Catalene was left behind in the centre of the ring.

"Vault, Asteria!" M'boola shouted to Asteria, who was standing next to her, "I'll catch for you."

They were all close to breaking point and the fine precision of their performance was gone.

But Asteria did not move.

"I'll take him," Paulius yelled, "catch for me, M'boola."

At the moment that Paulius vaulted, Asteria lost her head completely and ran blindly into M'boola, who was preparing to catch for Paulius. They collided and Asteria, shrieking wildly, tripped M'boola and they both fell to the ground. Asteria was up first. As she struggled to her feet, she trod on M'boola's face and then ran toward the line of dancers on the opposite side of the ring.

Meanwhile, Paulius had vaulted successfully and leaping off the bull, found Catalene at hand to steady him.

As the bull turned again to charge at Paulius, M'boola was directly in his path. The audience was suddenly quiet, gripped by the terror of that moment. Only Chloe's warning "Watch out M'boola!" rang out in the auditorium.

M'boola got quickly to her feet and turned aside to escape the bull. As she did so, she received a blow in the ribs from the flat of the horn. The sharp tip of the horn caught in her arm and ripped the flesh to the bone.

Freyna screamed when she saw the blood spurt out. Leander shouted at her to keep calm, but the wild roar of the audience drowned his voice. As Catalene ran to her, M'boola clutched at the wounded arm.

"Are you badly hurt, M'boola?" Catalene said.

M'boola could not answer. Paulius, who had vaulted once more with Sardi, the Cilician, standing by to catch him, now reformed his group and snapped at Catalene to return to the line.

"Are you all right, M'boola?" he asked.

She nodded but was still confused.

"Go off and wait by the gates," he ordered.

M'boola staggered from the centre of the ring as a trail of blood dripped across the sawdust. Murmurs of sympathy came from the spectators and many applauded her.

Paulius knew he must rally the dancers and end the performance as creditably as possible. He did not realize that M'boola was seriously hurt.

The dancers noticed a change in the bull, after M'boola was injured. His rhythm was different, his pace variable. Leander lined up for a vault, then, without apparent reason, the bull stopped dead in the middle of the charge, turned aside and charged half-heartedly at Sardi as though undecided on what to do next. The dancers began to hope that having drawn blood, their adversary was satisfied.

We've slowed him down, Paulius thought with relief. He signed to the dancers to regroup, the musicians responded to his signal to play again, and whirling and leaping, the dancers found a last reserve of energy. They sensed victory. The well-earned rest and the banquet that awaited them could be close at hand. The audience sensed it, too, and began once more to stamp their feet and cheer.

The Chief Trainer, Naxos, watching anxiously, was suddenly afraid for he thought that the dancers had misjudged the bull. This was no ordinary beast, supreme only in courage and strength. He was that rare phenomenon — an animal of cunning and intelligence. The danger was by no means over. The bull certainly was tired, but he was trying to deceive the dancers, to catch them off guard.

"Don't trust that bull!" Naxos shouted across the arena, but his warning was drowned in the crescendo of music and applause.

Leander vaulted once more and this time balanced for a second or two on the bull's back as Nino stood by to catch him. The audience roared appreciatively. Paulius turned and put out his hand to Asteria.

"Catch for me, my love, this is our last bull dance."

Asteria stood beside Paulius, her eyes wide with terror. When the bull came slowly towards them she did not move. Paulius had to push her aside to await the vault. But then she suddenly darted behind him. For a fatal moment Paulius turned to look at her. With terrifying speed, the bull thundered forward. Too late, Paulius turned to vault. The bull was on him. The great curved horn ripped into his body, under the ribs. He was gored and tossed several times. He screamed in agony. The bull then savagely trampled his victim. It was all over in a moment.

A great cry rose from the crowd. Women screamed and covered their faces. Men waved their arms helplessly. Many yelled in bestial pleasure — they had witnessed the ultimate climax, a violent, bloody death in the Bull Ring. The uproar continued as the bull galloped from the ring. The dancers watched, horrified, as the ring attendants ran on with a stretcher and carried the dying man to the Crypt of Sacrifice.

When they were gone, Leander gave the sign for the ritual dance of death. The crowd suddenly became silent. The musicians played the slow dirge and the dancers, like automatons, moved slowly from the arena, solemn in the knowledge they had participated in a ritual which had occurred frequently throughout the centuries in Crete.

# CHAPTER 35

As the heavy doors crashed behind them, Naxos confronted Asteria, his face distorted by rage and sorrow.

"You cowardly bitch! You are responsible for this disaster. Go to Paulius in the crypt and keep vigil there until he dies — it's the least you can do."

Asteria ignored him and fled to her quarters.

"I will go," Belia said quietly.

Naxos took her arm and led her gently to the door. Fearfully she moved down the narrow stairway which led to the Crypt of Sacrifice.

Paulius lay on a stone bench. A single candle burned nearby and in its wavering light she saw the deathly pallor in the young dancer's face.

The crypt was a small chamber, its walls stained with the smoke of a thousand candles. It had two closed doors, one of which led up a flight of stairs to the Bull Ring.

Paulius lay with one hand over the mortal wound in his side, scarcely breathing. He opened his eyes, but closed them again, realizing she was not Asteria and his disappointment distressed Belia almost as much as the sight of his terrible wounds. She knelt beside him.

"Paulius, Asteria is overcome with grief, we all are."

A faint smile touched the corners of his mouth. He gave a barely perceptible nod.

"I don't wish her to see me like this." He groaned. She took his hand and held it, not knowing what to say. He was so uncomfortable without even a pillow to support his head. She looked around the crypt and noticed, before the altar, a fine mat intended for those kneeling to pray. She folded it several times and gently placed it beneath his head.

"Thank you, Belia," he whispered faintly.

They were silent. She knew he would not live till morning.

"Paulius, I wish I could help you." Her voice was sad and tender. He lifted his hand and stroked a wisp of fair hair that escaped from her headband.

"It will be soon," he murmured, "I must prepare to face the Gods."

"They will welcome you. They will be proud of you, as we all are, Paulius," she said, fighting back her tears.

The dying bull dancer closed his eyes and began to pray, his lips framing the words though there was no sound. Belia lowered her head to pray with him.

After some moments, she became aware that they

were not alone, though she had heard no footsteps. She looked up and saw a priest staring intently at them. His expression showed a strange blend of pleasure and malevolence. He appeared to be sensually moved by the dying man's suffering and he was also annoyed by Belia's presence.

"What are you doing here?" Eburninos said. "Leave at once." His tone was cold and menacing.

"One friend is allowed to offer prayers," she replied, her voice trembling.

"Say your prayers and go back to your quarters."

"Naxos gave me permission to come," she replied stubbornly. Belia did not intend to leave Paulius until he was at peace. Her defiance sparked anger in Eburninos.

"Leave at once or you will be in trouble."

The voice was familiar but she could not recall where she had heard it before. Belia returned to her prayers. Suddenly, she remembered this man's voice in the Labyrinth when she was running with the semi-conscious Timon! The voice of her pursuer — it was this priest! Anger exploded in her.

"You, you are the child murderer!" she turned and shouted at him. "You monster!"

They faced each other across the body of Paulius. The priest stared into her eyes but did not speak. Then, muttering under his breath, he turned his back on her.

The silence became absolute. She sat motionless and then saw that Paulius was no longer struggling to breathe. She felt for his pulse. But there was none. Gently she closed his eyes and folded his hands over his chest. Belia felt a great weariness. She could weep no more and was thankful Paulius was at peace and free from suffering.

The priest Eburninos had not left the room and stood in the shadow, outside the small pool of light thrown by the candle.

"I am going now, Paulius is dead. You should go, too. You are not worthy to be here." She heard the priest gasp as she turned and ran quickly up the stairs.

"You will be sorry, when we meet again!" Eburninos hissed after her.

Asteria collected her belongings and went to Naxos for the money due to her. When it was paid she complained boldly that it was not enough.

"Paulius would have wished me to have his share," she said, "as his wife I would be entitled to it."

"You were never his wife," Naxos checked his anger with difficulty, "you will have what is yours — no more."

Asteria left the Bull Halls and was never seen again in Knossos.

The banquet was cancelled, the food and wine lay untouched, but M'boola insisted they should go and eat. Theseus and his Greeks ate heartily.

M'boola was expected to recover soon. The gashed arm was painful and she had lost much blood, but Naxos assured her that many had recovered from far worse injuries.

"I never thought I'd survive this —" he slapped his thigh and showed them the long white scar, "it was a big, yellow bull, high on his feet, with horns from here to Mallia!" The trainer chuckled. He was sitting by M'boola's bedside reminiscing about old times — a rare occurrence in the bull girls' quarters.

"He was a clever bull," Naxos continued, "strong, too. We danced the whole season with him. We regarded him as a friend but it's dangerous to get too confident. Well, M'boola, you'll be on your feet in no time. What's this I hear about a circus?"

M'boola smiled weakly. She tried to sit up, but lay back again exhausted.

"When you're better," Naxos said, "we'll have a farewell party for you." Everyone applauded this idea.

"Rest and get well," Naxos said as he departed.

Later that evening Scarron inquired about M'boola.

"It's sad, I don't think there's much hope for her," Naxos said gruffly.

M'boola did not recover. The wound in her arm healed quickly, but the doctors said the blow from the horn on her chest caused internal injuries. It was distressing for all of them. In constant pain, after the sixth day she coughed blood and in the second week she began to give away her possessions.

M'boola's protege, Shahali, wept helplessly. She, who had not wept at her own misfortunes, was inconsolable as M'boola grew weaker. When the famous vaulter could endure the pain no longer, Naxos had her carried down to the Crypt of Sacrifice.

The tragedy affected them all, but none more than Freyna. She had had no opportunity to speak to

Leander as his mind was totally occupied with the task of reviving the dancers' shaken confidence, of impressing his own authority on them and of welding them once more into a successful team. He knew it would be difficult to restore the affection and trust they had in Paulius. But he knew he must try. It was several weeks before he could meet Freyna again in the lamp-room.

Their second encounter was strange for both of them, and quite unlike their first. He noticed a difference in Freyna. She was calmer, more mature. He feared that she had changed — that she no longer loved him. For a moment they faced each other in silence.

"Well ..." Leander said quietly. He held out his hands, hoping she would come to him as before. Freyna approached him slowly and looked into his eyes.

"Leander, I have thought deeply since that awful day in the Bull Ring."

"Freyna, my dear, we must forget the past. It's the only way."

"I know," she replied, "everything is different now."

He nodded sadly, thinking she meant a renunciation of their love. He was surprised when she said quietly, "Leander, my dearest, we must be lovers."

"Freyna!" he began to protest, but she quickly placed a hand over his mouth.

"Listen to me, Leander."

He had never heard her speak like this and sensed that in the tension and shock of the past weeks, she had acquired new strength.

"All I want is to belong to you, to hold you in my arms. Our lives are so uncertain. If we are to die — if I am to see you injured or torn to pieces — at least we will have fulfilled our love for each other."

Leander knew that she no longer believed they would survive. He was grief-stricken at the death of his friend, Paulius, and weighed down by the responsibility of leading the group.

"Freyna, dear, do you know what you're asking? I'm supposed to be impartial. I shouldn't be so personally involved..."

"Are you not already?" she asked, smiling.

Leander was distraught. His desire for Freyna was as strong as ever and although he was determined to avoid causing her more suffering, he no longer had the will to resist her.

"No matter what happens, it's better my way," she pleaded, "if I become pregnant we'll have to leave Crete. Councillor Micalidos will help us, he promised because Belia saved his son, Timon."

"Please Freyna, I have to think this out," Leander said hesitantly.

She turned away from him and spoke sadly.

"I see you don't love me any more, it's finished. I don't care if the bull kills me."

"Freyna, please don't say that, I love you with all my heart." They kissed passionately and he continued, "What you ask could bring disaster." But he knew he would not resist her.

There was a knock on the door.

"Look out, someone's coming!" Belia warned.

Footsteps approached and the lovers embraced and parted. Immediately after Leander hurried away, two of Theseus' Greek girls came to fill their lamps. They stared curiously at Freyna and Belia who had no lamps with them.

"We must remember to bring a lamp next time," Belia said, as they left the lamp-room.

"How was Leander?" she continued in a low voice. "Was it a good meeting?"

"Yes, but we must escape from this nightmare, Belia. We must get away from this terrible place," Freyna said as they hurried back to the dormitory.

# CHAPTER 36

The skies were ragged and stormy. Squally winds blew down from the mountains and weather prophets forecast heavy falls of snow.

Nearly four months had passed since Andreas had borrowed the gold from the merchant Senthios, and the repair and rebuilding of the ships was proceeding. The date for the repayment of the loan was imminent and Andreas was short of money.

It was the Council's first meeting after the summer break and Andreas had worked on his speech for hours, aware that the fortunes of his family depended on the Council's willingness to reimburse him.

In the draughty Council Chamber, charcoal braziers provided some warmth, but the priests wore thick, woollen tunics and the King and Councillors were attired in fur-lined cloaks.

The sky was continually overcast and the light well gave little benefit. Many oil lamps were lit in the long chamber and the scribes had to draw their table lights closer to take the minutes. The Chief Priest, Pasterion, had taken to his bed and was not expected to survive the winter.

When the Priests and Councillors took their places, Minos entered and he signed to Arcanos to recite the opening prayers. When the formalities were completed, the Chancellor called for a report on the Days of Sacrifice.

One of the senior Priests, Chitos, gave a long and tedious account of the ceremonies performed throughout Crete and concluded with a paean of praise for the King. His Majesty had inaugurated a magnificent and solemn rite and he, the speaker, sincerely hoped that it would become a permanent, annual celebration.

"It is indeed a most efficacious and salutary initiative," Chitos enthused, "involving as it does the entire population of the island ... "

Andreas shifted irritably as the priest's voice droned on. He was eager to begin his address. At last the priest finished and took his seat to murmurs of appreciation.

Andreas then arose to address the Council.

"Your Majesty, King Minos, and Honourable Councillors and Priests. When we last met here, just prior to the summer recess, I put before you some vitally important information that to my certain knowledge threatened the security of Crete. I recommended urgent and immediate action to increase our defence capability to meet the threat of invasion."

Andreas referred briefly to his notes. Murmured criticism followed his remarks, probably, he presumed, from Councillors Brecchius and Xanthios.

"At the last meeting of this Council certain proposals of mine were agreed to unanimously. One of these, which I wish to discuss in some detail, concerned the purchase of timber, vital for the maintenance of our Fleet, from the merchant Praxitor in Amnissos. This timber has been delivered. It is now in the shipyard of Amnissos. I will speak more of that in a moment."

His words brought a growl of annoyance from Markos, the Navy Minister. Andreas ignored it. Taking a roll of papyrus from his cloak, he untied the cord and unrolled it.

"Your Majesty, I have here a report from Captain Keridos, Commanding Officer of the Flagship *Griffon*."

Andreas then read out a list of repairs carried out on the *Griffon* and the *Eagle*. To this was added a list of new ships, ordered last year, now under construction and their probable date of completion.

"Captain Keridos," he continued, "is concerned by the lack of fully qualified seamen to man these new ships. I agree with him and recommend that the Council deal with this problem urgently. At my own shipyard at Nirou-Khani, five new ships are being built. This activity, and the timber supplies, of course, can be inspected by any member of the Council who wishes to do so."

Until now, Brecchius had restrained the Navy Minister, albeit with some difficulty. But Markos could control himself no longer and leaped to his feet. Gesticulating angrily toward Andreas, he shouted, "Councillor Micalidos' interference in my department is totally without precedent! What right has he to board my ships and question my officers? And now, by all the Gods, he has the infernal impudence to tell me — me, the Minister for the Navy — that I can inspect my own ships, that I can view the timber in my own shipyards! Sacred Zeus, he's generous!"

His anger vented, Councillor Markos sat down, while Brecchius and Xanthios applauded enthusiastically.

Andreas resumed his address.

"Your Majesty, Honourable Councillors, how different is our position from only three months ago. Then we were in imminent danger of invasion, but now the situation has changed. The winter storms and the wild seas are our allies! No enemy now will risk his fleet till early spring. We have acquired not only timber, my friends, but precious time to prepare for war! And now I should explain my involvement in this vital project. Although it was agreed that we should purchase the timber, no action was taken. As you know, the Court was absent for a month in the Summer Palace. The Days of Sacrifice, propitious and invaluable as they were, further interrupted our business. Again I stress the importance of this project, our entire fleet must be prepared for wartime service by early spring. It was imperative to supply the naval yards with timber.

"Therefore, as the Council was absent, I ordered and purchased these supplies myself, on your behalf, carrying out the decision made by this Council some months ago. I now request that you ratify the Council's agreement and reimburse me for the timber supplied to the naval yards at Amnissos. I wish to make it quite clear that I'm not asking repayment for timber purchased through my agents in Byblos last summer and sent to my yard. Your Majesty, Honourable Councillors, I now present to you an account which details the quantity and type of timber supplied. I assure you that these figures are correct and the quality first class. If Your Majesty and members of this Council have further questions, I will be pleased to answer them."

Andreas handed his accounts to a scribe and took his seat. After a moment's silence, the High Priest, Arcanos rose and, assuming there would be no further comment, called on the Council to ratify the agreement to purchase the timber. But before he finished speaking the Minister for Supply, Xanthios, brusquely interrupted him.

"Just one moment, High Priest. Your Royal Majesty, Honourable Councillors, there are some other matters that need to be looked into before we agree to pay out some exorbitant sum to a member of this Council in what, I must say, are most unusual circumstances. Never, to my knowledge, has any Councillor taken it upon himself to purchase goods out of his own pocket and then demanded reimbursement from the Council."

Xanthios' clear, dry voice was empty of emotion.

"As I already stated," Andreas interjected, "this project was authorized by a unanimous vote —"

"The Council did not authorize you personally to purchase the timber," Xanthios countered, "the Council authorized the purchase of the timber at some future date as yet undecided."

"By which time it might not have been available," Andreas snapped, "timber is in very short supply throughout our island. No more will come in, now the ports are closed, so it was absolutely essential to obtain this timber. Without it we would have faced catastrophe in the spring."

"Catastrophe — always catastrophe!" Xanthios threw up his hands in mock horror. "What a dramatic picture Councillor Micalidos creates. Sir, you should have been an actor."

Andreas ignored the sarcasm, but the subdued laughter that followed Xanthios' remark angered him. "However," the Minister for Supply continued, "there are other more serious matters which must be raised here. Matters as personal, though not as selfless as Councillor Micalidos would have us believe." Xanthios paused and referred to some notes, which he withdrew from his sleeve. The atmosphere in the chamber had become ominous. All faces were turned towards the Minister for Supply, some surprised and curious, others with a tension which betrayed complicity.

"We should, I think, begin with timber, as that seems to be of particular interest to Councillor Micalidos."

The veiled scorn in Xanthios' voice aroused curiosity among the Councillors but Andreas was apparently unmoved. He was mystified.

"Your Majesty and members of this Council, it has come to my knowledge that, whilst bemoaning the lack of timber for ship building and inveighing against the rumoured misuse of timber from His Majesty's Storehouse, Councillor Micalidos saw fit to obtain it by bribery for the construction of his family villa in Mallia!"

A murmur of incredulity and disapproval greeted this statement.

"That's a lie. I have never obtained timber, or any other goods, to which I was not entitled from the royal stores," Andreas shouted.

"The facts prove otherwise, Councillor Micalidos," Xanthios hissed, "the merchant, Agidor — your agent, I believe — will testify that he provided timber for Madam Micalidos —"

"That is also a lie. I can't believe that Agidor will testify to anything. He is now wanted to answer for a criminal attack on my son, Lieutenant Antonius, an officer in His Majesty's Palace Guard. An attack made, I emphasize, within the Palace precinct while my son was on duty. That same merchant is also required to answer charges in Phaestos on the illegal abduction of Cretan children."

As he spoke, Andreas glanced at the King. He was surprised to note that Minos' face bore an expression of alarm and fear. He now understood from Xanthios' behaviour and the reaction of other Council members that this was a deliberate plot to undermine his position on the Council. He was shocked at the venom of the attack, the reason for which was not clear to him. Andreas bitterly resented his wife's complicity in dealing with Agidor. But self-doubt disturbed him. He had been too much involved in public affairs while his amoral wife supervised the building of that damn villa in Mallia. He despised those who opposed him and cared little whether the Council appreciated him or not. Unfortunately, the reimbursement of money spent on the timber was essential for his family's future welfare and he optimistically believed that would occur when reason prevailed.

However, for Andreas the defence of his good name and his integrity as a member of the Council and a public figure was paramount, and he knew he was facing a serious challenge.

Xanthios cast a malicious glance at Andreas and changed his attack.

"Your Royal Highness and Members of the Council, I regret to say Lieutenant Sartis brings a grave matter to our notice concerning our friend, Councillor Micalidos. The Councillor has been implicated in the harbouring of two escaped slaves in a hospital for the indigent sick. A broken-down place, in a low quarter of the city, owned by Micalidos and run by immigrant labour in his pay. These people broke the law and concealed these two slaves. Gentlemen, Councillor Micalidos must surely answer for this."

Andreas, embarrassed, rose to defend himself.

"Your Majesty, Honourable Councillors, an Egyptian physician, Dr Ahmed, an eminent man of the highest character and a valued friend of mine, conducts a surgery for the benefit of the poor and needy.

I understand this unfortunate couple — the runaway slaves of whom you speak — went to this hospital for treatment. No doubt Lieutenant Sartis neglected to tell you that in his greed to obtain the reward money for the slaves, he caused the death of these two young people and their newborn infant. Their only crime, as far as I know, was to fall in love and to desire the same freedom we enjoy. They suffered a grievous penalty and I most certainly did not know of their presence in the hospital. I myself, have been confined by illness in my own house for some time. Had I known of their plight, I would have informed their owner, Madam Doxa Grinkos, and offered her compensation. This woman's harsh and brutal treatment forced them to flee from her house with terrible consequences."

A murmur of sympathy came from the assembly. Xanthios was no fool and sensed he had lost some initiative.

"Enough of this sentimental rambling! The law was broken and Councillor Micalidos must surely answer for it!"

The Minister for Supply's rage stirred Councillor Markos. He rose to support Xanthios but clung to his own grievance.

"My colleague, Councillor Xanthios is right, Councillor Micalidos is at fault. What right had he to provide timber for His Majesty's Fleet at his own expense? This is unheard of!"

Xanthios scowled. Markos had reintroduced the very point that might influence the Council in Andreas' favour. The purchase of the timber was certainly an altruistic act and the interjection confused everyone. Before Xanthios could renew his attack, General Imanos rose to speak. He had not heard all that had been said, but he had grasped a few salient facts, including Andreas' purchase of the timber. The General cheerfully proposed a vote of thanks to Councillor Micalidos and called on the Council to ratify their agreement and reimburse him.

Xanthios was furious. He slammed his fist down on the scribe's table in front of him, nearly causing the man to fall off his stool.

"Your Majesty, Councillors, there is a third and even more serious charge against this Councillor..." Xanthios pointed to Andreas. "This man, this honourable Councillor, was seen leaving the Throne Room at the Royal Reception with a young woman, a bull dancer, a votaress of the Mother Goddess under the strictest vows of purity. This Councillor abducted her! We are men of the world. His motive is not hard to imagine!"

"Not if you have a mind like a cesspit," Andreas growled as he rose once more. This time he laughed. A genial, good-natured laugh. "Your Majesty, Honourable Councillors, the bull dancer is perhaps sixteen or seventeen years old — almost young enough to be my granddaughter. She needed some fresh air, not surprising in His Majesty's crowded reception room," he bowed to the King, and continued. "This girl was subjected to an insulting attack by a young man, whose behaviour disgraced himself and his family, not for the first time, I believe." Andreas glared at Markos. The Navy

Minister flushed, leaped to his feet and shouted, "How dare you insult my son and my family name! I demand a retraction!"

Andreas felt sympathy for Markos. He was a stupid and hotheaded man, but probably the only honest Councillor among those who opposed him.

"I did not say it was your son, Councillor Markos," Andreas said quietly and sat down. The Navy Minister remained standing, silent and embarrassed while Xanthios once again attacked Andreas.

"The Council has heard my accusations," he hissed, "the explanations offered by our honourable colleague are totally unsatisfactory. I demand Councillor Micalidos' immediate resignation."

"Resign, resign!" shouted Eburninos and urged his fellow priests to support him. Some shouted in agreement. The Councillors however, hesitated. Chancellor Darian looked anxiously at King Minos, who stared ahead blankly and seemed hardly aware that the Council meeting was in chaos. Councillor Brecchius, who had designated Xanthios as spokesman, now hesitated. He was unsure that the attack on Andreas could succeed.

The Navy Minister, Markos, was confused. He was angered by Andreas' interference in naval matters but he had no wish to see him expelled from the Council. Markos would have been satisfied with an apology. He perceived that he was being manipulated by his colleagues for a purpose he did not understand.

The High Priest, Arcanos, who resented Eburninos, remained silent. General Imanos was very annoyed because his motion of thanks to Andreas had been so rudely cast aside. He rose and repeated it. Xanthios and Eburninos and their few supporters, however, continued to shout for Andreas' resignation. The uproar was prolonged but eventually subsided. It became clear that Xanthios had failed to win a majority. He looked angrily at Brecchius and sat down.

Andreas got to his feet and spoke with quiet intensity. "Your Majesty, Honourable Councillors, my family has served the Throne and our nation for three generations and our loyalty and devotion has not been surpassed by any person in this chamber. During the past few months, I have been aware of an undercurrent of conspiracy against me, and more recently, against my sons. I have already spoken of the unprovoked attack on Antonius. My other son, five-year-old Timon, was abducted by a priest or by someone masquerading in a priest's habit and held prisoner in this Palace for several weeks. A reward was offered for his return, without result. He is now, thank the Gods, restored to his family, by what means I do not choose to divulge at this time. It has also come to my knowledge that many other children have been abducted and brutally murdered — here, in this Palace. I intend to bring those criminals to justice."

The atmosphere in the chamber was tense. All eyes were fixed on Andreas.

Suddenly the Priests and Councillors were horrified by an agonised cry from the King. Minos was obviously distraught. His eyes stared wildly ahead, his hands gripped the armrests of the throne.

"No ... no ... no!" he cried and struggling to his feet, he ran abruptly from the chamber, followed by Eburninos. After an uncomfortable silence, the High Priest Arcanos muttered a prayer and led the priests from the chamber.

The Councillors stared at each other in amazement. Too shocked to leave the Chamber, they stood in small groups speaking in hushed voices. All were stunned by this highly dramatic end to the meeting. Markos scowled and Xanthios glared coldly in Andreas' direction. Having no wish to remain in this hostile atmosphere, Andreas departed and returned thankfully to the villa.

Dr Ahmed was waiting for him and as the evenings were now too chilly to stroll on the terrace, the two friends met in Andreas' rooms before dinner. Andreas related the events of the Council meeting and the King's extraordinary behaviour.

"You have had a most unpleasant experience, sir," Ahmed commented. "Minos is a sick man and needs help."

"Only the Gods know how many children have died in that hideous place," Andreas said grimly, "those criminals must be brought to justice."

"It will be dangerous," Ahmed cautioned, "you'll have to protect Timon."

"Korynna's looking after him. She won't let him out of her sight," Andreas assured the doctor, "I'm concerned about Antonius," he continued, "I don't believe he's fully recovered. I'm surprised Captain Senthios didn't insist on his taking more leave."

Captain Senthios had been less cordial toward Antonius after Andreas had sent Shep-Anep and Senka to demand the return of Zanthope's necklace. He naturally resented the implication that Chryssa had stolen the jewels. After sending for his wife, Chryssa explained everything to his satisfaction. She declared she had no idea the necklace belonged to Zanthope Micalidos and had only worn it to oblige Papa Senthios — it was a precaution, she said, against it being stolen during the Royal Reception.

"Nasty jealous people are telling cruel lies about me, it's so unfair," she complained.

The Captain sympathized.

"Where is the necklace now?" Shep-Anep inquired.

Chryssa's pause was momentary. "I understand that my father-in-law, Papa Senthios, holds it as security for a loan." She smiled at her husband. Senthios gazed into his wife's beautiful eyes. She was perfect and he was the luckiest man on earth.

The necklace remained in Chryssa's jewel case. Shep made his report to Andreas, who then began proceedings to obtain a warrant to search the merchant Senthios' Palace apartment.

# CHAPTER 37

The island was in the grip of winter. The snowline on the mountains had moved down into the valleys, where the sheep huddled together for warmth. Wild northern gales sent huge waves crashing endlessly over the rocky headlands. The bitter chill, which penetrated even the wealthiest homes and most secluded courtyards, sent the citizens of Knossos scurrying for shelter.

On a cold, blustery morning Shep-Anep was surprised to receive a command to call on the merchant Senthios, at his earliest convenience. The Ambassador had no immediate need of his services, so Shep donned a woollen cloak and crossed the Palace Courtyard. As it was almost deserted, it seemed vast and lonely. On such a day, only those who were obliged to stirred from their fireside.

Lieutenant Antonius Micalidos, bound for duty at the North Gate, gritted his teeth, cursed the weather and thought longingly of the hot, spicy wine that awaited him when his stint was over. He glanced at Shep, but the Egyptian did not see him. Shep was preoccupied as he followed the steward who had brought the message, wondering what could be the reason for this unexpected summons.

He found old Senthios seated on a silk divan in an overheated room, dressed in a flowing robe of fine wool with an immense collar and cuffs of white fur.

"So you came at once. That was wise," the merchant said.

Papa Senthios liked to impress his visitors with his wealth and he enjoyed flattery. Shep, however, paid no heed to his surroundings, the luxurious furnishings and exotic ornaments crowded together in tasteless profusion. His indifference irked Senthios. His quiet "What do you want with me?" annoyed him even more.

"Address your betters as 'sir'," Senthios snapped.

"I do," replied Shep, looking directly at him, "why did you send for me?"

The two men faced each other, one gross, vulgar and ill-bred; the other tall, poised and ascetic.

"I'm told you act for Micalidos," Senthios snarled, "I have a message for him."

Shep inclined his head slightly but made no reply.

"Yes," Senthios said, leaning back against the silk cushions, savouring a particularly pleasant thought, "Yes," he repeated smoothly, "a message which I have no doubt my friend the Councillor will be relieved to hear."

Apart from the enjoyment of his wealth, Senthios was obsessed by two passions. One was sensual, involving his daughter-in-law, Chryssa, the other was a craving for power and position.

He proceeded to outline his scheme in the greatest detail, repeating himself continually, which tried Shep's patience. The implication that he was too stupid to take in simple facts was irritating. Shep bore it without comment because he realized that the message he was asked to convey was of vital importance to Councillor Micalidos and his family. His disgust and loathing for Senthios increased. As the circumstance of the loan for the timber was unknown to him, he was mystified how Andreas could have had dealings with this man. Now, having heard the merchant's proposal, Shep wondered how he could bring himself to relate Senthios' insulting terms to the Councillor. It would be a difficult and unpleasant task.

On arriving at Andreas' villa, he said as much, with some embarrassment. Andreas tried to put his visitor at ease.

"Please sit down, Shep. You know you're welcome here, no matter what news you bring."

He offered a cup of wine, which Shep declined.

"Well, let's have it all," Andreas said genially, "insults, as well. I'm thick-skinned enough to take anything Senthios could hand out."

"He has a plan to release you, sir, from your debt, but on certain conditions." Shep paused, embarrassed.

"Go on, Shep," Andreas said encouragingly, "nothing could surprise me."

"He wants you to resign from the Council on account of ill health. He will then be elected as Minister for Trade in your place. He maintains he has the support of Councillor Brecchius and Councillor Markos for family reasons, and Councillor Xanthios who owes him money. There are other votes he will buy — the Chancellor Darian — so he says, and some of the Priests, more than enough to ensure his appointment. He will cancel the debt, but you will make annual payments from the trading galleys, the oil harvest and the pottery, and these will be negotiated. Senthios says he's not interested in the family homes here or in Mallia. They are of no use to him. He has a dozen properties, which he regards as larger, more imposing. But there could be an arrangement about rent. That's about it—"

"Is that all, the bastard!" Andreas muttered.

Shep frowned. He felt wretched. While Shep was speaking, Andreas had reflected that his own actions had contributed to his present troubles. He had played into their hands and must now pay the penalty. Yet desperate as the gambit was, (the purchase of the timber), he still believed it was warranted.

"Shep, don't distress yourself," Andreas said, "have some wine, you've earned it." Andreas poured two cups. He dismissed Senthios' terms out of hand.

"The man is a pig, born in the gutter. Now, he wants my place on the Council and me and my family as his tenants! Over my dead body!"

Andreas had no special love for high office. He valued authority and power for what it could achieve for the good of Crete and the community. If Senthios had been motivated by similarly high ideals, Andreas could have relinquished office without regret. But he knew Senthios only too well.

"Power carries obligations and responsibilities, in my opinion, anyway," he continued, "it should not be a vehicle for greed and self-aggrandizement. This man must never be a Councillor. Shep, did Senthios say anything about the necklace?"

"No, sir, he did not."

Andreas frowned. Old Senthios had agreed, too willingly perhaps, to a search of his Palace apartment, but, of course, no necklace was found.

"Is there anything I can do to help, sir?" Shep inquired after a few moments.

"No thank you, Shep. I'm very grateful to you. I'll write to this man and Senka will deliver it. After that, we'll just wait and see. Senthios has appointed overseers in the shipyard and at the pottery. He's also sent an agent to inspect the farm and the olive groves. No one's been sacked and the wages are being paid so the people are all right."

The two men were silent for a moment. Shep was about to speak but hesitated. Andreas looked at him with some admiration.

"Oh, I know all that could change, Shep. He'll try to force my hand. The money is owed to me by the government. Who knows? If the Gods smile on us, they may pay up!"

"I pray they do, sir," Shep said, finished his wine and rose to leave. "Your two sons, are they quite recovered, sir?" he added.

"Antonius is back on duty, too soon, we thought, but he's tough. Timon, I don't know..." Andreas shook his head. "He had no physical injuries — a few bruises on his wrists and ankles — but his whole personality has changed."

Andreas leaned back wearily as he mentally compared the silent, nervous child, clinging to his father or aunt, unwilling for any reason to leave the house, not even to play on the terrace, with the happy, mischievous boy who played truant by the river or wandered the streets visiting his friends whenever he could slip away from the house.

"Timon seems to be enclosed in a world of his own. He won't say a word about it," Andreas continued bitterly, "he's obviously had a frightening experience. Ahmed advises that we should not press him. 'Let the mind heal as the body would after a wound' he says. Well, who am I to argue? Korynna tried to question him but he began to scream and then woke screaming in the night, we can't have that."

"There's corruption in the Palace, sir," Shep said.

"I know," Andreas said grimly, "but what is the remedy? We have no evidence to take to court. We must be alert. I've warned Antonius and Timon is safe here and I know you'll respect our confidence in these matters."

"Of course, sir. I am happy to serve you in any way."

Andreas summoned Credon to show his visitor out and then, almost as an afterthought, he said, "If you should receive a message from the Bull Halls, Shep, it could be of great importance."

Shep returned to the Palace wondering how many more surprises might come his way in the service of Andreas Micalidos.

# CHAPTER 38

Andreas had always been a wealthy man. Now, although he made light of his problems, he was practical enough to understand that there must soon be a change in his family's way of life. He discussed his affairs frankly with Ahmed in his rooms.

They sat by a brazier for the weather was cold. Credon had placed a screen across the opening to the little courtyard and had just brought them a bowl of hot onion soup.

"I'll miss Deva's cooking," Andreas said, "she's the best cook we've ever had."

Ahmed was astonished. "Surely things are not that bad, sir?"

"My credit's good for the time being," Andreas replied, "but I can't ask people to work without pay. This may well limit yours and Iros' good work in the surgery, I'm afraid. I realize new supplies of medicines are needed. I can meet one more order, Ahmed, but after that I think ..." Andreas raised his hands and dropped them with an expressive gesture, "I don't need to say how much I regret this, old friend."

"I think Iros and the staff will carry on as usual," Ahmed said cheerfully.

"But they must eat," Andreas said.

"We must do the best we can. Don't worry. I'm sure the government will pay its debt to you. They surely would not refuse."

Andreas believed they would, if it was worth their while, but he did not say so. He had managed, with some difficulty, to convince Zanthope that he had not surrendered the ruby necklace as collateral for the loan. He refused her demand to dismiss Dr Iros, whom she had accused of assaulting her.

This had been a bad time for Zanthope. Doxa Grinkos had told her, sweetly, how upset she was — they *all* were — to see her jewels around another woman's throat. And of all people, that woman, Chryssa Senthios!

Zanthope's torment and humiliation were complete. She shut herself in her room, brooding and plotting revenge against the thief, who she believed was her husband's secretary, Senka. She was obsessed and sent for the agent, Agidor in Phaestos. He would know how to deal with Senka. However, Agidor was nowhere to be found and it was rumoured that after Andreas had obtained a warrant for his arrest, he had fled to Africa.

Zanthope wept, tore her hair and bruised her body. Her passion for Senka was genuine and she hated him the more because of it. She began to drink a great deal and was often under the influence of strong Cretan wine.

Senka had an inkling of Zanthope's suspicion, but he lacked the courage to confront her and proclaim his innocence. Unaware of the intensity of her malice, he decided to wait until she calmed down.

When Andreas told Senka a week later that he had arranged a post for him at the Egyptian Embassy, (through Shep's good offices), he was delighted. Zanthope had long wearied him as a mistress and he departed from the villa with relief and without regret.

Dr Ahmed was less optimistic about the future of the surgery than he had let on to Andreas. Late one afternoon, when the last patient had gone and Damon had closed the street door, he and Iros discussed their future prospects.

"Why doesn't Micalidos apply through the courts for his money?" the younger man said.

"He's a proud man," Ahmed replied.

"He'll be all right. They won't bankrupt him. The ruling classes always stick together," Iros said laconically. He had been bitter since the death of the slaves, Arkos and Tyra, and had himself been arrested and interrogated. But, after the last Council meeting, the charges had been dropped and he was released.

Ahmed was dismayed by the young man's attitude.

"Councillor Micalidos has been very generous to us," he said reprovingly.

"He can afford it," Iros muttered.

"Well, now he cannot. Not until the government repays him."

There was an uncomfortable silence between the two men. They were sitting in the small courtyard between the surgery and the staff house, on the same stone seat where they had sat with Arkos and Tyra. The bench where she had worked was nearby.

"I know you cannot forget those two young people. Neither can I," Ahmed said sadly, "but Councillor Micalidos was in no way to blame. If anyone was at fault, I was. I should have told him they were here. If I had, they might still be alive."

"Don't blame yourself. If you must find a culprit, blame the Gods. It was fate."

Iros shivered. "It's too cold to sit here. Come inside, sir."

"No, Iros, I must return to the villa. It's a sad house now. Both Old and Young Madam keep to their rooms. Antonius lives in the officers' quarters in the Palace and Senka has gone to work there, too."

"Good night then, doctor."

"I'll come tomorrow, Iros. Try to give the medicines sparingly. I have a little money, enough to keep us going for a few months."

"Why doesn't Councillor Micalidos appeal privately to the King?" Iros said, just as Ahmed was about to step into a chair. "Or the Queen, for that matter surely he has some influence. Isn't his daughter married to the King's cousin?"

As the chair carriers jogged up the Street of Doves, panting as the gradient grew steeper, the doctor considered Iros' suggestion.

He felt sure that Andreas would not press the family connection. It would be taking advantage of privilege — Ahmed understood Andreas' pride and sense of justice. The money was owed. It should be repaid openly, freely and without any hint of patronage. That was how Andreas would see it. But then, an idea came to Ahmed. If *he* went to the Queen she could petition the King and Andreas need not know! The idea pleased him, but he hesitated as he was a shy and reserved man. But when he considered how much Andreas and his family had suffered, he was determined to go to the Queen and ask for her help.

After the tragic death of Paulius and M'boola in the Bull Ring, the strict routine of training and performance had resumed. One evening, after supper, Freyna and Belia met Leander in the lamp-room. Freyna had asked him to come and dissuade Belia from further exploration in the Labyrinth.

"Leander, make her promise not to go there again. That horrible priest has threatened her," Freyna said anxiously.

"I'm going to find a way out of here. I'll be careful," Belia said obstinately. She pointed to the ventilator shaft.

"Yesterday, I took the shaft to the left — it winds around and where do you think it ends up?"

Her friends waited in silence.

"Above the stables! I could look down on the bulls in their stalls!"

"I'm sure that passage is too narrow for Freyna or myself," Leander said wearily.

Belia agreed reluctantly.

"It was too narrow even for me!" She showed them the cuts and abrasions on her hands and knees.

"Belia, it's pointless," Leander said impatiently, "we cannot leave the island until the spring when the ports reopen."

"But Theseus goes through those passages," Belia persisted, "he's been meeting the Princess down there for weeks. There must be a way in from the men's quarters."

"No, I've searched. He must go out through the trainers' quarters and then, perhaps, there's a stairway leading down to the Labyrinth somewhere in the Palace," Leander said adamantly.

"Of course ... a stairway which the Princess uses!" Freyna said. "Why didn't we think of it before?"

"But how does Theseus get out through the trainers' quarters?" Belia said.

"Probably bribery," Leander replied, "and if *he* can bribe the guards, so can we."

"Then we don't need the passages ..." there was disappointment in Belia's voice.

"We may need them. Escaping from the Bull Halls is one thing, getting out of the Palace another. We are too well known. And there is something else ..."

"What is it, darling?" Freyna asked.

"Money," the young dancer said. "I want my pay. I've earned it — and we must have money. We shall have to bribe people and pay for passage on a boat. Without it we'll never escape or make a good life for ourselves somewhere else."

To escape had always been a dream, a fantasy for Freyna. The young bull dancers had never discussed it seriously but she now began to comprehend the difficulties. She sighed.

"Don't worry, Freyna. We'll be all right," Leander said firmly, "we'll keep in training and take no risks."

"Paulius tried to obey the rules," Freyna murmured bitterly.

"Yes, but Paulius broke the most important rule of all, and paid the penalty," he said.

"What do you mean?" Belia was ready to defend Paulius.

"He failed to concentrate. He allowed Asteria to distract him."

"May the Gods punish her!"

"They probably will. But she alone did not cause Paulius' death and he would be the first to admit it. How many times did he lecture us to always be alert and never lose concentration."

"And he broke his own rules," Freyna said sadly.

"Well, we must try not to grieve. I have to go now." Leander held out his arms and embraced them both.

"Don't forget what I said, Belia, no more explorations in the Labyrinth."

"I won't go to the Labyrinth again, not until the spring, anyway," Belia said. She went to the door and smiled at them. "You don't need me to help you say good night." Belia left the lamp-room and Leander and Freyna were alone.

Winter was nearly past when Madam Brecchius died. She was in her forty-fifth year. The doctors could not diagnose her illness or provide a remedy. Her death was a relief to all who were close to her.

At the funeral procession the family followed the coffin, Leda and Chryssa in hired chairs, the latter wrapped in furs, and the men, Councillor Brecchius and his son-in-law, the Captain, in a chariot loaned by old Senthios. The Markos', father and son, as Leda's future family, attended also. She wept in genuine grief while the others were dry-eyed.

In her final dying moments, Madam Brecchius had pressed Leda's hand. "Thank you, Leda, you're a good girl. May the Gods protect you," she whispered.

Leda was so weak from her long attendance on her mother, she found it difficult to walk to the chairs, waiting at the South Gate. Councillor Markos had suggested that she be carried in the chair from the apartment door. But Brecchius declared that the passages were too narrow. Also, though he did not mention it, the chair carriers would charge more. So he half carried, half dragged his younger daughter down to the South Gate, intruding on her grief with whispered plans for her forthcoming marriage "as soon as may be decent".

The brief mourning period he envisaged was hardly decent but Leda was too weak to protest.

Lieutenant Antonius Micalidos met the procession as it moved from the South Gate down the steep paved road from the Palace. He raised his hand in respectful greeting. Leda saw him as she peered through the chair curtains, but he did not see her.

It was now more than seven months since they had been together at Mallia. Leda saw that Antonius was changed; toughened and matured by his military training which suited his good looks and personality. Leda felt almost as if she were seeing him for the first time. The sight of him filled her with eagerness and delight and all the tender and passionate feelings she had renounced returned to overwhelm her. She thought with anguish of the hateful marriage her father was forcing on her. How hopeless it all seemed. She believed Chryssa's cruel story of Antonius' engagement. In her exhausted state she could see no escape and wept bitterly.

Ahmed's plan to call on Queen Kara to seek help for Andreas was easier to conceive than to fulfill. Antonius and Senka were absent, Korynna was busy caring for Old Madam and management of Andreas' concerns was mostly taken over by agents of old Senthios. Andreas now depended more than ever on Dr Ahmed for companionship. He even began to accompany him on his daily visits to the surgery now that he had more time on his hands.

It was Iros who thought of the plan. The Egyptian Ambassador, User-Amon, occasionally paid courtesy visits to the Queen. The Ambassador's steward, Shep-Anep was approached and willingly agreed to arrange an invitation for Dr Ahmed to accompany the Ambassador on his next visit to Her Majesty.

Queen Kara received the Ambassador and Dr Ahmed formally but graciously in her salon in the East Palace. User-Amon was accompanied by his retinue and also, to Ahmed's surprise, by Chancellor Darian. Ahmed noticed that Darian seemed tense and thoughtful, and the Queen, though as cordial and charming as ever, was pale and ill at ease.

The Ambassador sat at the Queen's right and the Chancellor sat beside him. The other members of the party remained standing and Ahmed doubted if he would have the opportunity to speak privately with the Queen.

User-Amon, fond of the sound of his own voice, spoke at length, extolling the greatness of Egypt and of her undying friendship for Crete. The Queen replied diplomatically and the interview continued for some time in this vein.

When the Ambassador turned to address the Chancellor, the Queen cast a quick and despairing glance toward Ahmed. She seemed as eager to speak with him as he with her.

Once the wine had been served and the Chancellor continued to hold the Ambassador's attention, Ahmed took courage, approached Queen Kara, bowed and paid his respects. She beckoned a servant to place a chair on her left and invited him to be seated.

After a mutual greeting, he lost no time in telling her the reason for his visit. He saw she was concerned, though she affected indifference and spoke rapidly in a low voice.

"I much regret, doctor, I cannot help you. I have not seen His Majesty since the last Council meeting. He has become a recluse. I believe he is ill and I fear the Priest Eburninos is influencing him. I feel sure King Minos is no longer in control of the government." She paused and smiled at the

Ambassador, raising her wine cup. "I think you must own to some merit in our Cretan wines, Your Excellency."

"Yes, indeed," User-Amon replied, "you and Dr Ahmed were discussing them?"

"Dr Ahmed also enjoys our wine. He has lived here many years," she said with a disarming smile. The conversation continued informally, the Chancellor and the Ambassador offering opinions on the different wines of Crete and Egypt.

As the audience was about to end, the Queen turned to Ahmed.

"Others are in control, I fear there may be trouble," she whispered. "I believe Princess Ariadne is involved. I wish I could help Councillor Micalidos but I do not think even the King can help him now. I believe Crete may be facing a grave crisis!"

She turned away from Ahmed and bid the Ambassador farewell and Ahmed returned home with a heavy heart.

Andreas was eager to have an account of his visit to the Queen. The doctor related what she had said, without, of course revealing the true reason for this visit.

Queen Kara's anxiety and her remarks to Ahmed reawakened all Andreas' doubts about the ability of the government to deal with such a crisis. He could see no clear way ahead but he took some pride in the knowledge that the fleet was now re-equipped and ready for action.

For Ahmed, the situation at the villa was embarrassing. Andreas, despite his financial problems, insisted on paying Ahmed's salary and the wages of the surgery workers, maintaining that he still had some reserves to draw on. Ahmed, however, knew that this arrangement could not continue. He was afraid that he would soon have to seek another position or return to Egypt.

# CHAPTER 39

Senka was in a gloomy mood as he sat at his desk in the Egyptian Embassy. The new job Andreas had arranged for him gave him no satisfaction and he groaned when he compared the comfort and luxury at the villa with his cramped quarters in the Palace. Although his salary had not changed (Andreas had seen to that) he had to work twice as hard and pay for his food and wine. His small room, shared with two disagreeable clerks, revolted him. Worst of all, there was little free time to attend to his own affairs.

He was already planning to escape. He reasoned that if he could regain favour with Zanthope, she could help him to obtain a better position. His first step must be to convince her that he did not steal the ruby necklace. As she was aware of his past relationship with Chryssa, a simple denial would not be enough. He would have to find the real thief —

that would be sure to please her. He recalled every moment of the time spent in Mallia, where he was convinced the jewels were stolen.

Each day, at the Noon Sacrifice, he listened to the gossip in the crowded Courtyard, hoping for a hint that would solve the mystery. He made the acquaintance of a Palace slave, a strange, stunted fellow named Krino, who took bribes, ran errands and could always relate the latest scandal. Through Krino he learned that Doxa's friend, Olivia, now had the good fortune to live at the Palace. This reminded him of his conversation with Vasca, the harlot some weeks previously. When Krino informed him that the previous owner of Olivia's apartment was a relative of the merchant Senthios, the pieces of the puzzle began to fall into place.

One day in the Courtyard, seeing Olivia, Senka joined the group of people around her. Since moving into the Palace, Olivia had become a very grand lady indeed and when Senka greeted her, she pretended not to know him. Angrily he skirted around the group, came up behind her and whispered.

"Stolen any jewels lately?"

She turned on him viciously.

"Fool!" she hissed. Then she recovered her composure. "Why, it's young Sharim Senakor, isn't it? I didn't recognize you. You used to work at the villa, I believe. What a pity you lost your job."

"I'm very well placed, thank you, Olivia," he replied, smiling, "I always wanted to live in the Palace. How did *you* get your apartment here, my dear?"

"That's no business of yours." She spoke softly but there was malice in her look and he rejoiced.

"It is my business. I'm investigating a theft. You were at Mallia, Olivia, when Zanthope's jewels were stolen."

"You'd better watch your tongue," she said icily, "Micalidos and his wife can't protect you now."

"*I* don't need protection." He smiled but his eyes were cold. Olivia was unmoved. Her nerve was not so easily shaken.

"If I hear any more of this, I shall report you to the Council," she said and turned her back on him and began talking to her friends. Then he watched her move through the crowds and disappear into the East Palace.

Senka returned to the Embassy and was reprimanded for overstaying his lunch period, much to the glee of his fellow clerks. Tight-lipped, he sat down at his desk and decided to write a letter to Zanthope. He would not mention Olivia by name, but would tell her that he knew who the thief was and how the stolen jewels could be recovered. He invited Zanthope to meet him in the Palace. For this project he needed help from the slave, Krino.

At noon the following day Senka saw Krino in the Courtyard and spoke to him.

"Where can I take a woman in this rabbit warren? A first class place — she's not a whore."

Krino's eyes narrowed.

"You could rent a room."

"I can't afford that," Senka groaned.

Krino took a vicarious interest in all forms of love-making.

"There is a place," he said with some consideration.

"Where?"

"It'll cost you something."

"Show me."

"Not so fast."

Senka reluctantly placed a coin in the outstretched hand. Krino led him across the Courtyard towards the North Gate, down the sloping footpath and past the shrine where departing visitors left their tributes. A passage, concealed by the wall of the North Keep, led to a narrow, spiral stairway that descended some distance below the level of the Courtyard. As they progressed down the stairs, Senka believed he was being taken to a cellar. The light became dim and the air musty.

"Where the devil are we going?" he asked, but the slave did not answer.

Krino took a lantern from a wall niche, lit it and continued further on to a wooden door which he unlocked. Senka had to stoop to pass through. Krino locked the door behind them and led the way into a passage that ran at right angles. Bending down, he picked up a cord out of the dust. When he glanced at Senka his eyes gleamed, but Senka could not tell whether this was from amusement or malice.

"Others use this way, so you'll have to watch your step!" Krino said.

"Where are we going?" Senka asked nervously. The place did not appeal to him.

Krino went ahead without answering and presently stopped outside a doorway.

"Here you are — perfect!" he said, as though he had produced an apartment to suit any lover's dream. Senka peered into a small dusty cubicle.

"You fool!" he shouted angrily. "I can't bring her here to this filthy rat-hole!"

Krino shrugged.

"Please yourself. It's private and it's free, well, almost. You need a key."

"For a price."

"Of course. Then you clean up, get a carpet and a mattress and away you go!" He winked and made a rude gesture. Senka smiled in spite of his annoyance. He considered. It was a possibility and he had no alternative.

"All right, how much for the key?"

They haggled for a few minutes and agreed on a price. The next day Senka cleaned the place, bought a second-hand feather mattress, a strip of carpet and a coverlet from an old woman in the market. Then he paid a messenger to take his letter to Young Madam Micalidos.

Three days later, to his surprise, for he had begun to despair, Senka received a message that Zanthope would come. He was to meet her that evening under the portico of the North Gate at sunset. He waited impatiently.

A veiled figure alighted from a chair, paid the carriers and walked slowly up the ramp to the gateway. Zanthope wore a heavy cloak. Senka greeted her but she remained silent. He led her down the winding stairway. After a few moments she stopped short.

"Why are you bringing me here? This is an awful place."

"We can be alone here, Zanthope. I must talk to you," Senka pleaded.

She did not reply so he lit the lantern and hurried on. He held the low door open for her and locked it behind them. When they reached the room he had prepared, she stood on the threshold for a moment.

Hanging the lantern up, he said, "Zanthope, I know this place isn't worthy of you but what I want to say is important and we won't be disturbed here."

"This place may well be entirely suitable," she said in a tense voice and threw off her veil.

Senka was shocked. Her skin was blotched and puffy, her long golden hair dull and lifeless. The bitter resentment and anger over the loss of her jewels, which had tormented her, and continual drunkenness, had devastated her beauty. She watched him closely. Senka did his best to conceal his distaste and even managed to flatter her, assuring her of his continuing devotion. "You despicable creature! Where are my jewels that you hung around that whore's neck?" she screamed at him suddenly, her eyes blazing.

"I didn't steal them, Zanthope. I swear I didn't, but I think I know who —"

"You're a liar, liar!" she shrieked in a frenzy of rage, not listening to a word he said. Without warning she took a step towards him and drew a knife from beneath her cloak.

"You bastard!" she hissed.

Senka backed away from her. He saw that she was mad. She lunged towards him and the knife flicked past his face. With surprising speed she slashed at him again. As he raised his arm to protect his throat, the knife ripped into his forearm. He tried desperately to escape and ran towards the door but she raced after him and struck again. The knife grazed the edge of his skull, just above the ear. As he crawled through the door, she raised the knife again. With blood streaming from his arm and down his face, he turned and ran into the darkness of the Labyrinth.

Her screams echoed after him. "I'll kill you, you thieving bastard!"

Senka grasped his arm trying to stem the flow of blood as he stumbled down the passageway. Presently, a light flickered and he realized that Zanthope was chasing him. She had paused only to unhook the lantern. Gasping with fear, he ran on, desperately seeking a place to hide.

The passage seemed to turn to the right, but Senka felt an opening in the wall on the left. As the light grew brighter he saw it was an archway leading to a spiral stairway. He hesitated, crouching in the shadows.

The light flared for a moment as Zanthope hurried past, following the main passage. Senka saw her face contorted with hatred and fury. Her blonde hair shone dully in the lamplight and the bloody knife was still clutched in her hand.

Senka waited for some moments, his heart pounding then he heard Zanthope cry out and a clattering as if the lantern and knife had fallen. Then a harsh sound of men's voices echoed and re-echoed down the passage, followed by Zanthope's screaming protests. She shrieked out Senka's name. He stood in terror, unable to move. Then her screams grew fainter. She was apparently being dragged by force deeper into the Labyrinth.

Overcome with horror, Senka hurriedly retraced his steps, feeling along the wall for the opening which led to the door and escape. After some moments of panic, he found it and with a trembling hand he took the key, opened the door and escaped into the cold night air.

Early the following morning, a labourer on his way to work found the body of a woman on the river bank, near the bridge where Timon and Luki had once played. Her throat had been cut. Soon all Knossos was buzzing with the strange and horrible story of the murder of Zanthope Micalidos.

Andreas and his family were shocked and hardly able to believe it. There seemed to be no motive for the crime and in spite of intense inquiries, Zanthope's death remained an unsolved mystery.

Senka lived in abject terror for weeks. He was afraid that his letter to her would be discovered, but evidently she had destroyed it.

Few people knew that the angriest man in Knossos was the priest, Eburninos. He discovered that his paid thugs had killed not Belia, for whom they had lain in wait, but Zanthope, wife of Councillor Micalidos. It was the golden hair that misled them.

# CHAPTER 40

The first hint of spring came with turbulent, salty winds from the south. The seas were drab and grey. The atmosphere was clouded by strong air currents carrying yellow dust from Africa.

This was a melancholy season for the Micalidos family. Zanthope's death had shocked everyone and there was the ever-present threat of foreclosure by the merchant Senthios.

Andreas, Ahmed and Antonius had attended Zanthope's sombre funeral with her father, old Aeschyton. Korynna had wished to go with them, but Old Madam and Timon could not be left alone. Hyacinth, who was soon to give birth, stayed in Mallia while Prince Lerintos simply refused to go.

Andreas and Antonius drew closer together at this time.

This was a welcome change, Andreas thought, as they returned to the villa after the ceremony.

Aeschyton politely declined their invitation to dine, so Andreas, Ahmed, Antonius and Korynna dined quietly together. Korynna excused herself when the meal was over and the three men stayed on to finish the wine.

"How could one foresee this calamity?" Andreas muttered.

Antonius angrily struck the table with his fist.

"I don't understand it. Who could have wanted her dead? And what could she have been doing wandering along the river bank so late at night?"

The question remained unanswered. "Credon told me about a letter which was delivered a few days before your mother died," Andreas said.

"A letter? From whom?"

"We don't know and it cannot be found."

Dr Ahmed looked up in surprise at the mention of a letter. "Maybe it was to lure her away from the villa," he suggested.

"Perhaps," Antonius said, "but who would do that and for what purpose?"

Andreas sighed.

"Zanthope lived her own life. We have always accepted that."

The wind outside slammed against the house, moaning through the tall trees in the garden. The silence in the room became uncomfortable. The doctor and Antonious exchanged glances but neither could find the right words to say.

Andreas then looked up and said firmly, "Maybe it's just as well we don't know what happened. It certainly won't bring her back, nothing will do that."

Antonius was about to continue, but Ahmed dissuaded him with a gesture.

"There are other things we must face, less painful but more urgent," Andreas went on. "Senthios is determined to get my place on the Council and if he succeeds, I doubt if they will ever repay me. He could influence them all. I am sure he has already done so." Andreas paused and drank some wine. "My deepest regret, Antonius," he added quietly, "is to have robbed you of your inheritance. I was faced with a terrible alternative — to choose to risk my family's welfare in order to safeguard Crete."

"Father, for Zeus' sake," cried Antonious, "I believe you made the right decision. I don't care about the money!"

"By the Gods I've no wish to be proved right! But I may well be — spring will soon be here." Andreas smiled as the wind buffeted the house and penetrated the room. The lamp flames dipped and trembled on the wall. "When the ports reopen, we will know our fate," Andreas muttered and poured the last of the wine.

"Will Senthios try to take our house?" Antonious asked.

"He told Shep he wasn't interested," Andreas replied, "but he may change his mind."

"I'm sure he wouldn't do that," Ahmed said, "he wouldn't risk public censure."

"He could charge a rent we couldn't afford to pay," Andreas said, half in jest.

"Doesn't the house belong to grandmother?" Antonius asked with some warmth.

"Technically it does," Andreas agreed.

"Well, then, we could fight Senthios on that. Grandma doesn't owe him money."

"We can't afford to challenge him. We can only wait and see what eventuates."

"Truly, sir, I am convinced the Council will honour its obligation to you. I cannot believe they are all without any sense of gratitude, decency or justice." Ahmed spoke with simple sincerity. He admired Andreas and could not comprehend the envy and malice of others.

"Have some more wine, dear friend," Andreas said dryly. But he took comfort from the doctor's confidence.

"If only we could get that necklace back," Antonious said with a frown.

The question tormented him. Did Chryssa steal it, or was she simply a pawn in an elaborate scheme to embarrass and ruin his father? The thought nagged at the young man like a toothache. Ill feeling over the necklace had almost poisoned his friendship with Captain Senthios.

"Indeed, the necklace would strengthen our position," Andreas agreed, "but if Senthios has got it and keeps it, then he will have to cancel the debt. He can't have it both ways."

"Do you think Senthios might have it?" Ahmed asked.

"I wish we knew," Andreas answered. "He denied any knowledge of its whereabouts and even invited Senka to search the apartment in the Palace, which he did without success. But that could have been a bluff.

Senthios may have hidden the necklace somewhere else."

"Didn't Chryssa say her father-in-law had it?" Antonius persisted.

"I know she did," Andreas agreed, "and not many people besides Senthios could afford to buy it from whoever stole it."

"Then you don't think Chryssa did?"

Antonius looked so concerned that his father raised his eyebrows in surprise.

"I don't think so," he replied, "she would hardly have worn the necklace in public if she had stolen it herself."

They speculated on the problem for some time more before retiring to bed. Andreas spent a restless night, listening to the wind in the tall trees and pondering the uncertain future.

Theseus' plans to overthrow the government of Crete were thwarted partly by the King's refusal to leave Knossos and also by disagreements between the Greek and Mycenaean authorities. Andreas Micalidos was in some measure responsible for this.

Toward the end of summer he had sent his agent, Tarsis, to Mycenae on a mission to spread rumours that the Cretan Fleet had returned north from Phaestos and to encourage belief in Crete's preparedness for war. Tarsis had been successful. He had fostered ill will and suspicion between the enemies of Crete whose rivalry and antagonism were easily aroused.

For Theseus the delay was intolerable. He had hoped to conquer Crete before the winter closed the ports. He reproached Ariadne for her failure to persuade Minos to leave Knossos and he began to cast doubts on their marriage plans. In spite of her passion for him, Ariadne had never been blind to her lover's ambition and his unbridled arrogance. On several occasions he failed to keep his tryst with her in the Labyrinth. The lamps guttered and her eyes stung with tears. Apparently Theseus had other affairs on his mind.

Soon, however, the gales subsided and the days became mild and sunny. Even in the enclosed world of the Bull Halls the change of season brought a new sense of optimism and enthusiasm.

The schemes Theseus had cherished for so long would soon be put to the test. However, there were many problems to overcome and Theseus was determined to leave nothing to chance. He sent a messenger for the priest Eburninos.

Leander had been wrong in assuming that Theseus bribed the guards in order to leave the Bull Halls. There was no need for him to bribe the guards for there was a door in the Crypt of Sacrifice leading directly into the Labyrinth — the same entry that enabled Eburninos to discover Belia with the dying Paulius. Here in the Crypt the conspirators, Theseus and Eburninos, could meet undisturbed.

When Eburninos arrived Theseus was restlessly pacing back and forth.

"Eburninos, we must be careful. We can't make our move too soon. The Palace Guards have been increased and we could easily be overpowered," Theseus said in a low voice.

Eburninos sat on the stone bench where Paulius and M'boola had died, after their benefit performance at the end of summer.

"What do you intend to do, Prince Theseus?"

"The Athenian Army will land on the north coast and march on Knossos soon after the ports are opened. I will take command when the Palace falls." Theseus stopped pacing and stood with his arms folded looking down on Eburninos. The priest was about to speak but Theseus continued, "Now — lookouts — how many men have we posted along the north coast?"

"About ten," the priest said.

"Not enough. We need thirty. See to it."

"The signal fires will warn us ..." Eburninos argued.

"We can't depend on the fires. The sentries could be taken by surprise or it might pour with rain. It is vital that we know immediately when our forces have landed. Nothing must be left to chance. We need help inside the Palace. Have you bribed any of the officers?"

"Lieutenant Sartis loves money," Eburninos said with a sly grin.

"Can he be trusted?"

The priest looked doubtful.

"What about the Libyans and the slaves? There must be some who dislike the Cretans."

"They'll all desert when the looting begins."

"What a rabble," Theseus said contemptuously. "Eburninos, find me twenty men we can depend on. Promise any reward they ask. Sartis can be their leader. Tell him I'll make him a General. Now, what weapons have we?"

"At considerable expense I have obtained some swords and spears and ..."

Theseus flared up angrily.

"How many? We need daggers and shields too. I told you what was needed ..."

"Don't make so much noise," Eburninos looked anxiously up the stairway, "I can't buy too much at once. We don't want to attract attention and I'm going to have difficulty in hiding such a quantity of arms."

"That's your problem," Theseus snapped, "put them under the shrines in the West Palace, you've got enough in that damned rabbit warren. Use your head. Must I plan everything?"

"I shall need more money," whined the priest.

"Money," Theseus said with a short laugh, "write promissory notes, you'll never have to meet them. The Mycenaeans will cut every merchant's throat. Now, listen and don't interrupt. I want a key to the women's quarters so my Greek dancers can get out when I give the signal. We'll assemble here, follow the thread through the Labyrinth to the West Palace, pick up the weapons and then we must have a place to hide until our troops are in control."

"You'd be safer to stay underground," Eburninos said.

"No. We can't hear what's going on."

"I could give a signal," the priest offered.

"No. No waiting for a signal. When the moment comes, we strike."

"The shrines will be too small to conceal you and your bull dancers. You must split up ..."

Theseus was adamant.

"No. We shall keep together."

Eburninos thought for a moment.

"There are ante-rooms," he said, "near the Council Chamber, usually empty. You could wait there."

"Is it far?"

Eburninos looked puzzled.

"From here?"

Theseus kept his temper, speaking between clenched teeth.

"From where we shall emerge in the West Palace."

"No, but it's easy to get lost. There are many passages."

"Show me now. I'll see for myself."

"At this hour?" Eburninos said nervously.

"No one will be expecting to see me."

Eburninos rose, pale and tense.

"You haven't forgotten that I am to be Chief Priest."

It was both a statement and a question.

"I've told you. You'll be rewarded. How many times do I have to say it?"

"I want it in writing."

"Don't you trust me, Eburninos? *I* have to trust *you*. If you fail me, your death will not be pleasant. Let's waste no more time."

They left the Crypt together and set off through the darkness of the Labyrinth.

During that same month, while Senka was sweating over the nightmare of Zanthope's murder and Theseus and Eburninos were plotting the overthrow of Knossos, Leander had sent an urgent message to Shep-Anep at the Egyptian Embassy. The messenger boy returned with the news that Shep was away in Phaestos on business for the Ambassador and it was not known when he would return.

This information filled Leander with great anxiety. Freyna had become pregnant and she was frequently sick. They knew some action had to be taken urgently before her condition was suspected.

Belia was concerned for her friends but tried to be cheerful. She remembered with horror the skeletons in the Labyrinth cells. She had told Leander of her discovery but both thought it wiser not to tell Freyna.

"Don't worry, Freyna. Nothing shows yet. We must keep our heads and play for time. If Vanna sees you being sick, we'll say it's food poisoning. I'll start vomiting too. That should satisfy her!"

The three dancers met in the lamp-room after the evening meal. The lovers sat on the low cupboard that concealed the grating, their arms around each other. Belia remained near the door. Despite morning sickness, Leander believed Freyna had never looked more beautiful. However, he was gloomy and desperate and blamed himself. Freyna knew that in the eyes of the authorities, she had committed the one unforgivable crime. But her love for Leander and the joy of carrying his child gave her great strength. She was strangely calm and was quite sure that all was predestined.

"Councillor Micalidos is our best hope," Belia said, "he promised to help us. Let us write a letter to him and explain our problem. Leander, you could pay a messenger boy to deliver it."

They all agreed and composed the letter to Andreas.

A few weeks later the Brecchius family, father, daughters and son-in-law, sat down together for the evening meal. It was the night before Leda's wedding to Vaden Markos. She was pale, calm and silent.

Chryssa made an effort to keep the conversation going with little help from either of the two men. Dino Senthios was not talkative and her father veered uncertainly between moodiness and outbursts against Leda.

"Look at her!" he stormed. "You'd think she was going to a funeral! Ungrateful wretch!"

Leda was unmoved. She had heard it all before. After the meal was over, Brecchius asked Chryssa to look at her sister's clothes.

"She's made no preparations the lazy, selfish girl. Make sure she won't disgrace us, Chrys. Lend her anything you think she needs. I'll make it up to you," her father growled.

The two young women withdrew and Brecchius and the Captain were left alone.

"Is it wise to force Leda to marry against her will?" the younger man remarked.

Brecchius was amazed.

"Force? Who's forcing her?"

"I understood ... she's obviously not happy."

Brecchius growled irritably.

"Ugh! Happy, it's a splendid marriage. A fine family, plenty of money, land, everything. She doesn't know what's good for her. I'm sorry for young Markos, but don't repeat that. She's no use to me and I'll be glad when she's gone."

"Perhaps when they have a child things will be better," Captain Senthios said. He longed for Chryssa to have a child. At this moment he looked forward to going on duty to escape from his father-in-law.

Chryssa returned to the salon. The apartment was dull now without the flowers Madam Brecchius had loved. During her long illness they had been neglected and the plants had dried up and withered.

"Leda's lying down," Chryssa said in response to her father's inquiry, "you were right, she's made absolutely no preparations, she hasn't even a veil for the ceremony. I'll get my maid to find something in the morning."

"Sacred Zeus! Don't leave it till the morning, Chrys," her father complained, rolling his eyes to heaven, "everything must be ready tonight. I don't want any excuse for delay."

The Captain took his wife's hand.

"Leda misses her mother. Do what you can, sweetheart," he said quietly.

Chryssa smiled and patted his hand. She yawned and stretched.

"Let's play cards. I'll play you, father, and the winner can play my dear husband."

"No. I'll play your father. You go and get the clothes and when you come back the winner will play you," Senthios said.

"All right," Chryssa agreed with a sigh. She rose, stretched again and pirouetted just out of reach of her husband who made a playful attempt to catch hold of her.

"Don't be long," her father said, setting up the game, "I'll beat this fellow in no time."

But it was Senthios who had won when Chryssa returned half an hour later with the maid carrying an armful of clothes.

"Hurry up, if you want to play," the Captain said, "I should be on duty soon."

They played and he won. Chryssa and her father paid up their forfeits in mock despair. Senthios prepared to leave.

"Good night, dearest Chrys," he said with unexpected feeling. He took her in his arms and kissed her on the mouth. She yielded passively as she always did, her dark eyes smiling their own secret smile, the look he found so captivating and so baffling.

"Sleep well, my love," he said tenderly, "I always long for the morning, when I must leave you like this."

"You really need not go," she said softly.

"I must set an example," he replied, straightening up at once, "I can't ask others to do what I'm not prepared to do myself."

"Have some wine to keep out the chill?" Brecchius was pouring it out.

"No thank you, sir. Not before duty."

The Captain put on his helmet, saluted his father-in-law and departed.

"You'll have a nightcap, Chrys?"

"Thanks, Father."

The old man looked tired and worn. She shuddered as she wrapped a shawl about her shoulders. This place smelled of death. Leda was best out of it. He's old and finished, she thought, regarding Brecchius dispassionately.

They drank their wine, while he rambled on, complaining about Leda, the servants and the King's illness.

"He's been cooped up in the West Palace all these weeks — ever since the last Council meeting — that was a strange business! Why don't the doctors help him? Why doesn't he send for his Councillors?"

Chryssa was not at all interested. She finished her wine, refused a second cup and took her leave.

On leaving his father-in-law's apartment Captain Senthios descended to the Palace Courtyard and crossed toward the Guard Room at the South Gate. The night air was cool and refreshing. Another officer approached and the Captain recognized Lieutenant Micalidos.

Dino Senthios was an amiable man, not given to bearing grudges. He was no longer angry over rumours that his wife, Chryssa, had stolen Zanthope's necklace. He greeted young Micalidos cordially.

"I'm glad to see you, Antonius. How is your father now?"

"Much improved, thank you, sir."

"Antonius, we haven't seen you for so long. You must dine with us soon."

"Thank you, I should like that very much."

"Well, I'm due to inspect — oh, damnation! I have a letter for Major Ortis. I meant to ask the man at Councillor Brecchius' to deliver it."

"Where does the Major live?" Antonius inquired.

As General Imanos' aide, Major Ortis had a Palace apartment.

"Not far from my father-in-law," Dino replied, "how stupid of me to forget."

"I'd be pleased to deliver it, sir."

"But you've been on duty all day."

"That's no problem, give me the letter."

"I'm most grateful, Antonius. It's Apartment 50 on the second floor. I wouldn't trouble you but it may be important." They saluted and parted. Antonius was tired after a long day but he welcomed this opportunity to renew his friendship with Dino Senthios. He soon found Major Ortis' apartment and knocked on the door. The servant accepted the letter and invited him in though Antonius hesitated.

"There may be an answer, sir," the man said.

Antonius hoped not. He had not bargained for that. Major Ortis appeared.

"Ah, Micalidos, what do you want?" he said in his usual abrupt tone.

He opened the letter, read it and snapped.

"There's no answer."

Antonius disliked Ortis. This man has the

manners of a pig, he thought. He bid Ortis good night and turned to go.

"Where are you stationed, Lieutenant?" Ortis called after him.

"The North Gate, sir."

"Ah, yes. Good night," the Major said bluntly.

The door closed and Antonius moved toward the stairway. As he did so, a woman came from an apartment along the passage and walked ahead of him. As she turned to ascend the stairs he recognized Chryssa Senthios.

Tired and nettled by Ortis' rudeness, the sight of Chryssa disturbed Antonius even more. It brought to mind the loss of his mother's necklace and his suspicion that Chryssa was in some way involved. For some time he had also been concerned that the loss of the necklace was inevitably linked with his father's serious financial problems and his mother's tragic death.

Like many beautiful women, Chryssa possessed an aura of mystery and an awareness of power. It was probably Chryssa's air of unassailable confidence that triggered in Antonius an irritation, almost fury, which robbed him of self-control and commonsense. The memory of his mother's death and the suspicion that Chryssa had stolen the necklace tormented him greatly. He decided to follow Chryssa. However, she was eager to be home and he was only able to confront her at the door of her apartment.

Chryssa smiled and showed no surprise and with an elegant gesture she invited him in. Antonius entered, scarcely aware of what he was doing. His heart was pounding violently.

Chryssa closed the door and preceded him to a room off the hallway. He followed her in a state of agitation. Chryssa offered him a glass of wine, which he declined.

Antonius tried to express his thoughts rationally, but he began to stammer which added to his embarrassment.

"Chryssa, I came — I wish to ask — Chryssa, I have to know —"

She watched him intently, amused by his discomfort.

Antonius was determined to discover why this woman had worn his mother's necklace. Suddenly, he stepped forward and grasped her shoulders as if he would shake the truth from her.

"Chryssa," he began again.

Her smile was mischievous and inviting and he found it hard to take his eyes from her face. To his surprise she calmly removed his hands from her shoulders and stepped back. With a quick movement she threw off her shawl and unclasped the belt from around her waist. Her gown fell to the floor and she stood before him naked.

Suddenly, all those things that had concerned him ceased to be important. He was aware only of her beautiful body and her dark eyes and he was possessed by an ungovernable rage and lust. He fumbled with his tunic. He saw that she was laughing as she helped him to undress. She tried to lead him to the bed but he grasped her passionately. She giggled when his feet became entangled in her gown and they both fell to the floor. They coupled there, rolling and gasping.

Finally, when the storm was over, they lay together on the cool tiles and he gazed at the curve of her throat and the dark shadow of her eyelashes against her cheek.

Antonius sat up with his head in his hands.

"Holy Zeus! Chryssa ... oh, Chryssa!"

She rose and put out her hand to him.

"Come, Antonius, let us talk and be comfortable."

She drew him over to the bed. They lay down and she pulled a fur coverlet over them.

"Antonius, it was always you. Why did you make me wait so long?"

"I should never have come. It was not for this."

"Why then?"

"Chryssa, I wanted to ask you about my mother's necklace, to hear your side of it."

"What do you want to know?"

Her tone was so innocent that he felt reassured even before he questioned her.

"Where did you get the necklace, Chryssa? Did you steal it?"

"I? Of course not." Her dark eyes reproached him.

"I was told you wore the necklace at the Palace reception. Chryssa, I've been so tormented since my mother died."

"Poor Antonius. How tragic it's been for you all. I understand, for I have lost my mother, too."

She began to talk to him softly, explaining how her father-in-law had insisted on her wearing the necklace.

"I did it to humour him. He said he was worried in case it was stolen from his apartment during the reception. I had no idea it was your mother's necklace. It was only later, after I had returned it to Papa Senthios, that I learned the truth."

"How did he get the necklace?"

"I really don't know, Antonius. I swear it."

Antonius believed Chryssa. He was convinced of her innocence. He had always avoided acknowledging his desire for her, denying it out of loyalty to his friend Dino. Now, close to her under the warmth of the coverlet, he found his desire overwhelming. The distress he had experienced had weakened his defences and the barrier he had placed against this temptation had been swept aside. Chryssa was in his arms again, her mouth on his and he could not tear himself away from her. Trying to ignore his feelings of guilt was near impossible.

"When will he be back?" he asked.

"Not until morning, the night is ours," she said with a smile.

They abandoned themselves to pleasure. Later Antonius lay exhausted and fell deeply asleep.

It was an uneventful night for Captain Senthios. He made his inspection rounds, the sentries reported nothing unusual and yet the Captain felt an unaccountable anxiety. Not given to nervous imagining, he was annoyed with himself. Everything was in order, why should he feel this sense of unease and foreboding? It was a cold night. A few hours before dawn, he shared a hot drink in the guard house with a young soldier from the mountain district near Jukto.

"Everything is quiet, Corporal," Senthios remarked as he drew off his helmet and warmed his hands at the brazier.

"Yes, sir, all in order."

"The night air still has a breath of winter."

"It's blowing off the mountains tonight, sir," the young man said with a smile, "my father will be out in the snow looking for newborn lambs."

"City life is new to you then. What made you join up?"

"The recruitment officer made it sound like a great adventure."

Senthios laughed.

"And here you are on sentry duty. Not much adventure in that!"

"I don't know, sir. The Palace is wonderful. I've never seen anything like it."

"So you find it entertaining?"

"I much prefer it to herding sheep!"

Senthios finished his drink and put on his helmet.

"Carry on, Corporal."

At the northern end of the West Palace there was a lookout post on the second floor level. Senthios would have preferred a lookout on the roof and he made a mental note to have something done about it. He kept returning to this particular post, straining his eyes into the darkness toward the coast, looking for the tell-tale flare of a signal fire.

As the wind dropped, an eerie mist descended on the coastline. Senthios' incessant pacing unnerved the sentry. When the Captain asked if he could smell smoke, the man sniffed the air.

"Could be, sir. Probably home fires. It's a cold night."

"Keep your eyes on the coastline, sentry. If you see so much as a flicker of light, yell as you've never yelled before. Understand?"

"Yes sir. I will."

# CHAPTER 41

The Egyptian Ambassador, User-Amon, was a poor sleeper. He would leave his bed late at night, light his lamp and read and occasionally dawn found him still awake. In recent weeks he had been more than usually affected by insomnia. His Excellency was more concerned by rumours of invasion than other Ambassadors and officials in the Palace and he had made contingency plans.

Early this morning he saw from his second floor window the lurid glow of signal fires. Soon after he heard sentries shouting, "Fires to the north! Fires to the north!"

Immediately there was a general call to arms. The Ambassador gave brisk orders to his steward. His household was roused and his servants ordered to pack. It was not long before his chariot and baggage cart were harnessed outside the West Palace.

The Ambassador was concerned for the Queen's safety. He sent Shep-Anep to the East Palace to advise Queen Kara and her son to return with him to Egypt.

"Try to persuade Her Majesty, Shep," he said, "Crete is finished. She will be safer with us."

The Queen received Shep in her salon. She wore a long woollen robe and her dark hair fell loosely over her shoulders. Shep informed her briefly that warning fires were burning on the north coast and that the Ambassador was leaving as an invasion of Crete was at this moment taking place.

"His Excellency is most concerned for your safety, Majesty. He earnestly entreats you and His Royal Highness, Prince Nikos to accompany him back to Egypt. A ship has been commissioned in Phaestos and is ready to sail immediately."

After some thought Queen Kara replied calmly, "Would you please thank his Excellency, Shep, but my place is here, with His Majesty, the King."

"And the Prince, Your Highness?"

Queen Kara had a moment of uncertainty, but her resolution returned.

"His place is here with us. He is the heir to the throne and we must stand together. The Cretan forces will defend us and I feel sure the invaders will respect the holiness of the Priest-King."

"As you wish, Majesty," Shep replied. He bowed, but paused before taking his leave.

"You are troubled, Shep?" she asked sympathetically.

"I am concerned about Councillor Micalidos, Your Majesty, I . . ."

"I'm sure he can take care of himself, Shep. Do you wish to give him a message?"

"I would like to be of service to him, but the Ambassador has ordered me to accompany him to Egypt."

"Then that is your duty. Councillor Micalidos will understand."

Shep seemed satisfied.

"May the Gods protect you, Madam," he said with emotion.

"May they protect us all," she replied quietly.

The Queen ordered her people to help her dress in her finest clothes. Then she woke her son and the Princesses, Ariadne and Phaedre, and told them of the disaster which threatened their country. Queen Kara returned to her salon and sat down. Gazing at the solid walls of the Palace, she tried to draw strength from them.

The Earth Shaker had done his worst in the past but the Palace and Crete had survived. She prayed they would also survive this calamity.

Presently her young son, Prince Nikos, came to the salon and sat beside her. She kissed him and put her arm around him. Together they gazed at the beauty and elegance of the frescoes that decorated the walls of the Queen's salon.

"Which painting do you like best, Nikki" Queen Kara asked.

"The dolphins," he replied at once.

"They are beautiful, Nikki. They're my favourite, too." she said.

Together they gazed at the fresco of the black

dolphins plunging joyously in the cool green sea and Queen Kara prayed that the dolphins and her son would survive.

The noise and bustle of packing in the Egyptian Embassy soon disturbed the Cretan staff. Senka got up, dressed hurriedly and went to see what was going on.

"What is happening?" he demanded. "Where is Shep-Anep?"

The Egyptian servants shrugged their shoulders. They were too busy to bother with him. By now all the Ambassador's Cretan staff were awake, hovering in the passageways, perplexed and worried by this sudden exodus. A stream of baggage was being hastily carried down the stairway to the West Gate. When Shep returned they surrounded him.

"What's going on, Shep?" Senka demanded.

"Crete is being invaded. We must leave." The tall Egyptian spoke quietly, with his hand on the Ambassador's door. He opened it and went in, ignoring the babble of questions that his words had generated.

Senka ran to his room and quickly gathered up the few possessions he valued. When he returned to the hallway the Ambassador was departing. He had waited only to hear the Queen's decision to remain in Crete. Senka pushed his way through the excited crowd and grabbed Shep's arm.

"Please let me come with you," he begged.

Shep was embarrassed. He shook his head and brushed Senka aside

"No Cretan staff — the Ambassador's orders. There's no room in the chariots."

"I'm Phoenician, one extra won't make any difference," Senka shouted.

Shep, however, was moving quickly down the stairs, following the Ambassador and the Egyptian diplomatic staff. Senka followed too with the Cretan clerks and servants, who were shouting angrily because many of them had not been paid.

At the West Gate, which opened out into the city, there was an uproar. The Ambassador and his staff, clutching their baggage, pushed and jostled the guards as they tried to close the heavy gates. In the mêlée a few Cretans managed to escape but Shep was held back by Senka, who kept shouting, "Take me — please, take me with you!"

Shep struggled and finally threw Senka violently aside. Pushing his way through the screaming mob of Cretans, the Egyptian steward managed to pass through just as the gates were closing. Those who were left behind shouted hysterical abuse at the guards who barred the gates and clutched their weapons nervously.

Furious, Senka raced to the central Courtyard. Determined to escape from Knossos, he remembered that Antonius was in command at the North Gate. He quickly made his way there, confident that their friendship would help him. But Antonius had not arrived on duty and the post was commanded by Cadet Nimos.

Nimos suggested that Senka should join the defenders of the Palace but the idea of shedding his

Phoenician blood in a battle between Cretans and Greeks did not appeal to Senka. He returned to the now empty Egyptian Embassy where he found some food and wine in the Ambassador's rooms. He sat down to consider the best course of action.

After ordering the general alarm, Captain Senthios hurried to the Chancellor's apartments in the West Palace. He pushed past the slaves at the door and entered without ceremony.

"I regret to disturb you, Chancellor, but we are being invaded from the north. The Palace will soon be under attack."

Chancellor Darian did not at first grasp the full meaning of the Captain's words. He grunted sleepily. Then, seeing the officer standing over him in full armour, he was startled out of his drowsiness.

"What's that? What's that you say?"

Senthios repeated his statement more forcibly, adding, "The signal fires are burning along the coast. We have perhaps an hour."

The Chancellor's jaw dropped, his hands trembled.

"Have you sounded the alarm?"

"Yes, sir. The guard is called out. The Palace gates are locked."

"The Council must be summoned, Captain. The King must be informed."

"You will attend to that, sir?"

"Of course I will," Darian snapped irritably. It was difficult to maintain his dignity sitting on the edge of his bed in his brief night clothes.

The Captain saluted and hurried back to the Courtyard satisfied that he had done his duty. He knew that it would take the invaders at least an hour to reach the Palace gates. His thoughts turned to his beautiful wife, Chryssa. She must go to the mountains. There would be time if she left immediately.

The alarm had not yet penetrated the upper floors of the East Palace. It was still dark and the residents slept on unaware of the danger threatening them. Captain Senthios dashed up the stairways and into his apartment. A lamp was burning in the hallway. He removed his helmet, took the lamp and entered his bedroom. He was horrified to see his wife asleep in the arms of Lieutenant Micalidos.

Senthios' sudden entry awoke the lovers. Chryssa immediately rose, wrapped a robe about herself and stood as far from the bed as possible.

"Ye Gods! Chryssa — and you, Antonius!" Senthios stammered, aghast and pale.

Antonius, naked and embarrassed, got up from the bed.

"Senthios, I'm sorry, I didn't intend this to happen." Sick with shame, he gathered his clothes, his sword and helmet and moved towards the door. As he reached it Senthios said harshly, "Go to your post at once, Micalidos. Crete is being invaded."

Antonius went to the hallway, struggled into his uniform and raced to the North Gate. He was consumed with misery and regret and would remember this moment of shame for the rest of his days. Chryssa, meanwhile was trembling. For the first time in her life, she feared her husband.

"Dino, he broke in here, he really forced me —"

"You're a liar! You are also a harlot — I should leave you to the Greeks!" His voice shook and his eyes filled with tears. She thought he would break down but he controlled himself.

"Go to my father and warn him. Tell him the island is being invaded. He'll know what to do. Leave at once for the mountains, before the roads are blocked and take your sister with you." He left her abruptly and went immediately to the command post at the South Gate.

Having sent messengers racing through the Palace to summon the Council, Chancellor Darian wrapped himself in a fur robe and set off to advise the King that the island was being invaded. A slave with a lantern led the way through the maze of darkened corridors in the West Palace.

When Darian reached the suite of rooms above the Council Chamber where King Minos had lived in isolation since the last Council meeting, the Chancellor found the door to the ante-room locked. He knocked, softly at first, out of deference, and then more urgently, calling in a trembling voice, "High Priest Arcanos, wake up! Wake up, Arcanos, we are being attacked!"

Eventually the door opened and Eburninos confronted him.

"What is the meaning of this disturbance?" the young priest asked rudely.

Darian was greatly taken aback but he managed to stammer out his message about the signal fires and the imminent invasion. At the same time he tried to enter the ante-room but Eburninos blocked his path.

"Who brought this message?"

The Chancellor was dumbfounded.

"I ... I do not think any messenger has come. The sentries have reported fires along the coast."

"And who says we are being invaded?"

"Captain Senthios has given the alarm."

"Isn't that rather premature?" Eburninos asked coldly. His manner amazed Darian.

"Before disturbing His Majesty, who is far from well, would it not be better to have definite proof that this invasion will occur? Captain Senthios may be mistaken. We have lookouts all along the coast. Surely they would have been aware of the invasion — if indeed it has occurred — they would have warned us as soon as the signal fires were lit."

The Chancellor was now in a quandary.

"But, Eburninos, I've called a meeting of the Council..."

"Would you like me to cancel those orders?" Eburninos said blandly.

"Certainly not," Darian snapped, taken aback, "you had better wait here, Eburninos. You will be given further instructions."

The Chancellor hurried away, endeavouring to persuade himself that this alarm may not in fact be a reality. When he returned to his apartment he sent messengers to summon Captain Senthios. He also cancelled the meeting of the Council. A short time later, thoroughly confused, he changed his mind and cancelled his previous orders. Darian then decided to eat breakfast before making any further decisions.

When the Chancellor had departed, the priest Eburninos made sure that no one was awake. Locking the ante-room door behind him, he hurried silently through the passageways, down the dark stairway and into the Labyrinth. With the aid of the cord which Ariadne had left for Theseus, it took him only a few minutes to reach the Crypt of Sacrifice beneath the Bull Halls. He moved silently up the spiral stairway, across the hall where the dancers had waited to enter the Bull Ring and down the main stairs to the men's quarters. He knew the bed in which Theseus lay asleep and placed a hand over the bull dancer's mouth before awakening him.

The Greek Prince opened his eyes, heard Eburninos whisper "It has begun" and knew instantly that his hour had come.

"Go ahead, Eburninos you know what to do. Leave the doors unlocked," Theseus said.

The priest nodded and left as silently as he had come.

In the women's quarters, Belia sleepily opened her eyes and yawned. Someone was knocking softly on the outer door of the quarters. She saw that three of the Greek bull girls were awake and dressing.

"What's going on? What's the matter?" Belia asked sleepily.

"Nothing," replied one of the Greeks, "we're just going to the bathroom."

Freyna was also awake.

"What's happening, Bee?" she asked drowsily.

"Nothing, Frey, the Greeks are going for a piss," Belia murmured. Yawning she went back to sleep.

A few hours before dawn, the Cretan sentries from the coast rode up the steep narrow roadway to the South Gate of the Palace. On being admitted they reported to Major Ortis and told their story. All along the north coast a great fleet of ships was disgorging invading armies from Athens, Mycenae and Tiryns. The Cretan fleet was destroyed and the Athenian army was marching on Knossos.

In an ante-room near the Council Chamber, Theseus, Prince of Athens and his band of Greeks, waited their moment, armed and determined to conquer Crete.

King Minos, in his suite of rooms above the Council Chamber, slept fitfully, his mind confused by drugs administered by Eburninos, unaware of the disaster threatening his country and its people.

When Lieutenant Antonius Micalidos arrived at the North Gate he found his men assembled under Cadet Nimos. The Palace Gates were closed and the sentries reported that all was quiet in the city.

"Well, Nimos, it won't be quiet for long," Antonius said grimly, "by the Gods my father was right — why didn't they listen to him? Nimos, we must warn him immediately."

"Who shall we send, sir?"

"Telmos is from Knossos, isn't he?"

"Yes, sir."

"Call him over."

When Telmos stood to attention, Antonius inquired if he knew the district where Councillor Micalidos lived.

"I know Councillor Micalidos' villa, sir," Telmos said.

"Good. Telmos, go to the villa and warn the Councillor we are being invaded. Tell him we may have only one hour before we are attacked. Return here immediately."

"Yes, sir."

Telmos saluted and set off through the silent streets. The young soldier was deeply concerned for the safety of his wife and their two small children and was convinced that the mountains would be their only refuge from this impending catastrophe. By the time he had reached the villa and delivered his message to Andreas, Telmos had made up his mind. He returned to his home and after a short time set off for the mountains with his family and their few belongings hastily thrown into a cart. He never returned to the Palace.

Andreas, meanwhile, had called his household into conference. He, Dr Ahmed, Korynna and Credon met anxiously in his apartment to consider the best plan of action.

Dorcas, the cart driver, was sent for and ordered to ride with all speed to Mallia.

"Dorcas, warn the Prince and my daughter that our island is being invaded. Hyacinth and her children must leave Mallia immediately. Then bring me news of the situation there as soon as possible."

Dorcas hurried away.

"The King will call his Council and of course I must be there," Andreas continued.

Korynna did not want him to go to the Palace.

"Oh, Andreas! It will be dangerous for you," she said.

"Don't despair, Korynna, our ships and the Army will protect us. Now listen to me carefully, all of you. Ahmed, my very dear friend, this war does not concern Egypt or its citizens. I have no doubt His Excellency, your Ambassador, is packing his baggage right now, if he isn't already on the road south! We will understand if you wish to leave. How can I help you?"

Ahmed frowned.

"Sir, I have no wish to flee. Crete is my home. I can help the people here. However, I am concerned," he paused.

"I think I understand," Andreas said, "you are thinking of Queen Kara."

"Yes, I am," Ahmed nodded.

"I'm sure the Ambassador will have some kind of proposal to make to her," Andreas said, "however, I would be very surprised if she were to leave Knossos. It would be out of character."

Ahmed agreed. "But, sir, I am also particularly concerned about the surgery, Dr Iros and the rest of them..."

"We can attend to that shortly," Andreas said impatiently, "but first we must arrange things here. Credon, order the grooms to harness up the cart and the large chariot. Korynna, you organize food, blankets and warm clothing for yourself, Timon and mother. I want you to set off for the farm as soon as possible. You will be safe there, at least until we see how events turn out. I am certain the Greeks and Mycenaeans will regret invading our island."

Andreas' confidence gave them hope, though in truth he was pessimistic. Korynna, however, was not convinced.

"It is your own safety, Andreas, yours and Antonius', that concerns me," she said anxiously.

"Antonius and I cannot leave Knossos, Korynna. We have our duty here. You must leave, my dear, immediately, and take Mother and Timon with you. You also, Credon."

"Master, I cannot leave without you!" the old servant spoke emphatically.

Andreas threw up his hands in despair, but he said kindly, "Can't I give orders in this household any more?"

He stared at each of them in turn — these gentle, kind, civilized people, he thought. What might this army of murderous invaders do to them? He forced a smile. He did not wish to frighten them. He realized they were unaccustomed to emergencies.

"Do the best you can," he added earnestly, "but hurry."

"Doctor, if you don't wish to leave Knossos, may I suggest that you let Korynna take those things you value? This house may very well be looted, by Cretan thieves, if not by the enemy."

Korynna and Credon went about their business without further discussion.

"I will accompany you to the Palace, sir, if you wish," Ahmed said.

"Of course, my friend," Andreas replied.

They parted, each filled with anxiety and some dread for the future.

When Chryssa left her apartment and hurried down the stairway, the passages in the East Palace were quiet and deserted. The prospect of invasion seemed fantastic. However, as she neared her father's apartment, she heard the sound of angry shouting. The door was open. Councillor Brecchius, in night attire and clutching a coverlet around himself, was berating a pale, frightened messenger.

"You must be mad, you lunatic, waking me at this hour! A Council meeting! Get out ..." He broke off when he saw Chryssa. "What on earth's going on, Chrys?"

"Dino said we're being invaded, Father."

"Zeus! Then it's true — there must be a Council meeting!" Brecchius became hysterical, shouting orders at the slaves, "Start packing, you worthless idiots. We must get away! Chryssa, we must go to the mountains."

Chryssa turned to leave.

"Don't go, Chrys, don't leave us, we need you here. Your sister can't manage the slaves. We must pack ... we must get away!"

"All right, Father. Dino told me to warn Papa Senthios, I'll come back soon."

Brecchius gripped the rail by the light well and tried to calm himself. His daughter, Leda, came into the salon.

"What's the matter?" she asked.

"The matter," her father replied, turning all the intensity of his fear and resentment on her, "is that we are being invaded. I am called to the Council."

"Then you had better get dressed," she said.

Chryssa turned in the doorway.

"O, poor Leda, I forgot. It's your wedding day."

"Another postponement," Brecchius growled, "they'll say it's a bad omen." Then he managed to control himself.

"Chryssa, I'm going to the Council Chamber. I'll see what plans Councillor Markos has. You order the horse and cart harnessed up, and get this dim-witted sister of yours to start packing our valuables."

Brecchius snatched his cloak from the slave and rushed out.

"Well, Leda, you heard what father said."

Leda stared vaguely about, still affected by exhaustion and shock from her mother's illness and untimely death.

"Are you awake, Leda?" Chryssa said.

"Yes, Chrys."

"All right. I must go and warn Papa Senthios."

"Of course."

"Send the man to get the cart ready and pack the valuables."

"All right, Chryssa. Take care."

Leda was left alone with the frightened slaves.

"Go and get the horse and cart harnessed," she said to the manservant. He left. He had a bundle tied up in a cloth.

The maidservants began to whimper. They were country girls who wanted to be with their families.

One of them fell on her knees and begged to be allowed to go. Leda nodded her consent and suddenly the apartment was empty. She stared about her. In her confusion she could not decide what to do first. She remembered their annual summer holidays in the mountains, her mother's endless fussing, the servants packing and re-packing. But they had never packed for an invasion. She was weak with fear and hoped that Chryssa would soon return.

When Chryssa banged loudly on her father-in-law's door, a slave opened the peephole to discover who was calling at this hour.

"Let me in. I'm Chryssa Senthios," she said irritably.

Chryssa found the old man in bed, enveloped in a voluminous silk robe. When he saw her, he pushed the young girl sleeping beside him out of the bed and told her to get out. She snatched up her clothes and ran from the room.

"What do you want, Chryssa?" he asked brusquely.

She told him Crete was being invaded and that his son had said they should leave the city at once. Senthios was immediately wide awake. He called his steward, gave curt orders and men went running to obey them.

"Chryssa, you'd better fetch the necklace and bring it to me."

"Those rubies are mine. I earned them, remember?"

He towered over her. "This place will be looted. The necklace won't be safe with you. Go and fetch it instantly."

"I might just decide to stay with my husband, like a loyal wife," she said sweetly.

His eyes narrowed. "Do you know what an invading army does to women?"

She rolled her eyes in mock terror. "It might not be worse than two nights with you!"

He went to a dressing-room nearby and returned dragging a heavy chest. When he clapped his hands, two servants came in and carried it out. Senthios then went to Chryssa, took her arm and led her to the door. He spoke quietly, but with an edge to his voice.

"Micalidos was right. We're being invaded and we can't defend ourselves. Your husband will probably be killed. Now listen, my little whore, I have a ship in Phaestos and for some strange reason I don't fancy life without you. We can be over the mountains before the Greeks get here and you'll find Egypt a pleasant and civilized place. However, I am not going to spend the rest of my days listening to your whining regrets for that necklace. So go and get it at once. Don't keep me waiting!"

Chryssa set off for her apartment to fetch the necklace. As she retraced her steps people in the Palace were beginning to stir. Slaves were running in the passages and many people were talking anxiously in doorways. On the stairway she ran into her sister.

"Leda, what are you doing here? Why, you're not even dressed!"

"O Chrys! I'm so glad I found you. Father sent to know if the cart was ready and the man hasn't come back yet. What am I to do?"

Chryssa led her sister back into the apartment.

"Leda, haven't you packed yet? Where is everyone?"

"I don't know where to start, Chrys. I ... I let the girls go," Leda said trembling and sat down on the bench. Chryssa was angry.

"You really are stupid. Pull yourself together, Leda. Pack your wedding dress, your veil, your best clothes and money and jewellery ..." A sudden thought came to Chryssa. "By the way, where are mother's jewels?"

"In our room, where she died. Her jewel box is on the table by the bed."

"You don't mind if I take something to remember her by?" Chryssa asked.

"Of course not, Chrys. Take what you like."

Chryssa went to the bedroom and emptied the jewel box on to the bed. She appraised each piece, made her selection and returned to the salon.

"Leda, I have to go. Dino said I was to go with his father."

"Yes ... yes, of course, Chrys."

Chryssa went down on one knee and took her sister's hand.

"Father and Councillor Markos will take you to Silamos. You'll have a country wedding. It will be much better for you there, Leda."

"The servant went to order the cart ... but he hasn't returned."

"So you told me," Chryssa said as she rose to her feet, "I really must go. I have my own packing to do. Now, get yourself dressed, Leda. When Father comes back he'll be angry if you're not ready," she paused in the doorway, "goodbye, Leda."

"Goodbye? Oh, Chrys, don't leave me. Don't go!"

But Chryssa had already departed. Leda went to the bedroom and she saw her mother's possessions tumbled on the bed. A small pile of trash. Chryssa had taken everything of value. Leda fell to her knees and wept, pressing her head into the bed, rocking her body from side to side in the intensity of her misery. She felt something hard and cold against her face. It was a small ivory carving of a monkey's head, a quaint little curio, half toy, half ornament, which had amused her as a child. She smiled through her tears as she remembered happy moments in the past. There was also a fine gold chain, which had luckily escaped Chryssa's notice. She hung this small memento on the chain around her neck, then dried her eyes and resolved to be brave. As she could not stop shivering, she dressed herself in a warm skirt and jacket and a woollen shawl. Feeling hungry, she ran to the kitchen, for she knew there was milk there and some meat, cheese and bread left from yesterday's evening meal. It was all gone. The servant must have taken it and drunk the milk. She knew now that he had never intended to return. Fear possessed her once again. The cold, paralysing fear that haunts victims of violence, bloodshed and war. She walked slowly into the passageway.

There were many more people about now. Women leading small children by the hand, slaves carrying heavy bundles and laden baskets, jostling men and women whose only desire was to escape from the

Palace and the city as soon as possible. There was a continual babble and murmuring of voices, and as more and more people decided to leave or to visit neighbours, the narrow passages became even more congested.

Leda found herself propelled forward and down the stairway in the direction of the Palace Courtyard. She had neither strength nor will to resist. She drifted on as in a dream, watching eagerly for her father. She felt so alone, so afraid, that even his scolding would be welcome. She had left the empty apartment forever.

When Chancellor Darian finished his breakfast and walked down to the great Courtyard, the scene astonished him.

A crowd of angry and hysterical people, laden with baggage, milled around, shouting and gesticulating. When he was recognized, they rushed towards him.

"Chancellor, open the gates, open the gates and let us go! We must leave Knossos!"

"Go back to your homes and apartments," the Chancellor shouted, but no one listened.

The great shrine in the East Palace was already crowded with tearful and frightened people, calling for the priests and the Council to save the city. Unmoved by their prayers, the great statue of the Earth Mother smiled benignly.

Chancellor Darian, stranded in the midst of this chaos, had a moment of acute self-doubt. He saw himself as a vain, incompetent old man. However, this unpleasant thought was swept from his mind by a terrifying sound. It seemed to come from the Merchants' Courtyard. It was the echoing crash of a battering ram. The panic-stricken crowd cried out in fear.

The Chancellor pushed and struggled his way towards the Council Chamber. There, the assembled Councillors, angry and confused at being dragged so early from their beds, also heard the relentless pounding of the battering ram. They stopped arguing and stood glassy-eyed with terror. When Chancellor Darian appeared they advanced on him angrily.

"What on earth is going on, Darian?" Councillor Markos roared.

"Where is High Priest Arcanos? Where is His Majesty, King Minos?" Councillor Xanthios screamed in his shrill voice.

"One moment, Councillors," Darian said, holding up his hands defensively. "Come with me, Councillor Markos, if you please."

Darian and Markos hurried into the shrine leading off the Council Chamber and up the stairway to the King's private suite where they roused Arcanos.

"High Priest, you must awaken the King immediately. We are being invaded!"

In the Chamber, Councillor Brecchius, who had been trying to persuade Markos to leave the Palace, now decided to do so alone. However, General Imanos confronted him in the doorway.

The General had hastily inspected the defences of the Palace and given words of encouragement to his aide, Major Ortis and his officers. He was angry that Arcanos had not appeared to comfort the people.

"Take your places, Councillors," Imanos said grimly, "no one leaves this Chamber without His Majesty's consent."

The Councillors obeyed him without a word.

"Where is Darian?" the General continued angrily. "And where is Arcanos?"

Before anyone could answer, Chancellor Darian and Councillor Markos returned.

"What's going on, Darian?" Imanos demanded. "Has His Majesty been informed of the situation?"

"Of course we have informed him," Darian replied tersely. "Where is Councillor Micalidos? He warned us and we did not listen."

In the confusion it had been forgotten that Andreas did not live in the Palace.

"I listened to him. Send for him immediately," General Imanos commanded.

"The gates are closed," the Chancellor moaned, wringing his hands.

"My daughter told me his son, Lieutenant Micalidos, is stationed at the North Gate," Brecchius said.

"He has my authority to leave the Palace," the General interjected, "let him go at once for his father."

A scribe was dispatched. Darian shook the astonished man by the shoulders, saying, "We need Councillor Micalidos here. Lieutenant Micalidos must go in person. Make sure he understands."

As the man set off for the North Gate, High Priest Arcanos entered the Chamber.

"Councillors, His Majesty Priest-King Minos of Knossos."

The Councillors turned, expecting to see the King enter in procession, as he always did, calm, aloof, self-possessed. They could not hide their dismay.

Supported on either side by two priests, the King was led, or more precisely assisted, into the Council Chamber. Minos' face was ashen, his eyes sunk in black shadows, his manner confused and hesitant. He was unable to comprehend what was happening, unaware of what was expected of him.

The King's robes hung loosely on his bent shoulders, and the jewelled, fur-trimmed hat had slipped over his forehead. He was a pitiable sight. His Councillors had expected something more inspiring in their hour of need. In the shocked silence that followed the harsh pounding of the battering ram seemed more than ever like the crash of doom.

At the North Gate, Antonius impatiently awaited the return of Telmos with news of his father. Time passed and the man did not appear. The sound of the battering ram echoed throughout the Palace.

"What can have happened? Telmos must be dead! I pray my father is safe," Antonius said to Cadet Nimos.

At that moment, the scribe sent by the Councillors and General Imanos came with their message that Antonius should conduct his father to the Council meeting.

Reluctant to leave his post, Antonius considered sending Cadet Nimos. However, the scribe repeated the Chancellor's order that Antonius must go himself.

"You take over here, Nimos. I'll take ten men to escort my father. We'll not be long."

The North Gate, with its solid, ancient Keep, had not yet been attacked by the invaders. The enemy was well briefed and the attack was concentrated in the south. The North Gate was quietly unbarred and Antonius and his patrol set off for the villa.

# CHAPTER 42

Captain Senthios faced the invaders with courage and determination. However, he was tormented by his wife's unfaithfulness with his friend Antonius Micalidos.

Senthios was a simple, uncomplicated soldier. His wife's betrayal sickened him, especially as he had trusted her completely. He suspected that in some way his father was involved with his wife's possession of Zanthope's necklace. But why? What had he received in return?

The Greeks advanced in a pre-arranged plan, focusing their attack at the southern end of the Palace. As the huge battering rams began to demolish the entrance to the Merchants' Courtyard, another large force marched up the long, sloping roadway from the city and assaulted the South Gate itself. Major Ortis sent reinforcements to the Merchants' Courtyard, certain that the Greeks were aiming at the

Treasury vaults. However, the South Gate was breached first. With a handful of men, Senthios fought with courage and desperation and as the pile of dead and wounded mounted at the South Gate, the Greeks lost heart and retreated. Not caring if he lived or died, Senthios followed with a few of his men. A young Greek, bolder than his fellows, stood his ground. He and Senthios fought, lunging and slashing on the narrow roadway. When the Greek was wounded in the thigh, Captain Senthios killed him with a sword thrust to the heart. The remaining Greeks fled in confusion toward the city.

The Cretans cheered their Captain and withdrew, believing he would now return to the safety of the Palace. They dragged the abandoned battering ram inside the Palace walls and began to repair the breach to the South Gate. However, the Captain, oblivious of danger, rushed after the band of Greeks and began to engage them. They surrounded him and before his troops could come to his aid, Senthios was mortally wounded. As he died, screaming, he saw his father hanging Zanthope's necklace around his wife's throat. His men retrieved his body and bore it back to the Palace.

Chryssa, struggling to return to her apartment, had a sudden moment of panic. Her slaves might have stolen the jewels and bolted!

To her relief, her treasures were safe in the casket. The slaves stood about nervously, waiting for orders. Chryssa dismissed them all, except her personal maid, who she instructed to pack some clothes.

"Go to Papa Senthios' apartment, hurry," she said, "I'll follow shortly."

When the girl departed, Chryssa turned to the jewel casket. It was large, made of embossed silver, with sharp corners. It was heavy but at this time of crisis she would not entrust it to anyone else. Chryssa opened the casket and placed her mother's jewellery in it. Despite the threat of invasion, she could not resist the temptation to admire her favourite pieces. She was aware that she should not delay, but she knew old Senthios would not go without her. She sat before the mirror and soon became engrossed in admiration of herself and the jewels. Zanthope's necklace was by far the most valuable piece in her collection and she was hypnotized by its perfection. The jewels were her children. She even thought of them when making love.

She was unaware of time slipping by, indulging in self-admiration and fantasy. But then, with a start, she heard the distant crash of the battering rams. She quickly replaced the jewels in the casket and ran out into the passage.

The crush of people was now almost impassable. Many, terrified by the sound of the battering rams, rushed from the Courtyard to barricade themselves in their homes. Chryssa, clutching her jewel casket tightly to her breast, pushed, shouted and struggled through the narrow corridors, panic-stricken in case old Senthios left without her.

In the Council Chamber the golden bull mask was placed hurriedly over the head of the unfortunate

King Minos. Weakened by his long detention and supported by two priests, he moved shakily down the steps to the Sacred Crypt. After much prompting, he muttered a confused version of the prayers.

Initially Councillors tried to pay attention. But, as the pounding and battering at the gates grew louder, they became restive. They began to argue again.

"We should go now, escape while we can!" Brecchius hissed.

"It's already too late," Xanthios muttered.

"We could leave by the North Gate," Brecchius insisted, "the scribe told us Lieutenant Micalidos has gone to summon his father."

After some discussion several Councillors rushed to the door leading to the ante-room and the Courtyard. However, General Imanos blocked their way, sword in hand.

"Consider your duty, Councillors," he said firmly, "remember your obligation to the people of Crete and the King."

His plea was ignored. Fear and panic possessed them and Priests and Councillors alike fled into the shrine, hoping to escape through the King's apartments on the floor above. Stools and lamps were knocked over, sacred vessels broken and trampled.

However, they found that the priest Eburninos had locked the door to the King's suite of rooms and it was impossible to escape that way. The traitor Eburninos alone remained calm, anticipating the arrival of Prince Theseus and his Greek conspirators.

The travesty of a religious ceremony came to an abrupt end when, with a tremendous crash, the battering ram burst through the gates of the Merchants' Court.

A soldier rushed into the Council Chamber.

"General, all is lost! They've smashed the gates — the Greeks are in the Palace!" he shouted.

After a moment of shocked silence, the cries of panic and hysteria began again.

"Control yourselves," Xanthios shouted, "they can loot the city! They'll spare us if we pay them well."

"You miserable cowards!" the General shouted, waving his sword, "we must support our Army. Councillors, follow me!" Markos drew a dagger from his belt.

"I'm with you, General."

Both men turned toward the ante-room but halted in astonishment. In the doorway stood Prince Theseus and his bull dancers, armed to the teeth.

"What's the meaning of this?" General Imanos demanded.

"Go back to the Bull Halls where you belong," Chancellor Darian shouted angrily.

"Where is the King?" Theseus snarled.

His abrupt question startled everyone. Minos had ascended from the Sacred Crypt and stood quietly.

"I am here."

Theseus took a step toward the King, but General Imanos intervened. With a sudden violent blow Theseus knocked the old soldier's sword to the ground and plunged a dagger into his throat. As the Councillors watched in horror, Imanos staggered, choking and fell to his knees.

"You Greek swine!" Councillor Markos shouted in a rage and rushed at Theseus.

The bull dancers cut him down mercilessly and he crashed to the ground beside the General. The Councillors and Priests drew back in terror as pools of blood spread over the tiled floor.

Theseus ordered them to leave the Chamber at once and none dared protest. The Greek bull dancers surrounded King Minos and led him into the Courtyard. The first rays of the sun, slanting over the East Palace rooftops, gleamed on his golden bull's head mask.

Hundreds of Greek soldiers were now in the Courtyard and many more were racing in through the breached southern gates. A few Cretan soldiers fought desperately but most were soon cut down and lay wounded or dying.

Cretan men and women, confused and terrified, ran in every direction, screaming and weeping. They were unable to escape or defend themselves.

When King Minos appeared, many surged forward to greet him and a great cry went up.

"The King — the King!"

Theseus saw at once that panic and hysteria in this vast crowd could upset his carefully laid plans. He raised his sword and called loudly for calm and order. He then directed the invading soldiers to form a barrier with their shields to hold the people back. At this, the crowd fell to their knees, calling on the Gods to protect them and save King Minos.

Theseus wasted no words.

In a loud voice he claimed the throne of Crete and

ordered Minos to remove the symbol of his power, the ancient bull mask.

Before the King could comply, the bull dancers on either side snatched it from his head. Minos stood bare-headed, pale and haggard, tears running down his cheeks.

Triumphantly Theseus held the mask aloft and the Greek soldiers cheered, waving their swords in the air. But the Cretans moaned and some protested. The enemy soldiers turned on them roughly, beating them with their swords. Women screamed and children cried out in terror.

But Theseus' strategy, his master stroke, was not yet complete. The Cretans must witness not only the fall of their King but also the destruction of his dynasty. The Greek leader gave an order to officers awaiting his signal.

Queen Kara, guarded by several Greek soldiers, entered the Courtyard from the East Palace. She held her young son, Prince Nikos, by the hand. Although terrified, she walked with calm dignity. She was followed by Princess Ariadne and Princess Phaedre. The people stood back to let them pass and called greetings to Queen Kara for she was much loved.

"Holy Zeus, save her! Earth Mother, look down in mercy, protect us all!"

As the Queen, Prince Nikos and the two Princesses moved slowly across the Courtyard, Cadet Nimos at his post at the North Gate heard the pre-arranged signal from Antonius. Hastily he ordered the North Gate of the Palace unbarred.

Andreas and Dr Ahmed entered quickly with Antonius and his soldiers. There had been no sign of the enemy.

"Thank the Gods you are all safely returned, sir," Nimos said.

"What's happened here?" Andreas demanded.

"It's a disaster, sir," Nimos replied, "Theseus and the Greek bull dancers have taken the King captive."

"Sacred Gods, how did they do that? How did they escape from the Bull Halls?" Andreas said bitterly. "Can nothing be done?"

"We can protect ourselves," Antonius replied and then addressed Nimos and his soldiers.

"The Palace has fallen — we must stand and fight together — what do you say?"

The men vigorously assented. From within the Palace the long narrow walkway leading down from the Courtyard to the North Gate was comparatively easy to defend. Nimos had placed his best swordsmen across it. Inside the Palace, the enemy had begun to loot the Merchants' courtyard and the luxurious apartments in the East Palace. They were not concerned with the North Keep.

"What's happening in the city, sir?" Nimos asked.

"It's quiet at the moment," Andreas replied grimly, "but not for long. We might escape to the mountains or by ship until the worst is over, what do you think, Ahmed?"

The doctor shook his head. He was confused.

"The roads will be blocked," Antonius said, "the sea is our best hope. I suppose we still have ships at Nirou-Khani?"

"If the Greeks haven't burned them," Andreas replied. "Antonius, I sent Dorcas to Mallia to get news of your sister and Prince Lerintos."

"Sacred Zeus! I hope they're all right," Antonius murmured.

"I must know what's going on," Andreas muttered impatiently.

He began to push through the Cretan soldiers guarding the walkway with Ahmed following close on his heels. When they reached the Courtyard level, the doctor was able to see over the heads of the Cretan people.

"Queen Kara and her son and the two Princesses are standing before Theseus!" he whispered to Andreas.

Ahmed raised his hand in greeting to the Queen. She saw him and acknowledged it. Andreas saw the King, his Councillors and Priests surrounded by the Greek bull dancers and he noted that all the dancers were armed. Among them was the Priest Eburninos. Andreas was surprised that the priest showed no fear or alarm. He suddenly realized that Eburninos had been in league with Theseus.

Black smoke was drifting from the West Palace and it appeared the invaders had fired the oil stores. Those who had stayed inside for safety were now driven out, choking and coughing from the acrid fumes. Hordes of rats scurried out, causing more panic and distress among the frightened people. Senka, Andreas' former secretary, was forced by the smoke to abandon his refuge in the Egyptian Embassy and he stood in the Courtyard staring around with smarting eyes. All these faces he knew so well — Olivia and her smart friends, the gossips, the rogues, the sycophants, what good does their money do them now? he thought cynically.

Prince Theseus called harshly for silence. Then, as the crowd listened dumbfounded, he accused the King of terrible crimes.

"He is a vicious criminal. Unfit to rule. Unfit to live! I therefore have no alternative but to pronounce judgement on him. I now sentence him to death!"

A groan of horror came from the Cretans and when a woman began to scream, a soldier knocked her to the ground. The High Priest, Arcanos, and the Priests and Councillors standing behind the King, were cowed with terror, too fearful and demoralized to raise any protest.

However, Andreas Micalidos, without hesitation, pushed forward at once.

"You cannot save him, sir!" Ahmed whispered futilely and grabbed Andreas' arm. Calling loudly to Theseus to justify his accusations, Andreas forced his way past the guards and stood beside the King and was immediately grasped by two soldiers. But his protest was drowned by a great cry from the Cretan people, for Theseus had raised his sword to kill King Minos.

The bull dancer, who held the King by the arm, quickly released him when he saw Theseus' sword descending towards him. The terrified King twisted his body away and the sword struck his right shoulder almost severing the upper arm. Minos screamed in agony and fell, half fainting, with blood spurting from the wound.

Andreas watched horror-stricken. A great moan came from the crowd. Queen Kara tried to rush forward to the King, but a Greek soldier held her back.

Theseus was about to strike again when Princess Ariadne intervened and pleaded with him not to kill Minos. Theseus turned on her angrily. While the conqueror and his mistress argued, Andreas was moved to pity by the King's suffering. His bitter anger over Timon's abduction was momentarily forgotten as he witnessed the wreck of this once proud man. Andreas understood that Minos had tried, in his own way, to fulfil a role for which he was in no way suited.

In this brief moment, the King turned his head with a look of agony and despair, as though pleading for one friendly face. He saw Andreas. Their eyes met. The King's lips moved. Andreas wrenched free of the soldiers and leant forward to hear the dying man's words, "I ... never hurt ... any of those children."

The soldiers dragged Andreas back just in time, for Theseus flung Ariadne angrily to the ground and thrust his sword through the King's heart.

A great cry rose from the people as word of the King's death was passed from one to another. Many fell to their knees, weeping and beating their breasts.

Leda, in the crowd, was unable to move. She glimpsed her father not far off but hardly knew him. His face was haggard and ashen with fear. She was moved by the great wave of emotion that swept through the Cretan people. Tears ran down her cheeks, and like her countrymen she beat her breast, though she cared nothing for the King.

However, worse was to follow. Theseus ordered young Prince Nikos to stand before him. Queen Kara, terrified, clung to the delicate child. She threw herself on her knees before Theseus, weeping and pleading for her son's life. She begged to be allowed to renounce all claim to the Cretan throne and return with him to Egypt.

To Andreas' dismay, Ahmed stepped boldly forward and addressed Theseus, demanding protection for the Queen and her son. His intervention probably saved her. Theseus had no quarrel with Egypt. The boy, however, was Minos' son and heir to the Cretan throne and Theseus was determined that the boy should die. In vain Queen Kara begged the Prince to take her life instead. In response, Theseus snatched the child and killed him with one cruel blow of his sword. With a scream of despair Kara fell senseless to the ground.

The Cretans shouted in fury on witnessing the callous murder of the young Prince. Fortunately, when the attention of the Greek soldiers was diverted, Ahmed was able to push forward and kneeling, lifted the unconscious Queen in his arms. With Andreas' help he carried Kara through the crowd to the small shrine at the North Gate where they placed her on a bench and after a few moments Ahmed was able to revive her.

Andreas was acutely aware of their extreme danger. He knew that now that the King and his son were dead, Theseus would turn on the Councillors and Priests and if he did not murder them, he would demand their allegiance.

Engrossed by the murderous drama in the Courtyard, the Greek soldiers were unaware of the small band of Cretans at the North Gate who had survived apparently by chance. Andreas believed any further sacrifice of life was pointless and that their only hope was to leave the Palace immediately.

However, Ahmed, usually so compliant, was adamant that he would not leave without Queen Kara and she would not leave without her son's body. She was determined that Nikos would have a proper burial.

Andreas discussed the problem with Antonius and Nimos and although both volunteered to fight their way into the Courtyard to retrieve the boy's body, Andreas firmly discouraged any such action. It would be futile.

"Don't throw your lives away," he said wearily.

They waited with mounting tension as Theseus' voice rang out again, calling, as Andreas had foreseen, for the Council, the Priests and the people to kneel and swear allegiance.

Beyond the Palace gates, the city of Knossos was in a state of panic and disorder as news of the invasion had spread quickly. The southern viaduct had been overrun by the Greek Army. The narrow bridge over the River Kairatos — the main highway east of the city — was blocked by laden, overturned carts. The streets were jammed with chariots and hysterical people, fighting each other in their frenzy to escape.

Old Papa Senthios, with his chariot, horses and chest of gold, waited for Chryssa with mounting rage.

He had no wish to abandon her and sent his steward to look for her, but the guards had closed the Palace Gates.

Realizing he could not escape south or east, Senthios ordered his men to hack their way north through the throng of shrieking, desperate people.

Madam Doxa Grinkos was screaming loudest, whipping her slaves mercilessly as they struggled with her heavy boxes. One of them, stressed beyond endurance, shouted furiously, "Why should we slave for this cruel bitch? Let her carry her own goods!"

Doxa faced her slaves with the whip, hard eyes gleaming.

"You scum, obey me!" she screeched. "Earn your keep, you miserable vermin!"

She raised the whip to strike but one of the slaves fought with her and grabbed the whip.

"Scum and vermin are we? What are you? You're a murderess! You drove Arkos and Tyra to their deaths, and poor old Talus! Come on, let's finish this cow!"

Grinkos shrank back in horror as the slaves attacked his elegant wife, kicking and battering her to death. Her screams went unnoticed, drowned in the cries of others being hacked down by the Greeks who were busy looting the laden carts.

Princess Ariadne, standing in the Palace Courtyard surrounded by angry Cretans, was horrified at Theseus' violent murder of her brother. She saw now the full consequence of her betrayal. She knew the people would judge her harshly but so strong was her passion for Theseus, she did not care.

Instinctively she put her arm around her younger sister, Phaedre, to shield her from the nightmare which had befallen them. In her distress, Ariadne failed to notice that Phaedre was not afraid. She had wept for her brother, Nikos, but now stood pale and tense, gazing at Theseus in fascination at his brutal strength.

While the people continued to cry out to the Earth Mother to help them, Theseus took the golden bull mask of Minos and showed it to them demanding their allegiance. The early morning sun flashed on the polished gold surface as he raised it over his head.

The great crowd was suddenly still and silent. Many of them now knew their proud and ancient history was coming to an end.

With both hands Theseus began to lower the mask onto his head. But he was never destined to wear it. At that moment a low rumbling began deep in the earth, which quickly became a mighty roar, an ear-splitting blast of noise, like the bellowing of a million bulls. The earth rocked and shuddered with a violent jolt that traversed the island from end to end. The paving in the Palace Courtyard rose and fell like waves of the sea, and Theseus staggered and fell. The priceless golden mask dropped from his hands and in the confusion and chaos it disappeared. He never saw it again.

As the convulsive shocks continued, Cretans and Greeks alike screamed in terror as they were thrown to the ground, the roaring noise adding to their horror and panic.

At the North Gate, Andreas, Ahmed, Antonius and Nimos and the Cretan soldiers staggered, clutching at one another for support. They feared that the North Keep would fall on them. Antonius tried to unbar the gate so they could escape into the open street, but he was thrown back as the earth shuddered and rocked beneath them. Ahmed ran at once to the crypt where Queen Kara sat alone.

"You had better leave this place, Madam," he said and together they joined Andreas and the soldiers at the North Gate.

As the shock waves beneath the earth intensified, the upper storeys of the Palace began to sway and disintegrate. Large blocks of masonry fell from the balconies, killing and injuring those looking for shelter below. Inside the Palace great walls cracked and fell and the passages and stairways became choked with rubble. Huge cedar columns crashed down, crushing those beneath them. Many people were trapped, including the Greek soldiers who had been murdering the inmates and plundering their apartments.

The violent earthquake lasted only a few brief moments but its duration seemed an eternity. It felled scores of cities and towns throughout the island and then as quickly as it had arrived, it was gone. The great roaring and quaking was followed by a period of unearthly silence but within minutes the piteous cries of the trapped and injured filled the air. Fires, spreading from damaged shrine lamps and braziers, brought more suffering to victims buried alive under tons of fallen masonry.

In the Courtyard, Prince Theseus called to his bull dancers and the Greek soldiers to stand firm. However, his fear that the Cretans might rally at this sign of anger from their Gods was unfounded. Too many soldiers and civilians had died defending the Palace and the people were dazed and stunned.

Leda Brecchius was one of the first to rise to her feet. Moved by a protective instinct, she clambered over the confused and injured people around her and ran to her father. Brecchius was on his knees trembling with fear. She took his arm gently and helped him to rise. Her beautiful face showed tenderness and concern and Brecchius had the impression that he was seeing his daughter for the first time. They embraced, weeping for joy that each was spared.

The invaders, robbed of their plunder within the Palace, fell in fury on the unfortunate Cretan people in the Courtyard, stripping them of their money and valuables. Women were raped unmercifully and men were butchered defending them.

Leda was snatched from her father's arms by a Greek, his sword wet with blood. She screamed and struggled as he and two others dragged her toward the northern end of the Courtyard and flung her to the ground.

Brecchius, in rage and despair, performed the first and last selfless act of his life, rushing at the soldiers and shouting in a vain attempt to save his daughter. Almost casually, one of them ran a bloody sword through his chest.

However, Brecchius did in fact save her. He had attracted the attention of the small band of armed

Cretans, led by Antonius, by the North Gate. Hearing Leda's screams and the shouts of Brecchius, they attacked the rapists and killed them.

Joy and relief flooded her heart when Leda recognized Antonius. He helped her to rise and together they ran to the North Gate.

"Leda, thank the Gods you are safe," Andreas said as soon as he saw her, "is your father alive?"

Leda shook her head sadly.

"I'm very sorry. Where is your sister?" Andreas went on.

"Chryssa left the Palace before the gates closed. She said her husband told her to go with Papa Senthios."

"I'm glad she's gone," Antonius said, "unfortunately Captain Senthios has been killed."

"Oh, I'm so sorry, poor Dino and poor Chryssa!" Leda said.

Poor Chryssa indeed — she had had to fight her way back to old Senthios' apartment, only to find that he had already left. Still clasping the heavy jewel casket in her arms, she had tried to descend to the Courtyard. Her path was near impossible as the passageways were even more congested with screaming people fleeing the Greek soldiers who were looting and murdering on the lower floors of the Palace. When the earthquake struck, the upper floors collapsed and they were trapped and buried alive. In an instant Chryssa was flung to the ground. She had no breath even to scream as the sharp corner of the jewel casket pierced her rib cage and she died, choking on her own blood.

In the city, the earthquake had brought even greater chaos to an already disastrous situation. Many tall buildings were totally wrecked, filling the streets with debris. In places the earth had gaped asunder, splitting houses apart and dropping them and their occupants into the yawning crevices. Some deep fissures opened widely and then closed abruptly, burying those who had fallen into them.

Many who survived were too shocked and dazed to do anything but wander aimlessly in the streets; some, searching for their loved ones, tore frantically at the ruins of their homes; a few, thankful to be alive and unhurt, congratulated themselves on their good fortune.

At the North Gate, Andreas held a short council of war with his son and Dr Ahmed while Antonius' troops guarded the narrow walkway to the Courtyard.

"Antonius, we must leave the Palace at once. Can you and your men escort us home to the villa?"

"Yes, of course, Father."

Andreas was deeply concerned for his family's safety. He suspected that Credon and Korynna would have delayed setting out for the farm, no doubt in the hope that he would soon return.

Dr Ahmed glanced toward Queen Kara. She was now standing alone and utterly dejected. "I shall try to retrieve the boy's body from the Courtyard," Ahmed said to Andreas with quiet determination.

Antonius immediately offered to go with him. They were a short distance along the walkway when they saw Cadet Nimos striding down from the Courtyard with Prince Nikos' body in his arms.

"Well done, Nimos," Antonius said.

"Now we must leave this place immediately," Andreas added and thanked Nimos.

"We need a litter for the Queen," Ahmed murmured anxiously.

Andreas approached Queen Kara. He spoke sympathetically but firmly.

"Madam, I share your grief, but it is absolutely vital that we leave here at once. Can you manage to walk?"

The Queen nodded. Dr Ahmed had taken the body of Nikos from Cadet Nimos.

"Madam," he said gently, "we must bury your son as soon as possible. We'll take him to the villa."

Queen Kara agreed and supported by Leda, she followed Ahmed.

The party set off flanked by the soldiers, with Lieutenant Micalidos leading and Cadet Nimos at the rear. Andreas fervently hoped this small show of strength would safeguard them. He was certain the invading Greek Army would quickly degenerate into lawless bands of cut-throats and looters.

As they progressed along the road toward the villa, Andreas' thoughts turned to the bull dancers and especially to Belia. Had she been injured or buried alive in the ruins of the Palace? He shuddered. He longed to help them. In fact, unknown to Belia, Freyna and Leander, Andreas had already arranged for a boat to be provisioned at Nirou-Khani to aid the bull dancers' escape from Crete. He had no intention of leaving Crete himself. However, he thought, Dr Ahmed and the Queen should certainly leave the island and sail for Egypt if possible. Meanwhile, they all desperately needed a haven until the madness of pillage, murder and violence had ended. Andreas hoped that the invaders would leave now the country lay in ruins. As these thoughts passed through his mind, he and his party hurried along the narrow paved road leading to the villa.

Senka had seen Andreas in the Palace Courtyard and sought to gain his protection. However, he was impeded by the crowd and the ring of soldiers holding them back.

Later, when the earthquake tremors had ceased, he lay in the Courtyard giddy and nauseated, unable to stand. Horrified, he saw Olivia raped, but could do nothing to help her. When he finally managed to stand and stagger toward the North Gate he was attacked by a Greek soldier. A blow from a sword left him senseless and his few possessions were stolen.

In the Courtyard, Prince Theseus stared about him in disgust. The carnage and destruction was appalling. Despite his plans and intrigues, he had failed.

The great Earth Shaker, the Bull of Minos, was the victor. He had tossed his mighty horns in rage and made the earth tremble, driving the invaders from Crete. Soon greed and lust would give way to superstition and fear. The invasion would quickly lose its impetus and the troops, laden with booty, would slink back to their ships. Theseus was suddenly afraid. He foresaw that Poseidon, the Sea God, in his fury could send a great tidal wave to destroy the ports and the Greek Navy.

It was time to go. The Greek Prince signalled to his companions to depart. Their captives lay dead or wounded and only Chancellor Darian sat in the Courtyard, with vacant eyes, mumbling like an idiot.

As the Greek bull dancers made their way toward the South Gate, a woman cried, "Theseus, don't leave us!"

Princess Ariadne stood amongst the dying and wounded with her sister, Phaedre, beside her. She held her head high.

"Theseus, please take us with you, we have no friends here." Her eyes pleaded, brimming with tears.

"Sergeant, take these two women to the boats," Theseus called to a Greek soldier.

He moved towards Ariadne.

"Take care of your little sister," he said to Ariadne without looking at her. He put a finger under Phaedre's chin and his eyes smiled into hers. "Perhaps we shall meet again one day."

Phaedre smiled back at him. "I hope so," she replied.

"We can't take you to Athens," Theseus said casually, "we'll land you at Delos on the way."

He left them. Ariadne, with her arm around Phaedre, stumbled after the sergeant, half blinded by her tears.

# CHAPTER 43

Some time earlier, in the dining-hall, the bull dancers were eating breakfast. There was much speculation about the fourteen empty places at the tables. Belia recollected seeing the Greek women dancers dressing before dawn.

"I thought it was strange then," she remarked.

"The Greek men are not here, either," Chloe said, "what's going on?"

At that moment, the Chief Trainer, Naxos and his assistant, Scarron, entered the dining-hall accompanied by the two guards normally on sentry duty. The dancers were now sure that something unusual was occurring.

Then, quite unexpectedly, the kitchen staff appeared in the doorway. They stared sullenly at Naxos. When he ignored them, the cook stepped forward from the group and stammered nervously, "Please sir, is it true Knossos is being invaded?"

"Of course it isn't. Don't be stupid, man. Get back to work," Naxos replied.

"We want to go home!" the cook shouted hysterically. "We want to look after our families — our women and children!"

The kitchen hands found their tongues and began shouting as they moved towards the outer door but the sentries barred the exit. Several of the bull dancers asked Naxos for further information, calling out. "What do you mean, invaded?" "What's going on?" and "Where are the Greeks?"

Naxos stood pale and angry. Accustomed to giving orders and being obeyed, he did not care to be interrogated.

"Silence!" he rapped out. "You should know better than to listen to stupid rumours."

"Naxos, tell us, where are Theseus and the Greek dancers?" Leander asked.

"All I can say is I believe there is some trouble in the Palace," Naxos replied, "the guards are investigating it now."

"But where are the Greeks?" Ali demanded.

"I don't know where they are."

"We want to go home to our wives and children!" the cook cried out again.

"Get back to your duties," Naxos snapped.

The kitchen staff stared obstinately back at him and did not move. Their complaints began again. Naxos fumed and hammered on the table for silence.

Before he could speak there was a loud and sinister rumbling from beneath the earth. The floor began to tremble and heave and the walls swayed and pots and crockery crashed down in the kitchen.

"It's an earthquake! Get under the tables!" Naxos roared.

Most of the dancers did not need his advice. The kitchen staff raced for the exit, falling over each other in the doorway. Some escaped only to be trapped under debris in the passageways.

Lamps swayed and toppled from the wall niches, plunging the dining-hall into darkness.

Two young bull dancers, Bruni and Dek, raced for the door but falling bricks and plaster drove them back. The violence of the earthquake was increasing. There was the crashing of huge baulks of timber. Dust choked the air and the earth-shattering noise reverberated throughout the confined space of the Bull Halls.

The bull girls clung together under their table, moaning and crying. Belia, Freyna, Chloe, Rhina, Catalene and Shahali were quite sure they would be buried alive.

Freyna heard her name shouted and recognized Leander's voice. He had crawled in the darkness from the men's tables, determined to find her. She shouted his name and soon they were together.

Suddenly, much to their relief, the quaking ceased and all was quiet. Then, in the eerie silence, the cook moaned that his leg had been broken.

Naxos cursed, feeling around in the dark for his walking-stick. When he retrieved it, he called for the lamps to be re-lit. Meanwhile, the cook was crying in agony and pleading for help.

"Be silent," Naxos growled, "you men, lift the beam off his leg."

It took six men to lever it up. The injured man groaned as Leander bound the limb.

Belia and Chloe went to the sleeping quarters. The door jambs were tilted at a crazy angle. They called repeatedly to Vanna and Asa and the rest of the slaves but there was no answer, only darkness and silence. The dormitories were all but destroyed.

The two sentries had tried to flee through the trainers' quarters, but returned shamefaced as the passage was blocked. The joy of deliverance soon faded when it became evident that all stairways and passages leading from the dining-hall were blocked with rubble.

"Trapped like bloody rats," Ali muttered.

The bull dancers knew they had lost everything and that they faced an uncertain future. The possibility of another earthquake, the choking dust, the groans of the injured cook, the fear of being buried alive, filled them with dread. The situation was too grave for one of the young kitchen hands who became hysterical and screamed to be let out. Naxos gruffly ordered the guards to restrain him.

Leander called for some lights and he, Ali and Sardi studied the two exits. One, through the trainers' quarters leading to the Palace Courtyard was hopeless as huge blocks of masonry had crashed through the ceiling and completely filled the corridors. However, the stairway, leading up to the hall behind the Bull Ring, held some promise as an escape route as the debris was more loosely packed.

They were obsessed with a desire to escape and trivial things such as possessions and worldly goods ceased to be important. The bull dancers and staff longed to leave the Palace before further quakes occurred.

Leander organized them into groups. The men were to tunnel into the debris and pass back broken bricks, rubble and splintered wood while the girls held lamps as they worked. Soon the collapsed stairway was reinforced with timber props and slowly a path was cleared. After some hours the bull dancers and the kitchen hands were able to crawl out into the space behind the great wood- and metal-studded doors leading to the Bull Ring. The tiled floor was littered with debris but the doors and the massive stone walls of the Palace were intact. Scarron and Naxos emerged last with the guards alternately dragging and carrying the injured cook.

Instinctively the bull dancers stood together. How often had they waited here preparing themselves to face the bull? Belia and Nino climbed on the bench and peered out into the arena through the narrow grille.

Part of the roof had collapsed and a shaft of pale morning sunlight illuminated the desolate scene. The Bull Ring was no longer level. It had heaved with the violent disturbance of the earth. Here and there a post lurched. Flags drooped forlornly. Much of the stone seating was cracked and out of alignment. The dark archway, through which the bull had galloped so proudly, had collapsed. Now, this place which had provided entertainment for generations of Cretans was derelict.

"Well, what are you all waiting for?" Naxos bellowed. "Open the doors to the Bull Ring!"

But the great doors would not budge. The surface of the arena had risen high above the normal level and it seemed escape through the Bull Ring doors was impossible.

Belia caught Naxos' eye and both had the same thought — the narrow, circular stairway which led down to the Crypt of Sacrifice. It could be their only way of escape. Fortunately the stairway was undamaged.

With some hesitation, for fear of the place was very great, the trainers, dancers, guards and servants moved down the narrow stairway to the Crypt. There, in that sinister vault, they huddled together. The spirits of the dead champions, Paulius and M'boola, seemed to hover there as well as those of other past bull dancers, dead and long forgotten.

However they were still trapped, for the earthquake had obstructed the door that led from the Crypt to the Bull Ring. They despaired. Chloe was weeping and the kitchen boy cried out to the Gods to help them. Belia pointed to the second door leading from the vault.

"That leads nowhere," Naxos said, "it's locked — or bricked up, most likely."

Belia went to the door and opened it. She saw a narrow passage sloping down into darkness and understood at once how Theseus had left the Bull Halls to meet Ariadne in the Labyrinth. The group waited silent and hollow-eyed in the dim light.

"There are passages beneath the Palace," Belia told them, "and there is a linen cord which shows the way to go."

The dancers and kitchen staff stared at each other doubtfully. Only Leander and Freyna understood what Belia was saying.

"If we can find the cord," she continued, "we may be able to escape. Are you willing to try?"

Naxos quickly made the decision.

"We certainly can't stay here. Lead on, girl, we'll follow you."

He ordered the guards to carry the injured cook.

"We need every light we can carry," Belia said.

Ali, Sardi and Nino took candles from the Crypt altar and Leander found a lamp.

"We must go carefully," Belia warned them, "and keep close together."

As she went slowly ahead with Freyna and Leander close behind, Belia's lamp revealed a passage which sloped downwards for some distance. Presently she paused.

"What is it?" Freyna said nervously.

"There's a steep, narrow stairway ahead. Leander, you'd better warn the others."

They waited while the message was repeated, then Belia, Freyna and Leander led the way slowly down the stairway, followed by Nino, the bull girls Chloe, Catalene, Rhina and Shahali, the men, Bruni, Dek, Ali and Sardi, the six kitchen hands and finally Naxos and Scarron with the two guards, who, much against their will, were carrying the injured cook.

At the base of the stairway Belia halted. She held her lamp high and peered ahead. The passage opened out and branched off in several directions.

"We must find the cord now," Belia said, "it's not safe to go on without it."

"How can we help, Belia?" Leander asked.

"You can hold my lamp," she handed it to Freyna, "and tell them all to wait a few minutes."

There were shouts from behind, "What's happened? What are we waiting for?"

Leander reassured them. However, the fear of being trapped in the darkness was in all of them. They waited for what seemed an eternity in mounting tension as Belia searched in the dust for the elusive cord.

Freyna, peering after her friend in the darkness, became more afraid and agitated.

"Are you all right, Belia?" she called at last. When there was no reply she said to Leander, "I'm going after her!"

"No, you are not," he said firmly, "we must stay together." She clung to him, near to tears.

"Come on, Freyna," he said gently, "we've a long way to go. Belia knows what she's doing. She's been down here before." At this Freyna grew calmer.

"What are we waiting for?" came Chloe's voice anxiously from the stairway behind. Leander told Nino to explain. While he was speaking they heard a voice somewhere ahead in the darkness.

"I've found it! Come on!"

"Thank the Gods," Leander muttered. He ordered those behind to proceed slowly and presently they came upon Belia, covered in dust, but triumphantly holding up the cord which Ariadne had left to guide Theseus through the darkness of the Labyrinth.

"Now we can go on safely," Belia said, her eyes shining with confidence, unmindful of the cobwebs in her hair and her unkempt appearance.

Every one of them now felt more confident they would escape from the Labyrinth. However, many of them and particularly Belia, were concerned that the earthquake could have damaged the underground passage. No one cared to voice these anxieties and Belia dismissed all speculation as she concentrated on following the cord, as it wound through the darkened tunnels. Belia had almost overcome her fear of the place, but it was a terrifying ordeal for her companions. The claustrophobic atmosphere, the weird shadows cast by their flickering lamps and the damp, foetid air were sinister and threatening. They strained their ears constantly for the terrifying rumble that would precede another earthquake.

Following close on Belia's footsteps, Leander was amazed by her courage in coming alone into this place. And she did it for us, he thought, for Freyna and me!

When Chloe's candle blew out, she screamed.

"Don't worry, light it from mine," Ali said, comforting her.

"I hope the oil in the lamps won't run out!" Catalene said in a trembling voice.

Sardi reassured her. "We've got the cord. We could follow it even in the dark."

"I'd go mad in the darkness," she replied.

Although they were unaware of their location, they would have been surprised to learn that they were about ten metres below the original foundations of the Palace of Knossos. They moved forward until Belia stopped suddenly. She gasped in dismay.

"What is it?" Freyna asked fearfully.

Looking over her shoulder, Leander saw what had halted their progress. The tunnel was completely blocked by a cave in of rocks, earth and rubble.

Freyna groaned in terror. Leander desperately hoped that they would not have to turn back but there was no way of knowing how far the obstruction continued.

While they stared in uncertainty at the huge pile of rubble, those behind began demanding the reason for the delay. Belia had already handed her lamp to Freyna and began to move stones from the path.

"Belia, be careful," Leander warned. He called to those behind him. "There's been a cave in. We must clear it and pass the rubble back as we did before on the stairway."

Cries of disappointment came from the semi-darkness and one of the guards suggested they should turn back. Scarron ordered him to be quiet.

While Belia and Freyna held the lamps, Leander had the men worked in shifts, some digging, others passing the rubble and soil back down the line. The work was slow and tedious. Leander insisted on the greatest care in case there was a further cave in. He sent Ali back down the line with a message for Naxos.

"Tell him to make those damn kitchen hands come up and do some work!"

However, they refused and wanted to turn back. Naxos and Scarron became very angry with them and a violent argument ensued. The young kitchen boy again became hysterical and his screams echoed through the dark passageway. A lamp spluttered and went out. One of the guards tripped and trod on the cook's injured leg. Naxos cursed him and the cook's yells of agony added to the uproar.

To escape the turmoil the women bull dancers edged forward, closer to Leander and their companions. Chloe was shivering with terror and the African girl, Shahali, who understood very little, rolled her dark eyes fearfully and prayed to her Gods.

Just when it all seemed hopeless, a cheer came from Nino and Bruni. They announced success. They had broken through the collapsed area of the passageway.

Leander ordered them all to form a line again. With raised spirits and passing the cord once more from hand to hand they moved one by one through the opening. It was little more than a narrow tunnel and required the greatest care to prevent a further subsidence. After a tense half-hour they all passed through into the undamaged section of the passageway.

As they continued through the winding passages there were some delays when the cord was buried in loose soil and stones. Nino and Sardi went ahead to clear the way, while Leander sent back messages of reassurance. He thanked the Gods silently that there seemed to be no more serious obstructions. He knew they were all near to breaking point.

Then suddenly, Belia, who was behind Nino, cried out, "Stop! Stop a moment!"

At first they all anticipated some new disaster.

"Now what's wrong?" Naxos growled. The old trainer was exhausted, struggling to keep going on his lame leg and to keep order amidst the alarm and hysteria threatening revolt at the end of the line.

However, all was well. The flame of Belia's lamp had wavered suddenly and she felt a cool draught of air on her face.

"Leander, fresh air! I can smell it — down this way!"

She indicated a narrow passage on the right. Leander hurried forward. In the flickering light of his lamp he saw a low doorway, half open. The key was still in the lock, just as Senka had left it when he fled in panic from Zanthope's murderers!

One by one they climbed the narrow, spiral stairway into the sunlight. From the Courtyard nearby they heard the groans of the dying and the lamentations of the living as they cried out and mourned their loved ones. They were told the King was dead and the Great Palace of Knossos destroyed. When Naxos led them out under the North Portico they stared in silence at the ruined city. Naxos ordered the dancers to stay together and the habit of obedience held them for the moment.

"Where can we go? What's to happen to us?" Ali spoke for all the dancers.

"One moment," Naxos said sternly, "Leander, all of you men, I need your help."

He explained to them that he was concerned about the bulls, probably trapped in their stalls under the East Palace near the Bull Ring.

"If they are injured, they may have to be put down."

The bull dancers agreed, concerned for Tauron, whom they loved, but of course they would have been pleased to see the demise of the black bull which had killed Paulius and M'boola.

Naxos led Leander, Ali, Bruni and Dek to the wide stable door in the Palace walls, leaving the two guards with Nino and Sardi to protect the girl dancers. Naxos and his men discovered that the stalls were empty and the doors were hanging on their hinges. The earthquake — the mighty Earth Shaker, God of the Bull Ring — had set his bulls free. Several of the grooms lay dead near the stalls, but Naxos could not tell whether their deaths had been brought about by the earthquake or the escaping bulls.

When he and his men returned to the street, the bull girls and two of the kitchen hands were comforting the cook. The guards had abandoned him and the rest of the kitchen hands had gone with them.

"Poor man, he's worried about his family," Catalene said. "He wants to go home to look after them."

A short distance away a carrying chair, surprisingly undamaged, sat upright on a heap of rubble. The chair carriers had evidently fled.

Naxos offered the kitchen hands some money to carry the cook home. They refused the money and, bringing the chair over, lifted the cook into it.

"He's our neighbour," said one of them. "We'll look after him."

They set off slowly, for the road blocks were uneven and twisted by the force of the earthquake.

The townspeople who had not fled wandered like sleepwalkers in the debris which had been their city.

The dancers were at a loss to know how to take advantage of their new-found freedom. Leander, however, was an exception.

"Naxos, from now on we must make our own way," he said gravely.

"Listen to me, all of you," the Chief Trainer said sternly, unwilling to surrender his authority, "you are still bound by your vows and dedication. Things will soon be normal again. This great city will be rebuilt ..." But his voice trailed away as he surveyed the devastation.

The girls looked at each other, not daring yet to defy him.

"It's all finished here," Sardi said brutally.

Naxos leaned heavily on his stick. He suddenly felt old and tired.

"We must stay together. We should be armed," Ali interrupted.

"This war is no quarrel of ours," Nino declared.

Leander was about to speak when a bugle sounded some distance away. Two soldiers ran out of a ruined house carrying heavy sacks of booty, their swords still bloody. Again the bugle sounded and one of the men shouted to companions who ran out from another house, carrying silverware and a money bag.

They paused for a minute to compare their loot and then set off up the road together.

"That bugle was sounding retreat," Leander said, "they are making for the ships. Naxos, we must leave Crete. Freyna carries my child. We can't stay here."

"Please yourselves," Naxos replied bluntly for he knew he could no longer control them.

"I think Ali is right — we should stay together. After all we have no money or food, how are we going to live? We must help each other," Nino said.

"We must find Councillor Micalidos. He will help us, I'm sure."

They stared at Belia in surprise.

"Who's Councillor Micalidos?" Chloe asked.

"A friend of mine."

Belia had to know if he was safe. She was concerned that he might be lying injured somewhere, and she also worried about the boy, Timon. She was determined not to leave Knossos without finding them both. The discussion might have continued for some time, but Freyna sank to the ground.

"I'm so tired and thirsty," she said faintly. Leander knelt beside her.

"Are you all right?" he asked with great concern. "I'll get you some water."

"The water pipes will all be broken," Naxos said, "we'd best all make for the river — it's not far off."

The sun was climbing now and they were exhausted and thirsty after their long walk through the dusty Labyrinth. Naxos, hobbling on his lame leg, led them toward the river.

"Take courage, my darling. We shall never be parted again," Leander whispered to Freyna as he helped her along.

Andreas and his companions arrived home without incident. The villa did not appear to be seriously damaged. The walls were solid, the graceful colonnade still ran the length of the paved terrace and the balconies were in place. None of the houses in this quarter had been looted, as they were located off the main thoroughfare.

However, on closer inspection, they saw that a large crack ran from top to bottom of the façade and the terrace paving had buckled. They found the peace and quiet of the garden unnatural after the turmoil and disorder in the city.

The absence of any sound alarmed Andreas and he began to dread what he might find. Antonius was eager to have his men search at once, but his father was more cautious.

"We don't know if the building is sound. Let's look at the back first." They walked to the far end of the house and crossed into the courtyard. The fountain no longer functioned.

"Hello there, Aunt Korynna, Timon — where are you?" Antonius shouted.

Then they heard a small voice calling, "I'm here."

The voice came from the direction of the low buildings behind the kitchen garden. Antonius and Andreas searched through the workshop, storehouse and finally the stables where they found Timon seated on one of the stalls feeding hay to Antonius' mare, Lorca.

"She was very frightened, Father, when everything shook. I fell on the ground, but she didn't tread on me. Is this shaking over or will it begin again?" the child asked.

Andreas took Timon in his arms and hugged him, not knowing whether to laugh or cry.

"I think the worst is over, Timon, my boy. There may be some little tremors, for a day or two."

"Were the Gods angry, Father?"

"Perhaps, — but not with you. Where's your Aunt?"

"I don't know. She said she was busy."

When Andreas, Antonius and Timon went outside, they saw the cart packed with clothes, blankets and food supplies.

"Credon and Aunt Korynna were getting ready to go to the farm," Timon said, "I haven't seen them since the earth started to shake."

The back of the house was a shambles. The kitchen ceiling had given way as the upper floor had crashed down.

"Korynna? Credon? Are you there?" Andreas called.

A faint quavering voice answered him from the kitchen area. "Master, I'm here."

Then Andreas and Antonius were astonished to see their old servant, Credon, crawling out of the wreckage on his hands and knees, his hair and clothes thick with dirt and plaster and his sleeve soaked with blood.

Antonius and Andreas quickly went to him and helped him to stand.

"Sir, sir, they've gone from us ... Old Madam and Madam Korynna and the kitchen girls. All gone. All passed away in the earthquake."

The old man was trembling and weeping. Andreas and Antonius tried to reassure and comfort him.

"What happened?" Andreas asked gravely.

"Aunt Korynna was here ... she was out there. We were loading the cart, getting everything ready," Credon began, "Timon was in the stable with the horses. Aunt Korynna went back into the house to fetch something — and then it happened! I was thrown against that rock," he pointed to a piece of ornamental stone, "and hurt my arm."

"I should have saved them. I should have cared better for them. I've been trying to dig them out." The old man was near to collapse. Andreas took him firmly by the uninjured arm.

"Now, Credon," he said, "you've done all you can. Nobody could do more. I want you to go and sit down over there on the grass. We have plenty of strong young men here. They can deal with this." Andreas turned to his son. "Antonius, I must get into the house to discover what has happened there. Can you organize your men to clear away this wreckage?"

"Of course, Father, but you must take care."

"Yes, I will. This is a sad day for our family, but thank the Gods Timon is safe."

Antonius' men immediately set to work to clear a way for Andreas to enter the house.

Meanwhile, Ahmed led Queen Kara to a stone bench under a shady tree and he gently laid the body of her son on the grass. She gave him her shawl with which to cover the dead body. Queen Kara's face was haggard, but she was now more composed.

Leda came and sat with her while Dr Ahmed went to the spring to draw water for them. He hoped there would be no difficulty in finding food. Weariness and hunger would soon sap their energy. He was also anxious about his assistant, Dr Iros, and the people at the surgery. The plight of the injured tormented him, but he accepted the fact that only the strong would survive. Many would probably die of disease or hunger in the weeks ahead but he tried to dismiss these thoughts and realized that his own hunger and weariness was partly the cause of his depression.

Now food was the primary need. He returned to the two women with some cool spring water in a large sea shell. They drank gratefully. Then he asked Leda if she would help to prepare a meal for the survivors, to which she eagerly agreed. The Queen said she would assist after she had sat with her boy for a short time.

Ahmed stood by feeling utterly helpless, longing to soothe her grief, but as usual he was shy and tongue-tied. Looking up she saw the concern and sympathy in his eyes. Her own filled once more with tears and she reached out her hand to him.

Leda left them together and went to find Andreas. The Councillor was now in the ruined kitchen directing the work of freeing the bodies of his mother, sister, the kitchen maids and servants. The task was difficult and hazardous as the kitchen was piled high with masonry, smashed beams and broken furniture.

When Andreas saw Leda standing shyly in the doorway, he went to her.

"How are you, Leda, my dear?" he asked.

"I am well," she replied, "so very thankful that you and Antonius are safe. What a terrible disaster — there are so many dead," she sighed. "The doctor wants me to help prepare a meal for everyone. He says we must keep up our strength. I must find some food."

"Why don't you speak to Credon, Leda, he'll help you," Andreas said.

Leda found the old steward seated on some stone steps in the garden, overcome with grief.

"I remember you. You dined here with the Minister and Madam Brecchius last summer," Credon said.

"Yes, I'm Leda Brecchius."

"Are they both safe?"

She told him of her parents' deaths and he shook his head.

"I am sorry, I offer my sincere condolence."

Leda thanked him and then asked, rather abruptly, he thought, where she could find some food and cooking utensils. He looked surprised at first that anyone could think of eating at such a time. But then, as she pointed out that the soldiers were working hard and would soon be hungry and thirsty, he understood there was work to be done and he could help.

"There's a big copper pot wedged just inside the kitchen door, and the storehouse is over there, next to the stables. I'll show you, miss."

Credon tried to rise.

"Your arm must be very painful," she said.

"It's nothing," he protested.

Dr Ahmed joined them. "Let me have a look," the doctor said inspecting the injury, "this wound is deep and must be cleaned." He led the old man firmly to the stone bench.

Leda persuaded one of the soldiers to drag out the big cooking pot, which was soon washed and set up on a tripod. As she worked she saw Timon watching from the stable door.

"Timon, you can help. We need some firewood."

The boy ran off and soon returned with an armful of sticks. The storeroom was well stocked with vegetables and grains. Leda also found some cheese and a batch of recently baked oat-cakes in the cart. After filling the pot with water, she chopped up the vegetables and threw in onions, beans, peas, lentils, barley, oats — in fact anything she could find.

"It will be a strong peasant soup," she said, laughing to Andreas, who came up to inspect.

"That's just what we need. A meal fit for the Gods," he replied smiling.

As Leda was stirring the soup, Queen Kara joined her.

"Madam, are you a little more comforted?"

Queen Kara gave a brief nod.

"You've done well, Leda, We shall not go hungry."

They were interrupted by Antonius informing his father that he and Nimos were about to bring the bodies of Old Madam and Korynna from the house.

The soldiers had already removed the bodies of the kitchen maids and servants.

Andreas watched tensely as his sister's body was carried from the house and then, Antonius and Nimos brought out the frail body of his mother wrapped in a sheet. The old lady was found in her bed. That side of the house had evidently collapsed when the earthquake struck. Korynna and the servants were making final preparations in the kitchen before setting off for the farm.

Andreas was very tired. He sat down and bowed his head in grief. Dr Ahmed, after examining the bodies, offered some comfort. They had both died instantly.

"Where is Deva, the cook?" Antonius asked, remembering his friend.

"She's away in the mountains, visiting her family." Andreas said.

"She would choose the right time to be away. I wish we had all been on holiday," his son replied.

"It would make no difference where we were, Antonius. The whole island has been wrecked."

"Do you think so, Father?"

"I'm sure of it."

Andreas thanked the soldiers for their help.

"We have a problem, Antonius," he began, taking his son aside. "My mother and sister, and these servants, must be buried as soon as possible."

"Of course, Father. And the Queen's son, too. But would it not be best to have a meal first," Antonius suggested, "then we can discuss what should be done."

Andreas agreed. After the meal, the sentries were relieved, and Andreas, Antonius, Queen Kara, Leda and Dr Ahmed sat down together under the trees. Andreas pointed out the impossibility of using the city burial grounds, which were several miles distant.

"This garden is peaceful and beautiful," he went on, addressing everyone but intending his words for the Queen in particular, "is there any objection to burying our loved ones here? I know it's not sacred ground, but we could fence off part as a private cemetery. There must be a priest in the city or the Palace who would conduct the burial rites. They cannot all be dead."

"Our Egyptian priests have gone with the Ambassador," Queen Kara said.

"I understand that, Your Majesty," Andreas replied patiently, "but if you would be satisfied with our funeral rites ..." He paused. As Kara hesitated he added, "When things are settled down, Madam, a memorial shrine will be built for the King and Prince Nikos will be remembered. However, if you prefer it, we could make a funeral pyre —"

"No," she interrupted. "Thank you for your kindness in considering my feelings." She faltered a moment and then went on firmly. "My beloved child will rest happily here."

No more was said and Andreas and Antonius selected a secluded spot where the soldiers were to dig three graves. A large one for the servants, a second where Old Madam and Korynna would lie together and a third — set apart — would be the last resting place of the young half-Egyptian boy who might have been the Priest-King of a great and powerful empire.

Then a settee was brought out from the loggia with some rugs and cushions to enable Queen Kara and Leda to rest. Timon soon settled beside Leda and Credon was persuaded to rest nearby.

Leaving Cadet Nimos and half the troop on guard, Andreas, Antonius and Dr Ahmed and the remaining soldiers set off for the city. Andreas was weary and would have enjoyed a rest himself, but he was determined that the burial rites should be properly observed for his mother and sister. He was also concerned for his father-in-law, Aeschyton, and asked Antonius if he could spare a man to check on the old man's safety.

"Let's hope he's not injured, Antonius."

"I'll go myself, Father," his son assured him.

Ahmed was eager to go to his surgery to discover if Iros had survived and to see what could be done to help the injured. As they approached the Palace he left Andreas, declining the offer of an escort and assuring the Councillor that he would return to the villa before nightfall.

In the Palace Courtyard the bodies lay as they had fallen. Bereaved families were left without consolation from the priests, for none were to be found. Andreas was grim-faced. He had always disliked the priests, now he despised them for deserting the people when they were most needed.

"There must be a priest somewhere," Antonius said, "perhaps they have gone into the city for food — the Palace storehouse is still burning."

As Andreas and his son debated their next move, they were surprised to hear the sound of applause, laughter and cheering. It came from the boxing arena situated outside the Palace not far from the North Gate.

"What's that all about? What's going on?" Antonius said.

Andreas shook his head wearily. "I've no idea."

Accompanied by the troop of soldiers, Andreas and Antonius passed under the North Portico to discover the cause of the bizarre and unexpected noise.

Before the earthquake, Old Senthios, having waited in vain for Chryssa, ordered his servants to clear a way for his chariot through the crowded streets of Knossos. They had made little progress when the first violent shocks began.

Almost immediately, Senthios was knocked senseless to the ground by falling masonry. When he recovered consciousness, some hours later, his servants and horses were gone, his chariot was overturned and the large chest of valuables burst open. All his wealth — his money and his jewels — was stolen.

Old Senthios staggered to his feet, cursing, furious at the loss of his possessions. However, he still had a considerable amount of gold in his money-belt. Returning to the Palace Courtyard, he searched briefly for Chryssa, but when he saw the mountainous pile of rubble which had been the upper floors of the East Palace, he concluded that she must be dead.

Shortly before Andreas and Antonius arrived at the Palace in search of a priest, Senthios set off on foot for Amnissos, on the north coast of Crete, with the intention of finding a boat to escape from the island.

When the bulls stampeded from the stables during the earthquake, they charged through terrified groups of citizens and scattered in every direction. However, one large black bull raced into the boxing arena near the North Gate and remained there when the quake was over.

As Senthios passed this arena on his way to Amnissos, he had the ill fortune to be waylaid by a troop of Greek soldiers travelling in the same direction who had celebrated their conquest with strong Cretan wine. When the Greek soldiers saw the bull, they remembered extraordinary tales they had heard about Cretans who worshipped bulls and dancers who enjoyed performing with them in the Bull Ring. They decided this was an opportunity to put these stories to the test and grasping Senthios they pushed him into the arena.

"Let's see you dance with the big black bull," one of the soldiers said drunkenly.

Senthios was terrified. He protested, offering them money. Laughing, the Greeks relieved him of his money-belt.

"Come on, fatty, let's see you dance!" one of them shouted.

When he hesitated they forced him at sword point to face the bull and Senthios recognized it was the savage black bull which had killed Paulius and

M'boola at their farewell benefit. He had never been so afraid and foresaw that he was doomed.

The bull pawed the ground and bellowed and the soldiers laughed and cheered drunkenly. Again they urged Senthios to dance with the bull and entertain them and the noise soon attracted a small crowd of Cretans.

Senthios, despite his faults, was no coward and for a large man was surprisingly nimble. The bull lowered its head and charged. Consumed by terror but with a strong instinct to survive, Senthios performed a ludicrous dance. His tormentors were delighted and the Cretans joined the soldiers in derisive applause.

For a short time the bull was confused by Senthios' voluminous cloak and his unexpected agility. This provided more entertainment for the spectators who cheered and clapped.

At this point Andreas, Antonius and their soldiers entered the arena. They heard a man's voice in the crowd shouting, "How does it feel, Senthios? Not so good when it's your own skin, eh?" For a moment the crowd was silent and the bull stood still.

"You yelled and applauded when my dancers risked their lives! Dance with the bull yourself and see what it's like!" the man shouted again.

Andreas recognized the voice of Naxos, the Chief Trainer, and beside him he saw the tall figure of Leander with his arm around Freyna. He was relieved and overjoyed to see the dancers had escaped from the Palace and looked eagerly among them for Belia's blonde hair.

Then the crowd roared as Senthios tried to escape by running through the spectators. The Greek soldiers stopped him and one put a sword between his legs to trip him. The old man fell heavily and the black bull rushed on him. Without apparent effort it lifted Senthios' bulk on its horns and tossed him several times in the air like a large rag doll. Senthios screamed horribly. The Greek soldiers and the Cretans watched in silence, hypnotised by the ghastly spectacle. Then the cloak became tangled in the bull's horns and the infuriated animal trampled and gored Senthios viciously as it tried to break free. The merchant was disemboweled and bloody from head to foot. He pleaded for death. A bystander shouted for someone to finish him off.

"Yes, for Zeus' sake!" Andreas said, sickened by the horrible sight.

Antonius ran into the centre of the arena and killed Senthios with a blow. He then turned immediately and shouted an order.

"Soldiers of Crete — kill these Greek pigs!"

The bystanders scattered hurriedly as Antonius and his troop rushed on the Greeks, brandishing their swords. Andreas, concerned for his son's safety, watched anxiously.

But the Greeks were taken by surprise and the fight was brief and bloody. When the few survivors ran ignominiously away, pursued by the soldiers and the black bull, the Cretan onlookers laughed loudly and applauded. Andreas crossed the arena at once to congratulate his son. They gazed on the mangled body of Senthios.

"What a frightful death," Antonius murmured.

Andreas, looking down on the man who would have destroyed him, felt no satisfaction or pity — only revulsion.

A light touch on his arm made him turn and he saw Belia smiling up at him and rejoiced.

"Belia, you are safe. The Gods be thanked! And your companions?" Andreas asked, holding out his hands to her.

"Yes, we are all safe," she said, laughing "and Timon? Is he all right?"

"Yes, Belia, the Gods have been kind. He is safe."

Suddenly she clung to him and tears filled her eyes. "Andreas, I was so worried about you and Timon. Isn't it wonderful to be alive."

Andreas could only nod in agreement. He was overcome by emotion and a feeling of enormous relief and gratitude. The three people he loved most in the world — his sons and Belia — were alive and safe. He held her for a moment in his arms, too overwhelmed to speak. Then, laughing, she took his hand and leading him over to her friends, the bull dancers, she proudly introduced him.

# CHAPTER 44

In the evening the citizens of Knossos who had not fled to the countryside huddled together around fires in the narrow streets. In the courtyard of Andreas' villa a large fire gave the illusion of safety to the friends gathered there.

After Senthios' death, Antonius had taken charge and persuaded his father to return to the villa with the bull dancers and most of the soldiers. With two men he went into the city in search of Dr Ahmed and a priest.

On reaching the surgery he found it undamaged. Ahmed and Iros, with the two assistants, Damon and Altheon, were attending to casualties. Among these was the High Priest Arcanos, whose broken arm was supported in a sling.

Antonius had no difficulty in persuading Arcanos to return to the Villa to perform the funeral rites for his grandmother and aunt.

"I hope you will accompany us, Dr Ahmed. My father will be concerned for your safety," Antonius said.

Sadly Ahmed agreed. He had been distressed to learn that his colleague Dr Iros' parents, Aptaeon and Nerida, were both dead. A stone block from the Palace walls had fallen, demolishing their small house and killing them instantly.

Ahmed loved Iros and the surgery, but he was exhausted. He was anxious to be with Queen Kara again and to help her in any way he could. He also knew that he was ill-equipped to deal with the disorder and barbarism that he believed would follow the destruction of the Cretan state. On the other hand, Iros was young and could face these problems. Ahmed took leave of his colleague who was as dear to him as a son and he promised that as soon as he was able to return to Egypt, he would send a regular supply of medicines to help Iros' work among the Cretan people.

While Dr Ahmed was making his farewells to the surgery staff, Antonius and his soldiers had made their way to his grandfather's house, which was not far from the surgery building. The small house had sustained only minor damage and Antonius found Aeschyton unharmed. The old man, independent as ever, thanked Antonius and his father for their concern but absolutely refused to leave his home.

"Thank the Gods you and Andreas are safe," he said.

Antonius returned to the surgery and was pleased when Dr Iros assured him he would look after Aeschyton.

"Thank you, doctor. My father and I are most grateful for your help," Antonius said. Dr Ahmed, Antonius and Arcanos then returned to the villa.

The afternoon shadows in the garden added to the melancholy atmosphere at the site of the three graves prepared for the burial. The Micalidos family, with Belia and Leda, stood with heads bowed as the High Priest recited the familiar and ancient words. Andreas was overcome with grief for his dear mother, whose courage and strength he had always admired; and his kind and gentle sister, Korynna, who would be so missed, especially by young Timon.

While the ceremony proceeded, the bull dancers and soldiers waited respectfully nearby.

Meanwhile, Dr Ahmed and Queen Kara stood alone at the grave of Prince Nikos. As the boy's body was lowered into the earth, his mother gave a cry of anguish and the tears gushed once more from her eyes. Ahmed put his arm around her as she leant against him, grateful for his support. Queen Kara prayed earnestly to Isis and Osiris to receive her child tenderly but her grief was beyond words, almost beyond bearing. The boy had been her only joy and delight through all the misery she had endured at King Minos' Court.

The funeral ceremony was completed with reverence and simplicity. Although Andreas had no love for the priests, he was grateful to Arcanos.

Belia had stood by Andreas at his mother's grave. Since their unexpected reunion, they had been constantly together.

"I'm sorry your mother and sister did not survive," she said.

Andreas nodded. "It's a disaster for the whole island and all our people."

"Timon and Antonius are safe," Belia said, trying to raise his spirits.

"Yes, and so are you, Belia, thank the Gods." He looked into her eyes. "When I saw Naxos in the arena, I looked for you. I recognized Leander and one or two others, but I couldn't see you anywhere."

He paused.

"I was there," she said in a matter of fact way.

He smiled. "Yes," he said, then added seriously, "When I thought, when I feared that you might not have survived, I was close to despair."

She took his hand. "I thought about you, Andreas, especially when we were trying to escape from the Labyrinth, wondering if we'd come out alive. I would never have left Crete without finding you again."

"Now, my dear, you are free." Andreas gazed into her eyes, entranced by her fragile beauty, as he had been when they first met in Phylon's workshop.

"Belia, what will you do now? Do you still want to be a bull dancer?"

"That depends," she said hesitantly.

"On what?"

She held his gaze steadily. "On you, of course, Andreas!"

He took her face in his hands. "I love you, Belia," he said simply, "but I'm an old man."

"Nonsense! You're not an old man, Andreas! I love you, too," she said softly, "the difference of our ages means absolutely nothing to me."

"Dearest Belia," he said with a smile and kissed her gently.

While they strolled hand in hand in the garden, she told him how the bull dancers had escaped through the Labyrinth. "They owe their lives to you, Belia," Andreas said, "thank the Gods you are all safe."

He told her of his anxiety for his daughter, Hyacinth, her husband and his grandchildren in Mallia.

"I sent Dorcas, early this morning to bring news, but he's not returned. I fear the worst."

"I'm sure they're safe. They will have gone to the mountains."

"Perhaps."

It was now some hours since the burial service. The evening shadows were lengthening and the air was cool. They all gathered around the fire.

Antonius had been totally concerned with the responsibility of ensuring the safety of this small group of survivors. He was thankful that they had not encountered the invading enemy in large numbers. Evidently the call to retreat had drawn them all to the coast.

Now, in the firelight, he relaxed for the first time. He watched Leda talking to Cadet Nimos and recollected the evening in Mallia when she had declared her love for him. She seemed more mature now and he wondered if her feelings had changed. He knew he had changed; the infatuation for Chryssa had gone, burnt out by the shame of that awful night and his betrayal of Dino. Leda's situation touched his heart deeply, a sweet young girl, alone in the world, and an uncertain time for them all. Cadet Nimos certainly found Leda very attractive. It occurred to Antonius that she might not stay single for long.

Small tremors had persisted throughout the afternoon and while they were discussing if it was safe to sleep in the house, a stronger aftershock, with the noise of distant thunder, shook the earth beneath them. They decided to sleep in the open. More rugs and cushions were found and a big fire was built to last through the night.

Andreas lay on the fleecy coverlet Belia had brought from the house and for the first time that day he was able to relax and ease the exhaustion that made his head throb and his limbs ache. Beside him, nestling in his arms, Belia slept peacefully. Her face, which he had kissed many times with great tenderness, was turned towards him. He argued within himself that he was selfish to take a young girl's love, but, gazing at her beautiful face and slender body, he wondered how he would ever find the strength to send her away if she did not wish to go. As these thoughts passed through his mind, he drifted into sleep.

He was awakened by a loud challenge from one of the guards.

"What's happening, Antonius?" he asked urgently.

"I'll find out," his son replied, moving forward, sword in hand.

It was the secretary, Senka, staggering, dazed and exhausted. He begged to be allowed to stay. Andreas rose and taking a lantern from a guard, confronted his secretary. Senka had a deep gash in his scalp.

"What happened to you?" Andreas said.

Not waiting for a reply he went to the stone bench some way from the fire and sat down.

"Something or someone must have hit me!" Senka groaned and smiled with some of his old charm. "I'm thankful you are safe, sir, and Antonius and the doctor, too."

"Yes, we are safe." Andreas stared coldly at the dishevelled young man. The spirit of Zanthope haunted both men.

"What do you plan to do, Senka?"

The question made Senka shiver. Andreas' voice was icy. It did not hold the warmth he remembered from the old days at the villa. As he struggled to reply, Andreas continued, "At first light tomorrow, you must go to Zakro to find your parents."

Senka was surprised. "Oh, yes, I know your parents well," Andreas said.

"I ... I didn't know, sir," Senka stammered.

"You've denied knowledge of a good many things in the past!" Andreas said sharply.

Senka flushed. He had not expected to be spoken to in this way.

"Your father," Andreas continued bitterly, "is my agent in Zakro. One of the most trustworthy and amiable men I have ever employed. Your father was concerned to help his clever young son, who had ambitions to better himself. Mainly to please your parents — both of whom I liked and respected — I employed you, Senka."

Senka regretted his deceit, his stupid lies and his betrayal of Andreas' trust, but he was stung by the contempt in Andreas' voice. He sought to justify himself.

"I did my work well."

"You did. But when you were not working?"

"I have never tried to harm you or your family."

"That may be so," Andreas replied, half inclined to believe it, "but you must know that your conduct has brought disaster and suffering to many people."

Senka wanted to shout, "I didn't kill Zanthope!" but of course he could say nothing. Andreas concluded the interview.

"You may eat and sleep here but tomorrow you must leave for Zakro, you have no future here. Maybe we can spare you a horse. See Antonius about that. Please give your parents my greetings and good wishes and do not return to Knossos."

Andreas left Senka abruptly and rejoined Belia by the fire. He tried to dismiss from his mind the bitter memories Senka's presence had evoked. Looking around at the sleeping forms, he reflected how strange it was that a few people could find happiness in the midst of so much tragedy.

Earlier that evening, Antonius had found a moment to draw Leda aside.

"I'm very sorry about your parents, Leda," he had said shyly.

"Thank you, Antonius," Leda replied, "I grieve for dear Old Madam and Aunt Korynna. But isn't it a miracle that Timon's safe?"

"Yes, my dear."

Antonius paused for a moment and then said abruptly, "Leda, did you know that those two dancers, Leander and Freyna, have asked Arcanos to marry them tomorrow?"

"Yes, I think it's wonderful for them," she said softly.

"Leda, it could be wonderful for us too. Let's make it a double wedding. Leda, will you marry me?"

Leda was overwhelmed.

"Oh, yes, dear Antonius. Of course I will marry you."

He kissed her, gently at first and then passionately as she returned his embrace. She was radiant with happiness. Antonius was surprised that he had never noticed how beautiful she was.

Hand in hand they went to ask Andreas' permission to marry and he was delighted. He had always hoped that Leda would one day be his daughter-in-law.

The two couples agreed that the ceremony would be simple and there would be no feasting or dancing.

"We can do that later," Freyna said happily and Leda agreed.

Now, in the dark and silent garden, they slept by the fire. The only sounds were the footsteps of the guards and their muttered exchanges as they passed each other and cursed as the night grew colder.

Andreas stared into the fire. He was still worried about the family in Mallia and was concerned that Dorcas, the cart driver, had not returned. Dorcas may very well be dead, he thought gloomily. He shuddered at the possibility of worse disasters.

A guard threw some more wood on the fire, a burnt log split and when the flame leapt up, Dr Ahmed saw that Andreas was still awake. He rose and went to him, stepping carefully over the other sleepers.

"You are unable to sleep, sir."

"I've slept a little, thanks, Ahmed," Andreas replied, "and you?"

"I've dozed. Would you like a sleeping draught, sir? I always keep some with me."

"No thanks, dear friend. I'll be all right. I'll need a clear head tomorrow. Is Queen Kara comfortable?"

"Yes, she's sleeping."

"Good. Good night, then, Ahmed."

"Good night, sir."

Andreas relaxed and in a short time, slept fitfully, Some hours later he was awakened by a hand on his shoulder.

"Father, wake up."

"What! Antonius, is anything wrong?"

"No, Father. Foreman Cibaros is here and he wants to speak to you urgently."

Out of the darkness came the lean, saturnine face of his foreman at the shipyard of Nirou-Khani. Andreas was wide awake at once.

"Sit down, Cibaros. What news have you?"

As the firelight emphasized the dark hollows of his

eyes and the furrows of his gaunt face, Cibaros began a graphic account of the day in Mallia.

"What of my daughter, Hyacinth and Prince Lerintos and my grandchildren. Have you news of them?" Andreas interrupted him straight away.

"I'm sorry to say, sir, I bring bad news. Your son-in-law was killed in a battle against the Mycenaeans. He led his people bravely but they were greatly outnumbered."

Andreas' face was ashen.

"And what of my daughter and grandchildren?" he asked, dreading the response.

"I was told they have escaped to the mountains."

"Thank the Gods for that," Andreas said fervently.

"I have it on good authority, sir, that the priestess Olykka gave the alarm. Apparently she spent a night vigil at the Temple in Mallia and went out very early to watch the sunrise. When she saw the Mycenaean ships moving in with the tide, she gave the alarm, even before the signal fires were lit. The Palace staff at Mallia harnessed every chariot and cart they could find and took the women and children to safety before the Mycenaeans landed."

Andreas mourned for his son-in-law but was relieved that there was a good chance that Hyacinth and the children were safe and would survive. His driver, Dorcas, had probably gone with them.

"Thank you for bringing this news, Cibaros. I'm deeply distressed to hear of the Prince's death. It will be a terrible blow to Hyacinth and my grandchildren as it is to all of us."

"Now, Cibaros, what of our ships? Is there news of the fleet?"

The foreman shook his head.

"Terrible news, sir. We saw the fires burning out to sea, a few seamen escaped and swam ashore, some had horrible burns. They were overwhelmed — three, four to one. I'll swear they fought bravely but it was hopeless."

"Did any of my ships join the fleet?"

"Two left, sir, a week ago but the rest were gutted at their moorings by the bloody Mycenaeans."

"The bastards! Things must be very bad in Mallia."

"Horrible, sir — murder and looting everywhere."

"Is your family safe, Cibaros?"

"I hope so, sir. I've hidden my wife and daughters in a cave."

"A cave?"

"Yes, sir, it's down by the sea, near that narrow inlet below your property at Mallia."

"Have you seen the villa? Is it damaged?"

"I didn't go inside, sir, but it appeared to be undamaged. Do you remember, sir, ordering a ship to be provisioned and ready for some people to leave Crete? From the Palace, I believe. Bull Dancers?"

"Yes, of course. Where is the vessel now?"

"The seamen moored it in the creek below your villa, sir. It's safe there — well hidden. The entrance from the sea is too shallow and difficult for war galleys."

"Thank you Cibaros for bringing me this news. I'm grateful. You've done well. You'd better rest here till morning."

"Thank you, sir. Good night."

Andreas' worst anxieties were set at rest. Hyacinth and his grandchildren had probably escaped into the mountains. More problems lay ahead, but they could be faced tomorrow. Thankfully he closed his eyes and relaxed beside Belia and he fell asleep at once.

# CHAPTER 45

The morning air was chill and the grass damp under their feet as the bull girls, Belia, Chloe, Rhina, Catalene and Shahali wandered through the quiet garden gathering spring flowers for the wedding. Jonquils and freesias perfumed the air, and they found crocus, anemones, daisies and myrtle. They made posies, wreaths and garlands, for this was the only adornment the bridal couples would have.

Some of the dancers began to prepare a festive meal; fresh oatcakes were baked in an oven, which Nino had built with flat stones, and Sardi and Ali raided the fowl yard. The aroma of chickens roasting soon filled the air. The garden yielded green salads and herbs and the storehouse still held a few treasures — dried fruit, nuts, olives and honey.

"What a wedding feast!" Belia cried, her eyes shining.

"I thought someone said there would be no feasting!" Leander said wryly.

Andreas suggested they should have some wine from the damaged cellar under the house but Antonius disagreed.

"No wine, Father. We are all short of sleep. It will be difficult enough to stay alert and even more difficult to keep the men here."

"I thought it was agreed that they would all stay together."

"Three men deserted during the night," Antonius said, "we can't risk losing the others. We may be confronted by the Mycenaeans on the road to Mallia."

"No wine then and we should have the wedding ceremony as soon as possible."

Andreas was convinced they should leave the villa immediately after the ceremony as further delays would increase the danger to the people in his care. There was no safe place on Crete. The Greeks might have followed Theseus back to Athens, but the Mycenaeans would certainly not leave until it suited them. In time, they could penetrate even to the mountain districts. Perhaps the high and wilder regions to the west would give sanctuary, but it was a long journey and many of the roads would be damaged and unsafe.

Andreas was thankful that he had ordered the ship to be made ready for the bull dancers. This would be their best opportunity to escape from the beleaguered island and the invaders who were overrunning it.

As to his own future, he could foresee no clear direction ahead. Life in a foreign country, however civilized, held little attraction for him. He knew the galley waiting at Mallia could not accommodate all the survivors gathered here, only about twenty people, according to Cibaros, and he clearly hoped for passage for himself, his wife and three daughters. The soldiers, who were to be used as escort, might then be left to chance and the cruelty of the Mycenaeans. This thought had probably occurred to those who had deserted in the night.

An altar, hung with garlands, was set up under the trees and the two couples stood before it to receive the High Priest Arcanos' blessing. The brides wore a chaplet of flowers and were robed in the soft colours which Korynna preferred. They had been given first choice of the clothing she had packed in the cart.

Each had their own thoughts. Freyna, carrying Leander's child, rejoiced in the fulfilment of all their plans. Leander, whose gloomy doubts had sometimes clouded their relationship, gazed at her with tenderness and admiration.

For Leda, her dreams had become a reality and the anguish and despair of the past year was at an end. Antonius experienced more complex emotions. He had always admired Leda's character and the gentleness and sincerity of her nature, but he had also known passion and he found it difficult to banish from his mind the guilt he felt over his betrayal of his friend, Captain Senthios. He now felt a great tenderness for this lonely and beautiful girl, soon to become his wife. He was determined to love and cherish her.

The High Priest called on the Earth Mother to bless the couples and to give them happiness and long life.

"Amen to that!" Andreas murmured.

He was sad that his mother and sister were not here to witness this ceremony, but he felt a deep and sincere happiness as he watched the four beautiful young people take their marriage vows. He regretted that there was much material wealth he could no longer provide, but as they sat enjoying the wedding breakfast, he reflected that the two couples were young and healthy. If the Gods were kind, they would survive.

During the meal, he rose and addressed them briefly.

"Antonius, Leda, Leander and Freyna, and all our good friends, you must feel great happiness as I do. This short ceremony has brightened the darkness of this tragic time. We wish these two young couples every happiness and good fortune in their future."

There was applause and cries of agreement. In spite of Antonius' veto on wine, a few jugs had mysteriously appeared. Andreas raised his cup and a bridal toast was drunk.

"Nothing would be more pleasant than to linger and enjoy this moment, but you must know we are still in grave danger. There will be looters and marauders attacking those who cannot defend themselves for some time. This house is no longer habitable, so unfortunately we cannot stay here and we cannot safely travel alone. My foreman, Cibaros, has told me that a ship is provisioned for a journey and lies hidden near Mallia. It was ordered last week when I received Leander's letter requesting my help. I understand this vessel will carry no more than twenty persons and the crew and unfortunately there are no other ships available at Nirou-Khani."

Andreas' audience sat in silence.

"I am sure that Her Majesty, Queen Kara, is anxious to return home to Egypt and my friend, Dr Ahmed, also. Those for whom the ship was originally intended — Leander, Freyna and Belia, must have passage on it, too, if that is their wish. I want you all to consider what I have said and discuss it among yourselves. Your decision should not be delayed. We must leave here as soon as possible."

Andreas sat beside Belia. The murmur of discussion began at once. He hoped fervently that the lack of accommodation on the ship would not cause grave problems.

When the meal was nearly finished, Naxos, the Chief Trainer, rose to his feet. He was pale and drawn. Although he had lost his authority, the dancers still loved and respected him. They were pleased he could speak for them. Naxos understood that they could not all travel on the ship waiting at Mallia.

"On behalf of the dancers and myself, sir," he said, "I wish to thank you for your generosity."

There was applause.

"Sir, amongst the bull dancers there has been true comradeship. It would be sad indeed if this terrible disaster should separate us. Those who wish to remain together intend to continue their careers as bull dancers and they have elected me as their leader. We intend to make our way to Amnissos, where I have relatives and friends. I am sure they will help us to find a ship sailing north to the mainland. I shall now ask the dancers who favour this plan to raise their hands."

The men, Sardi, Nino, Bruni and Dek, and the girls, Rhina, Catalene and Shahali, chose to go with Naxos. Leander asked for passage for himself and his wife on the boat at Mallia. Ali wished to return to Egypt and persuaded Chloe to go with him.

"Belia, what is your choice?" Freyna asked.

"To stay with Andreas," Belia said. This reply did not quite satisfy her friend but Freyna remained silent and to Andreas' relief, the question of who should travel on the galley was easily solved.

With the enthusiasm of youth, Nino spoke for the bull dancers.

"We shall continue to be the best bull dancers in the world! Who knows, we may one day take our dancing to distant lands far across the seas!" The dancers enthusiastically agreed.

The meal was over and there could be no further delay. They made preparations to leave. Andreas gave orders that the remaining food should be packed. Wine bottles were filled with water and the girls were given blankets. The time had come for farewells.

Naxos embraced Belia. She had always been one of his favourites. Nino looked long and sadly at her. They had been close friends, but he had come to love her truly. She embraced all the dancers in turn, wishing them joy and good fortune.

The men farewelled Leander and Ali, hiding their sorrow in jokes and rough embraces. Freyna and Chloe wept as they bid farewell to those with whom they had shared so much danger and drama for they knew in their hearts they would never meet again.

Then Naxos led the dancers away from the villa down the road toward Amnissos. Andreas and Belia sadly watched them go.

"Belia, are you absolutely sure you don't want to go with them? Nino is a fine young man."

"Andreas, I am content. I love you." He saw in her eyes that it was true and put his arms around her.

The journey to Mallia began shortly after Naxos and the dancers were out of sight. Antonius had the two chariots harnessed and the last of the food and bedding loaded into the cart. They had few possessions. After Zanthope's death, Andreas had placed her remaining jewels in a strong box for safe keeping and he took them and some gold in a leather pouch which he gave to Antonius. The remainder of his money he carried in his belt.

Antonius, riding his mare, led the group with ten soldiers. Andreas followed driving the large chariot, carrying Belia, Timon, Dr Ahmed and Queen Kara. Leander, Freyna and Chloe travelled in the small figwood chariot. Cibaros drove the cart, carrying the baggage, with Arcanos and Credon seated beside him. Ali rode Timon's pony. Cadet Nimos with twelve soldiers marched in the rear.

It was a slow and tedious journey, travelling on side tracks which fortunately had escaped damage in the earthquake. They avoided the guard station on the main road, which was probably occupied by Greek or Mycenaean soldiers.

Arriving at Zanthope's villa, near Mallia, they found the place deserted. Antonius directed that the chariots and cart should remain hidden in the trees while he and his soldiers entered the house. He sent Nimos and his troops around to the back.

While the rest of the party waited, a noise in the nearby woods startled them. Ali went to investigate. They heard him laugh and he was still laughing when he returned.

"Would you believe it! It's one of our bulls!"

As he spoke, the animal ran from under the trees and stood still, his roan and white colouring silhouetted against the darker undergrowth.

"It's Tauron!" Chloe cried and a cheer went up from the dancers when they saw their old favourite alive and well. As the big bull snorted and ran off, crashing through the trees and undergrowth, Antonius called that it was safe to enter.

The villa had been ransacked, furniture was overturned and the rooms were in disorder. Andreas noted that valuable ornaments and silver platters were missing but the building itself was undamaged. Only a few cracks in the walls gave evidence of the earthquake.

To their horror they discovered in the kitchen that the caretaker had been murdered. He lay on the floor in a pool of blood. His wife and the kitchen girls had been violated and brutally slain. Antonius covered the bodies and arranged for them to be buried and asked everyone to wait at the back of the house.

While the graves were being dug, Antonius drew Andreas aside.

"It's not safe here, Father. We must leave for the galley at once."

"You go with the others," Andreas replied, "I shall stay here." Antonius stared at his father in disbelief.

"You can't be serious, Father!"

"I am, Antonius, I've thought deeply about this. I want you to persuade Belia to go with you. She is so young, she can start a new life but my obligation lies here."

Antonius was shocked by this change in his father's plans.

"For Zeus' sake, Father, we're not going to leave you here alone!"

"Credon will look after me."

"Credon? He's injured and useless. You must be mad — why are you doing this?"

Andreas answered wearily but firmly.

"Someone must try to restore order here. Crete is my home and I could never be happy or content anywhere else. Besides, I must be certain that Hyacinth and her children are alive. When you are all safe on the galley I am going to look for them."

"Father, you are senselessly risking your life. You said yourself it was not safe to travel alone. Please change your mind."

"I have the chariot and the horses. Perhaps some of these soldiers will accompany me."

Antonius was exasperated. "This is ridiculous. If you insist on staying, we'll have to change all our plans."

The argument was interrupted by Cadet Nimos who informed them that the burial was completed.

Dr Ahmed, who had observed the discussion between Antonius and his father, saw that Andreas was pale and exhausted. "Dr Ahmed, talk to my father — he won't listen to me," Antonius said and walked angrily away.

"You are tired, sir. I'm sure everything will be all right now. We'll soon be safe on the ship," Ahmed said sympathetically.

Andreas repeated much of what he had said to his son and Ahmed was equally dismayed.

"Please reconsider, sir. We cannot leave you here. You will be most welcome in Egypt, my home will be yours for as long as you care to stay. There will be no problem about money, I have plenty."

"Ahmed, I'm very grateful..."

"Sir, it's not only your son who is upset — none of us could possibly leave you here. You are our leader, your wisdom and guidance will be needed as much in my country as it is here. And the Queen has influential friends and I'm certain you would find an honourable place in Egypt."

"Thank you, dear friend. I am most grateful." Andreas sighed. Emotionally drained and physically exhausted, he leaned against the handrail of the steps leading to the garden.

Queen Kara, the dancers and Cibaros drew near and they were alarmed when Antonius told them of his father's intention to remain in Crete.

Belia ran to him. "Andreas, my dear, are you all right? Is it true that you're not coming on the galley?"

"Yes, Belia. I must stay here. I hope you understand."

"Of course I do, Andreas. If you do not leave Crete neither shall I. Nothing you can say will change my mind."

"Belia, my darling, you have your whole life ahead of you ..."

"Andreas, I won't let you send me away. Antonius will not go without you, either and that means Leda and Timon will stay too. Antonius says that now we must hide, until it's dark. Then it will be safer to travel into the mountains."

Andreas realized that further argument was useless and he turned to Ahmed, Queen Kara and the dancers.

"Your Majesty, my dear friends, you must leave now, with no more delay."

"I hope you will accompany us to the galley," Ahmed said.

"Of course. I want to be sure you all leave safely," Andreas replied. He held out his hand to Belia who smiled and came close to him.

"Let us go," he said.

But there was yet another delay. Antonius ordered Cadet Nimos to parade the soldiers.

"If we don't go soon we'll have our throats cut!" Cibaros muttered impatiently and set off quickly along the path that led to the cliff head.

When the men were lined up, Antonius addressed them.

"My father's party will be travelling inland tonight. I want volunteers to accompany us."

Cadet Nimos and seven men stepped forward and two other soldiers, who had asked for passage on the galley, were assigned to serve Queen Kara and Ahmed.

Antonius thanked the men for their loyalty and gave each some money. The remaining soldiers were dismissed and left at once to find their families in distant parts of Crete while the seven who volunteered to continue service were ordered to guard the villa and the horses.

Antonius was ill at ease. He disagreed absolutely with his father's decision to remain in Crete, but he was more disturbed by a sense of foreboding — a premonition of disaster which he could not shake off.

The fugitives, including Andreas and Belia, set off on the last stage of the journey to the galley. Queen Kara was tired and walked slowly, leaning on Ahmed's arm.

Impatient to reach the galley, Leander placed his arm around Freyna and whispered, "Let's go on ahead, darling. I don't like these delays."

From the front entrance, the stone path led around the villa through the surrounding gardens. One fork turned off to the shrine where Olykka had danced the previous summer. The other passed through a lemon grove and meandered for some distance between the trees before opening on to a lookout on the summit of a cliff overlooking the sea. From here a steep path zigzagged down the face of the cliff to the beach far below. The blue sea and the deserted beach presented a tranquil scene that was in complete contrast to the turmoil and destruction in Knossos. The bay stretched westward for a short distance towards a low rocky headland that jutted into the sea. A narrow passage between the rocks gave access to the creek where the galley lay hidden.

As Leander and Freyna hurried through the lemon grove, the late afternoon air was warm and still. Freyna leant against Leander's shoulder, weary but happy. Leander was eager to reach the galley and leave Crete as soon as possible. Suddenly Freyna shivered. She stopped abruptly and looked around.

"What is it, darling?" he asked, feeling her brow, fearing she might have a fever.

"I had a strange feeling," she replied, "as if we'd been here before and something terrible was going to happen. It's probably nothing."

He paused as she spoke and saw that Ali and Chloe were close behind, followed by Ahmed and Queen Kara, then Andreas and Belia, arm-in-arm and Antonius with Leda holding Timon's hand. Further back, through the trees, Leander could just see Cadet Nimos assisting the old steward, Credon, and also Arcanos plodding wearily between the two soldiers.

"I hope we shall all be safe soon," Freyna said to Leander as they turned and walked on.

Andreas and Antonius continued their argument, the younger man pleading ever more vehemently with his father to join them and leave the island.

"Father, you will regret staying in Crete. You may not have another opportunity to leave for some years."

"Antonius, I've made my decision and I must stay. There's no alternative."

"You should consider Leda and Timon, Father, and Belia. She will leave if you do."

"*You* must take them both with you to Egypt, Antonius. You will have a better life there."

"I know that — we all know it — but we cannot go without you, Father."

"Antonius, let us argue no more. You cannot say anything that will make me change my mind."

As they approached the cliff summit, Antonius again experienced a sense of impending disaster. He tried to dismiss it by acknowledging the stress of recent events, but he failed. There was something else, something that he could not define or explain and he listened anxiously for any sound which would portend danger.

Evening was now approaching and already the sun was behind the mountains and the deep valleys were in shadow. As they came from the shelter of the trees, they could hear the sound of the waves and feel the cool sea breeze. At the top of the cliff, overlooking the beach, they stopped. When they saw the steepness of the rough track to the beach, Ahmed and the dancers realized that this should be the place for farewells.

Leander and Freyna embraced Belia. Freyna wept. They implored her to travel with them, but Belia was adamant that she would stay with Andreas. Ali and Chloe embraced Belia and wished her happiness. The dancers then bid Andreas farewell and thanked him for his generosity. Thanks to him, they would not arrive penniless in a strange land.

Andreas turned to Ahmed and Queen Kara and without a word the two friends embraced.

"Twelve years of one's life is a long time, my friend. Thank you for your care, Ahmed, but especially for your friendship. I shall never know a kinder or gentler man than you."

As Ahmed replied tears ran down his face.

"I hope you will look after yourself, Andreas. How I wish you would come with us. If you change your mind, my house will always be open to you. I'm so grateful for all your kindness to me ..." he broke off, unable to continue.

"Safe travel, Ahmed, and you too, Madam," Andreas replied, "may the Gods give you both joy and good fortune. Farewell!"

Ahmed and Queen Kara set off down the steep path with the two soldiers following. The dancers were already some way ahead. Antonius tried once more to persuade his father to travel to Egypt.

"Before it's too late, Father, I beg you — come with us. We can't possibly leave you, Belia and Timon behind."

"Antonius, my duty is clear —"

"Don't you have a duty to yourself and Belia and your son, Timon?"

"Antonius, *you* must take your wife and Timon to Egypt ..."

As they argued, Belia walked to the edge of the cliff and waved to her friends who were walking down the steep, winding path to the beach.

While the discussion continued, Leda, who was exhausted, relaxed beneath a tree and Timon lay with his head in her lap. Cadet Nimos stood some distance away, waiting patiently and the two older men, Credon and Arcanos, sat together, dejectedly nursing their injuries. No one showed much interest in the debate.

"Father," Antonius repeated, "Hyacinth and the children are safe in the mountains. They are among friends, with Olykka and all the Palace people to look after them. What more could you do for them?"

Andreas did not reply.

"I'm sure Hyacinth is as worried about your safety as you are for hers. If she were here, she would urge you, as I do, to leave this place."

"If she and the children were here, it might be different. We could all go. But Hyacinth might not wish to leave Crete — has this occurred to you, Antonius?"

"She would want what is best for her children. Everything is finished here," Antonius replied bitterly.

"Things will settle down, you'll see Antonius. These invaders will soon leave, with as much loot as they can carry and in time, the country will recover. Crete may never be wealthy and powerful again but the Cretan people will go on, trading, farming, fishing as they've always done. I may be the only surviving member of the Council — you must see, Antonius, that I have an obligation to revive some kind of government here."

"But, Father, you are alone. You are accustomed to peace, order and the rule of law!" Antonius was in despair. "This island will never be secure. The fleet is sunk and without it Crete is at the mercy of any invader who cares to attack."

They would have argued until it was dark and the galley, with its survivors, was only a speck on the horizon.

Cibaros, the foreman, was now on board with his wife and daughters. He was fretting at the delay and the Captain and seamen were eager to move out of the creek while some daylight still remained.

Leander and Freyna, with Ali and Chloe, had by now descended the steep, winding path to the beach. Queen Kara, Dr Ahmed and the two soldiers were a short distance behind them. Freyna looked up and saw Belia silhouetted on the cliff top. Belia waved and the dancers waved back. In the distance they could still faintly hear Antonius shouting at his father.

The argument then ceased abruptly. The two men heard the sound of hooves crashing through the trees and turned toward the lemon grove, fearing one of the horses had broken loose.

"Nimos, what's happening there?" Antonius called out.

The cadet peered into the trees and shouted, "Watch out, it's a big red bull!"

At that moment a huge bull raced from the lemon grove and Antonius instantly recognized it as the roan and white animal the dancers called Tauron. The bull halted for a moment and then turned menacingly toward Belia who was standing on the edge of the cliff a short distance away.

"Belia, look out!" Andreas screamed and ran towards her.

The bull, however, following its practice in the arena, bellowed, lowered its head and charged. Its hooves thundered over the rocky ground and the massive beast was almost upon her even before she'd had a chance to answer Andreas' warning. As he and Antonius watched horror-stricken, Belia stepped back to avoid the bull and lost her footing on the cliff edge. Clutching desperately at the cliff face she tried to grasp the clumps of grass and stunted shrubs growing there, but she could not gain a firm hold. The dry grass and twigs tore away in her hands.

The great bull, carried forward by the impetus of its charge, cartwheeled over the summit after Belia and landed with a crash on the rocks below.

Andreas cried out in anguish. "No, Belia, no!"

Racing to the cliff edge, he watched in helpless agony as the young dancer began to slide faster and faster down the steep hillside. Desperately she tried to stop her fall. About halfway down the rugged incline her leg struck a sharp rock and Andreas was appalled to hear the bone snap. Belia cried out and fainting with pain rolled helplessly over and over, her body tumbling through brushwood and slamming against rocks. At the foot of the cliff, near where the path curved onto the sand, some vegetation cushioned her fall. She lay there on the edge of the beach, apparently without life or movement.

Queen Kara, Ahmed and the dancers were shocked and speechless. The dancers raced over to Belia. The bull lay motionless nearby, its neck broken. The great head was bent low over a rock and the long curved horns, the once proud emblem of Cretan power, were now the symbol of its fall.

Dr Ahmed watched in horror as Andreas raced down the steep path, desperate to reach Belia, fearing such exertion was beyond Andreas' strength.

Antonius and Cadet Nimos rushed after him but none could have halted Andreas' headlong flight. As his momentum increased, he collided with trees, bushes and rocks on the edge of the path. His legs were cut and bruised but he ran as if he felt no pain at all. Thorn bushes on either side ripped his cloak and as he descended his speed increased. Andreas' lungs were bursting as he gasped for air and the pain in his chest was unbearable.

He blamed himself for the delays and arguments which had caused this terrible accident. They should have left at once as Antonius wished. Then, as the descent grew steeper, Andreas became panic-stricken when he sensed that he could not stop. His feet seemed hardly to touch the ground and again he shouted Belia's name. Closer to the beach he lost all control of his limbs and lurching from the path, he staggered the last ten paces over stony ground. And then, after a few convulsive steps, he catapulted on to the beach and fell heavily.

Ahmed ran to Andreas and felt his pulse. It was fast and thready as Andreas lay pale and desperately gasping for breath.

Antonius flung himself on to his knees by his father.

"Ahmed," he cried, "is he all right? Can you help him?"

"I believe he will recover, Antonius. Be patient. Your father must lie quietly. When he regains consciousness we must try to be calm and reassure him."

Leda and Timon came down from the path. The young boy ran at once to his brother. "Is father sick, 'Tonius?" The boy began to cry as Antonius and Leda tried to comfort him.

"Don't worry, Timon. The doctor says father will be all right."

"Leda, stay with them," Ahmed said and moved quickly to where Belia lay. She was beginning to regain consciousness and moaned with pain. Freyna and Chloe were weeping, stroking her hair and kissing her hands. She was bleeding from many cuts and abrasions and the girls tore pieces of their clothing to staunch the wounds and wipe the blood from her face.

Ahmed examined her and saw immediately that the bones of the lower right leg were fractured. He knew she must have many bruises and superficial injuries and would suffer severe shock. However, after a thorough examination he could not detect any other fractures. There was the possibility, he thought, of cracked ribs or serious internal injury — only time would reveal that. Her youth, excellent health and strong physical condition would make complete recovery a possibility.

The doctor reassured her friends, "Belia has had a miraculous escape but now we must do what we can to make her more comfortable. We will need splints and bandages for her leg."

The dancers were relieved. Leaving Freyna and Chloe with Belia, Leander and Ali accompanied Ahmed to where Andreas lay nearby. At that moment Cibaros came back along the beach to discover what was causing the delay. When he saw Andreas and Belia lying injured, he was horrified.

"Holy Gods! What's happened here?" he cried.

Ahmed explained what had occurred and asked Cibaros if there was any timber on the ship that was suitable for splints for Belia's leg.

"We'll find something, doctor," the foreman said and returned immediately to the ship.

Leander's anxiety for Freyna was now redoubled. He could not banish from his mind the image of the murdered women at the villa. He spoke urgently to Antonius.

"Lieutenant Micalidos, surely your father will come with us now. We must leave quickly without further delay."

Antonius agreed. He knelt and spoke gently but firmly to his father.

"Father, can you hear me? Press my hand if you can." He felt a slight pressure and continued. "Belia is safe, but she cannot walk, her leg is broken. We cannot travel safely to the mountains now. You must come with us on the ship."

Again Antonius felt the faint pressure on his hand and to everyone's relief the decision was made. They would all board the ship and sail for Egypt.

Cibaros returned with a seaman carrying pieces of timber for splints and some planks which were quickly improvised into stretchers. As Freyna tore up strips of clothing, Ahmed padded the splints and bound Belia's leg. Antonius asked Cibaros and the seamen to carry Belia's stretcher.

"All of you go to the boat as quickly as you can," he said. "Ali, will you help Leda and Timon?"

"Of course," Ali replied and hoisted the boy onto his shoulders.

Antonius then sent Cadet Nimos to dismiss the last members of his company and set the horses loose.

"Hurry, Nimos, we must leave as soon as possible."

"V-very good, sir." Nimos saluted and ran toward the cliff path while Antonius and the two Cretan soldiers lifted Andreas on the improvised stretcher and set off across the beach as fast as they could. They were near the rocky headland when a shout from the cliff top halted them.

"Lieutenant — watch out! The Mycenaeans are attacking!"

Antonius recognized one of the soldiers just as the man was struck by a spear and crashed headlong over the cliff. Nimos turned and raced back down the path to the beach.

Immediately a group of soldiers were silhouetted on the summit. Two Mycenaean leaders were easily recognisable as the last rays of the sun gleamed on their helmets. They wore cuirasses and greaves, and carried swords and shields. Some of the men were naked and armed with javelins and bows and arrows.

Antonius shouted to his friends. "Run for the boat! Run for your lives!"

The Mycenaean soldiers, their yells echoing harshly in the evening air, raced down the steep track in pursuit of the fugitives. For them, the last few metres of the beach seemed endless. On reaching the headland the sharp rocks cut their feet, but they dashed on, oblivious of the pain. Antonius and his men, carrying Andreas, lagged behind. Andreas struggled to speak. "Leave me, Antonius. Save yourselves!"

He was neither heard nor heeded.

The Captain of the galley, hearing the shouting, immediately ordered his men to cast off. The fugitives dashed through the gap in the rocks, ran into the water and scrambled aboard as best they could.

"We must go back and help Antonius!" Leander shouted to Ali.

Both men raced back toward the beach as Captain Tibor ordered the fugitives to go forward beneath the foredeck and Belia was carried to the small cabin below. They waited tensely as the yells of the Mycenaeans grew louder.

The light was now poor under the cliff face and the Mycenaeans, in their haste, impeded each other on the narrow path. Several lost their footing and tumbled down the steep cliff. However, the two officers and several of their men were soon on the beach and dangerously near to Antonius and the soldiers carrying Andreas. Nimos was racing ahead of them and as he rejoined Antonius, Leander and Ali appeared.

"Take my father," Antonius gasped, "we'll stop them until you get aboard the galley."

In desperate haste the exchange was made and Leander and Ali carried Andreas across the rocks toward the waiting ship.

# CHAPTER 46

Antonius, Nimos and the two soldiers drew their swords and faced the oncoming Mycenaeans.

They were attacked almost immediately. Their swords clashed and the sounds of blows on bronze-studded shields resounded along the cliff. The four Cretans fought grimly, lunging and slashing, struggling to keep their footing on the rocky shore.

Antonius knew that they could only hold out for a brief time and was sure they would soon be outnumbered. As they fought, they retreated toward the narrow path through the rocks. This desperate encounter, in the confined space, did not last long. When Antonius heard a shout from the galley — "All aboard" — he ordered his men to break off and run for the ship.

With Cadet Nimos and the two soldiers, he dashed through the narrow path and into the shallow water of the creek. The galley was now moving out into mid-stream as the oarsmen tensely awaited the command to row. Antonius and his men scrambled aboard.

"Row, row for your lives, you bastards!" Captain Tibor ordered and the sailors strained to get the galley under way.

The Mycenaeans had followed quickly after Antonius and his men and running into the shallow creek, they attempted to board the galley. From the deck the Cretans lunged, driving them back. A Mycenaean officer fell into the water with blood streaming from a gash in his throat while another soldier staggered away, clutching a wound in his shoulder. The second officer momentarily abandoned the attack and he ordered his men to fall back as he heard the remainder of his troops approaching.

Antonius realized that the galley was very vulnerable in the narrow creek. To those on board, the ship hardly seemed to move at all. As it drifted slowly into mid-stream, the Mycenaean archers and javelin throwers ran through the rocks to the edge of the creek, their officer shouting orders. The naked archers knelt on the creek bank and aimed at the oarsmen.

"Watch out! Take cover!" Antonius screamed, only too aware of their predicament.

Arrows whined over the galley and then spears and javelins as the soldiers and oarsmen crouched low behind the bulwarks. One of the soldiers fell to the deck with a scream of pain when he was hit in the shoulder and Leander quickly put his foot on the man's chest and removed the spear.

Meanwhile, the Mycenaeans had rushed into the water and attempted to stop the ship's progress by grasping the oars. As the oarsmen on the opposite side continued to row, the galley began to veer toward the attackers. Captain Tibor shouted orders to the helmsman and rowers to keep the ship further offshore into the channel.

A manic struggle ensued as the oarsmen heaved and strained to shake off the Mycenaeans. Antonius and Nimos fought to dislodge the enemy with their swords, but the Mycenaeans were cunning and stayed out of reach, ready to scramble aboard and slaughter everyone once the ship was grounded.

Below decks Cibaros had found the galley's store of tools, bronze spikes and spars. He also noted the rock ballast in the bilges. With the help of Leander and Ali, the ship's gear and ballast became defensive weapons.

"Aim at their heads!" Antonius yelled.

The spikes and rocks flew through the air as fast as Cibaros and Ali could throw them. Screams and howls of pain came from the Mycenaeans. Leander and Nimos, with the long spars, rammed and battered frantically at the Mycenaeans' hands and heads.

A sudden shout from Ali brought Nimos leaping across the deck. One of the invaders had succeeded in swimming unnoticed under the bow and as he climbed up to the deck and was about to stab an oarsman in the back, Nimos slammed his sword on the man's neck and he fell with a scream into the water.

Meanwhile the women, with Timon, Credon and Arcanos, crouched under the small foredeck. They were terrified but tried to remain calm and still as the Captain had ordered. Ahmed had done what he could for the wounded Cretan soldier, who lay faint from loss of blood.

Near the mouth the creek became wider. Antonius cursed because Captain Tibor did not steer toward the opposite bank, away from the attackers.

However, the Captain knew this anchorage well. He would have preferred to veer away from the Mycenaeans but he was sure that shallow water and large submerged rocks in that area made navigation impossible. Standing calmly at the mast he gave the helmsman sharp commands and encouraged his crew. He was concerned that a greater danger would face them before they reached the open sea.

At the mouth of the creek, a rocky shelf severely restricted the entrance. Here the creek was deep, but at this stage of the tide the bar reduced the channel to less than two boat length's in width. At this point they would be most vulnerable to boarding from the rocks. Beyond this lay a narrow sand-spit uncovered at low tide, and here the beach shelved steeply into deep water.

Without warning the attackers withdrew and the galley moved faster on the last of the outgoing tide. Cadet Nimos cheered, while those on board, believing their ordeal to be over, joined in. Captain Tibor ordered them to be quiet.

Antonius, seeing the Mycenaeans racing toward the creek mouth, saw they were not yet out of danger.

"They're making for the rocks at the mouth!" Captain Tibor shouted grimly.

A seaman ran up a gib, though there seemed to be no movement in the air. However, as they approached the mouth, a fitful land breeze came from the hills and the sail fluttered a moment and then filled. The Captain called the oarsmen for a faster pace while the helmsman maintained his course. He knew what his orders would be — steady ahead to the last minute, then, at the precise moment they approached the outlet, hard to port, then to starboard and then, if the Gods were smiling on them, they would escape to the open sea.

Antonius, sword in hand, stationed himself at the bow. He watched the Mycenaeans leaping over the rocks, intending to board the galley from the narrow spit at the creek mouth. The Lieutenant ordered Cadet Nimos and the soldier to take up their positions midships to repel the Mycenaeans. Leander, too, stood ready. He held the wounded soldier's sword and the enemy spear taken from his shoulder.

Ali and Cibaros, armed with daggers, watched tensely as the narrow outlet came nearer. The Mycenaeans were now level with the galley.

Leander hurled his spear and was gratified to see one of the Mycenaeans fall face down into the water. His comrades ignored him and raced on unheeding.

On board Captain Tibor shouted his orders.

"Hard to port!"

The helmsman gripped the rudder pole with both hands and heaved with all his might. Antonius judged the ship would pass through the gap with little room to spare. The sailors would have to raise their oars for a brief time trusting that momentum would carry the ship through.

As Antonius steadied himself on the bow, Nimos and Leander guessed his purpose.

"If he leaves the ship, he c-can't fight them alone," the young cadet said.

"He won't have to," Leander replied grimly.

"I agree," Nimos said, grinning.

They moved across the deck and stood beside Antonius. On the rocks, a short distance away, about a dozen Mycenaeans led by their officer clambered toward the ship. A moment later Antonius leapt from the deck on to the slippery rocks. He was immediately confronted by the Mycenaean officer. The two men attacked each other savagely, struggling to keep their balance on the uneven surface.

Cadet Nimos, Leander and the Cretan soldier leaped ashore and faced the oncoming enemy. The Mycenaeans attacked ferociously and a violent struggle began on the rocky promontory. The encounter was chaotic, for the light was failing and space so limited that movement was difficult. Although outnumbered, the three Cretans and Leander were, in fact, assisted by the contours of the promontory, which narrowed considerably. They were able to stand abreast and fight so resolutely that the Mycenaeans could not penetrate their defence. Shouting with rage, the enemy soldiers pressed from behind, forcing their comrades forward towards the Cretans' swords. When one of the Mycenaeans slipped, he was cut down by Nimos and fell screaming into the creek. Another immediately took his place. Three more enemy soldiers were wounded and their fallen bodies increased the difficulty of combat in the restricted area.

Antonius concentrated all his mind and strength on overpowering his adversary. Both men had abandoned their shields as too cumbersome and with swords and daggers each lunged frantically to effect a death blow. When the Mycenaean officer tried to force Antonius back into the creek, the young Cretan braced himself against a rock and held his ground.

Leander was wounded by a sword-thrust on his temple. He felt no pain but would bear the scar for the rest of his life. He and his companions had only one aim — to prevent the invaders from gaining access to the galley. They succeeded and the ship glided safely through the narrow channel.

Captain Tibor then ordered the oarsmen to cease rowing. The passengers now appeared anxiously on deck. Concerned for the safety of Antonius and his men, they listened with increasing alarm as the conflict continued on the rocky promontory.

Although many Mycenaeans were accounted for, the Cretans were still greatly outnumbered. Those on board shouted to Antonius and Leander to disengage and rejoin the ship, but this was impossible. Ali and Cibaros, fearing there would be a tragedy, urged the Captain to bring the galley closer to the rocks but Captain Tibor needed no persuasion. He and many of the seamen had been employed by Andreas, some for more than a generation. Their loyalty and affection for the Micalidos family was strong and they did not intend to stand by and see Antonius and his companions murdered.

At a command from Captain Tibor, the helmsman manoeuvred the galley closer to the beach near the rocks. Ali, Cibaros and several seamen who could swim, dropped overboard and swam underwater to the sand-spit. Their surprise attack disconcerted the Mycenaeans and although their officer tried to rally them, they lost heart and realized it was now almost impossible to defeat the Cretans. As they faltered, Ali and Cibaros shouted to Antonius and his companions.

"Run for the sand-spit! Run! Swim for the galley!"

The Cretans began to withdraw toward the shelving beach but the Mycenaeans, urged by their Captain, continued to harass them.

Antonius, snatching the opportunity of this brief distraction, plunged his dagger in the Mycenaean leader's arm and raced for the beach. However, his opponent was not so easily shaken. Enraged at the failure of this foray, he tenaciously pursued Antonius and they continued to fight, lunging and slashing at each other in the shallow water.

Meanwhile the Cretans followed Leander into deeper water, making for the galley and the Mycenaean soldiers had no inclination to follow them.

"I c-can't swim!" Nimos called out.

"Neither can I!" the Cretan soldier shouted.

Leander, Ali and Cibaros immediately went to their aid. Distracted by this, they were not aware that Antonius had not followed. The crewmen swam back to the galley and Cibaros came next, assisting the soldier. As Ali and Nimos were climbing aboard, they saw that Antonius was not with them.

He was still fighting in the shallows with the Mycenaean Captain! The two soldiers, hampered by the steep angle of the sandy beach, continued their vicious struggle, and the clash of their swords echoed across the water.

The Mycenaean Captain shouted to his men for assistance, but they hesitated.

"Leander, help Antonius — please help him!" Leda cried from the galley.

Leander needed no urging and at once swam back toward the combatants who were now fighting waist-deep in water. The stress of the last two days had weakened Antonius. He lost his footing and as he lurched toward the water, his helmet tipped back, held only by the chin-strap. The Mycenaean, seizing his advantage, lunged forward and struck Antonius a glancing blow to the forehead. The blood gushed out and, stunned, the young Cretan fell back into the sea. It was now almost dark. The sun's last glow faintly lit the western sky behind the mountains.

The Mycenaean Captain, determined to complete his victory, kill Antonius and acquire his enemy's sword and bronze-studded helmet as spoils of battle, strode into the deep water. He was unaware that Leander, swimming underwater, was also searching for Antonius. Suddenly, the Mycenaean felt strong hands crushing his windpipe.

The professional soldier and the bull dancer struggled violently in the deep water, but try as he could, the Mycenaean was unable to break Leander's grip on his throat. The bull dancer had the advantage and as he managed to snatch a breath of air, he saw Antonius in the water a few feet away. The wounded Cretan had risen to the surface dazed after his heavy helmet and sword had fallen from him in the water and now he was weakly trying to stay afloat.

Wrenching back the Mycenaean's head, Leander found the man was no longer a threat. He had drowned.

Swimming quickly to Antonius, Leander brought him safely to the galley and they were lifted aboard.

Freyna, weeping with joy and relief, flung her arms around Leander while Leda cried out in despair when Antonius collapsed on the deck and she saw the bloody wound on his forehead. She feared he was dead. But as he lay in her arms, she was overjoyed to see his eyes open.

"How are the others?" he asked.

"They are safe," Leda assured him and he saw that it was true.

"Thank the Gods," he said and lay back, exhausted.

Captain Tibor ordered his men to hoist the big lateen sail, and, as the land breeze strengthened, the ship came to life.

In the last gruelling hours all had seemed lost, but now the weary fugitives gave thanks for their survival.

Ahmed and Queen Kara talked quietly together. The doctor had stitched Antonius' wound and Leda bound it with a strip of linen which Queen Kara tore from the hem of her dress.

Andreas had been carried below and he and Belia lay together in great discomfort in the dark, airless cabin — but they did not complain. Each was so full of joy and thankfulness that the other had survived.

Presently Antonius came to find them.

"Father, Belia, how are you? Holy Zeus, you can't stay here!" Antonius at once asked Captain Tibor if a place could be found on deck for Andreas and Belia. He agreed and they were soon carried up into the fresh air. Andreas was still very weak but he gave one hand to Belia and the other to his son.

"Well done, Antonius," he whispered hoarsely, "you saved us all."

"Not I alone, Father," his son replied earnestly, "all of us together." He indicated the whole company on the ship. Andreas nodded.

"The Gods have been with us today," he murmured.

The voyagers gazed for the last time at the receding shore and they saw the dark mountains of Crete silhouetted against the pale sky and the blue smoke drifting from fires in the ruined city. The survivors found it hard to believe that all they had experienced on the island — success and hardship, disaster and great loss — might now fade into the past as the outline of Crete slowly receded.

"Father, we shall see Hyacinth and her children again. I'm sure we shall return to Crete."

"Of course we will, dearest Andreas," Belia agreed.

Andreas smiled and closed his eyes.

"Perhaps," he murmured, "perhaps."

The sea rose and fell in a steady rhythm, the eternal and mysterious sea which was to wait another thousand years for Homer's *Iliad* and its wine-dark name.

Despite their weariness, they began to feel hope and optimism. They were free and grateful for the gift of life and the joy of love. The fresh, strong air revived their spirits.

The crew carried out their routine tasks. The helmsman set course for Egypt and the new life that lay ahead of them.

# BIBLIOGRAPHY

For readers interested in exploring the time of the Priest King Minos and Minoan Crete:

The Aegean Civilization, G. Glotz, 1925/1968, publisher unknown.

Ancient Crete, Francis Wilkins, New York, N.Y., John Day Co, 1966

The Archaeology of Crete, J.S. Pendlebury, London, Methuen, 1967

The Archaeology of Minoan Crete, Reynold Higgins, London, The Bodley Head, 1973

The Bull of Minos, Leonard Cottrel, London, Evans Bros, 1961

Dawn of the Gods, Jacquette Hawkes, London, Chatto & Windus, 1968

The Greek Islands, L. Durrell, London, Faber, 1978

Prehistory and the Beginning of Civilization, Jacquette Hawkes & Sir L. Wooley, London, Allen & Unwin, 1963

**For information on bulls:**

Mort dans l'apres-midi, Ernest Hemingway, London, Cape, 1962

For Whom the Bell Tolls, Ernest Hemingway, London, Arrow, 1993

# AUTHOR BIOGRAPHIES

JOHN RAGGATT was born in Riverton in South Australia in 1922 and was educated at Adelaide High School. In 1941 he enlisted in the Royal Australian Air Force and became a Cypher Instructor during WWII. After demobilisation, John worked in the English theatre with Sir Donald Wolfit's Shakespeare Company. In 1946, on a six-month tour of Italy, Yugoslavia and Austria providing entertainment for the Occupation Forces, John met Pam.

PAM RAGGATT was born in London in 1919 and was educated at St Mary's Priory, a Benedictine Convent in Warwickshire. Pam did a two-year diploma course at the Royal Academy of Dramatic Art in London and worked in the theatre until called up for

National Service. She joined the Women's Royal Naval Service and worked as an electrician on torpedo boats and mine sweepers in Weymouth dockyard.

John and Pam married and both continued to work in theatre until 1952 when they returned to Australia. John worked for the Australian Broadcasting Commission in Adelaide and Melbourne before they shifted to Townsville with their three sons. John worked as Public Relations Officer for the Townsville City Council from 1967 until his retirement.

John and Pam have always had an interest in literature and art. They worked on this book together for some three years. John also painted landscapes in oils and won a number of art prizes — his paintings hang in State and regional art galleries and in private collections. Pam has always been a writer and has won prizes for her poetry.

John Raggatt died in 1994.